Daniel Sutka

Chris Merritt is a clinical psychologist and former diplomat.
As a member of the British foreign service, he completed
postings in Jerusalem and Iraq. He has also lived
and worked in the US. *Committed* is his eighth novel.

www.cjmerritt.co.uk
Twitter: @DrCJMerritt
Facebook: @chrismerrittauthor
Instagram: @cjmerritt81

ALSO BY CHRIS MERRITT

COMMITTED

CHRIS MERRITT

WILDFIRE

First published in paperback in 2023 by
WILDFIRE
an imprint of HEADLINE PUBLISHING GROUP

2

Cataloguing in Publication Data is available from the British Library

ISBN 978 1 0354 0729 3

Typeset in 10.75/13.75pt Carre Noir Std by Jouve (UK), Milton Keynes

Printed and bound in Great Britain by Clays Ltd, Elcograf S.p.A.

MIX
Paper | Supporting
responsible forestry
FSC® C104740

Headline's policy is to use papers that are natural, renewable and recyclable
products and made from wood grown in well-managed forests and other
controlled sources. The logging and manufacturing processes are expected
to conform to the environmental regulations of the country of origin.

HEADLINE PUBLISHING GROUP
an Hachette UK Company
Carmelite House
50 Victoria Embankment
London
EC4Y 0DZ

www.headline.co.uk
www.hachette.co.uk

To Max

PART ONE

DAY ONE

1

SHE'S SEEN THE guy before, she's sure of it. Two sightings in the space of twenty minutes, a mile apart. First at 69th Street station, when she arrived on the train into Philly, then again coming out of the 11th Street metro, reflected in a store window.

The guy's maybe 5-10, 170, moving like he's in good shape. Like he could run or fight if he needed to. Sports coat and open-necked shirt over jeans, soft shoes. The jacket just loose enough to hide a sidearm at his hip or in the small of his back, if he's carrying.

There's nothing remarkable about him, and that's precisely why he's caught her attention. It's like he's trying to blend in, and that's what makes him stand out to her. Because if it looks out of place, then it probably *is* out of place.

That was what they'd taught her at The Farm.

She'd learnt anti-surveillance theory in a classroom at Camp Peary, Virginia. Then the practical stuff on the streets of Williamsburg and Norfolk. Exercises trained and drilled until spotting someone following you was as automatic as breathing, until you couldn't switch it off.

Even when you'd left it all behind and had a totally new life outside the CIA.

Her shrink had said that, when we've been under extreme

stress, our bodies can still behave like we need to be on high alert, long after the event has passed. When we're safe. We imagine threats that don't exist. Hypervigilance, she'd called it.

Ellen McGinley understands that, because it's happened to her a lot.

But she also understands that, if there's one thing you can't afford to do, it's ignore your instincts: that little voice in your head that tells you something's not right. The same voice that's talking to her right now.

She needs to change her plans.

Instead of going straight to the restaurant where she's meeting her contact, Walter — a UPenn professor who knows more about US domestic terrorism than almost anyone in the country — she makes a detour.

She needs to flush out her surveillance, expose the guy, lose him.

She can't put her contact in danger.

Making a left on Chestnut Street, she heads east, past Thomas Jefferson hospital, past the Bank of America, towards Independence National Historical Park. She cuts south and east a couple times before she hits the corner of the park.

Midway over the crosswalk, she glances behind — a natural action — and glimpses the guy again. It's all the confirmation she needs.

Two sightings alone would be suspicious. But maybe, just maybe, the guy's heading to the same place as her for his lunch. After all, their roast pork hoagie is about the best in Philly, worth a train ride in from the suburbs.

But three sightings is no coincidence.

He's tailing her, and she can only guess it's because of what she knows, now.

What she *thinks* she knows. What she needs someone she trusts to make sense of for her.

Her heart rate has already rocketed. Her palms are sweaty.

It's the familiar anticipation of having to act on those instincts she's learnt to trust.

Learnt the hard way.

She heads for a group of tourists gathered outside Independence Hall. Weaves in between the bodies, blending into them. Brushes right by a lady speaking Korean and plucks the compact umbrella poking out of the tote bag on the woman's shoulder. Reaches inside her own purse for the pepper spray she always carries. Then slips through the arches to the side of the building and behind one of the tall red-brick pillars, where she's away from the bustle and cameras, alone.

Waits.

Tries to slow her breathing.

She guesses that the guy will parallel her to avoid being seen, and hope to catch her again on the other side of the arches. But when she doesn't appear on the other side, he'll need to come through and look for her.

She waits some more, pulse pounding at her temples. Pepper spray in her left hand. Umbrella in the right.

Ready.

It's maybe a full minute before she hears footsteps behind her. Cautious at first, the movements of someone searching.

She stays absolutely still.

Then he appears. A few strides and he's in front of her, now, with his back to her. He stops dead in the shadow between the two rows of arches.

"Hey," she says.

The guy turns.

Their eyes lock and she knows that she's made the right call. That what she heard last week must have been for real.

And she has just a couple of seconds to act.

*

Washington, D.C., one week earlier

Ellen has just finished talking to the babysitter on her cell phone, a minor thing about a misplaced bedtime book for her six-year-old son, Josh. But she didn't mind the interruption; she liked that the young woman bothered to call and ask because she wanted to read Josh his favourite story. In any case, the function she's at with Harry is kind of dull, full of political donors he's schmoozing, so she takes a minute in this quiet little nook of the sprawling five-star hotel to check her WhatsApp messages before she has to step back in for another round of smiles and small talk.

And that's when she catches the words, spoken softly in the corridor around the corner from where she's sitting. A moment of conversation between two men. She can't see them, but she can hear they're walking.

"Keystone Boys are on for the big one," says the first. "It'll be a game-changer. Like nothing we've ever seen here before."

"Is that right, son?" drawls the second. His accent is southern. He sounds impressed.

"Yes, sir," replies the first. "Real soon, they're gonna need more graves out there than when the pandemic hit. Boom!"

"Well, in that case, God bless America."

Both men laugh and she hears their steps fade.

Slowly, she rounds the corner. They've already gone. If she'd had a little more wine, she might've thought she'd imagined it.

But Ellen knows what she just heard, because she's heard something a lot like it once before, in France, back when she used to work for the Agency. When it was her responsibility to stop it, and she failed.

A terror plot.

*

Present Day

Ellen doesn't hesitate. She hits the guy who's been tailing her full in the face with a burst of pepper spray.

He gasps, his hands rushing to his eyes, leaving his neck completely exposed. And that's where she plants the umbrella. Hard. Right in his Adam's apple.

A single backhand jab is all it takes. He gives a choking sound, his tongue out like he's going to puke.

He folds forward a little, as though he might collapse, but steadies himself. Then his hand goes to his hip and that's when she sees the pistol.

She recognizes the shape of a Sig Sauer. The exact model doesn't matter. The fact that it's one of the few 9mm handguns made without an external safety catch does.

She drops the spray cannister and the umbrella and lunges for him.

But he's already drawn the gun.

There's a single scream from somewhere behind her, then raised voices.

She wraps her hands around the weapon, turns her shoulder into him so the barrel points away from her — away from the tourists — toward the wall.

His finger is on the trigger.

She grasps the pistol grip and twists, bending his index finger the wrong way. She hears his tendon snap at the knuckle right before the shot rings out. It's loud as hell.

She doesn't know where the bullet goes, only that it hits the 250-year-old brickwork someplace, and next thing she's got the Sig out of his hand and in her control.

His eyes are red, half-closed, streaming with tears. He can't see properly. He throws a haymaker at her with his left. She rocks back and the punch catches nothing but air.

She aims a hard kick between his legs and this time he goes down. Standing over him, out of striking range, she holds the gun steady in both hands. Points it right at his chest.

"Who are you?" she demands. There's a buzzing noise in her ears, tinnitus from the gunshot, and she can barely hear herself speak.

He groans on the floor, clutching his groin.

She raises her voice. "Why are you following me?"

He doesn't answer.

The sounds behind her are getting louder, now, and she can feel the movement of a crowd. She throws a glance between the arches and sees a dozen people watching, dozens more running for cover. She turns back to him, knowing there's not much time to make it out of this.

"Who are you working for?" she growls.

"Fuck you," he hisses.

"I'm not playing." She takes up some slack on the trigger. "Are you one of them?"

"Put down your weapon!" The order comes from the other side of the arches.

She keeps the Sig trained on the guy but takes a second to locate the new voice. Two uniformed cops have drawn their Glocks, the black eyes of their square barrels looking right at her. They're ready to shoot.

Goddammit.

This wasn't supposed to happen.

"Drop it right now!" the cop yells.

She briefly considers her options. Decides she doesn't really have any.

Still aiming at the guy, she adjusts her stance, clenches her teeth. Closes her left eye. Feels her trigger finger tightening.

And then she lowers the weapon. Puts it slowly on the flag-stones at her feet.

Raises her hands. Gets on the ground like they're telling her.

Next thing, she's being arrested. Cuffed behind her back, manhandled to her feet by the cops. There are more of them now, and she sees one working his radio, kneeling by the guy she just took out. Another is moving the tourists back, away from Independence Hall.

"That guy was following me," she says. "He pulled a gun on me. You gonna arrest him, too?"

But they don't answer. They're marching her towards a cop car that's pulled up on the sidewalk of South 6th Street. They open the rear door and shove her in. She cracks her head on the doorframe. Next thing they're on the move, the radio up front bleeping, callsigns given and received. The vehicle smells of old takeout and male sweat.

"This is a mistake," she says. "I'm the victim."

Neither of the cops up front respond. She guesses they've heard that one before.

Her head is throbbing where it hit the doorframe.

"Officer, am I bleeding?" she asks.

The cop in the passenger seat swivels back, his gaze sweeping up and down.

"Nah, you're good," he replies.

As the streets flash past, she thinks of Walter, sitting in the restaurant, waiting for her. Not knowing what she wanted to talk to him about, but knowing it was important. Wondering how long he'll stay, what he'll make of her no-show. She hopes he'll be safe. At least she didn't lead the guy right to him.

She'll find a way to contact Walter later on and explain, rearrange. She still has questions to ask him. Questions whose answers could save a whole lot of American lives.

Her next thought is of her son, Josh.

She needs to pick him up from his baseball camp in three hours.

She's not sure she's going to be able to do that.

2

SHE'S BEEN SITTING in the little airless room for almost two hours when the door opens.

A bald-headed, middle-aged man in a suit walks in, carrying a thin folder and a notebook. He has deep, dark bags under his eyes, like he hasn't slept in a week. She guesses that comes with the job. Being a detective in one of America's most violent cities would be enough to give anyone insomnia.

"Can you please tell me what's happening?" she says.

"Good to meet you, ma'am," he replies. "I'm Detective Brennan, Homeland Security Unit. Get you anything? Water? The drinks menu sucks, but as I always say, this ain't the Ritz Carlton." He chuckles and places the file and notepad on the table between them as he sits.

She knows what he's doing, trying to build rapport. The 101 of interview techniques. 101 is probably also the number of times he's used that line about the drinks menu to give the impression he's a nice guy. But she's not in the mood for any B.S.

"Homeland Security Unit?" she queries.

"Yes, ma'am."

"Why does this require Homeland Security?"

"Any incident involving firearms at a national landmark

comes straight to us. We're based out of south Philly. That's why it took me a while to get up here, what with the traffic."

She's heard about the unit. A 'fusion center' featuring Philly P.D., FBI and DHS.

"So, you guys think I was the victim of a terror attack?" she asks.

"Let's not get ahead of ourselves." His smile is going for reassuring. It's anything but. She wants out.

"Am I free to go?"

"I'm afraid not, ma'am. You've been arrested."

"Am I being charged with anything?"

"That depends."

"On what?"

Brennan tilts his head. "On whether we can establish why Independence Park almost turned into the Battle of Gettysburg today."

"Do I need a lawyer?"

He shrugs. "You have a right to one, as I'm sure they told you, but if you've got nothing to hide, you got nothing to worry about."

That's exactly the problem. She's got a whole lot to hide.

"Besides," he adds, "if you want an attorney, it's gonna take them a while to get here. And you did just ask if you could leave . . ."

"My son's at a baseball camp, out in East Norriton. He's six. I've got to collect him at three thirty."

They both look at the clock on the wall.

"Well, that's gonna be a little tight," Brennan says. He glances at her engagement ring and wedding band. "Do you want to call your husband? Maybe he can pick up—"

"He's in D.C." She doesn't tell him what Harry does. Not yet. She'd also prefer it if Harry didn't know about this until it's sorted out. Embarrassing would be an understatement, given his job.

Hell, this might even *cost* Harry his job if it goes really bad. The situation she encountered today is exactly why she left her old life behind. She left it for Harry — whose profile is a little more public, now, than when they first got together — and for Josh, to be the mom he needs.

And for her own sanity.

"Okay," Brennan says. "There anyone else who could help?"

She knows that her parents would drive a half-hour from Doylestown to collect Josh in a heartbeat. But she doesn't want them knowing she's here, either. Not if she can help it. They'd just worry. That's what parents do, no matter how old their kids are. And she wants to keep this as low-key as possible.

"I can come back tomorrow," she offers. "Make a statement or whatever."

"I think it's a little more complicated than that, Mrs," he opens the file, checks the top sheet inside, "McGinley. Can I call you Ellen?"

"Sure."

"All right, Ellen, why don't you just tell me in your own words what happened at Independence Hall, and we'll see if we can sort this thing out, quick as we can?"

"Great. I want to help."

"I'm glad we're on the same page." He spreads his hands. "Go right ahead."

The first rule of CIA interrogation training is seared into her memory: *don't get caught*. But, if something goes bad and you do, you have two options.

Option one is to say absolutely nothing at all, don't even give them a *yes* or a *no* to work with, and wait for the cavalry to arrive. Option two is to play nice — make them think you're cooperating, but still don't give them anything of value.

Ellen's problem is that there is no cavalry on the way. No one's got her back, and there's no one in an operations room at

Langley watching out for her. Not anymore, not since she quit. She's been on the outside ever since Paris. So, she decides option two is her best bet right now.

"So, I'm downtown, and I see this guy behind me," she begins.

"Okay." Brennan nods.

"I get on the metro and, when I come out, he's there again. The same guy."

"You're sure about that?"

"Positive."

He makes a note, gestures for her to continue.

"Then I'm walking to get some food, like six blocks away, and he's still behind me, following."

"How do you know he was following you?"

"I just . . . did."

"All right." He purses his lips, clearly unconvinced. "And why would he be doing that?"

She hesitates. Thinks, *because of what I heard about a possible attack on US soil. Because I'm a target now, and I don't even know who for.* She knows it'll sound crazy if she tells him that, though. She's only told one person so far, and that's Harry. Walter would've been the second.

"Uh, I don't know. You'd have to ask him. Maybe he was going to assault me."

Brennan clicks his pen a couple times. "And, yet, *you* assaulted him. With pepper spray."

"He came right up to me, I was scared."

"You put him in a medical center."

"It was self-defence."

There's a moment's silence while Brennan makes another note.

"Is he hurt?" she asks, not because she feels sorry for the guy, but because it could be a problem for her if he is.

"Not seriously. He isn't pressing charges." The detective pauses a beat. "I think his ego's taken a bruising, though."

"Because he got his ass kicked by a woman?"

"Something like that." There's a flicker of amusement in his expression. "So, what about the gun?"

"He pulled it on me."

"After you sprayed him in the face?"

She hesitates. Can't really claim it happened any other way. "Yes."

"All right. Then what?"

"I took the gun off him and that's when it fired. Then the officers arrived."

"You *took the gun off him*, huh?" Brennan blinks. "Just like that?"

"Yeah." She realizes he wants an explanation of how a 5-6, 130-lb civilian woman in her late thirties could do that. She doesn't blame him. And telling him she does CrossFit won't cut it. "I've taken some classes," she adds.

"No kidding." He looks like he doesn't quite believe her, though. "How did the weapon come to be discharged?"

"He had his finger on the trigger when I grabbed it."

"Mm-hm. And did you give a thought to the potential public safety impact of that action, given your location?"

"No. But I *did* give a thought to him shooting me." She leans forward. "Have you asked him why he was carrying a concealed weapon, anyway?"

Brennan doesn't look up from his notebook. "His license checks out. He doesn't need a reason. This is Pennsylvania."

So, they've traced the guy. It's an opportunity for a lead that might connect to what she heard last week. The thing that started all this. A potential threat against the US, from within. From among its own citizens.

. . .they're gonna need more graves out there than when the pandemic hit . . .

"What's his name?" she asks, trying to ignore the chill that those remembered words just sent through her.

The detective frowns. "I can't tell you that."

"Does he have a record? Is he a terror suspect?"

"I can't tell you that, either."

"Look, I just want to know who was following me. Whether I'm in danger or not."

"We haven't established that he *was* following you."

She rubs her eyes. "Jeez, okay."

"And you'd never seen the guy you attacked before today?"

"It was self—" She stops, decides to play nice instead. "Not that I'm aware of. But if I don't know who he is, I can't really be sure."

"Hm."

Brennan goes quiet. He opens the file, licks his fingertip and lifts the corner of the first page, just for a second. She scans the text upside-down and catches the words: *Michael John Smith.*

Is that the guy's name? It has to be. But it's so generic, it sounds to her like an alias. *An alias firearms license?* She wonders what opposition she's up against here.

"Any history of violence?" The detective's voice snaps her out of the thought.

"Excuse me?"

"Do you have any history of violent behavior, Ellen?"

A bunch of film clips flash through her mind. Times she's had to defend herself or someone else. Enemies who wound up worse than the guy today. But the secrecy agreement she signed on day one at Langley means she can't tell Brennan about that. She doesn't even want to tell him where she used to work, but she's running out of options.

"No," she lies.

"Any membership or contact with extreme groups, either past or present?"

"No . . ." That's not strictly true, either. But she sees what he's getting at here. He thinks *she's* a potential terrorist, not the creep who was tailing her.

"Just standard questions for an incident like this. Trust me." He's flashes her a crocodile's smile. "How about your psychiatric history? Ever had any diagnoses?"

She wonders if he knows, already. Whether he can find out. "Yes," she admits. She's not ashamed of it. "Post-Traumatic Stress Disorder, a while back."

"PTSD?"

"Yeah."

"Like, all the flashbacks and stuff?" He's writing more, now, and quicker.

"That's part of it," she replies, cautiously.

There was a whole lot more besides. Enough to put her in hospital on anti-psychotic medication at one point. She misinterpreted harmless, everyday stuff as danger. Like the time she heard a loud bang at home one day and threw herself under the kitchen table, thinking a bomb had gone off in the street. But it was just her neighbor's old station wagon backfiring. Harry found her hiding, shaking, cell phone in hand. She'd called 911.

"And thinking people are out to get you, right?" Brennan continues.

"Not necessarily," Ellen says, recalling how she'd had that symptom, too. She's sure that's not the case this time. It can't be.

"PTSD is no joke," he says. "It's a serious condition."

"I know."

She doesn't like how this is going. She needs to put a stop to it before they start talking about locking her up in a psychiatric ward again. Because she's not going back there. And she has one more card to play before asking for an attorney.

"Listen, uh, Detective Brennan. Can I ask you something?"

"Sure."

"This might sound a little odd, but can you call your colleagues at the fusion center and ask them to check my name, please?"

"We already did."

"On classified channels."

"Oh." He sits back in his chair, like this has changed everything. Sighs, as if she's been wasting his time. "Right, it's like that. And you can't just tell me right now what I'm gonna find?"

"I can't. Sorry."

"Okay. You got it." Brennan slowly gets to his feet, picks up the file, and leaves.

Getting his team to check with Langley isn't ideal, but she held out as long as she could. Hopefully, the confirmation of her old job will make Brennan see that they're on the same side. That she's one of the good guys. Then he'll let her go home.

Go and pick up little Josh.

She decides she'll make him his favourite for dinner: mac 'n' cheese. She imagines his reaction when she tells him what he's having. His big grin, those cute dimples in his cheeks, and that fist-pumping celebration he does whenever a treat is announced.

She pictures herself smothering him with a hug, stroking his hair, telling him he's safe.

Hoping that it's true.

*

It's forty minutes before the door opens again and she's about to start complaining when she sees it's not Brennan.

It's another middle-aged white guy. This one is pretty similar to the detective, except he's a little older, got a little more hair, and his suit is a little nicer. She wonders if he's a fed. Maybe she'll be able to tell him about the threat she overheard.

She has to tell someone else, sooner or later.

"Hello, Ellen," he says gently.

"Who are you?"

"I'm Doctor Schulz," he replies, sitting down opposite her. "I've been asked to conduct your psychiatric evaluation."

"Psychiatric? But ... Detective Brennan was supposed to check—"

"Classified channels, yes."

"So, what happened?"

"He checked."

"And?"

"There's no record of you ever working for the United States government."

3

S HE FEELS AS though the floor's dropping away beneath her. There's a tightness in her chest, a churning in her belly, and her head is starting to hurt again where it hit the doorframe of the cop car. She tries to process what's gone wrong, but her thoughts are racing so fast it's hard to think straight.

"That can't be right," she says. "You sure?"

"That's what they told me," replies Schulz.

"But . . . there must've been a mistake," she protests.

"I'm not with law enforcement, I'm afraid." His tone is almost apologetic, but not quite.

"They checked classified channels, though?"

"Oh yes." The psychiatrist gives her a benevolent smile. "I'm assured of that."

No wonder they sent a goddamn shrink to evaluate her, she thinks. They obviously figure she's crazy because she's claiming to be a spook after attacking a man — apparently an ordinary citizen — at a national monument.

She realizes it's actually worse than that. They believe she's crazy *and* dangerous.

Which is a not a good look when you're under arrest.

"This is so fucked up," she mutters to herself.

"I'm sorry?"

"Nothing."

She wonders how this could have happened. Forces herself to go through the logical steps. Most likely, they made the wrong check. Brennan called a junior colleague, who spelled her name wrong, checked the wrong box on the search app, maybe read the wrong result.

Because she *should* be in the system at Langley.

So, why wasn't she?

Even as a NOC — a non-official cover operative — she has to be on a list, someplace in the building. One that can be checked in case of incidents exactly like this one. She *knows* she's on that list — hell, they must've checked it when Harry got his new job — so it's probably just human error that she wasn't found.

That's the simplest explanation, and the most probable.

But she acknowledges that there are two other possibilities. Both a whole lot worse than some junior analyst pressing the wrong key because he's watching the Phillies highlights on his second monitor while he works.

One is that the people she's onto here — the group whose name she heard whispered by two men in D.C. last week — have friends in high places. Friends who can, say, dictate what happens to someone once they're in custody. That frightens the hell out of her. But the other possibility is just as bad.

That the Agency has scrubbed her from its books.

They must've done it right after they forced her out.

After what happened in France.

Covering their asses. Accusing her of "freelancing" and "incompetence". Standing by their public assessment that Paris had been totally unpredictable. Putting distance between Langley and any future investigations or congressional hearings. Delete, deny. That's what they do.

They'd effectively washed their hands of her. Put her on

gardening leave pending an investigation. Then offered to terminate the investigation if she just quit. She'd wanted to fight her case, but she didn't have the energy. Her mental health was shot to pieces, her career was over, and she was done with the Agency.

So, she quit. And, after Harry had wrapped up his charity work in France, they returned to the US and started over. Which meant a whole lot of therapy for Ellen as she tried to work through her trauma.

As she considers which is more likely, she wonders if Paris is, in fact, the real reason for her *no trace*. That churning in her belly has turned into full-blown nausea, now, as bad as the first trimester of her pregnancy with Josh. She thinks she might throw up.

It could be a symptom of concussion from where she hit her head earlier.

More likely, it's the memory that's just come back to her. A scene she'll never forget for as long as she lives.

*

Paris, France, five years earlier

The noise hits her from a half-mile away, long before she can see the chaos. It's loud enough to be heard over her Vespa engine and through her helmet. She slows to take the corner as a fire truck blows right by her, blue lights flashing and siren screaming. It races ahead of her, towards the crowd a few blocks down. There are a bunch more of the *sapeur-pompiers* — the city's paramedic firefighters — already here. They're always the first to be dispatched to an accident.

But she knows this is no accident.

"Jesus Christ," she says to herself as the scene ahead comes into full view.

It's Armageddon.

Ambulances, cop cars, emergency services everywhere. Hordes of people, yelling, weeping, spilling out from the mass of vehicles. She brakes hard, drops the kickstand on her scooter. Doesn't bother locking it, just grabs the keys.

Then she runs toward it all.

A cop tries to block her path, but she dodges him like a running back heading for the endzone. Except there's no endzone, only a war zone.

A war zone in the middle of Paris.

Her sprint becomes a jog when she gets close to the movie theatre. The place where one of her sources had told her all hell was breaking loose.

They were right.

A woman is rushed past her on a stretcher, oxygen mask on her face, carried by four guys in the orange uniforms of the French Red Cross. That's bad news, because it means they've already got too many casualties for the regular paramedics to deal with.

And those are the victims who are still alive.

The ones who didn't make it are lying on the ground, outlined beneath white sheets. She starts to count the bodies and stops when she reaches twenty. Some of the corpses haven't even been covered yet. Maybe they've run out of sheets. Because no one in Paris was prepared for this.

Blood is splashed on the sidewalk and the walls. It's even sprayed on the big glass doors of the movie theatre, like it's a Jackson Pollock canvas.

A young woman has clamped a hand over her mouth in silent grief, her eyes wide with shock. She's unsteady on her feet and leaning into the man beside her for support.

A guy with a tinfoil blanket and blood splattered over his t-shirt is using a cell phone. She tunes into his voice just long enough to realize he's American.

Ellen slows until she's standing still amid this carnage, like she's the eye of an apocalyptic storm.

She knows her life will never be the same. This — all of this — is on her.

Because she could have stopped it.

*

Present day

"Are you all right, Ellen?" Schulz's question pulls her back to the room. Across the table, he's studying her with obvious concern. "I lost you for a moment there."

"I was remembering something."

The psychiatrist nods. "What were you remembering?"

She swallows. Her mouth is dry. "Um, I . . ."

"You have a history of trauma-related dissociative episodes, don't you?"

She stares at him. *Go to hell*, she thinks, *you have no idea*.

"I need a break," she says. "I want to speak to my parents and ask them to pick up my son."

"Okay."

"And I want to call a lawyer," she adds.

"Of course," replies Schulz. "I'll pass that on."

"Thank you."

"Don't worry," he says. "We have plenty of time to do your psych evaluation."

But she *is* worried. Because she can tell he's already making his diagnosis.

*

"So, what you're saying, Ellen, is that you believed this man intended to kill you?"

"Well, probably not there and then," she replies. "Eventually, perhaps. I think he wanted to find out how much I knew. Where I was going, who I was meeting. But I couldn't take that risk, once I realized he was tailing me."

"Right. I see." Schulz notes the details of her story, same as Brennan did, his disbelief just as obvious as the detective's.

"If you investigate the guy — what's his name, again? Michael John Smith? — you'll probably find it's an alias," she tells him. "The question is, what's his true identity?"

"I'm not an investigator," the psychiatrist says. "I'm here to understand what's going on for *you*."

"I'm telling you what's going on for me. A guy with a concealed weapon was following me to a lunch meeting in downtown Philly, for Christ's sakes."

She feels her cheeks flush with anger. He's not *listening*, same as Brennan. He's just hearing what he wants to hear.

Schulz taps an expensive-looking pen on his notepad.

"What I don't quite get, Ellen, is how you can be so confident this man meant you harm," he says.

"Instincts, I guess."

"What instincts?"

"From my old job." She takes a breath. "In the CIA."

"But we've already established that you had no such job."

"No, I don't work there anymore, I—"

"You never worked there, though," he cuts in, "did you?"

She shakes her head. She can't believe this is happening. Damn straight, he doesn't *get it*. She needs to make him see how serious this is. Why she did what she did.

"Look," she says, "I heard something, last week, okay? About a possible terrorist threat."

"Really?" The shrink narrows his eyes. "What did you hear?"

"Only that . . . there's going to be a mass-casualty attack."

"Where?"

"Here, in the United States."

"Where exactly?"

"I don't know."

"By whom?"

"I don't know."

"Hm."

That's not the whole truth. She did hear a name: *Keystone Boys*. But she'd never heard of them before, and there was no mention of them online when she checked the surface web. That's why she wanted to ask Walter; if anybody's heard of them, it'd be him. But that'll have to wait. In the meantime, she doesn't want to give the name out to anyone she doesn't know. If the people who sent a guy to follow her — maybe even kill her — have any role in her detention, then they less information she gives people like Brennan and Schulz, the better.

For all she knows, they could be a part of it, too.

"Has anyone explained to you what a persecutory delusion is, Ellen?" Schulz peers over his notebook at her.

"Yes. But that's not—"

"The kind of paranoia you're describing is quite common in people who experience delusions like yours, along with a loss of their connection to . . . how to put it? Reality."

"I haven't lost my connection to reality."

"And you say you were in D.C. when you heard this?"

"Yes, I was out with my husband. He's a congressman."

The psychiatrist nods. "Fantasies of connection to powerful people are often a feature of the disorder, too."

"It's not a goddamn fantasy." She can hear the hostility in her own voice. Tries to calm herself down. "My husband *is* a congressman. Harry Flanagan. Democrat, Montgomery County, PA. Google it if you don't believe me."

"My phone is outside."

"Where's my lawyer?"

"I'm sorry, I don't know."

Something in her snaps.

"What the fuck is going on here?" she demands.

Schulz leans back, holds up his palms. "You need to relax, Ellen, okay?"

She shuts her eyes, takes a breath. Fights to keep control.

"I'm not crazy, doc," she says, quietly. "I'm telling you the truth. I swear."

"A lot of psychiatric patients lack insight into their condition," he responds. "It's very normal."

"But I'm not—"

"And," he continues, talking over her, "in view of your violent behavior today, and the risk you pose to the public at large, I'm going to recommend you be transferred to a safe place."

"What are you talking about? What safe place?"

"A Community Mental Health Center."

"No, no, no. Wait—"

"They'll make sure that you get the care you need. Medication, further assessment, therapy . . ."

"This is bullshit!" she yells. "I'm telling you about a threat to the United States, and you wanna have me committed? Let me speak to the FBI, for Christ's sake. They'll listen."

"I'm afraid it's too late for that." Schulz doesn't look at her as he gathers his things, pushes his chair back and stands. "The decision's been made."

She stands, too. She feels like she could kill this guy with her bare hands. She *knows* she could. But that'd only make things worse, since she's inside a police station.

"Who made the decision?"

"Don't worry," he says. "I'm sure it'll only be a short stay."

4

PETER LOGAN SLIPS his bank card into the jukebox beside the bar. Used to be, you put real money in the machine at the Toby Tavern and chose real records. But a lot of things ain't what they used to be.

Jukeboxes turn digital, stores close down, iron and steel works shut, people move out. Same story across the whole damned Rust Belt, from here on up to Wisconsin. The oil and coal refineries have gone, too, and the jobs with them.

The closest Peter can get to those industries now is his part-time work at the local gas station that pays minimum wage and gets him no respect. Even thinking about it makes him tense up with rage like he wants to smash someone's face in. The betrayal that caused it all. But he snaps out of it as the machine spits his card back and the big screen tells him he's got three choices.

"Hey, Pee-Wee," calls Leanne, from behind him. "No Nickelback, remember?"

He looks up at the handwritten sign taped to the wall by the jukebox, saying pretty much that. Leanne stuck it up there after he kept playing Nickelback. The staff left it there.

"Some people don't appreciate good music," he replies, but his words are drowned out by laughter around the bar. Even Angie, the barmaid, who has a soft spot for him, is quietly chuckling as she pours their first round of beers from the tap. Screw them all, he thinks.

Especially Leanne.

Thing is, he'd like nothing more than to *actually* screw Leanne. The problem is that she's his big brother, Mitch's, girl. So, it ain't happening, even if Leanne was interested, which she's not, and even if Peter could bring himself to go all Cain-and-Abel on Mitch like that, which he couldn't. Not after everything Mitch has done for him. It wouldn't be right. Besides, if he touched Leanne, Mitch — who has six inches and sixty pounds on Peter — would beat the living crap out of him. None of that stops him *imagining* screwing her, though. Like, every day, for the past sixteen years, since they were in ninth grade together.

The laughter dies down and he's left staring at the jukebox screen, suddenly aware that everyone's going to judge his selection. For a moment, he considers picking "How You Remind Me" — which is still one of his favourite songs — but instead he goes for the safe option of AC/DC. Classic rock, timeless. No one can give him shit for that.

As Brian Johnson starts belting out "Back in Black", Peter turns and heads back over to their table. He's almost there when Randy looks up.

"Yo, Pee-Wee, go grab our beers. Save Angie the trip." Randy jerks a thumb towards the bar and the tray of five glasses.

Go get 'em yourself, you lazy fuck, Peter wants to say. But Randy Kowalski goes 6-6 and 290 pounds, and Peter knows better than to talk back to The Dozer. People in Clarion started calling Randy that when he was just a sophomore in high school, but already as big as a grown man. As a defensive end, he bull-dozed enough opposition on the football field to win himself a full ride to Penn State. Some even had him tipped for the pros, until torn knee ligaments brought him back here to sit on a tractor in soybean fields, still without a college degree, but a whole lot angrier than when he left. And Peter doesn't want to provoke that anger now, so he swallows his pride.

"Uh, okay," he says. "Sure."

He fetches the tray and sets it down like he's a server. The others reach in and take their drinks without acknowledging he's even there.

"That's why the attack on The Capitol didn't go far enough," says Sherman. "They had the government right by the balls, and they just let it go."

Leanne and Randy voice their support, but Peter says nothing. Sips his beer. It's not that he doesn't agree — the government are a bunch of corrupt, hypocritical motherfuckers who need to be strung up by their necks — it's just that he doesn't much like Sherman.

Sherman Schweinsteiger — or "Sherman the German", as he's known, because no one can pronounce his last name — is the newest member of their group. He ain't from Clarion, and he ain't German, either, not really. His ancestors emigrated from Bavaria like a hundred-something years ago. He don't even speak German. But he plays up that background because of the whole Aryan, Nazi shit he's into. Sherman's even got a small swastika tattooed on his chest, though he knows better than to show it off.

Peter's no seig-heiling, Mein Kampf-reading Nazi, he's just a patriot, like his brother, Mitch. A patriot who believes his government has been destroying the American way of life, lying to the American people, and shitting all over the Constitution for years — and who wants to do whatever it takes to change that.

According to Mitch, that's where Sherman comes in. He's smart, smarter than all of them, even Mitch. He would've been a sciences major at Clarion College if he hadn't gotten kicked out.

He says it was the social justice warriors whining about his politics, but Peter knows it was because he made his own meth, got high all the time, then got caught selling his product on campus.

"You know what?" Leanne says. "Once they got inside The Capitol, they shoulda torched the place. That's what I woulda done. Started the civil war."

Sherman lifts his eyebrows. "Well, that's up to us now, isn't it?"

"Hell, yeah." Leanne grins. *God damn, she's hot*, Peter thinks.

"I'll drink to that." Randy raises his glass.

"To civil war!" cries Sherman.

"Jeez, keep your voice down," whispers Peter.

"What's the problem, Pee-Wee?" Sherman holds his arms wide, looks around. "No one's listening." Maybe he's right. At six thirty on a Monday, there's only a dozen people in the tavern, and most of them would probably agree that civil war was a good idea. Peter knows for a fact that one of the two guys shooting pool across the room has prepped a bunker with a shit ton of tinned food and ammo for exactly that situation. Still, he wants to be careful.

"Mitch told us not to talk about stuff like that too loud," he says.

"He made me delete the Instagram page I was making for us," Leanne complains.

"Whatever." Sherman shrugs, but he doesn't disagree. You don't challenge the alpha male, even in his absence, unless you're ready for a fight. And Sherman doesn't want that. No one who knows Mitch wants that.

Right on cue, as the song kicks into the power chords of the chorus, Mitch walks in.

Peter feels the atmosphere shift a little. The pool players stop, and the men at the bar turn in their seats. One of them, an old steelworker, tips his hat. There's respect — awe, even — and with good reason. Mitch is the man around here.

Okay, Clarion's just a small town that's only ever produced one celebrity — Chris Kirk-something, from that boy band NSYNC — but Mitch would still be the man if this was Pittsburgh or Cleveland or anyplace else.

His older brother is 6-2 and 200 pounds of solid muscle, the All-American boy. A gifted quarterback in high school, he passed up on playing college football with Randy to enlist in the Marines and protect his homeland. And that went pretty well, at least to begin with.

Mitch went off to Camp Lejeune in North Carolina, from where he completed tours in Iraq, Afghanistan, Somalia and Syria. He fought and killed America's enemies from Al-Qaida, the Taliban, Al-Shabab and ISIS. He took a bullet in Raqqa, stuck on his own field dressing and kept fighting. He was awarded the Medal of Honor *and* a Silver Star. The guy's a freakin' hero. Risked his life for his country more times than anybody could count. Lost a lot of fellow jarheads in the process. Which is probably why his motivation right now is stronger than any of them sat around this table. He had so much further to fall.

"What's goin' on?" says Mitch, as he sits down. He leans across, kisses Leanne full on the lips, bumps fists with Randy and takes a long pull on his beer.

"Got you a Bud, Mitch," says Peter. "Regular, not Light."

"Attaboy, Pee-Wee."

"Where you been, baby?" coos Leanne. She wants Mitch's attention. Dammit, they all do. But Peter knows that Leanne Spinoza needs attention more than most. She craves it, maybe because she never got it as a kid from her drunk dad and depressed mom. And she didn't find it on stage, either. He remembers when she left town for L.A., telling everyone she was going to make it big out west. Instead, she worked in a bar for six months and appeared in one porn film before coming home to Clarion and telling everyone she'd changed her mind about a career in acting. Peter still has the DVD of that film. More than one copy, in fact.

"Just got back from seeing our friend," Mitch replies. "And I got some news."

They all wait in silent expectation.

"We're confirmed for the Fourth of July," says Mitch. "Six days from now."

"Oh my God, yes!" Leanne blurts. She's wriggling with excitement, like a kid.

Sherman cracks a slow smile. "It's really happening."

"Let's fuckin' do this," adds Randy.

Only Peter is silent. He still ain't sure this is the right thing to do. Strike at government, yes. With a bomb? If necessary — that's sure as hell gonna get people's attention, just look at the Unabomber. But like *this*? He don't know, yet. He's trusting Mitch, just like he's always done. But he's scared, too.

"To the Keystone Boys." Mitch raises his glass.

"And girl," Leanne adds.

They whoop and cheer and touch glasses and everyone else in the tavern looks over, probably wondering whose birthday it is. But Mitch ain't happy. He's got that look in his eyes, the same one he'd have whenever he came back home from a military tour.

Like he wants to kill someone. Which is exactly what they're gonna do in six days. And not just someone. A whole lot of people.

Peter tries to drink his beer, but his throat's so tight, he can barely swallow.

*

Washington, D.C.

He's never been one for private clubs. They go against everything he stands for. Right now, though, he's got no choice. He needs the protection afforded by that exclusivity. A private room in a member's club, with no phones or cameras allowed, is about the safest location for him.

He's sitting in a deep Chesterfield armchair upholstered in green leather, surrounded by antique furniture and framed photographs of men — yup, he checks: all men — who have run the nation's capital one way or another since this place was founded, midway through the Civil War.

The Metropolitan Club has been home to political, military and business leaders since it opened its doors to the select few in 1863. People like the group he's sipping twenty-year-old scotch out of crystal tumblers with this evening.

"Heard we mighta had ourselves a li'l problem in Philly," says the man from Texas.

He's not sure if there's a question hidden in there, an invitation for him to respond. To justify himself to them. Before he can reply, though, the youngest of their group jumps in.

"I apologize, sir," offers the kid. He's maybe three, four years out of college. Slick hair and sharp suit, the kid reeks of ambition. A boy who wants to be king, or President of the United States, at least. "It wasn't supposed to . . ." he tails off, clears his throat. "There were unforeseen circumstances. I was assured that the man who was contracted for the job was more than capable of the task, but, ah——"

"That turned out to be wrong, didn't it?" This from the Californian woman. Her nickname is The Ballbreaker. He's scared of her. He thinks they probably all are, at some level, even The Texan. "He was *capable* of getting himself sent to ER by a woman, but clearly not a whole lot more than that," she says.

"It won't happen again."

"What I — what we — all want to know, son, is: has it been dealt with?" asks The Texan.

"Yes."

"You certain about that?"

"Sure, we are. Right?" The kid turns to him.

He feels the heat rise in his face. "Yes."

"It's been taken care of," adds the kid. "She's locked up, and she's not going anywhere, not until . . ." He doesn't need to finish his sentence.

"Speaking of which," says the fifth member of their group, an older man with a grey moustache, "how was your meeting with G.I. Joe today?"

"Good," he replies. "He says they'll be ready this time next week."

"I know we can trust *him*," says the man with the moustache. "But what about that bunch of rednecks he's with? Any of them ever done anything like this before?"

"No," he replies, thinking: *none of us has ever done anything like this before.* "But he's trained them."

"Has he? Hm." The older man sips his scotch. "Well, we'd better pray that's enough for them to pull this off."

He agrees with the sentiment. And if he believed in God, he'd be praying morning, noon and night. Because if it goes wrong, they're all done for. He drinks his scotch, too much and too fast, and it burns his throat. He's not sure how it came to this, how he found himself here with these people.

He only knows there's no way out of it, now.

5

A S THEY LEAVE the high-rise buildings of downtown Philly in the rear-view and hit the Schuylkill Expressway heading northwest, Ellen allows herself to think for a moment that they might actually be taking her home. That someone has realized this was all a huge mistake, and she's free to go.

She closes her eyes and imagines the scene as she arrives at the house. Little Josh is out front, tossing a baseball back and forth with her dad on the lawn, while her mom sits on the porch, reading the paper and watching her boys. Ellen pictures her son's open-mouthed shock as she steps out of the cop car, hears him demanding the story from her. *What happened, Mom? What'd you do?* She'd make something up about helping the police solve a crime and Josh would want her to tell it again and again as she put him to bed.

But she knows it's just a fantasy. Despite the fact that the two cops up front won't answer her questions — as if they're monks who've taken a vow of silence — she has some idea where they're headed. And it's not home.

They don't handcuff people they're taking home.

Back in the police station, her lawyer had explained over the phone that, because of some technicalities to do with public risk and police involvement, she couldn't access a clinic via the health insurance she was on through Harry's work. So, she was going to be taken to a Community Mental Health Center instead.

The lawyer assured her that it'd be safe and comfortable, that it was just a precaution after the incident at Independence Hall, and given her psychiatric history. That she'd stay there overnight, and they'd fix everything tomorrow. Ellen refused to go — she wanted this fixed *now*. But the lawyer said there was nothing more he could do for her. The system was the system. She had to go.

Ellen tried to fight it. But Dr Schulz wouldn't alter his assessment, Detective Brennan had already left the station, and the duty sergeant just shrugged and said his hands were tied. Didn't matter that they all knew by now that she was a congressman's wife. That she wasn't lying about *that*, at least. The decision was final. The whole thing was like some awful nightmare from which she couldn't wake up. She'd felt herself starting to panic as her control slipped away.

Her lawyer had assured her it'd be fine. All they needed was a different psychiatrist, another opinion, and the commitment order could be reversed. She just had to wait it out until the morning. Best not to go to the press, shouting about injustice right now, *for Harry's sake*. Ellen had wondered whose interests the lawyer was protecting. But, eventually, she'd had no choice but to accept it. Her parents were looking after Josh, and she'd call Harry from the clinic later. Tell him everything that happened. Tell him to do every damn thing he can to help.

Now she sees they're headed to Norristown, she figures that if she's got to stay under observation for a night, it might as well be at a clinic close to her house. That way it'll be a shorter ride back home tomorrow.

Then, without warning, the cops make a right turn and her stomach lurches as she realizes where they're going.

The wide, red-brick entrance, with sweeping lawns and tall

fir trees beyond them, makes the place look like a country club. Only the sign on the gate says otherwise: NORRISTOWN STATE HOSPITAL. And even that doesn't tell the whole story.

Ellen knows that this place — just two miles from her home — is a state-run psychiatric facility. And it houses a particular kind of patient.

"What's going on?" she demands from the back. She's starting to panic.

Neither officer answers.

"Why are we here? This isn't the Community Center."

Still no response.

Ellen kicks out at the panel separating her from the cops. "Hey! I'm talking to you." She kicks again. "Answer me, goddammit!"

Finally, one turns slowly in his seat. "Our orders are to bring you here."

A bolt of adrenalin shoots through her. "But this is a forensic psychiatric unit," she protests.

"Probably no bed space at the CMHC," replies the other cop. "That's usually the reason."

"Jesus Christ," she hisses, kicking the panel once more for good measure.

They roll past old, abandoned buildings, overgrown with foliage — relics of an asylum system from the last century. The kids in the area all think they're haunted and dare each other to come in here at night. Even Josh has heard ghost stories about this place. Ellen's never been here but she's watched videos on YouTube. It's creepy as hell.

But that's not what's making her pulse skyrocket.

She spots the notorious Building 51 from way down the road. You can't miss it. She's seen it on local news reports. A solid brick block, featureless except for the rows of narrow, barred windows, and surrounded by a high metal fence that curves inwards as it rises. It's designed like a prison, to keep people in. Which makes sense, because this is, effectively, a prison. A place to put criminals who aren't mentally fit to stand trial. Who don't understand what they've done. Now — for a night, at least — she's one of them.

She knows she doesn't belong here. And yet, a little voice is whispering to her that maybe she does.

Reminding her that she *was* in a place like this, not all that long ago.

This is all just a mistake, she tells herself.

She's not crazy.

Not this time.

*

The first thing Ellen hears when the two male orderlies escort her through the locked door to the ward is screaming. It's coming from a room off the third-floor corridor they're leading her down. Screams and thumping, as if someone's trying to break out.

She sees another orderly come to the door. He peers through the glass, tells the occupant to calm down, and walks away. But the piercing, raging noise continues and, as they pass the door, she glimpses a woman through the little window, back turned, gripping and twisting her own hair in both hands as she paces. There's nothing else in the room.

Ellen reads the small, printed sign beside the door handle: SAFETY SUITE. There's a lock on the outside of the door, same as every other door, she notices. Her anxiety surges again, pooling in her belly and spreading out through her guts. This is a prison.

They're putting her in a prison.

Down another identical corridor and through a further locked door, they finally stop in front of a room. As one orderly beside her extends a key card clipped to his belt and opens the door, the other tightens his grip on her arm. A woman in a different uniform appears from behind them. She's about Ellen's age and height and is wearing glasses over small, cold eyes. She starts to explain to Ellen about the bathroom and the showers and lights out and breakfast and she's talking really fast and it's too much for Ellen to take in.

They may have removed her cuffs, but bottom line is that they're still locking her up. They've already taken everything from her, including her cell phone. Now they're taking away her freedom. And it has to be because of what she's heard. *They* must be behind this. The same people who created an alias firearms license and sent a man to tail her through Philly this morning. Who are they? The Keystone Boys? Or another group of more powerful people? The ones she overheard at the hotel in D.C., maybe. Whoever they are, they've engineered this, she's sure of it, because she's a threat to them. For all she knows, the staff here could be part of it, too.

Her mind is racing, now, and the only thing she's sure about is that she doesn't want to be here, she wants to get out, wants to be back home tucking Josh into bed and reading him a story and then making sure her contact Walter is okay and arranging to see him again and finding out who the Keystone Boys are before they . . .

Suddenly she's picturing a bomb site, she's seeing bodies and blood and debris and it feels like her nerves are electrified and her heart's going a hundred miles per hour and next thing she's shaken free of the orderly's grip and is running back the way she came.

At the end of the corridor, she reaches a door and yanks the handle. It's locked. She hears footsteps behind her and spins.

"Stop right there," says the orderly.

"I shouldn't be here," she tells him.

"It's okay, ma'am," he raises his hands, steps toward her. "We're here to help you."

In a flash, she lunges across to the wall and grabs the fire extinguisher mounted on it. Pulls the pin and points it at the guy. He raises his palms, starts to back away. He's smart enough not to want a lungful of sodium bicarbonate powder. Behind him, the woman presses a button on her lanyard. An alarm sounds.

"Back up," Ellen commands them. She sprays a burst into the air to show she's serious. "Move!"

They do as she says.

Then she turns and smashes the glass in the door with the butt of the extinguisher. Reaches through carefully, making sure she doesn't cut herself on the glass shards, and punches the door release switch. Grabs the handle, tears it open and runs.

Breathing hard, she checks over her shoulder, but the staff aren't following her. She needs to find a way out, an escape route. She sees the green sign for an emergency exit up ahead and races toward it, still holding the extinguisher. But before she reaches it, the door at the end bursts open and two huge guys come through.

They're dressed all in black and jacked up like they've been taking steroids. Ellen knows she won't get to the exit door before they do. As they charge at her, she raises the extinguisher and hits them with a cloud of dry powder.

The guy in front slows and doubles over, hands on knees, coughing. The one behind him keeps coming and Ellen fires another blast. His eyes and mouth are shut, and he stumbles past his buddy, his arms flailing at her.

She sidesteps and smacks him in the head with the extinguisher, the force of her strike sending him to the carpet. She drops the extinguisher and sprints for the exit.

As soon as she hits the stairwell beyond it, she hears heavy, quick steps coming from above. The black boots and pants of another security guy come into view and she darts back, heading down.

Only now there are footsteps below her, more guys in

uniform running up, so she goes back through to the corridor. She's just reaching for the extinguisher again when the men explode through the emergency exit door and hit her like defensive linemen sacking a quarterback.

Then there are more guys, more thick arms and big hands clamping down on her, pulling at her limbs. She feels a knee in her back and next thing she's face down, pinned to the ground.

"Lemme go!" she yells. "Get the fuck off of me!"

But they don't budge an inch. She can hear coughing and wheezing from the first guy she took out with the extinguisher. The second one isn't making any sound; she guesses he's out cold.

She twists her neck just enough to see the woman with glasses approaching from behind her. She's holding a syringe.

"No!" Ellen cries.

"Hold her still," says the woman.

Ellen fights, kicks, bucks her body, but there are four men on top of her, and she can't move. Their weight is unbearable, compressing her lungs. She feels as though her ribs could crack at any minute. She can't even catch her breath. She knows she could die like this.

Then the needle stabs into her butt cheek and pressure builds behind it as the woman injects her.

She pictures the scene of the explosion in Paris, again, fragments of film playing in her mind, only this time it's in Philly and she's not even sure if it's real or not. Then the little voice tells her once more that maybe there is no mistake. Maybe she does belong here.

Her limbs start to relax.

Now she sees herself at home with Harry, curled up on the sofa, a glass of wine and a movie. He's stroking her hair and she feels safe. She tells him that she loves him. He says something back, but it's just a whisper she can't quite catch.

Then everything dissolves into darkness and silence.

DAY TWO

DAY TWO

6

Brrrrrp, Brrrrrp...
The ring tone seems to go on forever, and Ellen starts to think that maybe he's gone into one of those really long meetings and she's missed him.

She's standing in the corner of the communal area on the ward, in front of the payphone. Across the room, a few patients are sat around the TV, watching some talk show that's on way too loud. Others are in chairs, either gazing vacantly out of the window, or staring at the walls like zombies, or just asleep. Ellen doesn't blame them for their lack of energy; she feels pretty much the same. Maybe it's the effect of this place. More likely, it's the drugs they're being given. Amid all this lethargy, a young woman is pacing up and down on her own, talking non-stop, really fast, as if she's arguing with an invisible enemy.

A security guard prowls the perimeter of the room, eyeballing Ellen every time he faces her. She can't tell if he was one of the guys that wrestled her to the ground last night after she tried to escape. Even if he's not, she figures he's heard what happened and already has her marked. She holds his gaze; she's not scared of him.

To her left, an orderly doles out pills to an older woman,

sitting at a table in front of a pile of jumbled jigsaw pieces. The woman takes the tablets without a word and mechanically swallows them before gulping down some water. She doesn't even look up.

Ellen grips the receiver tightly and presses it hard against her ear, jamming a finger in her other ear to shut out the TV. Closes her eyes to focus on the call.

"Come on, Harry, please be there . . ." she mutters.

Brrrrrp . . .

She's about to hang up when there's a click, and the voice she'd know anywhere comes on the line, deep and clear.

"Hello?"

Just that one word from Harry fills her with hope. It's an instant connection to her *real* life, immediate proof that all this is just some temporary craziness that's going to be over soon. It's proof that she's right: it *is* a mistake that she's here. Proof that the people who put her here — and the doubting whisper in her head — are wrong. Then she realizes her husband won't have this number, and won't know who's calling.

"Harry," she says, hearing the longing in her own voice, already feeling the emotion rising inside her, threatening to overwhelm her. She pushes it down — she needs to hold herself together right now.

"Oh, sweet Jesus, Ellen!" he exclaims. "How are you? What the hell's going on? The hospital won't tell me anything. I spoke to the lawyer and your parents and . . . and I tried to call last night but they said you were asleep and . . . God, honey, I've been so worried, and I didn't know—"

"I'm okay," she replies, even though she feels anything but *okay*. "I'm fine, really."

"You sure?"

"Well, a little groggy, actually," she adds, almost smiling. "They gave me something."

"What — what'd they give you?"

"I don't know." She doesn't want to tell him it took four huge dudes plus a nurse with a syringe to give it to her, whatever it was, and even the memory of that is hazy. "Some sedative, I guess."

"Seriously? Are they . . . have they locked you up, like in a cell or something? They'd better be treating you right. Our attorney says you shouldn't even be in that place. He's filed for another medical opinion, a different psychiatrist, one he knows. They can evaluate you and then there's a chance they'll reverse the commitment order, and we can——"

"Wait a second." She cuts him off. "A *chance*?"

"Yeah, I know. He can't say for sure, because there's a process, legal issues, and it sucks, but . . ." Harry pauses, lowers his voice. "What the hell happened in Philly anyway? A guy attacked you? They said there were shots fired."

"One shot. It didn't hit anyone."

She tells Harry the story. He'll have seen some of it on the news. She caught the bulletin on TV first thing this morning: *Gunshot at Independence Park, Philadelphia PD arrest woman.* The headline was accompanied by some shaky footage from a cell phone, but you couldn't see her face, and she wasn't mentioned by name. Neither was the guy who'd been tailing her.

"Is it . . .?" he asks tentatively. "I mean, do you think it was . . .?"

"What?"

"You know, because before, when you——"

"I don't know." She can guess what he's about to say. Something about her mental health. Paris, PTSD, the previous episode, where she ended up in a place like this . . . imagining stuff that might not be real. "Maybe. But there's also that thing, you know, that I heard."

"Oh, that."

She recalls Harry's reaction when she told him, not as negative as Brennan or Schulz yesterday, but still sceptical. She doesn't want to get into that, now, though. She's not sure who might be listening. She clamps the phone between her ear and shoulder, suddenly exhausted, and rubs her eyes with both hands.

"Please just help me get out of here, Harry."

"I will. I swear."

She believes him. Harry has a way of doing that. She guesses it's a big part of how he ended up in Congress. You don't get a quarter million people to vote for you if you can't win their confidence. It was the same for her, in her old job. You can't develop an asset and get them to tell you secrets if they don't trust you. Ellen had spent a long time being trained not to give out her own trust easily — but Harry blew all those defences away right from when they met. She can recall the day with total clarity.

It was eleven years ago, in France. Not at a glamorous cocktail party hosted by the US Embassy, or in a beautiful Parisian art gallery, but in a camp for illegal migrants outside the industrial port of Calais. A place with dirt roads and open sewers where desperate people, fleeing poverty in Africa and war in the Middle East, lived in tents and huddled around oil drum fires while they waited for trafficking gangs to get them across the English Channel. A place where women sold sex and men sold kidneys for a new identity and a boat ride. A place full of drugs and weapons and fear, where you could disappear or die, and no one would know. A place without hope.

Ellen had been there under a charity cover to find new assets for the Agency; people she might convince to return to the country they fled and spy for the United States. Harry was there with a *real* aid agency, fixing the sanitation, clearing up trash, and making sure people had clean water to drink. She saw him across a stretch of wasteland, surrounded by kids, talking to each one in turn as he handed them food. He was tall, with broad shoulders and an even broader smile. Her first thought was: *damn, he's hot.* Her second thought was: *I could marry that man.* She went over to talk to him. And her instincts turned out to be right.

"I love you," she says now, a crack in her voice as the emotion surges inside her once more, fuelled by that memory.

"Love you, too," he replies. "It'll be okay. We'll get through this."

"I know."

There's a brief silence.

"How's Josh?" she asks. "Did mom and dad say anything to him?"

"He's good."

"Does he . . .?"

"No, he doesn't know where you are. We've just told him you had to go away for a couple days to do some important stuff."

"And he was cool with that?"

"After your folks distracted him with ice cream, sure. He slept like a baby, they said."

She lets out a laugh at the relief that her little boy isn't scared about her being gone, but it's tempered by the pain at being kept apart from him — and from Harry, too. From her whole life. She looks around her again. Wonders why the other patients are in this place. She knows that, even if she's not meant to be here, most people are locked in this ward for a reason. She doesn't want to stay a minute longer than she has to.

"I'm going to call Josh later," she says, "when he gets back from baseball."

"Hopefully you'll be halfway to getting out by then," Harry says.

"Can you come?" she asks. "Today, I mean."

"I want to," he replies. "But I'm still in D.C."

"At the committee?"

"Yeah. We overran yesterday. We're about to go into another session now."

"Oh, okay. Sure."

Ellen knows that part of a congressperson's life is sitting on committees. Harry once told her that committees are where the real work of Congress gets done, investigating issues, reporting to the house, drafting legislation. He's current chair of a subcommittee under Energy and Commerce. Which means there's no way for him to get out of a sitting, even in a personal emergency.

"But I'm going to get to you as soon as I can. I promise."

"Today?"

Harry sighs. "It may not be today, honey. We're not going to be done until this afternoon, then there's the travel back home, and the lawyer said visiting hours are pretty tight. It's not like a regular hospital . . ."

"No shit," she says, an angry edge in her voice.

"Sorry. I realize it's tough, but just hang in there. This'll all be over before you know it, and we can get back to normal."

Normal. Whatever that means, now — after this, and after what she's heard. The threat that nobody is taking seriously. That she needs to do something about.

"I gotta go," he says, before she can reply. "The psychiatrist should be there real soon, okay?" he adds.

"When will—?"

"Love you. Bye."

"Harry—"

But the phone's dead. Her connection to the outside world is gone. And she feels completely alone once more.

7

ELLEN'S READING A copy of *National Geographic*, which is so old it came out while she was still in college, when she sees the woman approaching in her peripheral vision. About the same age as Ellen, give or take, she's tall, thin, and black. Her hair's up in a bun and she's wearing a 76ers sweater, leggings and sneakers. Her eyes are wide, and her fingers are working overtime, picking at her nails. Ellen's gut feeling tells her: this is a good person.

"It's the one thing we've got a whole lot of, right?" says the woman.

It takes Ellen a second to process what she means. She's pointing at the title of the TIME magazine laying on the table beside Ellen.

"Oh, yeah. We sure do," replies Ellen, with a half-smile, although she hopes it's not true in her case. It reminds her that she needs to be getting out. Where the hell is the new shrink Harry promised her? Maybe she should speak to someone . . .

"Do you mind?" the woman asks.

Ellen gestures to the magazine. "Go right ahead."

"I'm Jada," she says, taking a seat at the table and sliding the magazine towards her.

"Ellen."

Jada cocks her head. "You the one gave them jailers a beatdown?"

"Felt like it was me getting the beatdown," replies Ellen. She's got the bruises to prove it, not least on her left butt cheek, where the nurse stabbed her with a needle.

"Well, sounds like you did what most of us'd love to do. And on your first night, too." She laughs.

"Jailers?"

"Make no mistake, girl, we in jail. So, that's what we call them," says Jada, her smile vanishing. "They supposed to be there for *our* safety. Truth is, we'd be safer without them. They just here to keep us in line."

"Kinda seemed that way last night."

"Hm. No offence, but you don't really seem like the type to give a beatdown," Jada observes. "Or to be here at all, for that matter."

"I, uh . . . I actually think somebody made a mistake. I shouldn't be here."

Jada leans in. "You know what? Me neither."

"No?"

"Hell, no." Jada frowns briefly. "I belong out *there*," she points towards the barred window. "With my babies. I got Marquis, he's ten, and Maya, she's eight. You got kids?"

In her undercover days, Ellen had to be careful about any information she gave out to people. Any detail of her life could be used against her, any slip might compromise her mission. But she knows you have to give a little to get a little: the reciprocity principle. Plus, she's in here now, and she likes Jada, so she chooses to be open.

"Yeah. I have a boy, Josh. He's six."

"Aww, cute."

"I've been here less than a day," Ellen says, "and I already miss him like crazy."

"Lemme tell you, it don't get any better." Jada presses her lips together, shakes her head. "It gets *worse*, the longer you locked down. Every day goes by you don't see them. You feel it here." She places a hand on her chest. "It's like a physical pain."

"I know what you mean."

"Let's hope you right about it being a mistake, then, and they let you out."

"Yeah." Ellen nods. "So, how long have you been here?"

"A year. Thirteen months, three days, to be exact. And they wanna keep me here a whole lot longer, too."

"Who, the shrinks?"

"No." Something shifts in Jada's body language. She looks around, gets closer. "The government," she whispers. "They put me here."

Ellen shrugs. "They put us all here. It's a state psychiatric unit."

"No, you don't get it." Jada grimaces, goes back to picking her nails. "I'm sayin', I was a *problem* for them. They had to get rid of me."

"Why?"

"Because of what I know. I had special agents followin' me, cameras in my house, wire taps on my phone, the whole nine yards."

"Seriously?" Ellen doesn't believe it. Then again, her own story isn't all that different. And *she's* definitely not imagining it. She knows what she heard. Knows she should've been on the system at Langley when they checked her name.

"Damn straight. But what they don't know," Jada continues, lowering her voice until it's barely audible, "is that I'm working for the CIA."

"You are?"

Jada nods knowingly.

"Okay," says Ellen. "Your secret's safe with me."

"Thank you," Jada says. "I'm protecting America. From the enemy within."

"Let me know if I can help."

They exchange a smile. Ellen's pretty sure Jada doesn't work for the CIA, because this is a secure psychiatric ward, with a lot of delusional patients. And because CIA operatives don't tell strangers about their clandestine job within a minute of meeting them. But Ellen also realizes that, without proof of her former career, her own situation is pretty much the same as Jada's. Why should anyone believe her story, either?

Jada looks pleased, maybe even relieved, like this is the first time no one's immediately told her she's crazy.

Protecting America.

That was basically what drew Ellen to apply to the Agency. There was no cloak-and-dagger, top secret James Bond stuff that brought her into it. Just a careers fair at Princeton, right around the time she was finishing up in grad school and looking for a job. She'd studied politics and international relations, she loved languages and travel, and here was a woman from Langley standing by a board and telling her she could get paid to do all that in cool places, while keeping the United States safe.

It'd been five years since 9/11 but global terrorism seemed a bigger threat than ever, with Islamic extremists from Morocco to the Philippines capable of blowing themselves up in public, anytime. Of kidnapping and killing US citizens, or anyone else, for that matter, who didn't deserve to die because of some twisted religious beliefs. She could save lives by doing this job. Stand up to the bad guys, help the vulnerable. Do something good. Make a difference, as much of a cliché as that sounded. The woman asked if she was interested.

Ellen's decision was a no-brainer: she submitted the application that same week. If she'd only known what it would lead to, in Paris, all those years later, would she have made the same choice, or would she have stayed away from that world altogether?

She doesn't know. It's easy to say how we might have done things differently, when we know how they turned out.

She did what she could in Paris. Tells herself to remember that, no matter how much a little voice tries to convince her otherwise.

Her career was spent finding and stopping America's enemies overseas. Now, she thinks about what Jada just said: *the enemy within*. Those words bring her to what she's facing today. The reason she ended up here. And why she needs to get out.

The Keystone Boys.

. . .gonna need more graves out there than when the pandemic hit . . .

"You okay?" It's Jada.

Ellen refocuses on her surroundings. Her new friend is staring at her.

"Uh-huh," she says.

"Cus you looked a little—"

The noise of a door slamming and chairs scraping makes both of them turn.

A woman has entered the communal area and is heading toward the TV. She's built like Ronda Rousey, only taller, and swaggers through as if she owns the place. People are literally getting out of her way, including staff. The security guard gives the woman a nod and steps back, as if to say: *you're the boss*. Her hair is pulled back in a tight bun, exposing a large tattoo of a skull on the side of her neck.

She makes a detour via the table with the older woman — who's been sitting in front of the jigsaw pieces for an hour without touching them — and takes her food. A bag of potato chips, two candy bars, and a can of soda. Then she crosses to the TV, tells two women to get off the sofa, and orders a third to give her the remote. They all comply immediately. She flips channels until she finds a UFC re-run, sits back and cracks open the soda.

Laughs out loud as one guy on screen repeatedly punches another in the face, blood spilling from his nose and mouth.

"Who's that?" Ellen asks.

"That's Shawna LeDuc." Jada gets closer. "A badass bitch."

"I can believe that. What did she do?"

Jada's eyes flick over to Shawna and back. "Murdered her husband, and his lover. Strangled them both. With her bare hands."

"Holy shit."

"That ain't the half of it. They found the pair of them cut up in a garbage bag. Just sitting in the trash can outside their home. She told the shrinks the devil made her do it. They bought it. So did the judge. Which means she's chilling here instead of spending twenty-three hours a day locked in an eight-by-ten cell."

"You don't believe her?"

Jada snorts. "She's as sane as you or me."

Apart from the stuff about the CIA, Ellen thinks. "How do you know?"

"Told me so herself," says Jada. "The devil didn't have nuthin' to do with it."

"Wow. Okay."

"You want my advice?"

"Sure."

"Stay outta her way. And if she wants something of yours, give it to her."

Ellen shrugs. "I don't have anything." She tugs on the plain old sweater they gave her. "I haven't even got my own clothes. The cops took 'em.'"

"That don't matter. I'm talking about your seat, your place in line, whatever."

"We'll see about that."

Across the room, Shawna barks at a woman who looks young enough to be a teenager.

Ellen didn't see her face last night, but she can tell this is the same person who was locked in the so-called 'Safety Suite' when she arrived.

At first, the kid pretends not to hear, but Shawna repeats her name, louder.

"Luz! I'm talkin' to you."

Luz raises her eyes. They're large, dark brown, and fearful.

Shawna crooks a finger, summons her. "Get your ass over here."

There's a brief exchange that Ellen can't hear over the TV, but she lip reads:

You got my money? Shawna asks.

I need it, please, implores Luz. *It's for my son. For his formula, diapers.*

The son you tried to drown in the bathtub? You must really love him.

Por favor, Luz protests, *my mother's coming today, and I need to give it to her—*

Give it to me, says Shawna, *right now. Or you know what happens.* She clicks her fingers, holds out her palm.

Reluctantly, Luz reaches into her jeans pocket and pulls out a small roll of notes. Steps forward and offers it to Shawna.

Something snaps inside Ellen. She can't stand bullies. And she's not going to sit by and watch this. She pushes her chair back, gets up.

"Wait, what'ch you doing?" Jada hisses, but Ellen is already halfway across the communal area.

"Stop!" yells Ellen.

The room goes silent, except for the crowd on TV, baying for blood as the referee separates the two fighters before telling them to engage once more.

Luz freezes, the roll of notes still in her outstretched hand. Her head jerks up to face Ellen.

Slowly, Shawna turns to Ellen as well. "Who the fuck are you?" she demands.

The security guard does nothing. Hooks his thumbs into his belt and looks over to the TV, pretending not to notice.

A roar goes up from the UFC fans on screen as the fighters go at each another. The guy with the bloodied face is immediately taken down to the canvas.

"Keep your money, Luz," Ellen says calmly, although her heart is hammering.

The young woman hesitates. Puts the roll of bills back in her pocket. "Gracias," she whispers. Then she's gone, heading quickly out of the room and down a corridor.

Shawna shakes her head. "You must be out of your mind. You know who I am?"

Ellen doesn't reply. She's near enough to Shawna to see the detail of her neck tattoo. There are worms crawling out of the empty eye sockets in the skull, and a bony finger held up to its mouth, as though it's asking for silence.

Ellen checks around her, sees the camera in the corner, the little box on the wall.

Shawna stands. She's even taller and bigger up close.

On the TV, the crowd goes wild. Ellen looks across for a second as the UFC fighter with blood all over his face is now somehow on top of his opponent, a flurry of punches turning into a choke hold that leads to a tap out. The bloodied fighter rolls to the canvas, badly hurt, but victorious.

"I'm talkin' to you." Shawna narrows her eyes. "You deaf, or just stupid?"

Ellen blinks. "It wasn't your money. Or your food."

They're facing one another, maybe ten feet apart.

"Do you have a death wish?" Shawna flexes her hands, steps forward. Now she's eight feet away, then six.

Ellen raises her palms in apparent submission. The non-confrontational stance they taught her at The Farm. You look as if you're surrendering, but you can still protect your head and strike if you need to. Turns her body slightly to the side, to make herself a smaller target.

Shawna's not stopping. She's five feet away, then four, three.

Ellen strikes. Not forward, but back. Throws her elbow into the little box on the wall beside her. The glass breaks and a fire alarm immediately rings out, deafening. Doors are thrown open and staff pour in. Within seconds, orderlies, doctors and nurses are escorting patients and sweeping everyone out of the room.

"You ain't goin' nowhere, bitch," Shawna snarls, as Ellen side-steps and is absorbed into the flow of bodies moving toward the emergency exit. "Your time's comin'."

Ellen doesn't doubt it.

8

Clarion, Pennsylvania

PETER'S NERVOUS AS hell, but he don't dare let anyone see it. Problem is, they're all gonna see it soon as it's his turn and he needs to step up and show them what he's got. Which is basically squat.

And the thought of that makes it even worse. The thought of his brother watching him screw up. Again. The thought of Leanne laughing at him. Again.

He's struggled to perform under pressure his whole life. Whether it was a school test or sports team try-out, a job interview or being alone with a woman — though it's not like that happens a whole lot — when the heat's on, it gets to him. He goes sweaty, nauseous, can't think straight. And the result's the same every time: he washes out. Flunks, big time.

Shooting guns is no exception.

Beside him, Randy's holding a Remington 870 12-gauge. The Dozer looks totally at home. And he should do — they're in a forest clearing in State Game Lands Number 72 that borders the soybean farm where he works. So, he knows the spot where they come for target practice like the back of his hand. And he's hunted deer in these woods every year since he was fourteen. Plus, he loves guns. He's got a camo jacket and pants on and the shotgun looks like a toy in his huge hands. Only it's not a toy. A slug from that sucker could put a hole in the side of a building, depending on the building. Randy racks the pump-action to open the barrel and glances in Sherman's direction.

"Why ain't you got no plates on your car, man?" he says, as he pops in his cartridges.

"Me?" Sherman is loading up his second mag of 9mm rounds at a folding table they've set up at one end of the clearing.

"Yeah."

"Because I don't believe in license plates. They're a violation of my constitutional rights. Same as taxes. Read the Fourteenth Amendment."

Peter wonders if that's true. He's pretty sure they didn't have license plates when the Fourteenth Amendment was written, but he don't remember much from his history class at high school, other than sitting right behind Leanne. So, as usual, Peter doesn't say anything. The German is full of shit, but maybe he's right about this. After all, Mitch keeps talking about how smart he is.

Thirty yards away, across the open space, Mitch is pinning a paper target to a board. It's black on white, the outline of a human head and torso.

Target practice.

"I couldn't agree more, brother," replies Randy. "Problem is, when you don't got plates, you drawin' attention to yourself. People notice you, look inside your car. Cops pull you over. That kinda thing."

"So? It's an opportunity to explain what bullshit these rules are. Artificial creations of an illegitimate government. Tools by which the good people of America are oppressed daily by self-interested tyrants in Washington and their federal minions."

"That's not the point," says Randy.

"Isn't it?" Sherman grins.

"The point," says Mitch, as he strides back over to them, "is that if you're on their radar, you risk screwin' up our mission. Put your plates back on."

Mitch picks up his AR-15.

His brother looks cool as fuck with the rifle, Peter thinks, in his cargo pants, black Under Armor tee and wrap-around shades.

"What about fake plates?" asks Sherman.

"Put your plates back on." Mitch repeats, staring at him, though his eyes are invisible behind the tinted Oakleys.

Silence hangs between them. Birds are chattering in the trees.

"All right," grumbles Sherman.

"Okay, then." Mitch holds up his gun, shows it's empty. "Randy's up. Everyone else made their weapons safe?"

They all confirm they have.

Randy takes his position.

"Ears," says Mitch.

They each put their ear defenders on. Peter has sensitive hearing, so he's got earplugs as well. His heart is racing faster than before. He'll be up, soon.

Randy holds the Remington steady, braced against his shoulder, takes aim, and pulls the trigger.

Boom.

Even with his ear protection, the gunshot is so loud Peter not only hears it, he feels it. Randy barely moves an inch, the recoil absorbed by his bulk. Peter remembers firing the 12-gauge once. The kick back almost took him off his feet. After that, he stuck to the smaller calibre guns. Peter realizes he's shut his eyes at the noise. When he opens them, he sees a hole in the target up ahead that's the size of a baseball. In the stomach.

Randy racks the rifle, adjusts his aim, fires again. Rack, fire, repeat. When he's done, he lowers the gun. The target's head has been blown apart, and its torso has three big holes in it.

"Attaboy, Dozer," says Mitch, who steps across and claps his buddy on the shoulder. "Go put a new target up."

Once Randy has replaced the target and lumbered back over to them, it's Sherman's turn.

The college boy is awkward with his handgun, his stance a little goofy, but his shooting is effective. Sherman the German's no gun nut like Randy, or soldier like Mitch, but he's practiced hard over their past few months of training, and almost all of his rounds hit the target. With the mag change and his slow, deliberate aim each time, it seems to take forever. Peter counts thirty shots.

"Good job, Sherman," says Mitch, when he's done. "Solid. Grab your target."

Next up is Leanne. She's chosen the AK-47 that Mitch brought back, illegally, from Afghanistan. Mitch gave it to her because it's the easiest weapon to use, but she likes it because it's *retro*. She's wired with excitement, a wide feline smile on her pretty face, like she's real horny or something. She's wearing a tight t-shirt and even tighter jeans, her hair up in a ponytail under a ball cap.

Watching her, Peter can feel himself getting a chub in his boxer shorts. He hopes it won't show through his pants.

The AK is powerful, but Leanne just about controls it. Tongue poking between her lips in concentration, she fires a mag's worth of 7.62mm rounds mostly into the target, though Peter hears some of them whistling through the trees behind their makeshift range.

"Not bad," Mitch observes.

Leanne swings to him, still gripping the AK at waist height. "Can I—?"

"Don't point that at us!" Mitch snaps. "Jesus Christ, Leanne. How many times have I told you?"

"Sorry, baby." She lowers the gun. Then pouts, cocks her hip, pushes her breasts forward a little. "But can I? Please. You know how much I love it . . ."

Mitch sighs. "Okay, sure. Just point it *that way*." He indicates the target.

Talking herself through it, Leanne ejects the magazine and puts in a new, longer one. A 'banana clip', with thirty rounds in it. Pulls the bolt to chamber the first one. Then she flicks the switch to full auto. That's one where you squeeze the trigger and it just sprays.

Peter knows what's coming.

Private citizens aren't supposed to own fully automatic weapons. But no one knows they have an Afghan AK. Probably no one around here would care anyway. And Leanne loves shooting like this as much as she seemed to enjoy her role in the movie Peter owns.

His chub gets a little bigger. It's almost a semi, now. Shit.

Leanne takes a deep breath, glances back at Mitch, puckers her lips, and winks. Then she turns to the target, pulls the butt of the AK against her belly, and squeezes.

Ra-ta-ta-ta-ta-ta-ta-ta-ta.

The force pulls the barrel up and left as spent casings rain down to her right, and in three seconds, she's out.

Peter squints at the target. Maybe three rounds have hit it, in a line arcing away from the center. Probably the first three. He guesses the other twenty-seven bullets are in the woods someplace.

Leanne's breathing heavily, her chest rising and falling, her mouth open, like she just came or something.

Oh Lord, now Peter's picturing that . . .

"Wooh! Fuck, yeah!" she screams. "How'd I do, baby?"

Mitch may have been a professional soldier for years, but no red-blooded male could resist this display. His lips curve in a half-smile.

"Pretty good," he concedes, as he walks over to her.

She grabs the back of his neck, pulls him in for a deep kiss. With tongues.

Mitch lets her do this for a few seconds before easing back and slapping her on the ass. "Why don't you go get your target?"

"Sure," she grins, walking off with a little extra wiggle, knowing they're all looking at her.

Peter adjusts his pants. Tries to look elsewhere. Fails.

When Leanne has replaced the target, Mitch steps up. He quickly preps his AR-15, smoothly pulls the charging handle. Pauses.

"What ammo am I using?" he asks.

"5.56," says Randy. "American Eagle, military grade."

"And why am I using that?"

"Greater mass, higher pressure, more velocity, and better stopping power than a .223 cartridge," says Sherman.

Peter knew that. Kind of.

"Right." Mitch turns back to the target and, faster than seems humanly possible, he puts twenty rounds into it, ten standing, ten kneeling.

Peter watches his brother in awe. The target looks almost pristine, except for two groups of shots, one in the middle of the head, the other in the center of the chest. Each group looks about the size of a quarter. There's less than ten holes per group, because some of the bullets have gone through the hole made by a previous round.

"Way to go, baby!" squeals Leanne. "That was frickin' awesome."

"Nice shooting, brother," adds Randy.

Even Sherman, still obviously sore from his scolding about the license plates, nods approvingly.

Brother.

It pisses Peter off that Randy calls Mitch his brother. He's *Peter's* brother, no one else's. Not that you'd even know they were brothers if you saw them together.

Back at high school, when Mitch was a senior and Peter was a sophomore, the other kids started joking that Peter and Mitch weren't *real* brothers. That they had different daddies. There was speculation over which little, weak, stupid, ugly old man in town was Peter's dad. It made Peter so mad, but he had to suck up the abuse, because there wasn't a whole lot he could do about it, personally. Leanne occasionally stuck up for him, but only because she was sweet on Mitch. In the end, Peter couldn't take anymore, so he told his big brother. And Mitch fixed it. Just spoke to a few of the guys in Peter's home room, and it stopped the same day.

But Peter knows everyone still thinks it.

And who could blame them? Basic biology alone would seem proof enough. Of course, they *are* full brothers. Their mom never cheated on their pop, or nothing like that. Peter's sure of it. It's just that Mitch won the genetic lottery, while Peter was left holding a useless ticket stub. Runts of the litter are just one of those things in nature. God's plan, some say. If that's right, Peter thinks, then God is an asshole.

Mitch returns after putting up a fresh target.

"You're up, Pee-Wee."

Peter takes a deep breath. He fumbles the mag insertion on his Ruger LC9 and then can't cock it properly. Hears the others shifting behind him. Someone coughs.

He takes aim. The target seems so far away now he's standing here. He can feel his hands shaking. He tries to swallow, his mouth dry.

He squeezes the trigger.

Misses.

"Don't shut your eyes," Mitch tells him.

"Okay."

His hands seem to be shaking even more, now. He fires again.

Misses again.

"Don't jerk it," says Mitch.

"That's not the only thing he's been jerking," Randy says, from behind him.

Peter hears sniggers, including a higher pitched one that belongs to Leanne.

Mitch just shakes his head. "Hey, Dozer. Let the man shoot."

"Am I stopping him?" asks Randy, spreading his arms wide.

Mitch comes closer to Peter. "Nice and smooth, now, Pee-Wee. Take your time. Remember, focus on your front sight, not on the target."

Peter takes a breath, steadies himself, fires.

Hits the target.

Okay, not the target-target, but the paper, at least.

"Attaboy," says Mitch.

With the confidence he's felt for a lifetime of having Mitch beside him, Peter repeats the process until his mag's empty. When he's done, he's three-for-seven, and one round is even in the torso. Just.

As Peter walks up to get his target — not that it particularly needs replacing — he thinks about what that one round inside the outline of a body means.

A hole in a person. Blood. Maybe death. If he had to pull the trigger with a real human in his sights, could he do it? He doesn't know. Just thinking about it sets his nerves on edge, again.

The other four seemed to have no issue with that. But, for Peter, it's just one of several things making him think twice about this whole . . . *mission*, as Mitch calls it.

And the guns are only a minor part of their plan. Like an appetizer in a restaurant.

Tomorrow, they start making the bombs.

9

ELLEN IS STANDING in the middle of the small office, in front of a desk. Behind it, her arms folded, sits the woman who stuck a syringe in her butt. Maybe she introduced herself to Ellen last night, maybe she didn't. Ellen can't really remember anything about that conversation, since she was already starting to have a panic attack when it took place. Her recollection after the injection is even shakier. But sign on the door — which she saw as the security guard dragged her in — said that the woman's name is Ava Ratkova, and her job title is Head Psychiatric Nurse.

Nurse Ratkova stares at her with those icy little eyes. Ellen realizes it's the concave lenses of her glasses that make her eyes seem so small. The lack of warmth in them, however, has nothing to do with short-sightedness.

"You've been here for less than one day," Ratkova states. "Eighteen hours, to be exact. And in that time, you've so far injured two members of staff, threatened several others, damaged property, tried to abscond, and initiated a false fire alarm, causing disruption to important clinical work, and distress to a number of the inmates."

"Inmates?"

"Patients."

Ellen has the feeling she's back at school, being scolded by a teacher. One of those sadistic ones you occasionally got, who was on a power trip and got a kick out of punishing kids.

"Sorry," she replies. Not because she means it, though. Ellen doesn't regret anything that's happened so far. Everything she's done, she did to protect herself. And she'd do it again in a heartbeat. The only thing she regrets is not actually getting out of the building last night.

Ratkova presses her lips together. Her nostrils flare. She's pissed. "Are we going to have a problem with you here, Ellen?"

"I hope not."

"So do I. Because what I need you to understand is that, under your commitment order, we have the ability to administer medication, alongside other measures, as we see necessary, in order to manage the risk you pose to yourself and others."

Ellen understands. It's a fancy way of saying that they'll jab her in the ass with another sedative if she steps out of line again. Or put her in that empty room and lock the door.

"Okay, then," Ellen says.

She needs to be smart about this. Her priority is getting back home to her family and investigating the threat she heard. For that to happen, she needs to play nice, let the new shrink do the evaluation, show them she's not crazy, and have the treatment order reversed.

"When's my evaluation?" she asks.

"What evaluation?"

"By the psychiatrist."

The nurse frowns. "It's already been completed. That's why you're here."

"Not that one. The new one, by the other doctor."

"Which doctor?"

Ellen feels her frustration rising. "The one my attorney arranged to visit me here."

Ratkova blinks. Her mouth twitches. "I haven't been informed of any visit."

This can't be right. Harry told her it was going to happen today. It must be a mistake in the system. Another one.

"There has to be," she insists. "Can you check?"

"Not now."

"What? Why not?"

Ratkova tilts her head forward. Now her eyes are barely visible at all. "Ellen, you need to keep your voice down, because—"

"Just check the freakin' schedule, will you?!"

Behind her, Ellen hears the security guard who escorted her in take a couple steps closer. She can smell his body odor, feel his breath on her neck. An attack dog, waiting for the command to go for her.

"You're not in charge here, Ellen," the nurse tells her. "I am."

"This is bullshit!"

Ratkova points to the open door. "Take her away."

The security guard reaches out, his meaty fingers coiling around Ellen's arm.

"Don't touch me!" she cries.

"Do as you're told," commands Ratkova.

Ellen blood pumps harder, and her muscles tremble as her fight-or-flight system kicks in. She wonders which of those two courses of action she should take: *fight, or flight?* Obviously, she knows the third option — the one suggested by Ratkova — is the smartest choice: stop resisting, give up and submit to this regime. But she's always been stubborn, and she won't be pushed around.

"Let go of me," she says.

"I can't do that," the guard replies.

He's got his hand on her upper arm and she knows that if she grabs his fingers with her other hand, she could turn his wrist and break his elbow before he has a chance to react. And maybe this time she could actually get out of here.

The guard tightens his grip.

Ellen tenses her body, ready.

Then a man's voice comes from the doorway. Deep, calm, and gentle.

"Is everything all right, Ava?"

Ellen turns. The guy who's just spoken is short, with jet black hair, an open-neck shirt, and a kind face that suggests East Asian heritage. She guesses he's mid-thirties.

"Fine, thank you, Dr Vang," the nurse answers.

The man looks at Ellen, his gaze travelling to the heavy hand wrapped around her arm.

Slowly, the security guard releases his hold on her. Takes one step back.

Ellen breathes.

"I'm Lee," he says, extending his hand toward her.

She shakes the proffered hand. "Ellen."

"I'm one of the clinical psychologists here."

"Nice to meet you. Vang? Is that a Hmong name?" she asks.

He looks pleasantly surprised that she's recognized it. Most Americans wouldn't. But Ellen knows that the Hmong helped the CIA fight the 'secret war' against the communists in Laos back in the day. It was basically the same as Vietnam, only it never officially happened.

"Yes, it is," he says. "My parents came here in the seventies." He gives a brief smile. "So, how are you finding it so far?"

"She's fine, Dr Vang," Ratkova replies quickly. "Other than some behavioral issues, which we're in the process of discussing."

He acknowledges this interruption with a glance before returning his attention to Ellen.

"How are *you* finding it so far, Ellen?"

"Honestly? Kinda hard."

Vang nods. "That's very normal. There's a lot of adjustment to be made in coming here. But we'll do what we can to help you feel settled."

Nothing about the psychologist is tripping her BS radar. He sounds absolutely sincere. Same as with Jada this morning, she takes an instant liking to him. Finds herself suddenly wanting to talk to him. To confide in him. To ask for his help.

"If you want to chat, anytime," he says, as if he's read her thoughts, "just ask the staff for me. I'm usually on the ward. We can find a quiet place, talk about whatever's on your mind."

"Okay," she says. "Thanks."

He gives a warm smile. "All right, then."

"Uh, there is one thing, Doctor Vang," she adds.

"Lee, please."

"Sure, Lee. I'm supposed to have another evaluation today, by a visiting psychiatrist . . ."

"There's no visit booked," says Ratkova.

"Could we at least check?" Ellen asks. "Maybe there's a message somewhere."

"Good point," Vang replies. "Ava, can we take a look at that, please? Speak to reception."

"Yes, doctor."

"Talk soon, Ellen," he says. Then he gives another nod, spins on his heels, and walks out.

Ellen watches him go, then turns back to Ratkova. The nurse is glaring at her with undisguised contempt.

"Take her out," she instructs the guard.

*

"I'll go get him right now," her mother says, "Can you hold on for a second?"

"Yeah, of course." Ellen glances behind her. There's a line of three other women, all anxious to use the payphone, but she's waited — listening to Jada talking sweetly to her kids just before — and now it's her turn. She's called collect in any case, so holding's not a problem.

She looks at the debris that's accumulated around the phone over the course of the day: a notepad, scraps of paper, a pencil, paper coffee cups. She thinks about all the women on the ward who've used the phone today, the conversations they've had with loved ones out in the real world. Then the little voice comes on the line and all other thoughts instantly vanish.

"Hello, mommy." Josh's tone is so casual, she can hardly bear it. He has literally no idea what's happening. What she's going through. And she doesn't want him to know, either. Not yet, anyway.

"Oh, sweetie!" she exclaims. "It's so good to hear you. Are you okay?"

"Um, yeah. I was playing with my monster truck and it was, um, it had to save Baby Yoda from the T-Rex cos he's the baddie and, um, then Batman came in and he fighted the T-Rex."

She can picture him kneeling on the rug, crashing the toys into each other and making all the sound effects as the story in his imagination played out. Another classic battle of good versus evil.

"Who won?" she asks, although she already knows the answer.

"Batman!" he cries.

Obviously, Batman won. Good always wins out over evil. Doesn't it?

"Mommy?"

"Yes, sweetie?"

"Where are you?"

"Uh, I'm . . ." The simplicity of his question breaks her heart, and she struggles to find the words to respond. "I'm just, uh, doing some work out of town."

"Work?"

Josh is smart. He knows she doesn't have a job right now,

although being a mom is just as demanding. She's talked at home about when she used to work.

"Uh-huh."

"But, your job is being my mommy."

She lets out a little laugh, even though she feels the tears coming.

"That's right, sweetie, it is. This is more like ... something from my old job, the one I had when you were a baby. And I just have to fix it real quick, and then I'll be home, okay?"

"Okay."

"You be a good boy for grandma and grandpa, and then we'll—"

"I miss you," he blurts.

It's more than she can take. She begins to cry, silently so that she doesn't scare Josh. The muscles of her face squeeze tight and warm tears flow down her cheek. The receiver is shaking in her hand.

And then it's not in her hand.

The attack comes so fast that it takes her a second even to realize what's happening.

The metal cable connecting the receiver to the payphone is around her neck, a body is pressed against her, pulling her back hard.

She can't breathe.

"Bitch," Shawna growls behind her.

Ellen scrabbles for the phone wire, can't get a purchase on it. Shawna pulls tighter. No one's stopping her. No one's helping.

"Mommy? Are you okay?" Behind her ear, Josh's voice rises from the receiver, small and distant. Frightened.

Her son is listening to her being strangled.

Something in Ellen's brain kicks in. A memory of self-defence classes at The Farm during her training. Their instructor, E.J. — a former Navy SEAL — teaching them how to escape holds and chokes. *Drop your chin*, she hears him say. *Release the pressure on your trachea, then strike and twist.* They drilled it over, and over, and over. For exactly this situation. Because she knows it's life or death if she can't get out of it.

And she only has seconds to act.

Survival instinct takes over.

She dips her chin and claws the fingertips of one hand into the wire. Feels the force on her neck drop just a little. But she's getting lightheaded, her vision blurring at the edges. Time's running out.

Frantic, she looks for anything in reach. Sees the pencil. Flails her arm at it, misses.

Shawna tightens her grip. "I knew you had a death wish," she snarls, her mouth right by Ellen's ear.

Ellen stretches once more, using everything she's got. Grabs the pencil. Sets her grip. Then stabs directly behind her.

The pencil isn't even sharp. But it connects with something soft in her attacker's face.

Shawna lets out a scream.

Ellen stabs again. And again.

She feels the pressure around her neck release a little more, enough to get her fingers in deeper. But Shawna is hanging on with the rage of a woman possessed, and Ellen's vision is still closing in.

If she blacks out, it's all over.

She stamps backward, aiming for Shawna's kneecap, but her heel doesn't hit its target. Tries again, but just rakes the big woman's shin instead. Ellen knows she's got maybe one more chance if she wants to make it out alive.

"Say goodnight," hisses Shawna.

Ellen drops the pencil so she can grab the phone cable with two hands. Summons the energy into her legs, then springs off the ground. Plants both feet on the payphone, then pushes backward as hard and fast as she can.

The cable rips off the base unit and she drops to the ground on top of Shawna. The impact knocks the wind from her. But the force around her neck is gone. She twists and pulls the cable free, gasping as she takes a lungful of air.

She rolls to one side and looks over.

Shawna lets out a groan. She's dazed, but still moving.

Ellen needs to finish this. She may not get another chance.

She sees the pencil lying on the floor beside her. Lunges for it.

Takes it in her grip, lead end down.

Kneels over Shawna, ready to strike with a hammer fist.

Lifts her arm higher to get more force.

A hand clamps around her wrist.

Then another grabs her arm, vice-like. Two more, then four, and before she knows it, she's being lifted off her feet, her arms and legs no longer in her control. She rages against it, but there's nothing she can do. There are too many of them, and they're too strong.

Ratkova appears, looks from Shawna to Ellen. There's no needle this time. Instead, she calmly says, "Get her into the safety suite."

Ellen protests, tells them she was attacked, but she's already being carried away by a small army of guards.

She twists her neck to look back.

Sees a smile on Ratkova's face.

10

Paris, six years earlier

THE DAY ELLEN meets one of the bravest women she'll ever know started just like any other. They say in intelligence work that you don't recruit the best assets, they recruit themselves. Ellen thinks that's only half-true. Yes, the top assets are usually the ones who are motivated enough to seek you out. But the other half of it is putting yourself someplace where they can find you.

It would have been useless if Ellen had spent her time in Paris swanning around diplomatic receptions looking for assets who could provide intel on French Islamist extremists. The whole point of her being undercover was to get away from the embassies and be out there in the field. She knew too many NOCs who took the easy option, wherever they were sent. Swanky downtown offices, high profile conferences filled with PhDs and college professors, boutique think tanks who could pay their well-connected "advisors" thousands of dollars for off-the-record material of interest. All of that had its role. But not for Ellen.

It wasn't money that was the issue. Sure, the CIA was accountable to the taxpayer, just like any other part of government, and she had to double check every dollar that came in and went out of her cover charity. But her bosses in the Agency had made it clear that she had all the financial resources she needed to get the job done. Whatever it took to get under the skin of the Parisian jihadist scene. And Ellen knew that money would only take her so far. The rest was choosing a base, and building a profile there to meet the right people.

That was why she'd set up her office in Vitry-sur-Seine. It's not the Paris from movies and picture postcards, the city of lovers, of the Eiffel Tower and Champs-Élysées, Chanel and Louis Vuitton. It's a run-down district on the outskirts of the city, where thousands live in high-rise housing projects and one in three people was born outside France, many in the Muslim nations of Africa.

At first, Harry was worried about her working there. Ellen assured him it was safe; she trusted her local fixers who helped her find a place to rent. Her French was good; she could navigate her way around the community. And besides, it wasn't like she was hanging out with angry bearded guys in martial arts clubs and kebab shops. Her strategy was to meet women. Women who knew men who were involved in bad stuff. And who, despite the risk it might pose to them, had enough empathy to want to stop a terrorist attack that could claim civilian lives. Who didn't want murder committed in their name, or in the name of their religion.

It took a while, but her instincts proved right.

Slowly but surely, Ellen got to know women in the community. Her charity offered everything from emergency financial assistance and a food bank service to health and education advice. She employed four women from the neighborhood, and had a bunch of others volunteering to help out. Gradually, people came to trust *l'Américaine*, whose funding from an "anonymous donor" in the US was helping make their lives better. No one knew the money was from Uncle Sam, and the idea it actually came from Langley was unimaginable.

At some level, she felt bad about deceiving them all. But the aid she gave was real, and so was the difference it made to people. And the deception was necessary, for that ultimate purpose drummed into them since day one of training. The mantra used — and sadly abused, at times — by many an American defending the homeland over the decades: *the greater good*. It may have been a cliché, but that didn't stop it being true.

It's a Friday morning when she meets Nadia for the first time. Ellen's reading through a bunch of resumés she's been sent ahead of an upskilling workshop for women trying to find jobs. She's entering names, phone numbers and email addresses so she can send them back to Langley to be cross-checked against NSA databases of known extremists. Any that look interesting she'll forward to the vetted hacker-for-hire the Agency has set her up with — a guy called Ricardo back in the US, who knows the dark web better than anyone. It's the long, often thankless process of turning over stones that's the bedrock of intelligence work.

Josh, just six months old, is in a little carry cot beside her desk, asleep. The rain is pounding at the windows, the sky beyond the color of lead.

Then the door flies open and a woman almost stumbles through it. She's wearing jeans and sneakers, but has a hijab over her hair. She's young, small, fragile looking. When she stops inside the door, Ellen can see that she's trembling. Maybe it's because she's soaked from the rain, maybe because she's scared. Probably both.

"I need your help," the woman says. She holds it together for a few seconds before her face crumples and the tears start to flow in big, jagged sobs.

Ellen stands, walks over to her.

The young woman reaches out with both arms and, before Ellen knows it, she's holding her in an embrace.

*

Present day

Ellen doesn't know how long she's been in the safety suite. When they first threw her in here — literally — she was so wired she just paced around, smacked her fists against the padded walls a few times, yelled for someone to let her out.

But nothing happened.

Eventually, she realized that she'd be locked inside this little airless box for a while. So, she decided to get used to it. Save her energy. She sat on the floor, with her back to the wall, and slowed her breathing. Closed her eyes and travelled back in her mind to Paris.

In the absence of anything else to do, the memories are a distraction. Ultimately, though, any recollection of her time in France always ends up in the same place: the mass casualty attack at the movie theatre. The one that happened on her watch. The one Nadia warned her about.

It's a reminder that every minute she spends here is a minute she's not investigating the threat she overheard last week. A minute closer to the Keystone Boys unleashing the same kind of violence here against ordinary American people. She's sure of it.

And she needs to do something about it.

There's a knock at the door.

She looks up.

Dr Vang is at the narrow window, his palm raised in greeting.

She lifts a hand in reply, manages a half-smile.

He gestures like he wants to come in, and when she nods, he unlocks the door and steps inside.

"Ellen, I heard about the, ah, situation in the communal area with Shawna," he says. "Are you okay?"

She traces her fingertips across her throat. "I'm fine, I think. Apart from a psychopath trying to kill me, obviously."

"We should get you seen by a medical examiner," he suggests.

"I'd prefer to be seen by the new psychiatrist," she replies.

"About that," he begins, awkwardly. "I checked with reception just now. Apparently someone did show up — a woman — but they weren't allowed to see you."

"Why not?"

"Because you were in here."

"Seriously?" Ellen wipes both hands over her face. "What the fuck?"

"I'm sorry."

"So, where is she now?"

"She was sent away."

"Jeez. It gets better."

Vang sighs. "Like I said, I'm sorry. I was supposed to have been informed."

"Who denied her entry?" she asks.

"Nurse Ratkova," he says. "According to our risk protocol, technically she did the right thing, but she should've come to tell me first. I'll take that up with her."

"Goddammit."

"We can reschedule."

Ellen gets to her feet. "There may not be time for that."

Vang frowns. "What do you mean?"

She glances past him, to the open door. She can't see any security goons. Vang has come here on his own, and that means he trusts her.

"Can I tell you something?" she asks, lowering her voice.

"Sure."

"I think there's going to be a terrorist attack. And a lot of people are going to die."

His eyes widen. "What? Where?"

"Here," she says.

"In Norristown?"

"No. I don't know. Maybe. In the US, I mean."

"Okay. But you don't know where."

"No."

"Right."

Ellen considers her options. Makes a decision. Then tells him everything: the conversation in the D.C. hotel corridor, the talk of graves. The guy who followed her through Philly as she went to meet someone who might know about the Keystone Boys. The speed with which her past life was denied by Langley, before she was branded delusional by a shrink hired by the cops, and sent here.

Vang listens without interrupting.

"We need to act," she concludes. "Before it's too late to stop it. Whatever *it* is."

The psychologist blinks. Opens his mouth, but doesn't say anything.

"Can you help me?" she asks.

"Ah, I . . ."

"Please, Lee." She looks him right in the eye.

"Well, uh, if you have details, we can report them to the police," he offers. She can't yet tell if he's convinced, or just playing along to keep her sweet.

"That won't work. I tried that already. FBI, too. This is where I ended up."

"I don't understand," he says.

"Nobody believes me," she states. "They think I'm making it up. That I'm crazy. It's like they don't want to listen to me. Which makes me think there's something else going on. Something bigger."

"What do you mean?"

Ellen can tell this is way outside of the doc's experience.

"You have to trust me," she tells him. "I used to work on this kind of thing for the US Government, a few years back. I know what I'm talking about."

He nods. "We have contacts in law enforcement. Perhaps we could—?"

"No. That's just gonna give the system more reason to keep me in here." She jabs at the air with a finger. "What I need is to be out there, finding these sons of bitches."

"Ellen," he says gently, "I want to help you, but there's a process with a commitment order that's the same for everyone. You're due for review the day after tomorrow, when your 72 hours is up."

"This is time critical."

Vang studies her. Gives a long breath out through his nose.

She meets his gaze and asks, "Do you believe me?"

"It's not about whether I believe you or—"

"Yes, it is. Do you believe me, yes or no? Simple question."

"I believe you're sincere in your belief about this."

"That's not the same thing."

There's a long pause.

Eventually, he says, "Yes, I believe you."

"Okay, good. So—"

"But," Vang holds up a finger of caution, "I'd also like you to consider the possibility that there might – *might* – be another explanation for what you heard."

"There isn't."

"There might be," he counters. "Even if it's, like, a one per cent chance."

"One tenth of one per cent," she acknowledges, grudgingly.

"Deal."

"So, if we're ninety-nine-point-nine per cent confident the threat is real, we've gotta do something, right?"

Vang scratches his beard. Stares at the linoleum floor. Rocks on his heels.

Ellen's seen this before. The moment where someone needs to make a choice. She asked a dozen assets in her career to cross a line and help her out, to take a personal risk for a shared mission. Now she's asking Vang. He looks up at her.

Before he can speak, though, Ratkova sweeps into the room.

Ellen didn't hear her approach. Had she been standing outside the room, listening?

The nurse looks surprised to see Vang there, her small eyes bulging behind the thick lenses of her glasses.

"Sorry to interrupt, doctor," she says. "Ellen, it's time for your medication."

"What medication?"

"To calm you down," replies Ratkova.

"I am calm," Ellen insists. "Right, Lee?"

Vang snaps out of a trance. "Ah, yes, I would certainly say so."

"Psychiatrist's orders," Ratkova says.

"If Doctor Nyborg considers—" begins Vang.

"I don't need any medication." Ellen interjects, her tone firmer, now.

"That's not the opinion of our head doctor."

"I've never met the guy."

"You don't need to meet him. He's read the reports."

"What reports? Anyway, I don't *want* any meds."

"It's not up to you."

"Wait a second," says Vang, holding out his hands, as if he's separating Ellen and Ratkova in a bar fight.

"Don't make this harder than it needs to be, Ellen," says Ratkova.

Heavy footsteps approach from the corridor. Two security guys fill the doorway. She glances at Vang, who shakes his head.

Ellen knows she can't run. And, after defending herself against

Shawna, she doesn't have the energy left to fight. Maybe she needs to give them this one. Lose a battle to win the war. If she volunteers to take the pills, she has a little more control, at least. And she won't get a syringe in her butt again.

"Okay, fine," she says, and allows herself to walk out with the guards.

On her way out, she shoots a glance at Vang, nods.

He nods back.

DAY THREE

DAY THREE

11

FINALLY, HARRY'S HERE. It's only been two days since Ellen last saw her husband, but it feels like a lifetime. When the orderly brought him through the locked door into the ward, and she spotted him, they ran to one another and he put his arms around her. Held her tight, stroked her hair. Whispered over and over that he loved her, and everything was going to be all right. Even just the sight of Harry made it all seem so much better. It's given Ellen hope that she's going to get out, maybe even today. After all, if a congressperson can't make something happen here, who can?

Now, they're in a small room with plastic chairs off the main corridor, sat opposite one another. The door's open, and they're alone, but Ellen knows a security guy is somewhere outside. He's probably been briefed by Ratkova to listen in.

Harry's wearing a suit, and he's still got his jacket on. He looks uncomfortable, like he really doesn't belong here. Like he doesn't want to stay long. She doesn't blame him. It's exactly how she has felt since the second she walked in.

"They told me you got into a fight yesterday," he says. "Are you okay? I mean, what the hell . . . how did it happen?"

"I was using the payphone," she begins slowly, still feeling groggy from the sedative pills last night. "I was talking to Josh and a woman jumped me from behind. She pulled the phone cord around my neck."

"What? Why?"

"Because she's a bully. And I stood up to her."

She tilts her head back to give him a full view of the bruising.

"Oh my God, sweetheart. Does it hurt?"

"It's not that bad," she replies. Maybe the sedatives have taken the edge off the pain.

"Have you seen a doctor?"

"Yeah, last night. I don't remember a whole lot about that, though. Apparently, I'm fine."

"Jesus." Harry shakes his head. "Who was the woman?"

"Her name's Shawna LeDuc. She's in here for double homicide."

"Homicide? What— Why's she even here? Shouldn't she be in prison?"

"She claims the Devil made her do it."

"Are you safe?" Harry leans forward. "Because I can talk to the staff. I'll make sure they get you some protection."

"Actually, they've kind of already been doing that."

He nods. "Okay, good."

"No, it's not good. They stuck me in a fucking box, Harry. The so-called *safety suite*. Maybe you saw it on your way in here? It's an empty, padded room."

"Is it safe, though?"

"Christ, Harry!" Ellen slaps her hands on her thighs. "They didn't put me in there for *my* safety. They put me there to get me out of the way!"

"But . . ."

"They didn't let the shrink see me last night — the one you arranged through the lawyer. They sent her home. Because they think I'm 'risky'." She makes quote marks with her fingers at the last word. "Did they tell you?"

"Shit. No, they didn't."

"Yeah. So, I'm still here. Can you speak to our attorney, reschedule the visit? For today?"

Harry bites his lip. Lowers his eyes to the old, stained carpet.

"Listen, honey," he says, "they told me they're, ah, concerned about you."

"Concerned? Who told you that?"

"The guy in charge. Doctor Nyborg."

"Who the hell is he?"

"I just told you, he's the guy in charge, and—"

"Have you spoken to Vang?" she blurts. Her head is starting to hurt.

"Who?"

"Doctor Lee Vang. Shorter guy, dark hair, Hmong heritage. He's a psychologist."

"Uh, no, I didn't meet him . . ."

"He gets it," Ellen says. "He believes me. At least, I think he does. He's, like, the only one here who's not trying to sedate me and lock me in a room."

"Nyborg told me that was standard practice when someone's been involved in a violent incident."

"They left me in there for three hours, Harry!"

"Apparently they're short-staffed at the moment."

"Bullshit," she says.

"Well, I complained to Nyborg, obviously. But he said the report showed that you started the fight."

"What? Whose report?"

"A nurse. What was her name? Ratched, maybe?"

"Ratkova. Fuck, she wasn't even there. Was it on tape? There are cameras, right?"

"Apparently, there was a problem with the video recording. They were switching over the hard drives in the office and . . ."

"At the exact same time that psycho tries to strangle me? Come on, Harry."

"What?"

"Think about it." She drops her voice. "Think about what I know. Who I'm a threat to."

"Ellen . . ."

"People are talking about the Keystone Boys in D.C. Powerful people. People who move in your circles. People who can make phone calls that sway the cops. Maybe they're giving orders to this Nyborg guy."

"That's ridiculous."

"Is it? I'm telling you, Harry, they want me gone. First the guy in Philly, now this."

There's silence as they look at one another. Ellen is searching her husband's face for that hope she felt when he came in this morning, for the support he's always given her. But it's not there. In its place is an expression that's somewhere between sadness and fear.

"Harry? What's going on? Can you please just help me get out, so I can go home, look after our son, and do something about this goddamn terror threat that no one else seems to think is real?"

He looks away for a long moment. When he turns his face back to her, she can see that his eyes are wet.

"Honey," he says, "you've been through a lot."

"What's that supposed to mean?"

"It means . . ." He lets out a deep breath. "You remember what happened after Paris?"

She remembers some of it, even though she'd prefer to forget. The lowest point in her life. The end of her career in the Agency. Nightmares, flashbacks, not wanting to leave the house. Somehow depressed and jumpy as hell at the same time. All the time. And the pills . . .

Harry reaches forward, lays a hand on her knee. Speaks softly. "The most important thing is that you get the right care, sweetheart. And that you get it right now, you know, early on, before . . ."

"Before what?"

"Come on, Ellen . . ."'

She studies her husband. *For better, for worse . . . in sickness and in health.* Weren't those the vows they made to each other? She's not thinking of their wedding day, though. That was just the public show.

For an intelligence officer, the more important step in a romantic relationship is the moment you "declare": when you choose to tell your partner what you really do for a living. When you confide in them that you're not exactly who you said you were. That there's a whole other part to your life. A world about which most people have no idea, except what they see in the movies or read in spy novels, most of which is crap, anyway.

It's a leap of faith, same as asking an asset to work for you, only worse, because you're so personally invested in it by that point. You don't just tell a random guy in a bar you're a Non-Official Cover CIA operative because you want to sleep with him. It takes time — years, in her case — to reveal that part of yourself to someone else. You have to be in love with them, first. And you have to take the chance that, when you share that secret with them, they might no longer accept you.

Ellen heard a few stories at Langley where the declaration had been the end of it. *If you can't accept my job, you can't accept me —* that was how the subtext ran — the implication being that the Agency wasn't just a part of your life, it *was* your life. And it was more important than any relationship. Well, that wasn't necessarily true. But she didn't need to worry about that. Because Harry had accepted her.

They'd been together for four years when she told him. After their first meeting, in the migrant camp at Calais, they'd started dating. Casually, at first, then a little more frequently. A few months later, they'd had the conversation about being exclusive. Just before their two-year anniversary, they'd moved in together. And by the three-year mark, they were starting to make big plans for the future. She couldn't put it off any longer. It was time.

She wrote back to headquarters to ask permission and, after Harry's records had been checked and all the boxes were ticked, she got the green light.

*

Paris, seven years earlier

Ellen's nervous as hell this evening. More scared than she'd been making any pitch to an asset. She's planned it out in detail, though. Done her recon at the restaurant, just like she would for any other meeting. Chosen an intimate spot in the back corner that's not in earshot of other diners, and been sure to reserve that specific table. Rehearsed her words, tested out different ways of saying it. Tried to make the bottom line – *I've been lying to you for four years* – seem like a positive thing – *I'm telling you because I trust you and I think we have a future together*. She's terrified.

They order their food and the waiter takes away the menus.

Ellen's heart is going like a jackhammer.

"Are you okay?" Harry asks her, reaching out to touch her hand on the table.

"Uh, yeah." *Now or never*, she tells herself.

"It's just, you seem a little quiet," Harry persists "Is it work?"

"You could say that."

"Right," he says. "It's not that thing with the office rent, is it? Because I was thinking, you could—"

"It's not that," she interrupts him.

"Okay." He gives a confused chuckle, like he thinks she's being a little weird. Which she is.

"Harry, there's something I have to tell you," she says.

He squeezes her hand, his brow furrowing. "What?"

"It's about my job."

He looks relieved, as though maybe he thought she was going to break up with him.

"Your job?"

"Yeah."

"Okay."

She takes a deep breath. "The women's charity isn't the only thing I do," she continues.

"What do you mean?"

Oh God. She decides to come straight out with it. Leans toward him.

"I also work for the CIA," she whispers.

"What?"

"The CIA."

Harry narrows his eyes, then a smile cracks at the corners of his mouth.

"That's funny," he says. "You got me for a second."

"It's not a joke," she replies.

The waiter arrives with their wine, shows them the label on the bottle, then uncorks it and pours a sample for Ellen. She sips, nods, and the guy fills their glasses, then leaves.

Harry tilts his head. "Really?"

"Yeah."

"Since when?"

"The whole time."

"But . . . you came here to set up the charity."

"For the Agency."

"So, your American donor, is—"

"The Agency."

"Wow." He sits back, blinks. Grabs his wine glass, takes a big gulp.

"Sorry I couldn't tell you before," she says. "I wanted to, it's just . . ."

"No, I get it," he says.

There's a long second where he seems to be thinking, then he reaches out to her, interlaces his fingers with hers. In that moment, she knows she's done the right thing. That she can trust him. And that they have a future together.

*

Present day

Harry left a half hour ago, to head back to D.C., promising her that he'd do everything he could to get the new psychiatrist to visit again, so that she could feed her evaluation into the review tomorrow afternoon. Ellen told him that was a day too late, that she wanted to be out today. Harry countered that, given what's happened since she arrived, and the concerns of the staff, maybe it'd be better to give her commitment order the full seventy-two hours before making a decision. She didn't like that one bit. And not just because she wanted to be out of this place and trying to find out what the Keystone Boys were planning. It was more than just that.

For the first time in their eleven-year relationship, it felt as though Harry was abandoning her.

Like he thought she was crazy, too.

Worse still, Ellen has no faith that they'll release her tomorrow evening. Ratkova is clearly determined to punish her for stepping out of line. This Nyborg shrink is writing prescriptions to sedate her. The guards all want a piece of her after she took two of them down. And whoever's pulling the strings doesn't want her let out.

None of that is her biggest concern right now, though.

"Shawna's coming back to the ward this afternoon," Jada tells her. "She had a night in the hotel."

"The hotel?"

"The medical center. Nice food, comfortable bed . . ."

"Shit."

Ellen knows she was lucky to escape Shawna last time. Psychopaths don't tend to let stuff like that go. Next time could be even worse.

There's only one thing she can do.

Break the fuck out of here.

12

State Game Lands Number 174, Indiana County, Pennsylvania

PETER LOST HIS bearings someplace east of Punxsutawney, when they took a right off the 36 onto a shitty forest track. Now, he has no idea where they're at. He's not exactly sure what they're doing, either. He only knows that whatever Mitch needs his help with, it requires the shovels in the truck bed. And it's illegal.

No going back from this, Mitch said, before they set out. Randy joked about them being sent to jail if they get caught. Only it wasn't a joke. Peter doesn't like the sound of the penitentiary, not one bit. He got to thinking that maybe his job in the gas station isn't so bad after all. But he couldn't say no to Mitch. He's committed, now.

Up until today, everything they've done — talking weapons, stocking ammo, target practice — could be passed off as a few buddies who wanted to shoot guns in the great American outdoors. Innocent enough.

Today, though, he feels guilty as hell. He knows they've crossed a line. And not even riding beside Mitch, in his brother's

Chevy Silverado, with Metallica turned up loud, is enough to stop him getting antsy. If anything, the music's making it worse.

"Yo, you okay, Pee-Wee?" Mitch glances at him.

"Yeah, sure," he replies. "Just a little, you know . . ."

"What? Nervous?"

"No." He shrugs. "Maybe. You gonna tell me what we're doing?"

"You'll see. The less you know about it right now, the better. For your own protection."

"Okay."

"We're just a couple of hunters," his brother says, "headed out into the woods to shoot us some deer. Ain't nothin' wrong with that, right?"

"Right."

"There you go." Mitch chuckles and gives him a punch on the shoulder.

Peter knows it's just playful, but it still hurts. He forces himself not to yell out at the dull pain in his arm. Instead, he says, "Got it."

"Trust me, you're gonna love this." Mitch grins at him.

They bump along the forest road in silence for a while.

"So, uh, you and Leanne?" asks Peter. He's not sure where the question came from, or if it's even a real question. But the words were out of his mouth before he could stop himself. He must've been thinking it and then just said it. He does that sometimes.

"Me and Leanne." Mitch nods. "What about us?"

"Uh . . ." He's got to say something now. "You, ah, you think you guys have a future?"

"A *future*? What are you, like, her dad?"

"Just askin'," replies Peter.

Mitch's eyebrows rise above his wrap-around shades. "You interested in her too, huh?"

"No way!" he splutters, too fast and too loud.

"Come on, Pee-Wee. I won't hold it against you. I've seen the way you look at her."

"I didn't—"

"It's all good, man. I get it. You guys have a history. You've known her a lot longer than me. You told me at high school you had the biggest crush on her, remember? And you gotta admit, she's still smokin' hot."

"I don't like her in that way," Peter protests.

"Okay, cool."

"I swear."

"I know about the DVD," says Mitch.

"What do you mean? What DVD?"

Mitch gives him a sly smile, shakes his head. "Whatever."

Neither of them speaks for a moment.

Peter hesitates, then thinks, *what the hell*. "It's just . . ."

"What?"

"Well, if you guys end up gettin' married or whatever, we will still, you know, hang out? You and me."

Mitch bursts out laughing. "That's what you're worried about?"

"I'm not *worried*, I—"

"Come here." Mitch reaches over, grabs Peter's head, and pulls him close in a one-armed hug that makes Peter feel as though he might choke.

"Listen," Mitch continues, "no matter what happens, you're my brother. Always have been, always will be. Nothin's gonna change that, not ever. That's blood right there." He jabs a finger in mid-air. "Understand?"

"Yeah." Peter shuffles in his seat, embarrassed. But he's also kind of happy.

Then Mitch says, "I love you, man."

Peter is stunned. He can't remember Mitch ever telling him that before.

"I'd do anything for you," his brother adds.

"You would? Really?"

"Sure. And you'd do the same for me, right?"

"No doubt."

"All right, then. And about me and Leanne . . ."

"Yeah?"

"Who knows what's gonna happen after Sunday. Nothing's gonna be the same again. For any of us."

That's exactly what Peter's afraid of.

Mitch spots something and pulls off the track. Kills the engine. "Here we are."

His brother takes a handheld GPS from the glove box, fires it up and taps the screen a few times. "Let's go," he says.

They get out, grab the shovels and trek through dense woods of maple, birch and hemlock for a half-mile or more. They haven't seen another person for almost an hour. Eventually, they reach a place that looks identical to every other patch of forest surrounding them.

Mitch checks the screen of his Garmin and scans the ground. Then he walks over to what looks like a little tree branch, sticking up out of the leaf litter.

"This is it," he says.

"What now?" Peter asks.

Mitch raises his shovel. "Dig, soldier."

*

It takes them maybe a half-hour, grunting and sweating, until they've dug a pit that's about five feet across and four feet deep.

"Stop," Mitch says.

Peter catches his breath and stretches his back, leans on his shovel. He's exhausted.

His brother, who looks as though he could've kept digging all day long, tosses his shovel aside and jumps into the hole. Squats down and starts to claw away the dirt with his hands. He stops, looks up at Peter, and a smile breaks across his face.

The tall trees are blocking a lot of the sunlight, but as he peers into the pit, Peter sees a layer of black plastic. It looks like a tarp you'd use to keep the rain off a truck bed.

"Come on." Mitch beckons him down.

After another ten minutes, side by side, their hands are black with dirt. But they've scraped away enough earth to reveal a box, about the size of a large crate of beer, wrapped in the tarp. Together, they lift it up, set it to one side of the hole and climb out.

"It's heavy as hell," Peter says. "What is it?"

"Just a little something I borrowed from work," Mitch replies, "after I decided to quit."

Peter takes a step back, looks at his brother. "Is it dangerous?"

"Depends who's using it," says Mitch, laughing.

Peter laughs too, but it dies quickly. He has some idea what's in the box, now.

"Come on." Mitch jerks a thumb towards the hole. "There's another one in there."

*

Clarion

They pull up outside Randy's parents' house. Well, his mom's house, now. Old man Kowalski passed about three years back. Heart attack — his third, after a double bypass. Randy's mom said it was hard labor that killed him. Long, physical days in the garage workshop he made after losing his job at the steel mill. But Peter knows that's not the whole truth. Kowalski Senior lived off bacon, sausage and burgers, washed down with bourbon, even at breakfast. He dipped tobacco, and was heavier than his son. It was a matter of time before his ticker gave out. Peter has never said that to Randy, though. He'd catch a broken jaw, or worse, if he did.

Leanne comes out of the little side door to the garage. That's not surprising — they're under strict orders not to open the main entrance. What is surprising is her obvious black eye. And she don't look too happy about it, neither.

"Holy shit, what happened to her?" says Peter.

His brother switches off the engine. "Dumbass walked into a door," he replies.

"What, last night—?"

But Mitch doesn't respond. He's already out of the truck. "Let's go," he says.

Together, they carry the two boxes across the front yard and through the side door. Peter notices that Leanne doesn't look at Mitch as they pass.

"Hey, Leanne," says Peter, softly.

"Hey, Pee-Wee," she whispers back.

"You okay?" he asks.

"Uh-huh."

Inside, Randy's working a metal disc at a lathe, visor down. Sherman's hunched over a table with a bunch of wires and electrical stuff. They both stop as Peter and Mitch bring the boxes in and set them down on a workbench. Leanne comes in last and shuts the door. She's real quiet.

Peter's thinking about that door she walked into, how she didn't see it.

"This the shit?" Sherman asks.

"Yes, sir." Mitch plants his hands on his hips.

"Hallelujah." Randy takes off his visor and walks over. "Let's open it up."

Mitch pulls a hunting knife from his belt, carefully slices the black plastic on one box, peels it away. There's a wooden crate inside. He plants the knife blade under the lid and pops it.

Sherman gasps.

"Sweet Jesus," mutters Randy, leaning over to get a better look.

"What is it?" asks Peter.

The three guys all stare at him like he's an idiot.

"These right here," says Sherman, "are M112 charges. Ninety-one percent RDX, five-point-three per cent dioctyl sebacate, two-point-one per cent polyisobutylene, and a li'l dash of oil." His lips twist in a smartass grin.

"Wait," Peter says, "ninety, no, ninety-one per cent . . . what?"

"C4," Randy states.

"A hundred pounds of it," Mitch adds.

"Forget trying to take TNT from a quarry, or shipping some shit off the dark web over here from Europe," explains Randy. He's hyped, pointing at the crate. "We've got the finest military-grade high explosive you can buy—"

"Or steal," offers Mitch.

"Or steal, right here in the greatest nation on God's green earth."

"Amen." Mitch claps Randy on the shoulder.

"Thanks to the US Marine Corps." Sherman runs a hand over the plastic-covered blocks inside the crate. He looks excited.

"High explosive," Peter repeats. "Is it, I mean, is there any chance it could—?"

"Catch!" yells Sherman, grabbing one of the blocks and tossing it to him.

Peter fumbles the catch, but throws himself sideways to get his body under the block. Screams as he falls to the ground. His ass and then his ribs smack into the concrete floor, but he manages to catch the explosive, hold it steady.

The others are laughing.

"You fuckers," yells Peter, his adrenalin surging.

Mitch reaches down, plucks the block from where Peter's cradling it in his arms. Flips it up in the air and catches it in one hand. "Don't worry, Pee-Wee, it's not goin' off," he says.

"Not without a detonator in it," adds Sherman.

"I knew that," Peter lies.

"Then why'd you shit your pants?"

"Fuck you."

As Peter gets to his feet and brushes dust off his shirt, he catches Leanne's eye for a second. She looks away quickly. He realizes she hasn't said a word since they stepped in. And she's normally the loudest one of them. Something's wrong. The black eye.

"Leanne," says Mitch, "go fix us some coffee, will ya?"

Peter watches her slink away into the house. He wants to follow, ask her if she's okay. But he can't do that, not right now, anyway. He turns back and takes another look inside the crate.

"What's taggant?" he asks, reading the label more closely.

"It's a chemical tracer," Mitch says. "It means that when all this goes boom, they're gonna know the US Marine Corps was the source."

"Poetic justice, brother." Randy holds up a fist.

Mitch bumps it. "Damn straight. All right, let's get cookin'."

Peter looks around. Explosives, wires, metal plates. Wonders what Old Man Kowalski would've made of his workshop being turned into a bomb factory. Maybe he'd have been happy, if the target was the steel mill that laid him off and the only folks inside it were the ones who fired him. That gets Peter thinking. His mouth is dry. He wets his lips, clears his throat.

"So, ah, what are we blowing up?" he asks.

The others exchange a glance.

"You'll find out soon enough, Pee-Wee," says Mitch. "But I'll tell you one thing. It's gonna be big."

With a hundred pounds of military explosive, Peter doesn't doubt it. He's absolutely terrified. He wants to leave and go work a shift at the gas station, pretend none of this is happening. But he remembers Mitch's words this morning.

No going back from this.

13

ELLEN BLINKS HER eyes half-open. It takes her a second to register that she's in her room in the hospital, lying in bed. Her body feels stiff and heavy, her head fuzzy. She figures she must've fallen asleep after lunch. The extreme drowsiness has to be a side effect of the medication. No doubt, that's exactly how they want her to feel. Slowly turning her into a zombie like most of the other patients locked up in here. She's less trouble that way.

As her eyes open wider, she becomes aware of a presence. There's someone else here. She twists her head to see better. Gives a sharp intake of breath as she realizes it's Ratkova.

The nurse is standing in the center of Ellen's little room, looking down at her through those thick glasses.

"What are you doing here?" Ellen demands. It creeps the hell out of her that Ratkova was watching her sleep. Not to mention the fact that Ellen's pretty sure she locked the door from the inside, as a precaution, since she doesn't know when Shawna is getting back to the ward. The nurse must have let herself in.

"You're late," Ratkova says.

"For what?"

"Your session with Doctor Vang."

"What sess—" she begins, but cuts herself off. Remembers that she asked for his assistance last night, right after she told him about the terror threat. "Uh, yeah, okay. Gimme a minute."

She forces herself out of bed and onto her feet. Slips on her sneakers, which have had the laces taken out for "safety" purposes, and follows Ratkova down a couple of hallways. They pause at each locked door for the nurse to open it with the key card attached to a retractable lanyard on her belt.

Vang has his door open. His office is pretty minimalist; two low armchairs facing each other on one side, and an office chair at a desk on the other side, where he's sitting now, working at his computer. He spins in the chair as Ratkova knocks on the doorframe.

"Come in, Ellen," he says. "Thank you, Ava."

"Do you need security, doctor?" the nurse asks. "I can call them."

"No, it's fine." Vang gets up, starts closing the door.

"I recommend keeping it open," says Ratkova.

"That won't be necessary," replies Vang. "Now, if you'll excuse us . . ."

"Of course, doctor." She lingers a moment, then leaves.

Vang shuts the door. "Please have a seat," he says, gesturing towards the low chairs. "Thanks for coming to see me."

Ellen sits down. "Sure. I mean, she just woke me up and told me we had a session."

"Yes, I scheduled it. Sorry for the short notice," Vang adds, sitting opposite her. "I just thought it might be useful for us to talk."

"Okay." She lowers her voice, in case Ratkova is still outside. "Is this about me asking for your help yesterday, you know, with the . . . thing?"

"Uh, well," Vang rubs his chin, "I certainly want to help you, Ellen."

"Great. Can you get me out of here?"

The psychologist tilts his head. "It's not quite that simple."

"You sound like my husband."

"In what way?"

"Just, that's basically what he told me this morning."

"I'm afraid he's right. Your seventy-two-hour commitment order is up for review tomorrow afternoon. I need to make the case for your release to the board. So, I thought it'd be good if we spoke a little more about your history."

"You mean my old job?"

Vang hesitates. "You know the police said you never worked for the government."

"Records can be changed," she says. "Especially by the CIA."

"Why would they do that?"

"A bunch of reasons."

There's a pause while he chews his lip. "Actually, I meant more like, your psychological history."

"Ah, right. That's a long story. It's connected to my old job, anyway," she adds.

Vang checks his watch, smiles. "Well, we've got some time. So, are you okay to talk about that with me?"

"I guess." *I'll talk about anything that might help me leave*, she thinks. Besides, same as when the detective asked her, she's not ashamed of her mental health issues. She knows that the police shrink ended up using them against her when he had her sent here, but Vang seems to be on her side.

He must hear a lot of crazy things in this place. Yet, somehow, he's not dismissing her as delusional, and it doesn't seem like just professional empathy. Maybe, unlike Nyborg and the others, he understands that even delusions usually have some truth behind them, and he wants to get to that truth. Maybe she's successfully built trust with him and convinced him she's for real, in the way she's been trained to do with assets. Or maybe his conscience simply won't let him take the risk that the terror threat she's describing is imaginary.

Whatever the reason, she's grateful he's listening.

So, they talk.

Ellen tells him about Paris, five years ago. About the terrorist attack on the movie theatre, and the carnage she witnessed in its aftermath. About the nightmares and the flashbacks she had from then on. About how depressed she was for a very long time afterwards. How crazy angry she was with everyone: the terrorists, obviously — who murdered a hundred and thirty-four innocent people — but also the Agency. How her colleagues in Langley betrayed her, although she doesn't give Vang the details of that right now.

She explains how, in the months following the atrocity, she'd get mad at Harry for no particular reason. How she'd snap at little Josh without warning. And how badly she beat herself up, more than anyone else, over the guilt she felt for not stopping it. The guilt at what happened to her asset.

Vang listens calmly, nodding, his full attention on her. She can see her own pain reflected in his face with each new detail. He asks the occasional question for clarification as she tells her story, but otherwise he doesn't interrupt her. She starts to relax, but as she does, a feeling of sadness begins to rise within her, like it's been allowed out of its box now that she's not on high alert.

"Thank you for sharing that, Ellen," he says, when she's done. "That's an incredibly traumatic experience to have gone through. You must've had to be very strong to come out the other side."

"I don't feel as though I have." She wipes the tears from her eyes. "I think I'm still in it."

"Were you given a diagnosis at the time?" asks Vang.

"Yeah, PTSD."

"And did you ever have any treatment for those symptoms?"

"I did see someone, for a while, after I got back to the States."

"Did that help?"

"Kind of."

"You still get flashbacks?"

"Uh-huh."

"How often?"

"Well, not all that much, the past couple years. But then it started again."

"When?"

"Last week, when I heard about the, ah, you know." Her eyes flick around the room, then to the closed door and back to Vang.

"I can see why that might trigger off those memories again," he says.

"No shit," she retorts. "And getting strangled by a psychopath last night didn't help a whole lot, either." She pauses a beat. "Sorry."

"That's okay. I understand you're frustrated — with being here, with what's happened since you arrived . . ."

"You could say that."

Vang inclines his head. "So, I'm wondering about when you first got here, and you . . ."

"Tried to escape?"

"Mm. Do you know what happened in that moment?"

Ellen pushes out her lips, shakes her head. "Not really. I just remember thinking those guys were about to put me in a prison cell, that they wanted me out of the way, and I felt this surge of, like, panic . . ."

"So, you ran?"

"Yeah. But I don't know what happened after that, until I got pinned to the ground by those assholes."

"Did you have any other episodes like that in the past week? I mean, times when you lost touch with your awareness of what you were doing?"

She recalls the guy pulling the gun on her at Independence

Hall. She knew exactly what she was doing there, start to finish. Same for defending herself against Shawna yesterday, even though she almost lost consciousness.

"I don't think so," she says.

"Okay. So, my plan for the review tomorrow is to argue that the moments where you've shown what they call *risky behavior* were triggered by the sense of being threatened or trapped, which this place is causing you to feel. So, if you're out, back home, you won't feel that, and you won't be a risk. The two other times you were involved in a violent incident recently, you were the victim."

"The reports say otherwise," she counters.

"Reports can be challenged. And I'll be sure to emphasize how much you could be at risk, now, from Shawna."

"You're filling me with confidence."

"It's mainly to back up the argument for you leaving. But I've already requested an additional security presence on the ward when she comes back."

"Thanks." Ellen feels her anxiety rise a little at the prospect of coming face to face with her attacker again. Tries to focus on her goal: getting out. "Will they believe you?" she asks.

"It's the truth — isn't it?"

"Yeah, but . . ." she shrugs, "truth doesn't always win out."

"Sadly." Vang blinks slowly. "But we can try."

"How likely are they to let me leave?"

Vang exhales slowly. "Our case will be strengthened if we say you'll agree to get treatment out in the community for your PTSD, but ultimately it's going to be Doctor Nyborg's decision."

"I still have literally no idea who he is. What's he like? Apart from thinking he knows me well enough to medicate me, having never met me."

"He's . . . old school."

"Meaning?"

"Meaning he likes to keep people in, when he can. Extend their orders."

"He does? So, my chances of getting out are, what — slim to none?"

"Maybe a little better than that."

Ellen tips her head back, lets it rest against the high back of the armchair. Imagines herself outside, reunited with her family, then following up on the Keystone Boys. It gives her an idea.

"Lee, I know this is probably against the rules, but could I use your phone?"

"Uh . . . before I answer that, can I ask what for?"

"I need to get a message to someone. Urgently."

"Is it your family? Because I know the payphone's out of action, but they're fixing it real soon—"

"It's not my family. It's my old college professor."

"Oh, I see," says Vang, although he's obviously confused.

"I need to message him on a secure app we use," she continues, "and ask him what I meant to ask him on Monday, about the group."

"The terrorists?"

"Exactly."

Vang looks away. He's obviously weighing it up. "I don't know, Ellen. I get why you want to do this, but it's totally against protocol, and it could seriously count against us at the review panel tomorrow if we're caught."

"How would we get caught?"

"Not to mention the possibility of me losing my job," he adds.

Ellen holds his gaze for a long moment. She can see how conflicted he is. She doesn't want to screw up his career, but she's confident no one will find out. And besides, what's at stake is bigger than any of their personal lives.

"Okay," she says. "Can I have a pen and paper?"

"Sure." Vang turns to his desk, tears a page out of his notebook and grabs a ballpoint. "Here you go."

She writes *Walter* and *Signal*, then a cell number. "Walter's a sociologist at U Penn. He researches and writes about US domestic terrorism. He's like a walking encyclopaedia of every far-right, white supremacist, prepper, anti-government militia group out there. And he has contacts. I need to ask him about the Keystone Boys — if he's heard of them, what he knows about them.

"We use Signal instead of regular texts, because it's harder to hack," Ellen continues. She jots the words *Wassup Walt* beneath the cell number. "This is the all-clear code. If you start the message with that — no question mark — he'll know it's me, and I'm not contacting him under duress."

"Right." Vang sounds unsure. He looks it, too.

She can understand his reaction; encrypted messaging and comms tradecraft probably aren't in his job description.

"Look, you don't have to decide now," she says, "but if you can ask him that for me, it would really help us. We don't know how much time we have."

She folds the paper in half and holds it out to him.

He hesitates, then takes it. "I'm not promising anything," he says.

"Thank you."

There's a knock at the door.

Vang folds the note again and pockets it. "Hold on." He gets up, cracks the door.

From where she's sitting, Ellen can't see who it is in the corridor, but she recognizes Ratkova's voice immediately.

"I just wanted to inform you, doctor," the nurse says, loud enough for Ellen to hear, "that Shawna LeDuc is back on the ward." She sounds excited by the news, like the return of an old friend.

Ellen's reaction is the exact opposite. She feels like a prisoner on Death Row who's just had her stay of execution overturned. And tomorrow afternoon's review — her best ticket out of here — now seems an awfully long way off.

14

ELLEN PICKS UP the jigsaw piece, rotates it one-eighty, and puts it into one of the many gaps in the puzzle they're working on together. It's supposed to be the Grand Canyon, but so far it just looks like a mess of reddish-brown rock. And even that's hard to make out.

"Wait, how'd you know that went there?" says Jada, pointing to the newly filled space.

Ellen shrugs. "I just, kind of, saw it."

"Damn. Okay." Jada's impressed. "You do a lot of jigsaw puzzles?"

"Not really."

But I did spend a lot of time piecing things together, thinks Ellen. Random stuff that didn't seem to fit until you turned it around and looked at it differently. She hopes she's retained that ability from her old life — she'll need it if she's to stop the Keystone Boys.

"My li'l girl, Maya, loves these. She's got the patience for it; Lord knows where from. Marquis, though, he can't stay still long enough. I'm lucky if I get him to sit down for ten minutes to eat his dinner before he's up and running again, grabbin' that basketball." Jada smiles. "He wants to play in the NBA. For the Sixers, obviously."

"Josh is already obsessed with baseball."

"What is it with boys and balls?"

They both laugh, but Ellen is acutely aware that Jada is trying to distract her from the stress of waiting for Shawna to show up. There are two guards in the communal area now, although Ellen isn't convinced they'd come to her aid in the event of another attack. But she didn't want to stay in her room, like a sitting duck, waiting for the inevitable payback. She figures here is as safe a place as any on this ward, which isn't saying much. For a secure hospital, it feels pretty damned dangerous.

"You miss him, huh?" Jada lays a hand on her arm.

"Yeah," replies Ellen softly. She knows Josh will be okay with her parents looking after him, but he must be wondering where mommy is and what she's doing. Why she's not at home.

Ellen feels an almost physical pull to get out of the ward and be back with him again. Which is more than she can say about Harry right now. But the thought of being reunited with her son is bittersweet, because she knows she'll have to leave him again pretty quickly to find the Keystone Boys and stop whatever they're planning.

"No matter how much time passes," says Jada, "they still your babies."

"If Nyborg keeps me in at the review tomorrow, I'm just gonna break out."

"You and everyone else in here."

Ellen doesn't respond.

"You serious?" Jada's eyes widen. "You know what happens if they catch you escapin'?"

"What?"

"More drugs, stronger, too. More time locked in the crazy room on your own. Maybe even restraints. And you don't want that. They caught Luz trying to get out the back door to the kitchens one time. Doctors cranked up her meds. She ain't never been the same since."

"Jeez."

"Yeah." Jada holds up a finger. "So, don't say I didn't warn you."

"Appreciated."

"Besides, where you gonna go if you do escape? The five-oh will be at your crib before you get there. They'll arrest you in front of your neighbors and bring your ass right back here."

"That's probably true," acknowledges Ellen.

"No probably about it. Even if you go on the run someplace, they'll get your picture up on the news. Then there's nowhere to hide."

Jada's right about the news. Ellen remembers seeing a bulletin or two like that in the past. But her friend is wrong about there being nowhere to hide. Especially if you know a thing or two about staying off the grid.

At Camp Peary, the CIA run a training exercise where recruits are dropped in the woods with nothing but the clothes they're wearing and a water bottle. They're given a half-hour's head start before a military team with dogs, drones — the whole nine yards — comes looking for them. Most trainees wind up getting caught after an hour. Not Ellen. Sixteen hours later, she was the last to be found out of her class of fifty students. First thing she did was assume the water bottle had a tracker in it (it did) and ditched it. Then she ran to the nearest road, hitched a ride with an elderly couple travelling to the coast, and persuaded a guy to lend her his motorboat. By the time the Coast Guard found her she was in Maryland, halfway to D.C. on the Potomac River, a hundred miles from where she started out.

"Oh shit."

Ellen snaps out of her memory at the sound of Jada's voice. She follows her gaze to the door where Shawna LeDuc has just come in, accompanied by Ratkova.

Shawna has a patch over one eye, and Ellen realizes it must

be from where she stabbed her with the pencil from the pay-phone. The bandage somehow makes her seem even more threatening than before.

The pair stop just inside the doorway when they register that Ellen is here. Shawna dips her head and Ratkova whispers something to her. Shawna nods and, surveying the security staff and the camera in the corner, strolls right through the middle of the room. She passes Ellen and Jada's table without a word and crosses to the TV. The sofa is immediately vacated by two other patients, one of whom automatically hands Shawna the remote. She drops heavily into the couch, flips channels until she finds a boxing match, and settles back with her feet up on the coffee table. It's business as usual.

"Stop starin' at her," whispers Jada. "You gonna get yourself killed."

"It's a little late for that," replies Ellen, still watching Shawna. The big woman is clearly playing nice, for now, but her brief chat with Ratkova has set Ellen on edge. It's almost worse that she didn't just charge at Ellen the second she came into the room. It means she's planning something, cold and calculated.

For Ellen, trying to escape now seems a better option than ever.

*

The patients from the women's secure ward are finishing up their dinner in the cafeteria. A beige meal of rehydrated powdered eggs and home fries soggy with grease, with a bruised apple for dessert. The men's ward are due in next for their sitting, so the orderlies are hustling everyone along to make sure they get out in time. Avoiding contact between the sexes for safety reasons, they told Ellen, and that's absolutely fine with her. She hopes they pay the same attention to the threats from inside the women's ward.

She's been keeping an eye on Shawna ever since she came

back a couple hours ago. But the murderess has barely looked at her. Ellen knows she's not ignoring her — that would be too good to be true. She's just biding her time. Ellen wonders if it'll be tonight, after lights out. Will Shawna find a way into her room, somehow? Will she have a weapon?

"Are you okay, girl?" Jada is looking at her, head cocked.

Ellen realizes she's hardly touched her meal, and it has nothing to do with the quality of the cooking. She lets go a breath she's been holding, feels her pulse thumping at her temple. The sense of danger makes her think of the guy tailing her through Philly, and that makes her anxiety spike even more. Her thoughts are racing, but she fights to keep calm. Grips the table, blinks, tries to stay in control.

"I know Shawna's up to something," replies Ellen. "She's too quiet."

"I hope you're wrong."

"I don't think I am."

"Well, you know what? She'll have to come through me, first." Jada squares her shoulders.

"No." Ellen takes her hand, squeezes. "You don't have to defend me. I got myself into this. I'm the one who picked a fight with her. Don't put yourself in harm's way for me."

"I'm sayin'—"

"You don't know what she's capable of. And you have Marquis and Maya to think about."

"I know. Either way, though, I'll be lookin' out for you," Jada says.

"Four eyes are better than two, I guess."

"True that."

"But no hero bullshit, okay?"

"Oh, what?" Jada pouts. "We leave that to you, I suppose?"

Ellen manages a smile.

"All right, ladies," says the orderly, approaching their table and gently clapping his hands. The ID card hanging from the lanyard at his waist says *Tommy*. "Let's move it along, now, please. Back to the ward."

"You got it, Tommy," Jada gives him a grin.

"Much obliged, Jada." Tommy nods his thanks and walks over to the rack where they stow their trays.

Ellen knows it's his job to make sure no one holds on to their cutlery. Even though it's plastic, the sharp edges could still do serious damage if a patient was determined to hurt themselves. Or someone else, in the case of Shawna.

"He's sweet," says Jada. "Obviously hasn't been here long enough."

Ellen pushes back her chair and lifts her tray. She sees Shawna stack hers and throw her cutlery in the garbage can, but instead of walking over to the exit, she makes for the kitchen and disappears. The two orderlies don't seem to have noticed; they're in a discussion with a woman, whose name Ellen doesn't know, over whether or not she can take a yoghurt pot and a spoon out with her. The spoon seems to be the issue.

Then Shawna's back. She was gone maybe all of ten seconds. She circles to the end of the line, like she wants to be last out. She doesn't so much as glance at Ellen.

But Ellen knows something's wrong.

Shawna's right hand is a fist, half inside the sleeve of her sweater. She adjusts the cuff, just a little, with her other hand.

It's enough for Ellen to see the glint of metal.

Shawna has a kitchen knife.

Ellen knows what's coming.

Back at The Farm, the self-defence instructor, E.J., used to say there was one tried and tested move to defend against a knife attack: run. To illustrate this, he showed them how dangerous it was using your bare hands to stop someone with a blade. Ellen remembers E.J. taking his shirt off and handing her a big red marker pen. She had to pretend it was a knife and go for him. He wrestled it off her in seconds, but not before she'd left a bunch of red marks on his arms and even one on his ribs. E.J. pointed out that, with all due respect to Ellen, if the person knew how to handle a knife, it'd be ten times worse.

So, she understands what she has to do right now.

Run.

15

THE ONLY PROBLEM with trying to run in a secure psychiatric hospital is that almost every door you come to is locked. So, Ellen can't run just yet. She needs to push down her growing panic and find a way to open those doors so that she *can* run. She guesses Shawna will attack in one of the corridors between the cafeteria and the ward, which means she has until they file out to do something.

As she dumps her trash before stowing her tray, she focuses on her peripheral vision, trying to locate Shawna without looking directly at her. Her attention flips briefly to Tommy as he checks her tray.

And that's when she has the idea.

Pickpocketing is not something Ellen has had to do a whole lot in her life. In fact, before the CIA, she'd never really stolen anything from anyone. At The Farm, though, it was one of the "dark arts" they had to learn, or at least attempt. A guy from Vegas, who was a one-time asset, had come in to explain the psychology of it to the recruits and show them a few techniques.

Fundamentally, pickpocketing is about two things. One, getting "inside the bubble"; close enough to someone that you can actually reach their pockets, bag or whatever, without raising their suspicion. And two, distraction and misdirection; shift their attention elsewhere and you can even disguise taking a watch right off their wrist or a ring off their finger.

Ellen was never much good at any of this in training, but that wasn't the point. It had been one of those sessions that was more about having a little fun and bonding over the ridiculousness of being trained to steal things. She never figured she'd actually need to use what they'd taught her as a matter of survival.

Now, as Ellen gets the signal from Tommy to stack her dinner tray, she makes her move.

"Should I put it here?" she asks, motioning toward a space in the rack.

Tommy leans across. "Yeah, right there's good."

Ellen lets the tray slip from her hand.

Tommy lunges to catch it.

Ellen steps to his side, leans into him, grabs the tray with her left hand while her right goes to his waist. Her leg briefly presses against his, masking the movement of her hand as it unclips the lanyard on his belt.

"Oh my God, sorry!" she says, as she palms the lanyard and badge. "You okay?"

"I'm good," Tommy replies, brushing a little egg from his sleeve. "You all right?"

"Yeah. I'm such a klutz. Must be the meds."

She stoops to grab a handful of the home fries that tumbled to the floor. Tucks the lanyard into her sock.

"It's fine," Tommy says. "The cleaners will fix it."

Ellen stands and moves aside as Jada comes through behind her and offers her tray to Tommy for inspection. He hasn't noticed anything yet.

She joins the line moving toward the exit. She doesn't have a lot of time, since she guesses Tommy will check for his lanyard pretty soon. Another orderly is holding the door open for them as they file out of the cafeteria.

Once she's passed him, she drops to re-tie her shoelace and extracts the ID pass. As she thought, Tommy has his key card on the reverse of it, clipped into the back of the plastic holder. They all do.

Aware that Shawna is somewhere behind her, Ellen continues down the corridor beyond. She knows that it snakes around a few times before they hit the ward. She's guessing Shawna will go for her at one of those points, out of camera shot. The first turn is coming up.

There's a convex mirror up by the ceiling in the corner of the corridor, where it turns left. She checks it, sees Shawna — a head taller than the women around her — striding up from the back.

Ellen knows she doesn't have long.

She hears the orderly at the cafeteria door call out, "Hey, has anyone seen Tommy's pass?"

It's time to move.

She waits until she reaches the corner, then breaks left.

Hears a commotion behind her, footsteps, an orderly shouting at her to stop. She heads for the door at the end, taps Tommy's key card on the reader and it clicks. Ellen rips the door open and bursts through it, starts running again as it closes behind her. Glancing back, she sees it's not quite shut yet. It's on one of those slow spring mechanisms. She has to keep going.

She can see the emergency exit sign up ahead that marks the stairwell. That's her best chance to put distance between her and Shawna. Between her body and that knife.

Ellen reaches the door and throws a final look over her shoulder. The first door she came through is almost closed. She watches it go the last few inches. Almost there.

It's as good as shut when the metal blade shoots through the gap, wedging the door ajar. It's looks like a filleting knife — long, thin, and sharp as hell. The door is thrown open and Shawna is standing there. Ellen guesses the look on her face is the same one that her husband and his lover saw before they met their deaths. It isn't hot rage, but something that's a lot more frightening – an absence of emotion. Ellen feels a shiver go through her body.

Then Shawna runs at her.

Ellen yanks at the emergency exit door, sprints through and down the stairs. She figures heading for ground level is her best way out, even if the orderlies have sounded the alarm and the security goons are on the way. All she has to do is get to the other side of a locked door and she'll be safe – from Shawna, at least.

She flies down the first set of stairs, jumping the last half-dozen, rounds the stairwell and carries on down. She's somewhere between the second and first floors, now, and there's not much more to go, but she hears Shawna's heavy steps before hearing her voice.

"Get back here, bitch!" growls Shawna from somewhere overhead. Her words echo around the concrete stairwell as Ellen starts to take the steps two at a time.

No sign of security yet. She can make it, if she just—

Her ankle turns underneath her. She sprawls forward, tumbling to the concrete. Hits the steps hard with barely enough time to get her hands out and break her fall. The lanyard and ID badge spill from her grip as she rolls to the bottom of the stairs.

Shawna is gaining on her.

"You can run," she shouts down, "but there ain't no one watching us here."

Ellen tries to get up. A burst of pain goes through her ankle, and she stumbles, hits the deck once more.

Shawna takes the last few steps slow, confident her prey isn't getting away. Her grip on the knife looks solid. "You're gonna die, now," she says.

Ellen gathers her strength, then dives for the lanyard, grabs it and roars in agony as she forces herself to her feet. Lunges for the door and bursts through it with Shawna so close she can hear the big woman's breath and smell her sweat.

There's the scrape of metal on concrete as the blade flies at Ellen, misses by inches.

Then she's half-running, half-hopping on her bad ankle. Grimacing against the pain, but telling herself that her life depends on keeping moving.

Ellen reaches a door — any door — with Shawna pounding the corridor behind her. Touches the lanyard to the reader. It clicks.

She opens it just wide enough to slip through, then turns and pulls with all her might to shut it against the pressure of the big spring.

Shawna is a just few yards away.

Ellen lurches backwards, driving through her legs.

Shawna launches herself at the gap.

Ellen gives one last pull, and the door clicks shut as Shawna slams against it.

Shawna's face appears at the narrow, reinforced window.

Ellen stares back at her for a second, knowing how close she just came.

Then Shawna breaks eye contact and starts looking up, down, around, checking for a way through.

Ellen turns and runs.

She's on the first floor, now, and she just needs to find her way out of the building. Then she can disappear into the grounds and get the hell out of this godforsaken place.

She follows one corridor, and another, glancing around her for any sign of Shawna. It's like a maze, but eventually she reaches another door that opens into a larger area. She realizes it's the reception.

Ellen clicks on the reader and goes through. Shawna isn't here. There's some movement a way off, from another corridor, but there isn't even anyone behind the reception desk as she enters and crosses to the main double doors, trying to keep the weight off her busted ankle.

Beyond the doors, she can see the fence and the road, leading out of the hospital, to freedom. To her family. To a chance to stop the terrorist attack. To redemption for Paris.

She holds the pass out ahead of her, aiming for the reader. Touches it to the plastic.

Nothing happens.

She looks at the mechanism, tries again.

Nothing.

"Shit," she mumbles. Taps the card a third time, harder. Turns it over, swipes it once more.

The sounds behind her are getting louder. There's indistinct shouting from a corridor.

"Come on," she says, tapping the card again.

It's not working.

There's only one thing for it if she wants to get out: she'll have to break the doors open.

She hobbles to the waiting area on one side, picks up a chair.

A door opens, and she glances back. It's the security guys. Four of them.

"Stop!" one yells.

Ellen raises the chair overhead, winds up to smash it through the glass.

"Last warning!"

She swings the chair forward.

Then it's like two sets of cat claws dig into the middle of her back. There's a crackle, and she shrieks as her spine goes rigid. The chair slips from her grasp and she collapses to the floor, shaking. She has no control over her body anymore. Her nerves feel like they're on fire and her limbs contort as her screams continue.

The crackling stops but she's still buzzing with pain, her muscles drained. She turns her head, sees the wires trailing out of her back and up to the taser in the security guard's beefy hands.

There's a second of silence.

Then his buddies are on her, fists, knees and handcuffs, more brutal than ever.

It's over.

*

When Ellen comes to, she's lying under bright strip lights that make her screw her eyes shut. She can't move her limbs or torso and wonders if she's somehow been partially paralyzed by the taser. She lifts her head — about the only thing she can move — and sees that she's in one of those hospital beds with folding sides and wheels. Her wrists and ankles are held tightly by Velcro straps, and a fifth restraint runs across her chest, pinning her down.

A man's voice behind her says, "She's awake."

Ellen twists her neck, straining to see who it is, trying to work out where she is.

"I need ketamine, three-hundred milligrams for IM," replies a woman's voice that Ellen recognizes as Ratkova's.

"Wait," says Ellen, turning as much as she can in the bed. She can't see them.

There's some movement that sounds like drawers opening and shutting, packets tearing. A whispered discussion she can't make out.

"Please, no more drugs," she protests. Her speech feels sluggish, like her mouth isn't working properly. The effort of fighting the restraints is too much and she lets herself relax, shutting her eyes against the glaring lights overhead.

Then there are footsteps approaching and before she can react, a hand clamps her shoulder and the needle pierces her skin.

"No, stop," Ellen says. But it's already done.

Ratkova pulls out the syringe, holds it up, checks it's empty. She looks down at Ellen and smiles as if she's enjoying herself. "Now go back to sleep."

"Let me out of here," mumbles Ellen, tugging feebly at her restraints even as she feels her strength draining again.

"You're not going anywhere," Ratkova tells her. "Not for a long time."

END OF PART ONE

PART TWO

DAY FOUR

16

Clarion, Pennsylvania

PETER'S MOM PUTS the plate of buttermilk pancakes in the center of the kitchen table. They're thick and fluffy, and they smell incredible.

"Here you go, boys," she says.

"Thanks, ma," replies Peter.

Beside him, Mitch grunts something and starts helping himself to the stack, loading his plate up and dousing it in maple syrup. His big brother's lack of gratitude pisses him off. He knows mom only made the pancakes as a special treat because Mitch showed up for breakfast. If it was just Peter, she wouldn't have bothered. She'd never admit that, but Peter knows it's the truth. He's lucky if he gets to reheat pop's leftover oatmeal.

"You okay?" Peter asks him.

"Yeah," says Mitch, through a mouthful of pancake. He doesn't look up.

Their mom returns with a frying pan and slides eggs onto their plates — over-easy, which is how Mitch likes them. His brother gets four, Peter two. It was always that way when they were kids, and now they're both grown men, nothing's changed.

He's bigger than you, mom would always reply whenever Peter complained. *Yeah, because you give him more food*, he would argue, though he knew there was more to it than that. The genetic lottery. Winners and losers.

"You boys need anything else?" she says now.

"Maybe some more coffee, ma." Mitch slides his mug over to the edge of the table.

Mom collects it. "Comin' right up," she says, crossing to the coffee maker.

"I'll do it, ma," Peter gets to his feet, but his mom shoos him back to his seat.

"Nonsense. Eat your breakfast, Pee-Wee." She sets about refilling the machine and adding fresh coffee to the filter.

"When did Pop leave?" asks Peter, partly to fill the silence because Mitch ain't saying much.

"Seven," his mom replies. "He had a lot of work on."

Their old man always has *a lot of work on* at his auto repair shop. He's had a lot of work on for thirty years. Pop was usually at the garage when they were growing up. He'd go out early and get back late, his hands and face stained with motor oil. But even once he was home, he wouldn't talk much. He'd just eat his dinner, then crack a beer and settle into his favourite chair to watch the Pirates, Steelers or Penguins, depending on the time of year. Mitch would get asked about his latest high school football game, and Peter got asked . . . well, nothing much, truth be told. Pop never used the word "disappointment" about Peter, but he didn't have to.

"He'll be sad he missed you," mom adds, squeezing Mitch's arm.

Mitch acknowledges this with another grunt. "Tell him I said hi."

They eat in silence while the coffee finishes dripping, and mom tells Mitch about the rent going up on pop's garage. Peter can see Mitch isn't really paying attention to her.

"It's so good to see you, honey," she says to Mitch as she refills their mugs.

"What about me?" Peter queries.

"You live here," says mom, replacing the carafe on the hot plate. "I see you all the time."

"That's not an answer."

Peter waits for a response, but mom simply announces that she's going to take a shower, and heads out of the kitchen. The bathroom door clicks shut.

"What's goin' on?" Peter asks.

"What d'ya mean?"

"Why'd you come over?"

Mitch shrugs. "I wanted to see ma."

"Bullshit. You wanted a free breakfast."

His brother pauses, shakes his head. It should be a signal for Peter to keep quiet, but he doesn't want to be quiet. He's sick of never being spoken to, never being listened to in this family.

"Leanne didn't make you any food this morning, huh?"

"Watch your step, Pee-Wee."

"No, come on. Let's be straight." Peter's been wondering about Leanne's black eye, and he thinks he knows what happened. "You guys have a fight?"

Mitch doesn't reply, just keeps eating.

"She didn't walk into a door, did she?" Peter persists.

"Shut the hell up."

"Did you hit her? Because if you hit her—"

Mitch's knife clatters against the plate. Then his hand shoots across the table, and grabs Peter by the throat, squeezes.

The shock makes Peter inhale sharply and he feels the food stick in his windpipe.

"What if I did?" says Mitch. "What are you gonna do?"

Peter stares at his brother as he feels himself start to choke, the blood rushing to his face. His throat feels totally blocked, and he jerks a thumb toward his back, gasping for air.

Then it's like a switch trips in Mitch's brain. He releases his grip, thumps Peter between the shoulder blades with an open palm. One hit is all it takes, and the chunk of pancake flies out onto the table.

Peter coughs, then retches. Takes a sip of juice and a couple breaths.

"Sorry," Mitch says, "I've just . . . there's a lot of stress for me, right now."

"No shit."

"For all of us, I guess."

Peter looks his brother in the eye. "Why are you doing this?"

Mitch blinks. "I told you."

"No, you didn't. Not really, anyway. Just some crap about hatin' the government, like we all do."

"It's true."

"But you never told me *why* you hate them. Enough to—"

"Don't say it out loud," his brother warns him. "Not with mom here."

"Okay. So, tell me."

Mitch puts his fork down. Closes his eyes a moment. When he opens them again, there's a hard set to his features.

"Two-thousand one, we invade Afghanistan. I'm twelve years old. Maybe you don't remember it, but I can see the US Army on Fox News, kicking the shit out of those terrorist cocksuckers over there, right after 9/11."

"I *do* remember."

"I felt so damned proud that our nation could do that. That we had the power — the weapons, the soldiers, and the leadership — to get the job done. The day our troops rolled into Kabul was the day I decided to enlist."

"Really?"

Mitch nods. "Fast forward six years, and I signed up. You know the rest, up to last year. Then it all changed."

"What changed?"

"We pulled out."

"Of where?"

"Afghanistan, dumbass. Twenty years. Two thousand, three hundred and twelve servicemen and women dead. More than twenty thousand injured, and a bunch of them ain't never gonna walk again. Some can't even take a shit without carers to wipe their asses now. Eight hundred twenty-four billion — *billion* — dollars of our goddamn money, and then what?"

"What?"

"We just fuckin' leave."

"Good. It ain't our country, anyway, it's—"

Mitch slams his hand on the table. "It's not good, Pee-Wee," he growls. "It's cowardice. It's politicians screwing us over to win votes. It's giving up on everything those soldiers lost their lives for. It's disrespecting their memory. And it ain't a red or blue thing, neither. The last guy in charge started the deal, this one finished it. They're as bad as each other."

Peter stays quiet. He can see there's a kind of wildfire burning inside his brother.

"Three hundred eighty-one US marines, dead," Mitch states.

Peter swallows. His throat hurts.

"Know how many of them I knew, personally?"

"Uh, no."

"Forty-two." Mitch is pressing his teeth together so hard, his lips start shaking. "Forty-two of my brothers," he adds. "Guys I trained with, fought with, ate meals with, lifted weights with, played poker with."

Peter never really stopped to think how many buddies Mitch had lost. "I'm sorry, man, I—"

"It's betrayal, pure and simple. And the more you read about it, the more lies you find. The United States has been bent over and fucked in the ass by its politicians. For years. They need to pay. We need to hold them accountable. And talkin' ain't gonna change nothin'. It's gone way past that."

He's never seen his brother like this, and he don't much like it. It's even scarier than usual. Like he could kill someone right now, if the wrong person walked through the door.

"Why are *you* doing this?" Mitch asks him.

Peter's been asking himself the same thing a lot this week. He's not sure he has an answer. Not one to justify the kind of craziness they're going to unleash in three days' time, anyway.

"Huh?" prompts Mitch. "You gotta have a reason, Pee-Wee."

What does he say? Because he's angry at somebody for the fact his life doesn't amount to much? Because he's sick of being a nobody, and he wants people to take notice of him? Because he wants to be a tough guy, like his big brother? Because he's too scared to say no? None of those seem like good enough reasons to kill a person. To kill a lot of people.

"Uh, well, I hate the government, too," he replies hastily.

"You sure about that?"

"Of course, I am."

Mitch studies him. "All right, then."

Peter looks out of the kitchen window. Sees the old rope swing still hanging from the big tree, where he and Mitch used to play until they got too big for it. Until Mitch got too big for it, at least. That seems like another lifetime, now.

"In three days' time," Mitch continues, "you're gonna be part of the team that struck the biggest blow for American freedom since independence. Ruby Ridge, Waco, Oklahoma City, The Capitol, then us. Shit, even the Unabomber is gonna seem like the goddamn tooth fairy compared to the Keystone Boys. We're their worst nightmare."

Peter nods. His stomach is churning.

"And this afternoon," Mitch adds, "when we test the EFP, you're gonna see what a little bit of hell looks like."

"What's an EFP?"

Mitch cracks a smile for the first time that day. "You'll find out."

*

Washington, D.C.

He walks through the revolving door of the Old Ebbitt Grill early, but the kid is already there. His associate has chosen the seat commanding a full view of the restaurant, while he gets the wall, forcing him to focus his attention on the younger man. A power play for a power breakfast.

At least there's a nice painting for him to look at when he gets bored of the kid's face. It's a huge canvas of the White House — which is literally across the road from the restaurant — lit up by fireworks. He guesses it's supposed to represent the Fourth of July, or maybe the inauguration of a new president, but it's like the explosions are coming right out of the building, as if it's being torched. Maybe better to look at the kid after all.

As he approaches the table, the young man rises and extends his hand, knuckles up. It's another stupid power move he's probably read about in some book on how to be "alpha".

He resists the urge to crush those soft fingers in his grip as he accepts the handshake.

"Welcome," says the kid, as if he owns the place. Maybe he does. "Thanks for coming."

"It's a great spot," he replies as they sit. "And you're buying." *With your parents' money*, he resists adding.

The young man flashes a set of perfect white teeth. "You know who used to come here?"

"Obama?"

"Teddy Roosevelt, youngest ever POTUS," the kid says proudly. "So far." It's no secret he wants to break that record.

"He only became president because McKinley was assassinated. He didn't win an election. Not at first, anyway."

The kid chuckles. "Doesn't matter how you get there."

A waiter comes over and they order. His young associate takes an egg-white omelette, while he goes all in with a full American breakfast. It's a heart attack on a plate. But he needs the fuel, and the comfort.

"She tried to escape, again," says the kid, once the waiter has gone.

He nods. "I thought she might."

"Our friends are concerned that she may not be under control."

"She is."

"You sure about that?"

"So I've been told."

"Hm." The kid leans back against the velvet banquette and smooths his hair, surveying his surroundings. "Our colleagues want reassurance. Can we give it to them?"

"Yes."

"All right, good." The younger man strokes his freshly shaven chin. "I'll tell them they have nothing to worry about."

"Fine."

"I hope you're right."

"I am."

"Because if you're not . . ."

The kid doesn't need to finish his sentence — its implication is clear: other means will be used. And Ellen McGinley will become the first casualty of the terrorist act in which he's somehow playing a role. The first casualty of many.

It's not long before the food arrives. But when it does, he's completely lost his appetite.

17

WHEN ELLEN WAKES up, she's still restrained on the bed. Only now, she's in a new room, one she hasn't seen before. At least, she *thinks* she hasn't seen it before. But her brain feels like it's made out of jello and she's not sure about anything right now. She doesn't even know how much time has passed since she was — oh God, she remembers — trying to get out.

There was the cafeteria and the ID card and Shawna and the knife and she's running and then . . . her body tenses involuntarily at the memory of trying to break through the main doors. Lifting the chair, then the taser, the electricity snaking its way through her, paralysing her, before the security guys descended.

After that, it's just fragments. Ratkova. Something about ketamine. Needles. Maybe she dreamed that last part.

But her left shoulder hurts like hell, so maybe not. She can't even move her hands to touch it or check it, though, because of the Velcro wrapped around her wrists. She figures that must be where they're injecting her. It's marginally less violating than a jab in the ass, at least.

Twisting her head to look beyond the strip lights, she sees a security camera in the corner of the room, pointed right at her.

They're watching her.

It's a few moments before the door opens and she hears footsteps from behind her. Bigger and heavier than Ratkova. Adrenalin stabs her belly and rushes to her limbs. Is it Shawna? She strains to see but can't move her neck enough. Tries to rip her arms and legs free, but they won't budge.

"Help!" she yells at the top of her lungs. "Somebody help me!"

The footsteps get closer. She braces for the assault, knowing she has no way of stopping it this time.

"Good morning, Ellen."

It's a man's voice. She doesn't recognize it. Seconds later, the owner comes into her line of sight, looming over her. He's really tall and wearing a black suit and a bow tie. He has dark eyes under large, equally dark eyebrows that stand out against his grey, slicked-back hair. He looks like Lurch from The Addams Family.

"I'm Doctor Nyborg," he says.

Okay, she thinks. *It's just the asshole in charge, not a psychopath trying to strangle or stab me.* Ellen allows herself to relax, but only a little. Her heart is still hammering, and her palms are sweaty.

"Where am I?" she asks.

He ignores her question. "You're being restrained and medicated for your own safety, and for the safety of the other patients here."

"She was coming for me," Ellen gasps, "with a knife from the kitchens. I had to take Tommy's pass, otherwise—"

"Who was *coming for you*?" Nyborg cuts her off, his tone sceptical.

"Shawna LeDuc. That's why I ran from the cafeteria," she says quickly. "I had to get out. She would've killed me."

The psychiatrist frowns. "No knife was reported stolen, or found, and Shawna hasn't been involved in any incident of which we're aware. At least, not since your attack on her two days ago."

"She tried to murder me. Twice!"

"Calm down, Ellen. Can we talk in a civilized manner, or do I need to give you something more to take the edge off this anger of yours?"

She wants to tell him to go fuck himself, but she forces herself to play nice. At least then she might have a chance of getting out of these restraints. She closes her eyes a second, takes a breath.

"I am calm," she says.

"Good." He looks her up and down as if checking her restraints are secured, although she notices his gaze lingering on her breasts.

"When can I go home?" she asks.

Nyborg presses his lips together, shakes his head. "You're experiencing what's known as a delusional psychosis. Apparently, you think that some sort of terrorist act is imminent, and you're the only one who can stop it, because you used to work for the CIA."

"That's true."

The shrink tilts his head, his expression more pitying than sympathetic. "I'm afraid it's not. It's already been confirmed that you never worked for the government."

"But—"

"Now, there are many people who have, shall we say, *unusual* beliefs. More than half of the American population believe that aliens have visited our planet, for example. Mostly, those beliefs are harmless. But when they result in physical threats and attacks on others, they have to be stopped, and treated properly."

"No."

"You're obviously very unwell, Ellen. And you need help."

"I need to go home to my family," she protests.

"Imagine if you'd actually got out of the hospital and into the community," he continues. "The harm you might have caused to others due to the state you were in. And that would be my responsibility. Our number one concern here is safety."

"But, I didn't . . . I was—"

"And until I'm satisfied that you can be safe, we'll be keeping you here."

"My review meeting, it's this afternoon, right? My attorney should—"

"It's been cancelled."

"What?"

"There will be no review. The risks if you leave are patently too high."

"Bullshit!" she cries, unable to hold her frustration any longer.

"The decision's been made. Your commitment order has been extended."

"You asshole."

There's no pity in Nyborg's face, now. "The things you think are happening are not real, Ellen. The sooner you understand that, the better. The problem here is your mental ill health, not some non-existent terrorist group you've been babbling about."

"They do exist. They have to," she says, as much to herself as to Nyborg. But there's a small seed of doubt in her mind, now.

"Large doses of ketamine, such as those we've had to administer to sedate you, can cause hallucinations. But since you admit to having had these fantasies prior to admission here, and this isn't the first time you've experienced psychiatric illness, I'm not inclined to attribute your delusional beliefs to the medication. And, in view of your safety issues, I'll be continuing the drug regimen."

He takes one final look down at her, then he's gone.

"Wait, Doctor Nyborg! Please . . ."

But the door's already shut behind him.

Ellen screams with rage.

Her will is starting to ebb away and there's a fog in her head. She can't think clearly, and it hurts even trying to work it all out. She's exhausted, mentally and physically. She needs to relax. A voice whispers that she should stop fighting and let them do what they want here. That if she just takes the drugs, they'll make her feel better, feel nothing . . .

As the tension drains from her body, she starts to get drowsy again, and images begin to crowd her mind, jumbled up like pieces of the jigsaw puzzle she and Jada were trying to solve. She sees the aftermath of a bomb attack . . . only it's here in the US, not in Paris, so it can't be real. And if she imagined that, what else did she imagine?

No, she tells herself: Nyborg is wrong and she's right. That has to be the truth. Because, otherwise, it would mean she really is crazy. And she's not crazy. She can't be. She knows she had problems before, but she's over them. Or she was, at least, until last week . . .

Ellen can picture little Josh, Harry, and her parents, all together, without her. She hears the voices that sparked this whole thing, the men in the hotel corridor. What did Doctor Vang say? Maybe there *is* another explanation for all this, and she's fighting ghosts, for nothing . . .

She starts to drift, feels as though the walls and ceiling are moving away from her. Then the room dissolves as she closes her eyes.

*

Paris, six years earlier

Nadia, the woman who stumbled through the door of Ellen's charity in the pouring rain that day, had good reason to be crying. Her three-year-old boy, Samir, was in the kids' ICU at the hospital. His congenital heart defect meant he had to be hooked up to a giant machine twenty-four-seven to pump blood around his body. But that was only a short-term solution. He needed a new heart.

Months had gone by and the public healthcare system in Paris had nothing. Then a heart became available in Switzerland. But Nadia's hopes were crushed when she discovered its price: $250,000. She made ten bucks an hour as a cleaner. Her husband, Jalil, was an unemployed ex-con with no job prospects. The family lived in social housing in one of Vitry-sur-Seine's high-rise blocks. There was no insurance. You didn't need to be a math genius to see they had no way to pay for it. So, Nadia begged Ellen to ask her donor in America: could they save her son's life?

Ellen talked it over with Harry, spent a couple of sleepless nights thinking about it. She had the money. But, ironically, she wasn't running a charity. She could pay, but only if there was intel to be had. She expedited traces on Nadia's cell phone and email, but they came back negative. Even Ricardo, her friendly hacker, couldn't find anything in the deep web. There were no ties to any known extremists. Put another way, as an asset, she was useless. Ellen tried making the argument that Nadia could develop access, but no "clean skin" was worth a quarter million dollars. Ultimately, Langley said no.

She thought about it some more. She had a chance to save a child's life. A child not much older than her own little boy. And she made a decision: she said yes.

As the account controller, she could make the transfer to Switzerland from her French bank before the CIA could block it at their end. She did it.

Her boss at Langley was seriously pissed. He demanded she get the money back. But it was too late. The op had already taken place. Samir had his new heart, and Ellen had a friend for life, as well as a bunch of enemies back home. She didn't care, though.

She'd done the right thing. Perhaps that single act of disobedi-
ence was the beginning of the end.

*

It's almost a year later when Nadia comes into the office, Samir
walking beside her, holding her hand. She drops by every so
often, volunteers a little, when she can, between childcare and
cleaning shifts. Her husband is still unemployed.

"Can I talk to you?" she asks Ellen. Her tone indicates it's a
private conversation.

They go outside.

"What's up?" Ellen asks, once they're alone.

"I'm worried about Jalil, and there's no one else I can tell,"
Nadia explains. "I think he has become a *jihadi*. And I believe
he's planning a terrorist attack, here in Paris."

There's something about the way she speaks that tells Ellen
this is real.

Her boss at Agency headquarters would grudgingly call that
a return on investment.

For Ellen, it's the opportunity to save lives.

It's what she came here for.

She needs to act.

*

Present day

Ellen wakes at the sound of movement by her bed. The first thing
she sees is the syringe by her shoulder. She's almost too tired to
resist it, this time.

"No," she mumbles, letting her head slump back against the
thin, hard pillow. "Please."

"It's okay," says the voice.

It's Vang.

Ellen blinks her eyes open and looks up at him. She can't really see him properly because he's standing behind her head. What is he doing? For a second, she wonders if she's read him all wrong, whether he's just another part of Nyborg and Ratkova's gang of bullies, drugging everyone to the eyeballs in the name of "safety". Then she realizes his body is blocking the security camera's view of her.

"Hold still for me," he says, placing a thick tissue between her shoulder and the syringe and squirting its contents into the paper instead of her arm.

"What . . .?"

"I figured you're better off without this," he responds. "But whoever's watching this needs to think I'm giving it to you."

"Thank you," she whispers.

"How are you feeling?" he asks, as he walks over to a trash can and disposes of the needle.

"Like I've got nothing left," she replies.

"Ketamine will do that to you."

"And . . . as if stuff might not be how I think it is."

"How do you mean?"

"As if, you know, Nyborg is right. Maybe I am imagining it all. Delusional psychosis."

"You're not imagining it," Vang says, returning to her bedside.

"But you said there might be an—"

"Look." He takes out his cell phone and, shielding it from the camera with his body, shows her the screen.

"Walter got back to me," he says. "And the Keystone Boys are real."

18

"HARRY, IT'S ME," she says, as soon as he picks up. She knows he takes lunch at noon, if he can, so her call is timed perfectly to catch him when he's not in a meeting.

"Ellen! My god, honey, how're you doing?"

She glances over her shoulder. Across the room, Vang is sitting in one of the armchairs. He looks up from the stack of papers he's reading, nods, and returns his attention to the documents. He's almost certainly breaking the rules by letting her call from his office, but he's accepted the risk of that. She knows he's on her side, now. He's made the choice. His decision to message Walter was the first step. And Walter's response was the confirmation he needed to continue.

"Uh, well, they've let me out of my restraints for the first time in like fifteen hours," she replies.

"What?"

"No one told you?"

"No," he says. "I called first thing this morning, but they said you were still sleeping. What are you talking about? Restraints?"

"The same woman tried to attack me again, yesterday. I ran. They caught me at the front door, shackled me to a bed and pumped me full of ketamine."

"Ketamine? Jesus, Ellen. Are you all right?"

"Just about."

"Where are you now?"

"I'm with my therapist."

"Oh, okay." He pauses. "That's great. So, you're getting some help, then?"

"I don't need *help*, Harry," she hisses. "Not the kind they're telling you I should have, anyway."

"But, uh," he clears his throat, "Doctor Nyborg said that, you know, what with your delusions . . ."

"They're not goddamn delusions, Harry!"

He thinks she's making it all up. The conversation she overheard in D.C., the secret she trusted him enough to tell. She realizes that the one person who should trust her, doesn't. For a fleeting moment, she wonders if she can trust herself. The Keystone Boys exist, sure. But do they represent the threat she's convinced herself they do?

She lowers her voice. "They're not delusions," she repeats, with a little less conviction.

"They told me you needed treatment, Ellen," he counters. "They're professionals. Who am I supposed to believe?"

"You're supposed to believe me. Your wife."

Harry doesn't respond. There's a brief silence between them.

"Do you?" she asks.

"Do I what?"

"Believe me. That the stuff I've been talking about is real."

"Ah," he hesitates, "I . . ."

"Christ, Harry!"

"Listen to me, honey. It's not a question of believing or not believing . . ."

"Don't give me your politician bullshit."

"Sorry." He sighs. "It's just . . . maybe they can help you there."

"Help me with what, exactly?"

"Uh, you know, unusual beliefs."

"How? By chaining me to a fucking bed?"

"They didn't tell me they were doing that. Maybe you should let them—"

"I suppose they didn't tell you that my review this afternoon is cancelled, either?" she says.

"No. Why is it—"

"Safety issues. That's their excuse, anyway."

"Well, I mean, they've got to assess the risks, and—"

"It isn't about that, Harry. They want to keep me here. You and I know why."

"Ellen . . ."

"But things have changed."

"They have?" He sounds confused.

She can't go into details, because she doesn't know who might be listening, even to Vang's phone. She can't tell Harry what Walter discovered. That — same as she found — there was nothing about the Keystone Boys in "open source" information on the surface web. But that was why she needed to ask Walter.

Her old professor knows his way around the domestic extremist underground. And today, that's mostly on the dark web. Militias, conspiracy theorists, QAnon types, sovereign citizens, neo-Nazis — they've all got wise to law enforcement infiltration of regular chatrooms. They've moved their "chans" — anonymous message boards — onto the darknet and out of sight. But Walter has contacts who trust him. Or, rather, they trust his alias persona, *ProfessorX*, who can give them more political rhetoric in support of their wack-job beliefs than they could ever want.

And he found what she was looking for. One single reference to the Keystone Boys, three months ago, on an internet message board called *Gigachan*, along with a username and, perhaps the most important detail, a date. *We're gonna light up the sky on the Fourth of July*, the final post had read.

It wasn't much. But it was enough for her to know she hasn't imagined it. That she didn't misinterpret the words she overheard at the hotel in D.C. last week. And that she has three days to stop this thing.

"Trust me," she tells Harry. "They've changed."

"Okay . . ."

"I swear to you, I am not crazy," she says firmly.

"Honey, I didn't say you were, I only—"

"And I need to do something about this . . . situation."

"But what about your treatment?"

Harry seems determined for her to stay here. Maybe he's just seeing the same problems she had after Paris and wants to help her get well again, like he did before. She remembers how crucial his support was that time. But she *knows* this is different.

"You don't get it. I don't need treatment. I need to sit down with someone like Ricardo and figure this out."

"Let me call our attorney," he offers, "I can get her to speak to Doctor Nyborg, arrange a meeting. Then I'm sure we can all just sit down and talk about—"

"That won't work, Harry," she says, cutting him off. "If they won't even review my commitment order, there's no way they're gonna let me out. They're set on keeping me here."

"Well, there's a system, which we have to respect and follow, and eventually—"

"That's too slow."

More silence.

"Besides," she continues, "I'm not sitting around and waiting for some homicidal psychopath to have a third go at killing me."

"Ellen, listen. There has to be a way out of this. Within the law."

"*Within the law?* Is that your primary concern? Is this about your public image?"

"It's not like that."

Yesterday, when her husband visited, Ellen felt as though the support he'd always given her wasn't there. She hoped that it'd be different today. That her assurances would change his mind. But it hasn't worked. He thinks she belongs here, end of story.

"What's your solution then?" she demands.

"We need to trust the process," he says.

"What does that mean?"

"It means that I remember what happened to you after Paris. Do you?"

She does remember: paranoia, panic attacks, flashbacks. The occasional feeling that her mind had been disconnected from her body. Things that have been coming back to her this past week.

"This is different. I'll prove it to you."

"Don't do anything stupid, Ellen. Josh needs you. I need you. We'll find a way to get you out and get our family back together. I'll call Nyborg right now and make sure you've got extra security on the ward to protect you from that woman."

"No. Don't do that."

"What? Why not? You told me a second ago—"

"Just make sure Josh is safe," she says. "I'll see you soon."

"Wait, honey, don't—"

She hangs up. Stares at the phone. She can feel tears prickle her eyes.

"He doesn't believe me," she says quietly.

Vang puts his papers down. "Can I help?"

"You've done enough, Lee. Really. I don't want to get you in trouble."

It was Vang who got her out of those restraints, with his idea of a one-on-one "behavioral intervention" to help her manage panic and anger. Nyborg had agreed, letting Vang escort her to his office, where they are now. And, thanks to him volunteering to deliver her ketamine shot, then not actually giving it to her, she's starting to feel halfway in control again.

"It's okay," he says.

She pauses, then asks him, "Why did you choose to help me?"

Vang blinks. "Let's just say that I know what it's like to be in your position. My community . . . we've suffered a lot. Racism, poverty, discrimination, mental health issues. That's why I become a psychologist, to help make a difference." He shakes his head. "I didn't sign up for some of the stuff that's going on here. I didn't become part of the system to keep other people down."

Ellen nods. She made the right call coming to Vang. And she knows she can trust him.

"Besides," he adds. "If these guys are planning something and, as you say, you can't go to the cops, then you've got to investigate."

"Right."

"And if the Fourth of July thing is literal, there's not a whole lot of time. Today's the first."

Ellen feels a wave of anxiety building inside her. It's Paris all over again. She fights it down, though: she needs to focus on getting out of here.

"What do you need?" Vang asks.

She shuts her eyes, thinks. Recalls something she noticed when she first arrived here. Sees the plan coming together in her mind's eye. After a minute, she looks up at him.

"This is going to sound nuts," she begins.

"Try me."

"I'm gonna need a disposable camera, with a flash."

"Uh, okay."

"That's important. It has to have a flash."

"Got it."

"Do you have any?"

He considers her question. "I'm pretty sure we ordered a bunch of them for a photography project last year. But if not, I can buy one."

"Plus, two medium screws, a flathead screwdriver, some wire and electrical tape."

"Maintenance will definitely have that."

"Can you get a hold of it?"

"Yeah. Should I ask what this is for?"

"Better not," she replies. "Oh, and a syringe full of ketamine."

Vang leans back in his chair, exhales long and slow. "You know what?" he says, checking his watch. "I think we should end our session here. I'll take you back to the communal area, collect you from there again at one-thirty, and bring you back here. Sound okay?"

"Perfect," she says. "Thank you."

*

Jada presses the jigsaw piece into place. There's still a lot of the picture missing, but the silver ribbon of the Colorado River, winding down the canyon between two steep, rust-red cliffs, is now discernible. She smiles at Ellen.

"It's startin' to come together, huh?" she says.

"Lookin' good," remarks Ellen.

"Mm-hm. That's teamwork right there."

They bump fists.

"Jada, can I ask you something?"

"Go 'head."

Ellen drops her voice to a whisper. "You remember when we first met, you told me about how you're secretly working for the CIA?"

Jada glances around her before turning back and meeting Ellen's gaze. "It's what put me in here. They caught me takin' documents from a federal building in Philly."

"Really?"

"Yeah." Jada leans in a little closer. "I got two years. But if they think that's gonna stop me completing my mission, they're wrong."

Ellen can tell from the intensity in Jada's expression that she's still totally convinced by the beliefs that brought her here. That there's that little bit of her that she can't see is beyond reason. But that's the bit Ellen needs to gamble on right now. She just hopes it's going to work.

"Well, I have kind of a mission myself."

"You do?"

"And I need your help."

Jada's eyes widen. "Are you . . .?"

"That's right." Ellen nods. "I'm CIA, too. At least, I was."

"Aw, shit." Jada shakes her head, a wry smile on her lips. She wags a finger at Ellen. "I knew there was somethin' about you, girl."

"Can you help me?"

Jada reaches out, lays her hand over Ellen's. "Whatever you need."

Ellen explains what she needs.

*

Ellen is being escorted to the ladies' room by a security guard when the bathroom door opens, and Shawna LeDuc steps out. She stops in the doorway and gives Ellen a dead-eyed stare. Ellen's heart rate instantly goes through the roof. She's due to be collected by Vang in ten minutes. She has to play it smart if she wants to have a chance of putting her plan into action. Now is not the time to stand up to the bully and get into another fight, maybe risk getting restrained again. She sidesteps, so that the security guard is shielding her.

Shawna acknowledges the apparent show of deference.

"I thought they strapped you down, li'l runaway," she says.

"Uh, yeah . . . temporarily," replies Ellen, slowly. She needs to pretend she's still under the effect of a sedative.

"Well, you ain't gettin' outta this place." Shawna's mouth twists into a sneer. "And I ain't goin' nowhere, neither."

Ellen looks away. She doesn't want this to escalate; she's not convinced the guard would help her out if it did.

"Can we get to the restroom, please, Shawna?" says the guard.

"Be my guest," Shawna moves out of their way. "It's all yours."

"In you go, Ellen." The guard steps aside, gestures for her to walk forward.

As Ellen advances, she can't avoid passing Shawna. The big woman dips her head as they draw level.

"You're not right in the head," Shawna whispers, "I get that. Everybody in here has somethin' wrong with them." She taps her temple. "And it's real sad how many of those folks end up killin' themselves. Happens every once in a while on this ward. Hangin', mostly."

Ellen tries to swallow, but her mouth is too dry.

"All right, keep it moving, ladies," the guard says.

"Usually they do it at night," Shawna continues, "alone in their rooms, with the lights out. No witnesses."

Ellen turns her head, looks up at her. Her eyes flick from Shawna's face to the skull tattoo on her neck and back up.

Shawna gives her a smile that reminds Ellen of an alligator. Then she walks away.

As the adrenalin pulses through her, Ellen can feel a panic attack coming on, but she needs to keep her shit together.

She's struck out twice trying to escape this place. Now she knows that if her next attempt fails, it'll be her third strike. Then she's done.

Time to get her game face on.

19

ELLEN IS ALONE in her room, lying in bed, with her back to the door and the blinds down, pretending to be asleep. She's trying not to think about Shawna's threat earlier, which isn't easy when she has nothing else to do but wait. She asked Vang this afternoon about suicides on the ward, and he confirmed that there had been three in the two years he'd worked here. And, just as Shawna had said, all of them were hangings, in patients' rooms, using the bedclothes.

Now Ellen can't help but imagine Shawna coming for her in the night, wrapping a sheet around her neck before she's even woken up, then staging the scene to make it look like suicide. She got the feeling from their encounter earlier that not only is such an attack inevitable, but that Shawna would enjoy it, too. Psychopaths' brains are wired to get a kick out of other people's suffering.

Ellen knows that, rather than freaking out and letting the panic take hold of her, she needs to use the fear to sharpen her mind and focus on the next few minutes. She's going to get one shot at making it out of here.

She needs to make it count.

Thanks to Vang, her preparations are as good as they could

be. She has a syringe under her pillow, with enough ketamine inside it to knock someone out cold. In her hand is the disposable camera she's modified.

Now it's just a question of waiting for the visit Ratkova has scheduled, and hoping that Jada can play her part at the right time.

During her training at The Farm, they'd taught recruits how to improvise weapons and explosives. Often, out in the field, you don't have the proper supplies, so if you need to defend yourself or create a distraction, you've got to use whatever is to hand. They learnt to build simple explosive and incendiary devices out of household products. It was like a high school chemistry class, only a lot more fun. There was a morning when Ellen had to pinch herself, realising she was getting paid to make and throw Molotov cocktails. In those moments, she hadn't appreciated that one day her life may depend on her ability to make something potentially lethal out of everyday objects.

But that's exactly the situation she's in right now.

A disposable camera with a flash contains something called a capacitor — a little box that can store electrical charge. To fire a flash, you need more power than a little 1.5-volt AA battery can generate. So, the capacitor draws it up and holds it and, by the time it's fully charged, it can put out a burst of 250 volts. More than twice what you get from a household electricity supply. All you need to do is open the camera's plastic casing, run the power from the capacitor through a couple of wires to screws that you poke through the casing, and you've got a home-made stun gun that delivers a bigger shock than putting wet fingers in a plug socket.

Ellen hears the footsteps approaching from the corridor outside her room. A small, quick *clack-clack* of heels. Ratkova.

Showtime.

She pushes the flash button to start charging the capacitor.

There's a pause, presumably while the nurse peers through the little window into Ellen's room to check she's inside.

Ellen needs her to come in and walk over to her, which is why she stays in bed. She wants Ratkova to think she's so beat that the nurse has to wake her up to deliver her afternoon medication.

Lying still, she keeps her breath steady.

The lock clicks, the door opens and Ratkova enters.

Then a second set of footsteps follows behind, bigger and heavier.

There's a delay of maybe a second before the adrenalin shoots through her. Is it Shawna? Was the stuff she said about night-time just a ruse to catch Ellen off-guard during the day? Every fibre in Ellen's body wants to twist to see what's happening, but she holds still. She can't lose the advantage of surprise.

"Do we need to take her to the clinic room?" A man's voice.

Ratkova's brought security with her. She clearly isn't taking any chances.

That's better than having to deal with Shawna, but it wasn't part of Ellen's plan. She didn't account for the possibility that Ratkova might bring reinforcements. Ellen has the means to subdue one person, but not two.

"Yes," replies Ratkova. "Let's get her up."

Both of them approach the bed.

The scream from down the corridor pierces the air. It's not the sound of pain. It's a battle cry. There's indistinct shouting. Ellen knows who it is.

Jada. She's precisely on time, and she's mad as hell.

Ratkova stops. "What's going on?"

Before the security guy can respond, his radio crackles to life. Ellen catches the words *code blue* and *communal area* and *backup*.

"I'd better go," he says.

There's an agonising pause before Ratkova agrees. "Fine. Meet me in the clinic room."

The security guard hustles out.

Then it's just the two of them: Ellen and Ratkova.

"Time to get up, Ellen," Ratkova announces.

Ellen doesn't move.

"Come on, let's go," the nurse insists. "You need your medication."

Ellen murmurs, shifts a little, then goes back to the deep breathing of her fake slumber.

"Don't waste my time," Ratkova adds, stepping closer. "You'll only make it worse for yourself."

Ellen reckons she's just a couple feet away now.

"Are you . . .?" Ratkova takes another step. The material of her clothing rustles as she reaches out.

Almost there.

Ellen feels the comforter being drawn back.

Ratkova's fingers touch her shoulder.

And that's when Ellen strikes.

In a single movement she turns over, grabs Ratkova's left arm and pulls her in close. The nurse loses her balance, tips forward onto the bed.

Ellen's right arm wheels around and plunges the screw tips of the stun gun she's holding into the base of Ratkova's neck. She hears the crack of electricity as the charge flows into the nurse's spine and her body goes rigid. She releases her grip on Ratkova's arm and clamps her left hand over the nurse's mouth to stifle her cries. Ellen knows she has just a few seconds to act while Ratkova's nervous system is overloaded with electrical impulses. She drops the stun gun and scrabbles under her pillow for the syringe.

She jabs the needle deep into Ratkova's shoulder, pushes the plunger all the way down and then holds her close, hand still over her mouth.

It takes maybe a minute for the tension to drop from Ratkova's body, and for her attempts at yelling to subside. A minute later, she's all but out cold. It feels like the longest two minutes of Ellen's life, as she wraps her limbs around Ratkova to pin her down — just like E.J. taught her in the self-defence classes — throwing a glance at the open door every few seconds.

Down the hall, Jada is making one hell of a racket and Ellen hears what sounds like furniture smashing, then male voices shouting. The way the security goons go mob-handed into any confrontation, Ellen's confident that Jada will keep them all tied up for a couple more minutes, at least. She just hopes she'll be okay at the end of it.

Finally, Ratkova's body goes limp. Ellen rolls the nurse onto her side, checks her pulse and breathing. She goes over to the door and shuts it, tucking her bathroom towel into the top so that it covers the window.

Then she gets to work.

*

Three minutes later, Ellen walks out of the room dressed as Head Psychiatric Nurse, Ava Ratkova. The idea came to her when she realized they were about the same height and weight. But that's where the similarity stops. Ellen's hair is longer and darker than Ratkova's, her feet are too small for the nurse's shoes, and her face is obviously different, even behind those huge glasses. She knows the disguise won't convince anyone up close, but that doesn't matter. Her disguise only needs to defeat a glance or someone watching a camera feed, and for that, it's good enough.

Crucially, the outfit also comes with her ticket out of the hospital: Ratkova's key card.

Ellen takes a final glance back at the bed. Ratkova is in the exact same position Ellen was in five minutes ago, her back to door, wrapped in the duvet. The only difference is that Ratkova really is asleep, literally given a taste of her own medicine. But there's no time for Ellen to enjoy the justice of that. She needs to get going.

Getting out of the ward isn't as easy as she imagined. Ratkova's super-thick glasses are screwing with her vision, she can't walk properly, and she isn't totally sure where she needs to go. She only knows that she's got to avoid the chaos that's still raging in the communal area.

She spots an exit with a card reader along the corridor and heads for it. On the way, she sees a small fire evacuation plan mounted on the wall. She rips it off and uses it to orientate herself as she walks toward the door.

She reaches the first exit and extends her key card. Sees the panic button on the lanyard that Ratkova pressed the first time she tried to get out. The memory of that episode briefly freezes her.

Then the yelling pulls her back to the moment.

"Last warning!" she hears. She knows what's coming for Jada if she doesn't surrender now.

Ellen touches the card to the reader and the door clicks open.

She hears the scream from down the hall and knows Jada is being tasered.

Part of her wants to go back, defend this woman who has shown so much courage to help her. Who, in different circumstances, could have been her friend. But right now, Jada is doing a job that Ellen needs her to do. Going back would be the end of her escape. And the green light to the Keystone Boys.

Ellen vows not to forget Jada's sacrifice. It's just possible that she may have helped to save a lot of innocent lives — though it's on Ellen to see that to its end, now.

She moves quickly through the door and down the next corridor, following the fire plan to head for the emergency exit. Reaching a different staircase, she removes her shoes, and runs down the steps barefoot. Remembers to slip the shoes back on before she exits into the first-floor corridor. She makes a final check of the evacuation plan and memorizes the sequence of turns to get to the main entrance, then discards the plan.

She's one corridor away when a voice behind her says, "Ava?"

She freezes. It's Shawna.

"Ava, where you goin'?" asks Shawna, walking toward her. "You told me that little bitch was headed to the clinic room, and . . . wait a second."

Ellen reaches into Ratkova's pants pocket, presses the flash button on the stun gun. Hears a little whining sound as it charges.

Shawna's right on her shoulder now.

"What in the hell's goin' on . . .?" Shawna says.

Ellen draws the stun gun and whips around, lunging for Shawna. The big woman is caught completely off-guard, and barely has time to raise her hands before the electrified screw tips connect with her solar plexus. She roars in pain and doubles over, giving Ellen a window of maybe two seconds.

There's no room for error.

Ellen swings her hand down on Shawna's exposed throat, the blade of bone at the base of her pinky finger connecting with the soft tissue between Shawna's windpipe and the muscle at the side of her neck.

The vagus nerve and carotid artery run down that section, linking the heart with the brain. If you strike the nerve or press on the artery, you can put someone to sleep in seconds by tricking their brain into shutting down. It doesn't require a whole lot of force, but you've got to be precise.

The effect is almost instantaneous.

Shawna drops like a sack of potatoes.

Ellen knows she doesn't have long before Shawna wakes up again. Frantically searching the corridor around her, she spots a store cupboard. Opens it with Ratkova's key card. It's full of cleaning equipment. Wedging the door open with a mop, she lifts Shawna under the arms and somehow finds the strength to drag her across the carpet and fold her into the cupboard. She has just enough time to stuff a cloth in her mouth and tie it in place with another cloth. Then she closes the door and walks away.

At the end of the corridor, she sees the main entrance. She clicks open the penultimate lock and proceeds through.

This time, though, there's a receptionist at the desk on the far side. An older lady whose glasses are even bigger and thicker than the ones Ellen is wearing right now. She's reading a newspaper, squinting and frowning at it, as if it's written in a language she doesn't speak.

Ellen moves quickly toward the doors, keeping her head down, praying the woman doesn't pay her any attention.

"That you, Ava?" says the receptionist. "Not the end of your shift, is it?"

Ellen freezes.

She shakes her head. "Personal emergency," she replies, mimicking Ratkova's voice.

"Oh, right. It's just, there's a couple envelopes for you here."

"Later," she mumbles. The doors are just a few feet away. She keeps moving.

"You forget your purse?" the woman asks.

"Uh . . ."

"And what about your jacket?"

Ellen reaches the doors. "I have to go," she says.

"All right, well, hope it's okay." The receptionist pauses. "Your emergency."

"Thank you," Ellen says, as she touches the key card to the reader. "Me too."

The doors slide open, and a draught of fresh summer air rushes in, thick and sweet.

"Have yourself a good night," the woman says, as she walks out.

Ellen imagines that the night she has ahead of her will be

anything but good. It's only a matter of time before they find out that the person in her bed isn't her, or discover Shawna in the janitor's cupboard. Then they'll come looking for her. She knows there's no going back from this. She hopes Jada and Vang will be okay. She owes it to them as much as anybody to take the opportunity she's got now.

She opens the final security gate and reaches the long road that takes her out of Norristown State Hospital, into the world beyond.

She keeps walking and doesn't look back.

20

Clarion, Pennsylvania

PETER SCANS THE horizon, but he can't see shit. He guesses that's the whole point of this place.

Randy's brought them miles out, to the farthest edge of the back field on the soybean farm where he works. The farmhouse, barn and grain bins are just specks in the distance, while in the opposite direction, the dense woodland of State Game Lands Number 72 stretches out. There ain't another human being besides them in a mile or more, whichever way you look. It's a landscape that makes a person feel really small. And that's something Peter struggles with at the best of times. It's peaceful, at least. But he can't even appreciate that because of what's about to happen.

Not for the first time this week, Peter wonders what the heck he's doing. Obviously, he knows why they're here: to watch the test of their home-made bombs. It's the bigger picture he's still not sure about, not by a long way, despite his brother's conviction. But he don't have time to think on that anymore right now, because the show's about to start. And he's got the best seat in the house, whether he likes it or not.

Randy has already moved a concrete block out here with his

John Deere and put it a couple hundred feet away at the forest boundary. It's sitting there between the soybeans and the trees like some crash-landed spacecraft. Now they're all gathered round, waiting in silent expectation for Mitch to return from his pickup.

A crow caws.

Then there's a gunshot behind them.

The noise makes Peter's heart skip and his guts clench. His body tenses, and he instinctively drops into a crouch, covering his head with his hands.

"Jesus H. Christ!" he yells. "What was that?"

He hears the laughter and slowly stands up again.

Randy points to the center of the field, where something that looks like a telescope sits on a tripod.

"That's the bird cannon, Pee-Wee," he says, still chuckling. "Just a li'l propane. Cover up the noise we're about to make. If it's too scary, though, one of us can give you a ride back. Cos it ain't gonna get any quieter."

Leanne isn't laughing at him, this time. Her black eye looks a little better than yesterday, although maybe she's just put more makeup over it. She's still quieter than usual, though.

He's trying to think of a good comeback to Randy when Mitch strides over, carrying a cylinder under his arm.

"All right," his brother says, holding the object in front of him. "For the uninitiated — and I'm looking at you two, Pee-Wee and Leanne — this right here is an EFP. Explosively formed projectile, or penetrator."

"I know what it is," Leanne says, like she's a teenager who's been asked about something her parents wouldn't want her to do. "I've been readin' about it online."

"You'd better not have left any traces," says Mitch. "Remember what I said about all that shit? The message boards and stuff like that."

"Don't freak out, baby. I know how to cover my tracks."

"Make sure you do." Mitch turns to him. "Pee-Wee?"

"What?"

"Jeez, man, are you even listening? Do you know what a fuckin' EFP is?"

"Uh, no. No, I don't." The first time Peter heard the letters *EFP* was at breakfast today. "I asked you this morning, but you didn't tell me."

"Well, this is an EFP," Mitch states.

Peter studies the device. It's maybe a foot long and six inches in diameter, with a metal disc at one end, like a smaller version of the ones Randy was lathing in the workshop yesterday, and a spool of cord coming out the other end.

"These motherfuckers killed a lot of good people in Iraq and Afghanistan," he continues, glancing down at the device in his hands. "'cause they're pretty easy to make, as IEDs go, they're easy to hide, and they're goddamned lethal."

Mitch pauses, perhaps thinking of his fallen comrades. What had his brother told him at breakfast? Forty-something marines he knew personally, dead.

"We've got a copper plate, hand-crafted by The Dozer," he nods at Randy, who grins, "and behind it, inside the pipe, we got two-and-a-half pounds of C4. That's two M112 charges. The blasting cap is in the base here, connected to the det cord, rigged by my man Sherman."

Sherman looks around the assembled group, raises his hand in mock acknowledgement.

"This is what we're gonna use on Saturday night," Mitch adds. "Only the real thing's gonna have a twelve-inch plate and thirteen charges inside."

"Hellfire," observes Randy.

"Let's see what it looks like," says Mitch. "Sherman, would you do the honors?"

"With pleasure."

Mitch hands the bomb to Sherman, who strolls over to the concrete block, like he's got all the time in the world. They watch him with silent anticipation.

"This is gonna be fuckin' nuts," Randy says.

Peter can see that the big man is geed up, breathing real quick, flexing his hands. He's probably got a semi, too. Not that Peter has any desire to see that.

"Everyone got their ears?" Mitch asks, looking around.

They all show him their ear defenders. Peter's got earplugs, too.

Over by the concrete block, Sherman sets up the EFP on the ground. It's a few yards away from the block, the copper plate end facing the concrete.

Peter watches him line it up carefully, then check its position from multiple angles. Apparently satisfied, he walks back over, unspooling the det cord as he goes. When he reaches them, he clips the end of the cord into a little device with a switch.

"Ears," Mitch tells them.

They all put the defenders on.

Sherman hands Mitch the device.

"Fire in the hole!" his brother yells, and presses the button.

The bang is instant and deafening, the flash blinding.

Peter feels a shockwave go through his entire body, almost strong enough to knock him off his feet. He realizes he's shut his eyes. When he opens them again, there's just a cloud of smoke where the concrete block was. Pretty soon, it starts to clear.

"Woo-hoo!" cries Randy, yanking off his ear defenders and pumping his fist. "You fuckin' see that? Holy shit."

"Let's go take a look," says Mitch.

When they reach the block, Peter's amazed to see that it's largely intact, except for a hole about the diameter of a basketball that's been punched right through three feet of solid concrete.

There are some low whistles and cheers as they inspect it, taking turns to get up close and look right through the gap.

"Not bad," observes Mitch. "Pretty clean."

"It's a thing of beauty," Sherman proclaims, high-fiving Randy.

"Never a truer word, brother," replies The Dozer.

Even Leanne looks excited. She smiles, the same hundred-watt knockout that made guys go weak at the knees even back in ninth grade. "I felt that inside me," she says, eyes wide.

"I'll bet you did." Randy chuckles.

Peter doesn't really get it.

"Uh, why are . . ." he begins, "why are we makin' a hole? Don't we wanna, you know . . .? I mean, most times you see an explosion, it goes up in the air."

"Up in the air?" queries Sherman, smirking.

"Yeah. Oklahoma City, that bomb kinda went up, you look at the photos," Peter says. "Or in the movies."

"This ain't a movie," says Mitch.

"You don't know?" Randy asks Peter, narrowing his eyes.

"Know what?"

"What the target is."

"Nope." Peter shrugs. "No one's tellin' me shit." He turns to Mitch.

Mitch thinks about it, then nods. "All right, Pee-Wee. It's about time. You know what Three Mile Island is?"

"Ain't that one of them craft breweries?"

"Jesus fu— no, it aint' no brewery." Mitch looks square at him. "It's a nuclear power plant, two hundred miles south-east of here."

"Nuclear?" Peter's pulse starts thumping in his neck. His hands are clammy.

"Yup."

"Nuclear," he repeats, trying to process the craziness he's picturing. He can recall some old film of a nuclear bomb going off. Maybe in the war, in China or someplace like that. A fireball and then a mushroom cloud the size of a whole town.

"That's right," Randy chimes in. "Atoms and shit."

"We're . . . we're gonna blow up a nuclear power plant?" Peter can hear the tremor in his own voice. Hell, his legs are shaking. He feels as though he might piss his pants.

Nobody answers him.

"Won't that kill, like, a million people or somethin'?" Peter asks. He feels sick.

"Not a million, no." Sherman grins. "Depends whereabouts in the power plant you put that hole, though. Right through the reactor core . . ."

"Oh, dear God." Peter feels his throat and face get tight, like he's gonna start crying.

Mitch steps over, puts his arm round him. "Listen, Pee-Wee," he says. "I didn't tell you before 'cause I didn't want you worrying. The fact is, this ain't about killing people. It's about sending a message. Yes, some people may die, but they're necessary sacrifices for the greater good. This is about showing the whole world that the American people can't trust their own government, inside their own country. It's about starting a revolution."

"Amen," says Randy.

Peter doesn't know what to say.

"We're gonna be famous," adds Leanne, her voice a breathy whisper.

"What?" Mitch whirls around to her. "What did you say?"

She stands a little straighter, tilts her chin up. "I said, we're gonna be famous," she repeats, louder.

"The fuck?" snaps Mitch. "Famous?"

"Uh-huh."

"That's not what this is about. At all." His brother glares at her.

Peter feels the urge to step in and defend her. But he knows that wouldn't end well.

"Ain't it?" she queries.

"No."

"Come on. Not just a li'l bit?"

"Crazy bitch." Mitch shakes his head.

"Hey!" blurts Peter. Before he can stop himself, he's grabbed a fistful of his brother's shirt. Then he stops.

Mitch is staring at him. So is everyone else.

He lets go.

No one speaks for a few seconds.

"Okay. Let's move the block out of sight," Mitch says.

"I'll go get the tractor," Randy offers, and lumbers off toward the vehicle at the other end of the field.

Mitch heads for his pickup.

"Here's the thing," Sherman says to Peter. "The real EFP's gonna have a plate three times the size of that one, with six-and-half times the explosive inside."

Peter tries to reply, but his mouth won't move.

Sherman claps him on the shoulder, harder than necessary. "You seen that TV show, *Chernobyl*, Pee-Wee?"

"No."

"Look it up." He starts laughing, and walks off after Randy.

Then it's just him and Leanne.

"At least there's one gentleman here," she says. She gives him a little smile, then sets off toward Mitch's pickup.

"Leanne," he says.

She turns around. "Yeah?"

"I don't want no part of this," he says, quiet enough so as the others can't hear him. "I ain't no killer." His voice catches with the last part.

She looks at him. "Me neither. But it's too late to quit, now. Just pray it ain't us doing the killin'." Then she turns again.

Peter watches her walk off. He tips his head back, looks at the big open sky. Then he lets his head drop until all he can see is soybean plants and tilled earth.

He wishes that earth would swallow him up.

21

East Norriton, Pennsylvania

ALTHOUGH SHE'S SWEATING and breathing hard and her adrenalin is pumping, Ellen tries to keep still as she watches her house from the cover of the trees out back. She's pretty sure no one's home but she doesn't want to break in to find her parents and Josh there. She'd give anything to see them, of course, to pull them close in a big hug and hold on for as long as she can. But she has to keep her family as far away from this situation as possible until she's fixed it. She swears she won't let any harm come to them because she's gone after the Keystone Boys. She wouldn't be able to live with herself if it did.

Ellen figures she has around a half hour before someone finds Shawna or Ratkova and realizes what's happened. She knows that one of the first places they'll send the cops is her home. But if she's to have a chance of succeeding, she needs some stuff, and this is the best place to find it. She just has to get in without being seen and be back on the move before anyone realizes she's escaped.

It's been twenty minutes since she left the hospital grounds. She snapped the heels off Ratkova's shoes and ran all the way here, on her bad ankle, through Norristown Farm Park. That leaves maybe ten minutes to do what she has to do.

She reckons she only needs five.

Scanning left and right to check that the neighbors aren't out in their backyards, Ellen jogs across the lawn to the storage shed, which she and Harry always leave unlocked. Their neighborhood is the kind where you can do that, and your lawnmower will be safe. Inside the shed, she selects a hand trowel, a rigid steel one with a sharp tip that Harry gave her for Christmas four years ago. She briefly remembers that time when things were calm. Harry hadn't yet started in Congress, and she had felt as though she was beginning to recover from the horror of Paris. Gardening had seemed like a good hobby to take up, active and outdoorsy, and they bought each other a bunch of tools. But neither of them could have imagined how or why she'd be using one of those tools now.

Ellen approaches the small window to the first-floor bathroom and jams the trowel in the crack between the window frame and the lintel. Then she yanks the handle down with as much strength as she can muster. It takes a few goes before the little lock pops and she can slide the window up. After a final check, she tosses the trowel and pulls herself up and in, hauling her head and chest through the window. She ends up in a kind of handstand on the toilet seat, her legs still dangling outside, before she can lower herself down and drag her feet through. She loses one of Ratkova's shoes in the process, but she doesn't have time to go back outside and get it.

She steps out of the little bathroom into the hallway.

The alarm triggers immediately. It's deafening.

She can't blame Harry or her parents — whoever was here last — for setting it. She's always on them about security and making sure they put it on when they leave. Right now, though, she wishes they hadn't, because she has fifteen seconds to enter the code before the alarm company gets an alert. They'll try her number, find her cell phone off, call Harry, probably find him busy, then call the cops, ask them to take a look. And she doesn't need that.

The countdown begins in her head.

Fourteen, thirteen, twelve . . .

She darts through the house to the front door where the keypad is mounted on the wall. Flips up the cover. It falls down again. She flips it back up. Sees the timer.

8, 7, 6 . . .

Punches in the number – Josh's birthday – too fast, gets a digit wrong.

4, 3 . . .

Keys it in again.

1 . . .

The alarm stops. The box gives a single bleep, and a little green light comes on.

Ellen takes a breath.

She moves back down the hallway, towards the basement door. On the way, a photo on the side table catches her eye.

It's her, Harry, and Josh – age two – on the porch outside her parents' house in Doylestown. Their first Thanksgiving back home after seven years in France. The memory is so vivid that she can smell the turkey her mom is carving in the kitchen and hear her yelling at them to shut the front door to keep the heat inside.

In the picture, Josh is gazing up at her rather than at the camera, despite her dad's best efforts behind the lens to get his grandson's attention. Harry is laughing, his eyes half closed, the skin around them wrinkled with crow's feet. It's not a perfectly posed family portrait, but it's her favourite, which is why it's in a frame on the wall here. She likes it because, rather than simply *looking* happy, she knows they *were* happy. Happy to be home, to be safe, to be together.

For a long moment, Ellen just stands and stares at it. Sadness starts to well up inside her, so deep that she can feel the ache of it, the physical absence of the people she loves. The family in the photograph seems a long way away right now. She vows to get that back. And her best chance of doing that involves putting even more distance between her and her family than there has been over the past four days.

With renewed purpose, she flings open the basement door and heads down the stairs.

*

Route 309, Pennsylvania

Forty minutes later, Ellen has left the red brick and white clapboard of her street behind and is passing through Quakertown on her way north. The I-476, the main road connecting Philly and Allentown, would have been a much better route, quicker and smoother than the cracked blacktop she's bumping over right now. But it's a turnpike, which means cameras and tolls. And even though the old station wagon she's driving has an E-ZPass, she doesn't want to give the cops — or anyone else — help following her movements. They'll track her down, eventually, but every minute that she can stay ahead of them counts. She's got the car radio on, listening for news bulletins about her escape. There's nothing so far.

The wagon belongs to her elderly neighbor, Mr Hamilton. She knows he doesn't go out it in much and hopes he won't mind her taking it. Okay, stealing it. But he doesn't lock it, and keeps the keys under the sun visor, because he kept losing them in the house, so she can kid herself it's just borrowing. She'd considered leaving a note for him, but thought it better just to make a clean getaway. She imagines Mr Hamilton coming out of his house, seeing it's gone and standing there, hands on hips, wondering what happened. She feels bad, because Mr Hamilton is good people. She resolves to explain it to him later, apologize. She hopes she'll get the chance to do that.

On the seat beside her is the main reason she broke into her own home just now: her grab bag. The rucksack she kept in the basement in case of needing to "bug out" fast, as the ex-military guys like E.J. would say. And that's exactly what she had to do.

The bag is another legacy of her training at The Farm. Despite leaving the CIA and becoming a stay-at-home mom in the Philly suburbs, she's always maintained a grab bag, just in case, and boy, is she grateful for that now. The pack contains everything you need to survive on the move, for a little while at least. Five hundred dollars in cash, food rations, a burner phone, flashlight, first aid kit, toiletries, multitool, GPS and batteries, as well as a bunch of other stuff — including lock picks, a handgun, and ammo.

She's also changed clothes, swapping Ratkova's work outfit and oversized, broken shoes for a black t-shirt, jeans, and her own sneakers, which actually fit. She's got a sweater in case it gets colder at night, and a ballcap to help hide her face, but not much else. She doesn't know exactly how long she'll have to stay mobile like this, although the words that Walter found on the dark web forum give her a clue.

We're gonna light up the sky on the Fourth of July.

She has tonight, plus two days, a little more if she's lucky, to find the Keystone Boys and stop their attack.

She wonders if the phrase *light up the sky* is reference to a bomb, or whether—

Her thoughts are interrupted by the radio.

A woman with a history of violent behavior has escaped from Norristown State Hospital. 38-year-old Ellen McGinley, from East Norriton, in Montgomery County, fled the secure psychiatric facility earlier today after seriously assaulting a staff member and a fellow patient. Police are searching for her and have warned the public that she is considered dangerous . . .

Ellen knew it was just a matter of time before this happened. She hits the gas.

*

As Ellen reaches Allentown, she's reminded of the Billy Joel song about the city. He sings about coal mines and steel plants being closed down, lines of people looking for work, promises of the American dream crushed. Folks let down by the country they fought wars to protect.

She knows there are a lot of places in Pennsylvania like that, towns hit hard by industrial decline after jobs went south to the Sunbelt, or overseas. A lot of angry people hurt by economic crisis, struggling to provide for their families. And their resentment is directed toward government, big business, foreigners and whoever else they see fit to blame.

She wonders about the Keystone Boys, and the forces beyond their control that shaped them into who they are today.

She wonders who they are.

Ellen's years in Paris, working on terror networks, taught her that there are three main types of person who get drawn into these groups, whether they're religious, political, social, or any other kind.

First, you have the guys who enjoy violence. The borderline-psychopaths who'd start a fight at a football game or in a bar, probably beat up on their partners, and are looking for any excuse to hurt others, especially those they believe have wronged them. They're dangerous, but they're a small minority. Most people who get drawn into extremist groups are actually vulnerable in one way or other.

That's the second category: abused, downtrodden, lost individuals looking for hope, who just want to belong. Some are ex-addicts or ex-cons who want a sense of direction in life. These are the guys who become foot soldiers, the ones who carry the weapons and bombs, who shoot and get shot at. Who are usually too dumb to avoid getting caught and ending up in jail. They fall under the spell of the third group: the leaders.

The leaders are the ones who know exactly what they're doing, who manipulate their recruits with words, money, identity and whatever else works. They're often wealthier and more educated, and they prey on the weak. Ellen thinks of the guys she overheard in the hotel last week. She guesses they're in the third group, running the show, and the Keystone Boys are mostly group two, following orders. She hopes they don't have anybody in group one.

North of the Little Lehigh Creek, it isn't just the size of the buildings that tell her she's downtown. It's the type of building, too. There are Latino restaurants, Indian grocery stores, even a mosque. Each tells a story about Allentown's new residents, the ones who moved here from Philly and New York in search of cheaper real estate, homes and businesses left vacant by the previous occupants. Allentown's population is now two-thirds people of color, including a large and thriving Puerto Rican community. It's one of them whom Ellen has come to see.

If Walter was one of the only people capable of confirming whether the Keystone Boys existed, this guy is one of the only people capable of actually finding them.

She just hopes he's home.

22

Allentown, Pennsylvania

ALTHOUGH SHE'S ONLY ever been here twice, and hasn't visited for a couple of years, Ellen finds Ricardo Reyes's house easily. The buildings on the quiet road just off North 7th Street all look alike — two-storey townhouses with faded white paint over their brickwork — but his is the only one with a ramp outside the front door instead of steps.

She buzzes and waits, holding her head up straight so that whatever camera feed Reyes is no doubt checking right now can get her face clearly. After a while, the faint noise of rolling wheels comes from behind the door and the relief washes over her. She hears a bolt slide back and a chain unhooking before the door opens wide. Reyes is sitting in his wheelchair, wearing a shirt over shorts, his arms spread wide in friendly surprise.

"Holy shit, Ellen McGinley!" he exclaims, grinning.

"Jesus, Ricardo, I'm so happy you're here." She glances down the street. There's no one around.

"I'm always here. What's up?" he asks, rolling to the threshold and following her gaze outside. "You okay?"

"I need your help," she replies.

"Not a social visit, then?"

"Nope."

His smile vanishes, and he's all business. "You better come in," he says.

Ellen shuts the door behind her and replaces the bolt and chain. She follows Reyes as he pushes himself down the hallway ahead of her. His back and arms are thick with muscle, and his haircut is as high and tight as it was in the photos she's seen from his military days.

She never knew Reyes when he could walk, before an Iraqi insurgent's IED hit his vehicle in Fallujah, back in '04, and paralysed him from the waist down. He was medically discharged from the army and returned to Allentown, where his parents, brothers, sisters and cousins all live. He never imagined he'd be coming home from war in a wheelchair, but he adapted to his new existence fast. More than that, he taught himself computer skills. And it turned out he was pretty good. So good, in fact, that a few years later, a veteran's organisation put him in touch with the CIA, who offered to pay him for deniable online intelligence gathering. Or hacking, as most people would call it.

Reyes was part of a virtual team working with Ellen when she was in Paris, supporting her with technical analysis and leads on their targets. The two of them shared a similar fate after what happened there five years ago, which is one reason why they kept in touch. Since he parted ways with the Agency, Reyes has been a hacker for hire. He's what's known as a "grey hat" — sometimes working for good, other times just getting paid. But, as he puts it, he never robs anyone who can't afford to lose a few bucks. In fact, the people he robs usually *deserve* to lose a few bucks.

Now he leads her through to a room full of computer kit. CPUs, keyboards, a half-dozen screens, laptops, and a server stack. Along with the fans keeping everything cool, and the stereo that's filling the room with loud reggaeton, Ellen guesses this place is responsible for about half the power use in the 7th Street neighborhood.

"Music off," says Reyes, and the beats cut out immediately.

Trust him to have some cool voice-activated piece of tech, she thinks.

He rotates his chair to face her. "What's goin' on?"

She tells him everything. The threat she overheard, the guy in Philly, her arrest, commitment order and escape.

He listens carefully, pursing his lips and nodding. He gets it right away.

"Not the first time they didn't believe you, huh?" he observes.

"Right."

"So, you want me to geolocate these *hijos de puta*?"

"Yeah."

"What've you got?"

She describes the *Gigachan* dark web forum Walter had accessed. The message he found referencing the group. And the username of the guy who posted it: *gotmilk2022*.

When she's done, Reyes raises his eyebrows.

"That's it?" he asks.

She nods.

He shakes his head. "Damn, you don't ask much, do you?"

"Is it enough to go on? Can you track this person down?"

Reyes runs a hand over the short hair at the back of his scalp. He looks up at her. "You think this is for real?"

"I wouldn't be here if I didn't," she replies, meeting his gaze.

He's quiet for a while before he responds.

"All right, then," he says. "I'm gonna need a little time, though. And I can't promise anything."

"Thank you. I owe you. And so might a lot of other people."

"You can buy me a beer when it's over."

"Find these guys, and I will buy you beer for the rest of your life."

"I'll hold you to that." He points at her. "Seriously."

"I'm not even joking."

Reyes gives a quick smile, then wheels himself up to the central desk and minimizes a window with swastikas and Klansmen on it. "I've been screwing around with those guys today," he explains, opening a Tor browser in its place.

"What'd you do?"

"Emptied their bank accounts, converted everything into crypto to make it untraceable, then wired the whole lot to disability charities."

Despite the situation, Ellen can't help but laugh. "That's awesome."

"I'd call it a slow day." He rolls up his sleeves, rubs his hands, cracks his knuckles. "Now for the real work."

Reyes gets started, typing and clicking and opening a bunch of new windows, one of which is full of code. Within seconds, she's unable to follow what he's doing.

Ellen knows this is a risk. Though Reyes is one of the best at what he does, every hour he takes is an hour the cops are closer to finding and stopping her, and an hour closer to the Keystone Boys' attack. But she has no choice. She needs intel, and right now Reyes is the only man she can trust to get it for her.

As she watches him working the web, a wave of tiredness hits her.

"I need coffee," she says.

"In the kitchen," he tells her. "Make mine black, two sugars."

She goes out and lets him get to work.

*

While the coffee machine does its thing, Ellen uses the bathroom, realising that she hasn't been for hours. She didn't even dare waste two minutes going at home. She returns to the kitchen, pours two mugs and carries them through.

"Got anything?" she asks, as she sets the black, two-sugar one next to Reyes.

"Are you kidding me? I literally just started."

"Sorry." She blows on her coffee, takes a sip. It's strong, which is good — it'll keep her going awhile. She has no idea how long she'll need to stay awake. "Hey, can I check the web?"

"Sure. Use that." He spins in his wheelchair and indicates one of the laptops before turning back. "It's unattributable."

She googles herself and filters the results by time, most recent at the top. The latest update is from the *Philadelphia Inquirer* website, added just ten minutes ago. It's like some nightmare, reading about herself like this:

'Dangerous' mental patient at large

Escaped psychiatric patient Ellen McGinley is believed to be on the run ... McGinley, 38, who is the wife of Democrat Congressman Harry Flanagan, had previously been hospitalized for mental health problems ... According to official sources, McGinley has been diagnosed with schizophrenia and repeatedly behaved violently while being held on a commitment order. She should not be approached under any circumstances ...

There are two photographs of her in the article. In the first, she's standing next to Harry on the night he was elected. They're smiling together and waving for the cameras. Next to this image is the mugshot they took of her on Monday at the police station in Philly. The grimacing, wild-eyed woman in the second picture looks like a different person. Then again, she remembers, someone had just pulled a gun on her; several people, if you include the officers who arrested her. This media attention was inevitable, and she knew they'd paint her as batshit crazy. But she regrets it all the same, not least for the effect it'll have on her family.

The cops will soon be calling at her parents' house in Doylestown, if they haven't already done so, looking for her. They'll be asking her mom and dad where she is and scaring little Josh, who'll be asking the same thing. The police will accuse Ellen of being a bad mother, of being unfit to look after her little boy. They'll suspect her parents of hiding her or helping her flee. She sees Harry being pulled out of an official meeting in D.C. and quizzed on her whereabouts, asked about places she might go. She imagines the concern on his face as they explain she's "at large" in the community. She hates doing this to her family, knows they'll all be worried sick for her safety when they find out what's happened. She wishes she could tell them she's okay, but she has to keep the bigger picture in mind. Taking a long drink of coffee, she reads on:

Local law enforcement has advised the public to be alert and report any sightings of McGinley by calling 911 immediately. She may be travelling via public transport or in a stolen vehicle . . .

A stolen vehicle. Do they know about the station wagon? Ellen tries to reconstruct the police's search process to see if it's possible. She guesses the hospital called the cops as soon as they realized she was gone. The cops probably then went to her house, since it's only a mile from the hospital, and discovered her break-in. If they were smart, they'll have spoken to the neighbors, asked if they saw or heard anything out of the ordinary. Asked them if anything's missing. If they figure out that Mr Hamilton's car is gone, they'll be tracing it every way they can. The clock is ticking.

"Found anything yet?" she asks.

"I'm good," Reyes replies over his shoulder, "but I'm not *that* good. I'm gonna need at least another hour, maybe more."

"I have to go."

Reyes stops typing, turns his wheelchair to her. "Why?"

"Because I think they could be onto the car. I need a new

ride." Wherever she needs to go next, she's sure she'll need a vehicle to get there.

"Lemme call my cousin, Luis. He can you loan one."

"I don't want to get your family involved in this, Ricardo. You're doing enough for me as it is. If the cops find out I've been here—"

"They won't find out. If they're looking for you, though, you're safer staying here until I've found some intel."

"No." She shuts the laptop, stands. "It's better if I hide the car I drove here in, and get a new one ready to go. Besides, no one knows I'm in Allentown."

"They might do. Don't underestimate the po-po."

She knows there's a possibility he's right, and Mr Hamilton's station wagon is compromised. A camera she passed might have clocked the license plate. Someone could be running that search as they speak.

"Maybe. But I also need something to eat," she says. "I'm starving, and there's not a whole lot in your fridge," she adds, managing a smile.

"I wasn't expecting guests." Reyes grins back. "Well, if you're going for takeout, *Flama Tropical* is two blocks north of here on 8th Street. Can I get a *tripleta*?"

Now Ellen feels even hungrier. Reyes introduced her to the *tripleta* – a sandwich that contains pork, chicken *and* beef – the last time she visited. She could really use one right now.

"With *arroz con habichuelas*. That's rice and beans—"

"Got it."

"And *tostones* on the side" he adds. "Plus a little hot sauce."

"Jeez," Ellen laughs, "anything else, sir?"

"No, I'm good."

She takes the burner phone out of her grab bag, and swaps numbers with Reyes. "You find something, text me right away."

"Sure. But you'll still get the food, right?"

"Depends what you find." Halfway to the door, she pauses. "Ricardo?"

"What?" He doesn't look away from the screen, his fingers flying over the keyboard.

"If you wanted to get your hands on a car around here, what would you do?"

"You mean besides going to the automobile dealer and paying for it?"

"Yeah."

He stops typing. "Are you seriously going to try jacking somebody's car, in my 'hood?"

"I didn't say that . . ."

"Good, 'cause you don't want that kind of trouble. Trust me."

Ellen realizes that trying to steal a car around here probably isn't the best idea. "I was thinking more of borrowing."

"I already gave you the answer to that. My cousin, Luis. He runs a scrapyard. They usually have like two dozen vehicles."

"Any that actually work?"

"Sure. I ask him, he'll give you one of them. It's just for a couple days, right?"

"Maybe three."

"Okay, then."

Reyes makes a call in Spanish, some of which Ellen gets, and when he hangs up, he gives her an address. It's about a mile west of here.

"Thank you." She pulls on her ballcap. "My picture's all over the news. You think people around here might recognize me?"

He shrugs. "If they do, you don't need to worry. They won't call the cops."

She nods. "All right. See you in, like, an hour. I hope."

"Don't forget the hot sauce."

Ellen takes the 9mm handgun out of her grab bag, chambers a round, stashes it back in the bag, and leaves.

23

Allentown, Pennsylvania

IT'S STILL DAYLIGHT as Ellen works her way north, and then west, through the back streets, to the scrapyard where Reyes's cousin Luis is waiting for her. She'd have preferred to wait until dusk to get a little more cover for her journey, but there isn't time. She hopes the vehicle will be solid enough to get her wherever she needs to go to find the Keystone Boys.

Pennsylvania isn't the biggest state, but if she's got to head way out west, toward Ohio or West Virginia, she could still be looking at a drive of five, maybe six hours. Breaking down in the middle of a forest is not an option. But neither is taking a cab, and switching cars is the smart thing to do. She just has to trust Luis.

She's on foot, now, having left the station wagon in a small, unattended parking lot a few blocks away from Reyes's house. Dropping it there gave her another stab of guilt at stealing from Mr Hamilton, but she has to move on. She's sure he'll understand.

Ellen has been to Allentown twice before, but the streets she's on now are unfamiliar. There are a couple of local stores on the corners, plus a barber's shop and a nail bar, but it's mostly housing and she's aware that, as a stranger here, she sticks out like a Buddhist monk at an NRA rally.

She passes a group of men, drinking beer on a porch, who notice her. She keeps her head down, but she can feel them watching as she walks by. It isn't them she's worried about, though. She recalls Reyes's warning about the possibility that the people who are after her already know she's here.

She picks up her pace, checking behind her every time she crosses the street or catches a reflection. She can't see anyone following her, but that doesn't stop her being on edge. Her pulse is racing, her toes are tingling, and her palms are sweaty. And it's not just the fact she's a target for the cops that's making her feel that way.

Seeing Reyes again has brough back memories of the work they did together when she was in Paris. In fact, this part of Allentown kind of reminds her of Vitry-sur-Seine, the district where she lived and worked. She can see through the windows that people here keep their homes neat and tidy, but the neighborhood itself has been neglected by those in charge, and needs a little love. There's uncollected trash, grass growing out of the sidewalk, and spaghetti heaps of tangled power lines wherever she looks overhead. Despite everything that's happened to her this week, it makes her thankful for her own home. She felt the same way in Paris, living around people whose lives were so much harder than hers.

People like Nadia.

*

Paris, five years earlier

When Ellen relayed Nadia's story to her boss back at Langley, he didn't believe her. Nadia's husband Jalil wasn't a jihadist, according to their assessment. He wasn't even a person of interest. They'd traced him on their systems, found nothing. No connections or contacts, no relatives linked to Islamic extremism, no record beyond his rap sheet for burglary. He didn't attend a radical mosque. Ellen told them that, according to Nadia, he had changed. He was praying at home, which he never used to do, with a group of guys who'd started coming over regularly. The Agency basically said, *whatever*. They wanted cast-iron proof of his involvement in a terror plot before they acted. *Validation*, they called it.

Ellen called it bullshit. Their inaction wasn't because her reporting was off. It was political. The guys at the local "base" — the CIA station housed within the US embassy in Paris — had a terrible relationship with their opposite numbers in the DGSI, France's version of the FBI, fuelled by years of mistrust. The guys in the DGSI — recently formed by a merger of two other agencies — didn't trust each other, either. No one was sharing anything with anybody else, and as a NOC, operating undercover, Ellen couldn't talk to any of them personally to make her case. The French didn't even know she was in their country, and Langley didn't want to admit that she was. On top of that, her bosses were still pissed at her for paying for the heart transplant without authorisation. They actively wanted her to be wrong. In one memo, her section chief effectively accused her of making it up to justify the money she's spent on a new heart for a kid who was *"of no value"* to the Agency.

But Ellen's instincts told her there was something to it.

Her only option was to ask Nadia to gather as much intel as possible on her own husband, and his friends, and see where it led them. Little by little, Nadia learned the names of the guys who were visiting her home and meeting with Jalil. She discovered that he'd got to know them at a nearby martial arts club that she didn't realize he'd been attending. She was even able to photograph a couple of these new friends subtly on her phone and send the images to Ellen.

Nadia reported back on the group's conversations about ISIS and how happy they were that an Islamic state — a "caliphate" — was being established in Iraq and Syria. That *kufar* — non-believers — were being executed. One of Jalil's new buddies, a big guy with a full Salafist beard, named Mehdi, was saying he wanted to go there and fight. And, if they couldn't do that, they should do something for the cause right there, in France. Still, Langley didn't pay any attention. *Guys like that are a dime a dozen*, her boss wrote her back when she told him that. *They're all talk*.

Ellen didn't think so.

Meanwhile, Nadia was becoming increasingly worried about her husband's mindset. He was getting stricter with her about how she dressed, even in the apartment, and where she went. He wanted their son, Samir, now four years old, to start memorising the Qur'an. He expected Nadia to make tea, fix food and clean up after him and his pals whenever they came over, despite the fact that she was the one working a job. And she was scared, too, about what would happen if Jalil became suspicious of her contact with Ellen.

Ellen did her best to reassure Nadia that she was doing the right thing. That she was protecting her city, her community, and her son by passing on this information. Ellen, in turn, gave those leads to Reyes who, back in Allentown, worked the computers. For weeks, there was nothing, and Ellen was beginning to think that maybe her douchebag of a boss in Langley was right. That it was *all talk*.

Then, one day, Reyes contacts her.

He's found something.

*

Present day

"I really appreciate this," says Ellen, inspecting the '96 Toyota Camry sedan, "but seeing as I might have to drive a long way, I need to know. What's wrong with it?"

Luis shrugs. "Nothing."

"It's in a scrapyard," she counters.

"It had a minor collision, right here," Luis says, pointing to the driver's door and wheel arch. They look a little bent out of shape, and the paint's a slightly different color to the rest of the car. "But it runs just fine. Got a decent engine under here, too." He slaps the hood as if that proves his point. "These babies are indestructible."

"So, why's it here?"

"Simple," he says. "You get in an accident with a twenty-five-year-old car, it doesn't matter how small the damage is, the insurance company's writing it off. Cheaper for them to pay out the value of the car, which is basically nothing, than drop five or ten times that amount on repairs."

She opens the door, perches on the seat, checks the pedals, then the wheel. The wheel feels a little tight.

"The steering okay?" she asks. She knows that collisions can bend the chassis and stop a car moving fully left or right.

"I fixed it myself," replies Luis.

Ellen doesn't know whether this is a good or a bad thing.

Luis seems to sense her concern. "It's what I do, in my spare time. I fix up old cars."

"Do you have any qualifications?" she says with a smile. She doesn't want to seem rude, but she has to know if she can trust his repair job.

"No," he chuckles. "But my uncle, Carlos, taught me. That's Ricardo's father."

She's still not sure. "Have you test driven it?"

"In the lot, sure."

That doesn't fill her with confidence, either.

"It's the best I've got," he adds.

Ellen gets out, plants her hands on her hips and surveys the vehicle, as if looking for a signal that it's going to fall apart someplace between here and Pittsburgh. She can't even tell if it'll get her back to Reyes's house in one piece. She looks around her at the other cars. One has a smashed windshield, another has no tires. She realizes she has no choice.

"I'll take it," she says, eventually. "Thank you."

"Whatever you're doing with it," Luis says, handing her the keys, "good luck. *Vaya con Dios.*"

He looks as though he means it.

Ellen slides the key into the ignition.

*

Paris, five years earlier

Ellen is in her apartment, studying the intel that Reyes found online. He managed to hack a local extremist forum that Nadia told them Jalil was using. Although Reyes doesn't know what the participants are talking about, because he can't speak French, what he has found are a bunch of connections. He has the logs of which users have messaged which other users. Most of them use aliases, but their underlying email and IP addresses let Reyes cross-check with their surface web use to identify them. And what he's discovered scares Ellen.

Nadia's husband, Jalil, has exchanged a handful of private messages with a guy whom they believe to be Moustapha El-Amin. He's an arms trafficker who specializes in bringing old Soviet weapons — mostly AK-47s — into France from Eastern Europe, typically selling them to big-city gangs who run the drug trade. What the hell is Jalil doing talking to him, Ellen thinks, if he's not trying to get hold of guns? Not just any guns, either. Fully automatic rifles. The kind terrorists use for mass casualty attacks against civilian targets.

Reyes has sent Ellen the transcripts and, although it's

Arabic-infused Parisian *argot*, she can just about understand it. The messages are about a delivery of *halal* meat. Jalil says he's hosting a party. Moustapha says he knows a good butcher. Ellen is sure it's code.

"You okay, honey?"

She looks up to see Harry standing in a doorway, holding two beers.

"Uh, yeah," she replies. "Actually, no."

"You look as though you could use one of these," he says, handing her one of the bottles.

"Thanks." Ellen takes a long swig, then presses the cold glass to her forehead and sighs.

"What's up?"

She shuts the laptop. Even though she totally trusts Harry, and he knows some of what she does and who she works with, she's not allowed to let him read her messages.

"Have you ever been certain that something bad was going to happen," she asks, "only no one else believed you?"

"I don't know, maybe." Harry frowns, sips his beer. "I mean, when the French government was staying out of those migrant camps on the coast and pretending they didn't exist, my aid agency told them things would get worse. And we were right. Poor sanitation, disease, crime. They didn't listen to us. But that doesn't mean they didn't believe us. You can know something but choose to ignore it."

"Right."

"What do you think's going to happen?" he says, laying a hand on her shoulder.

"I don't know," she replies. "Just something bad. Something really bad."

*

Present day

Ellen has placed the food order at *Flama Tropical*, making sure to remember the hot sauce for Reyes, and is waiting inside to collect it. She went for exactly the same combo as him, and she can't wait to eat a decent meal, especially after days of insipid hospital food.

The Camry felt okay as she drove back across town. At least, as good as an old car that's had an accident and been repaired by an amateur mechanic can probably feel. Now she just needs to know where to go next. For that, she's relying on Reyes.

The restaurant is busy, with plenty of people coming and going, and no one seems to be paying her much attention. She's relieved at having ditched Mr Hamilton's station wagon, and the new car will buy her some time keeping ahead of the cops. For a moment, Ellen allows herself to sit back in the chair at her corner table as she waits. She lets herself relax, just a little, enjoying the lively chatter of customers and the incredible smells floating from the kitchen behind the counter.

Ellen has just closed her eyes when the burner phone beeps in her pocket. Only four people have this number: her mom, her dad, Harry, and Reyes. She pulls the phone out, checks the screen.

It's a text message from Reyes.

Make sure you get some food for me. Cause I got something for you.

24

Clarion, Pennsylvania

"PEE-WEE! YO, EARTH to Pee-Wee, come in!" Randy gives a deep laugh. "Houston, we have a problem."

"Huh?" Peter snaps out of his daydream and back to the tavern. They're huddled around a small table with their beers. Peter has barely touched his. He's been too busy imagining what a full-on meltdown of the Three Mile Island nuclear power plant would look like. He watched some clips from that TV show that Sherman was talking about this afternoon — *Chernobyl* — and he can't get the images out of his head.

A burning, smoking wasteland that looks like something right out of hell itself. People stumbling around, screaming as their skin literally melts. A gigantic beam of light going up into the sky out of the reactor, or whatever it's called. Only it's not light — it's atoms that'll make your unborn babies grow three legs and two heads, if those atoms don't kill you first.

He pictures all that hitting fifty thousand folks in Harrisburg, just a few miles north of the plant.

He feels sick.

"So, would you?" Leanne asks, a hint of a smile on her lips.

"Would I what?"

"Get a Fauci ouchie?"

"Fowch—?" Peter has no idea what they're talking about.

"You know," giggles Leanne, "a little prick?"

Peter looks at her. Is she talking about his—

"A vaccine, retard," says Randy. "Would you get one, or are you with us?"

"Uh, I don't know." Peter rubs his hands over his face. He wants to go home and lie down, only he knows that he still won't be able to erase what he saw earlier. Another clip pops into his head: a guy covered head to toe in bandages, who can hardly speak, convulsing in a hospital bed. Doctors telling his wife there's nothing they can do for him. Some kind of poisoning has gotten into his blood or his bones, and maybe he's given it to his wife, too, like a disease. The idea that he could be responsible for doing that to someone scares the hell out of him like nothing he's ever felt before.

"You gotta have an answer," Sherman says. He seems to be enjoying the fact that Peter's on the spot. "In my view, the science is questionable."

Randy jabs a pointed finger on the tabletop. "The Chinese are making the vaccines as well as the diseases. They got factories over there. Bill Gates built them. The whole thing's designed to keep us under their control. Biden knows about it, too."

"You sure about that, Dozer?" asks Mitch.

"Yes, sir," replies Randy, his eyes wide. "I saw it on Infowars."

"I ain't lettin' no Libtard tell me what goes in my body," Leanne announces. She seems to have got some of her usual attitude back, although the bruise on her face is still visible.

Peter thinks about all the things she's let others put in her body over the years. He recalls the DVD he's got stashed away at home. For a second, he's picturing something other than a nuclear apocalypse. But he can't even enjoy that moment.

"What do you think, Mitch?" he asks.

"In the military," his brother says, "you don't have a lotta choice. You gotta get the jabs and take the pills, else they don't let you deploy overseas. And all I know is, I didn't ever get a disease."

"So, what do *you* think, Pee-Wee?" Sherman persists.

Peter is saved from having to reply by Angie the barmaid bringing them a huge basket of chicken wings. There's got to be four dozen on there, all doused in dark BBQ sauce.

"Fries are on the way," she tells them, as they all start digging in.

"And another round of beers, please, honey," Randy says.

"You got it." Angie gives him a smile and Randy returns it. Peter thinks The Dozer is sweet on Angie. He wonders if she shares the big man's views on the world, and if she'll want to date him after he bombs a nuclear power plant.

"Steady on, Dozer," cautions Mitch.

"What?" Randy takes a gulp of beer and wipes his beard with the back of his hand. "We're celebrating."

"That's right," Sherman adds. "That shit went to perfection today."

"It was pretty good," acknowledges Mitch. "We just need to keep our heads clear. It's not long, now."

"Okay, two beers," Randy concedes. "That's all."

"You just ordered your third," Mitch says.

"Three, then. I can handle it." Randy leans back, pats his ample gut. "Besides, it's not on an empty stomach."

Peter watches as the four of them grab wings, rip them apart and gnaw at them, all teeth and bones and red-brown sauce on their hands and faces. It's like a pack of hyenas stripping a carcass in one of those shows on *Discovery*. He knows the tavern's wings are about the best in town. He's been eating them his whole life. The sauce is Angie's grandma's recipe, and it won an award at some contest in Pittsburgh once. But right now, all he can see is chunks of meat covered in blood, blood around the mouths of his companions, and the pictures from *Chernobyl*. And all he wants to do is go to the bathroom and throw up.

Angie comes back with a bucket of fries for them, and it's another feeding frenzy. Peter doesn't touch them, either.

"You not hungry, Pee-Wee?" Leanne raises her eyebrows, as if Peter's lack of appetite is a real cause for concern.

"I'm just . . ." He falters, not sure how to express himself. Apart from the images, he can't get the smell of the explosion out of his nose. He took two showers after he got home, but it didn't make any difference, like the odor was now permanently in his head. Smoke and concrete dust and, beneath that, something more . . . human. "You guys are gonna think I'm crazy—"

"We already do!" Randy barks.

"But I swear I can smell blood," Peter continues, "and I can't *not* smell it, if you know what I mean. It's just there the whole time."

"Weirdo," Leanne says, although she gives him a little wink.

"It *is* blood," says Sherman. "Kind of."

"Huh?" Peter doesn't get it.

"What you can smell," Sherman explains, "is molten copper. That's the slug from the EFP that melts at the detonation. It releases vapors that we would have inhaled when we got close. So, you literally have particles of metal in your nose. Copper's got iron in it, and humans have evolved sensitivity to smell iron because it's in our blood. It's like a survival thing to be aware of you or someone else bleeding. Your brain thinks it's blood."

"Knowledge, brother," Randy shakes his head in awe and holds up a fist, which Sherman bumps.

Peter looks around, checks that Angie and the other handful of customers in the tavern are out of earshot.

"Why nuclear?" he asks, looking at Mitch.

"Because it's the perfect target," replies his brother, without hesitation. "Listen, Pee-Wee, I know you're shitting your pants about the death toll, but if we do this right, it doesn't have to kill a lot of people."

"How many is not a lot?"

"Nuclear is symbolic," Mitch says.

"Of what?" Peter asks. He can feel his bowels moving.

"Government power," Sherman answers.

"The lack of it, to be exact," Mitch adds. "Nuclear scares people, 'cause they don't understand it. They still think Cold War, Soviet bombs dropping out of the sky, mushroom clouds and all that."

That's exactly what Peter thinks.

"But the government tells us nuclear is the future, and they want a whole lot more of it," continues Mitch. "So, attacking a power plant is the perfect way to show the American people — and the whole world, for that matter — that the people in charge have no control. That they can't be trusted. And if we can't trust the government with nuclear, then what?"

"It could be the start of something even bigger," Sherman chips in. "Something that's been brewing in this country a long time. An uprising."

"Amen," says Randy.

"Fuck, yeah," Leanne adds.

"Besides," Mitch says, "if we hit the right spots with the right amount of C4, we drop enough radiation to cause a mass evacuation and a national emergency, without actually causing a meltdown."

"The only thing that's gonna be melting down is the federal government," says Leanne. The others laugh and she seems pleased.

But Peter's not convinced.

"So, it ain't gonna be like Chernobyl, then?"

Mitch hooks a thumb at Sherman. "College boy here has

done the math," he says. "Enough explosive to breach the plant walls, not enough to blow the whole fucking thing up. Right?"

"Right." Sherman takes a swig of beer. "It's basic physics and chemistry," he mumbles, sounding less sure of himself.

It doesn't sound basic, Peter thinks. And Sherman got kicked out of college. Peter figures they wouldn't give a college dropout a job running the Three Mile Island power plant. Especially not one who's probably still cooking meth and getting high on his own supply. So, does this genius really know how to do the math?

Peter studies Sherman. The German's face is buried in his beer glass and he's drinking real fast. Right now, he doesn't look as though he could do the math to divide up their dinner cheque.

*

Washington, D.C.

He pours himself three fingers of Scotch from the bottle in his desk drawer and downs the whole glass in one go, as if it's a dose of medicine. In a way, it is. A numbing antidote to the poison he's been swallowing for weeks, micro dose after micro dose, slowly killing him from the inside out. He's still thinking about the meeting they had earlier this evening. A quick, aggressive exchange, back in one of the discreet members' lounges at The Metropolitan Club. He'd been in no mood to enjoy the luxury of the surroundings; none of them had been. It was like a war council, of which he had wanted no part but had been unable to ignore.

The kid had tried to open the conversation with as much charm as he could muster.

"Now, I'm well aware that you must all be very concerned by this afternoon's events at the hospital," he had said. "But let me assure you that I've spoken to the relevant contacts, and every effort is being made to—"

"She's escaped," interjected The Texan. "And she knows too damn much."

"She needs to be stopped," added The Ballbreaker.

"That is very much in hand, ma'am," the kid responded, forcing a smile of reassurance.

"It was supposed to be in hand before," said the older man with the grey moustache.

"Only it wasn't." The Ballbreaker stared at the kid, as if he was personally responsible for what happened at Independence Hall.

"It will be," the young man responded, shooting his cuffs and looking away.

"What, ah, additional measures are being taken?" he asked, not entirely sure he wants to hear the answer. But he's in too deep already. He lost control a long time ago.

"We have a lead," announced the kid. "On a vehicle."

"And?" The Texan tipped his head forward, studying their young associate from under thick eyebrows.

"And," the kid said, "thanks to our own intel, we have a pretty good idea where she's headed. We've sent someone."

"Not that loser who got his ass kicked in Philly, I hope." The Ballbreaker had framed it as a statement, not a question.

"No, ma'am, somebody else. Somebody better."

"I hope you're right," the older man said. "Or else this is going to come crashing down on our heads."

There'd been a moment of silence as they all stared at the low table between them.

"We should send G.I. Joe to take care of her," said The Texan.

"No," The Ballbreaker countered, "leave him be. He needs to focus on the main event."

The Texan scratched his chin. "Maybe you're right."

"The new guy was recommended by G.I. Joe," the kid added. "He said he's done this kind of thing before."

"What's the new guy going to do when he finds her?" he had asked.

"Oh, just take her someplace safe," the kid replied, "find out how much she knows, who she's told. That's all." They were the right words, but delivered in the wrong tone. Too casual.

It had sounded like a lie.

Now he takes out his phone, checks his messages. There's nothing new.

He pours himself another whisky and shuts his eyes.

Tries to pretend that none of this is happening.

25

Allentown, Pennsylvania

ELLEN KNOWS SOMETHING is wrong at Reyes's apartment as soon as she sees the front door.

It's ajar.

She remembers the security when she arrived. No way would he leave his place like this, especially not right now. She freezes, like a cat that's scented a dog and is trying to work out where it might be. Puts the carryout bag of food on the sidewalk and scans the street. She can't see anyone, and there's no noise beyond the distant drone of a few TVs.

Ellen drops into a crouch, takes the grab bag off her back and unzips it. She removes the pistol, confirms it has a round chambered, and tucks it into her belt while she re-shoulders the bag, double-strapped so she has both hands free. Then she draws the handgun and holds it cup-and-saucer grip as she stands again and advances toward the entrance.

She keeps to one side of the door, using the brickwork as a shield in case a potential threat is waiting in the hallway. Listens.

She can't hear anything.

Slowly, gently, she nudges the door with her foot.

It hardly makes a sound as it swings open.

Ellen steadies herself and steps quickly around the door-frame, pistol-first.

No one's there.

She creeps down the hallway, transferring her weight care-fully from one foot to the next so as not to announce her presence. She heads for the computer room where she left Reyes. Still listening, still hearing nothing. The door is open.

Cautiously, she enters the room. The only person there is Reyes.

He has his back to her. His wheelchair is facing the monitors, but his head is tipped forward. The screens are all locked.

At first, Ellen's conscious mind tells her that he's just fallen asleep, nothing more. But her unconscious knows that's not true, because she can smell the gunshot residue.

Her fight-or-flight system kicks up another gear.

Then she notices the single entry wound at the top of her friend's skull. It's tiny, neat. Made by a small calibre bullet.

"Jesus, no," she whispers. "Please, God, no."

She takes a step closer. Sees the evidence of that bullet's exit on the desk in front of Reyes. Blood, brain, little fragments of skull, spattered across his keyboard.

She doesn't even call his name, because she knows he's dead.

And she's the one responsible.

It's that same feeling she had in Paris. That horrible realisa-tion of something that can't be undone. That same knowledge that it's on her.

The pistol suddenly feels heavy in her hands. She thinks she might start crying but then she's getting hot with anger, her teeth gritted, jaw set hard. She's going to make the person who did this pay. She wants to let that fury out, to scream and yell for Reyes, but she knows his killer could still be here, so she can't—

"Put the gun down. Now."

The man's voice comes from behind her. He's calm. Someone who's used to being in this situation.

Ellen curses herself for not anticipating this. For switching off and losing her advantage.

"Don't do anything stupid," he adds.

She doesn't need to look to know that he's pointing the same weapon at her that he used to execute Reyes.

She does as instructed.

"Turn around," he says.

Slowly, she pivots to face him, palms raised.

The first thing she sees is his mask. It's made out of clear plastic but with curved ridges that distort his face, like he's behind a warped windowpane.

He's six-feet, she'd guess, 190, all muscle. Cut from the same cloth as the guy who was following her in Philly — only an upgrade, version 2.0.

The pistol in his gloved hands is completely still. It has a long black suppressor on the barrel.

"Take two steps forward," he tells her.

She moves away from Reyes, away from her weapon.

"Start talking," he says.

"How'd you get in here?"

"I'll ask the questions."

"You picked the lock, right?"

He doesn't respond.

"Before the guy in the wheelchair could get there," she continues, her rage getting the better of her. "Then what, you tried to get him to show you what he was doing? But he wouldn't, would he? So, you shot him in the back of the head. How'd you find him?"

He ignores everything she's said. "What do you know?" he demands.

"About what?"

"Don't fuck around. I will kill you if I have to."

"Then you won't know anything."

"I didn't say I'd kill you right away," he replies.

Ellen's mouth goes dry. She guesses he's ex-military, maybe ex-private security. He probably waterboarded a hundred guys in black sites around the world during the so-called War on Terror. Maybe even killed a few of them in the process. She's met one or two guys like him before, men with literally zero empathy.

She's terrified, but she needs to think of a plan to get out of here. Somehow.

"Please don't do this," she says. "I have a six-year-old son. His name is Josh."

"I won't lose any sleep over that."

Ellen tries to swallow. She can't. Her guts clench.

"Tell me what you know about the Keystone Boys right now," he says, "and I'll let you walk out of here. Back to your kid."

She knows that's a lie. He's been sent to kill her.

There are only two ways this can end.

*

"Talk," the man commands, reaching behind him with one hand to close the door, keeping the gun and his eyes on her. He takes a step toward her.

"I don't know anything about them."

He sighs. "If you wanna play hardball, I can play hardball too. Your buddy here tried it," he says, gesturing to Reyes with the pistol, "and look what happened to him. Tell me what I want to know."

"I don't know anything," she repeats. "That's the truth."

She guesses that Reyes held out, didn't give this guy whatever it was that he'd found and wanted to pass to her. *I got something for you*, he'd said in the text message. The question is, what was that intel? She figures it's behind the locked screens in front of him.

"Last chance before I put a bullet in your knee."

She sees the stereo, off to one side behind the guy.

"Right or left?" He lowers the barrel and aims at one of her legs, then the other.

She takes a breath.

"Music on," she says.

The reggaeton beats start up. Loud snare drums. Deep bass.

The guy turns his head, just a fraction. It's a physiological reaction to the new sound that his training can't override. The sensitivity of a predator to its environment.

Ellen takes her chance.

She launches herself at him, going right for the suppressor, pushing it aside as the shot fires. She hears a window crack and some glass shatter but all she can see is the pistol and she's got both hands on it but the guy's really strong and he won't let go.

He throws a punch with his left but she's too close for it to have any power and Ellen is pressing inside his wrist with her thumb and pressing some more but then he's got his arm around her neck and he's squeezing. For a second the image of Shawna garrotting her with the phone cable flashes into her mind.

Then he yells out and she knows she's hit the pressure point, right on the nerve.

His right hand opens and the pistol clatters to the floor. She kicks it away, across the room.

But he's still crushing her neck and now he's recovered from the shock, he's trying to press the back of her head forward in a sleeper hold. It's game over if he chokes her out.

She shifts her hips to the right, grabs his arm with both her hands and — just like E.J. taught her at The Farm — she pushes her butt out and drops to tip him off balance then rolls him over her back to the ground.

Ellen pulls free of him and kicks him hard in the ribs, twice. The guy reaches into his boot.

She's about to stamp on his balls but then she sees he's pulled a blade, so she backs off. Ellen recognizes the distinctive look of a Ka-Bar — the US Navy and Marine Corps knife of choice. It's a serious piece of gear. Seven-inch blade, curved to a point, and no doubt razor sharp.

He springs to his feet, holding the knife in the backhand grip. E.J. always said watch out for anyone who does that, because it means they know what they're doing. You can stab as well as slash with a backhand grip.

He comes at her, and she stumbles backward. He wheels his arm at her, and she weaves back, the blade missing her by inches.

She needs something to protect herself.

She turns, just enough to see the laptop Reyes let her use, sitting on the coffee table. She reaches for it but hears movement and feels pressure and then heat in her side, right above her hip. She grabs the laptop and swings it just in time to block his next stab.

The knife glances off the laptop casing and then she's using it like a shield to parry his ferocious attack. She can feel pain at her hip, hot and wet, and she knows he's got her. It's just a matter of time before he slashes her again. And she can't afford to lose more blood.

But she's not going out like that.

She blocks the next strike and immediately swings the laptop at his head. She connects and knows she's stunned him. She swings once more, hits him a second time, full in the face. She hears a crack and knows the impact has probably broken his nose. She can see blood behind the mask.

Growling at the agony of her own wound, Ellen pushes him backward until he hits the wall.

He tries a stab but misses. As his arm moves aside, she aims the flat edge of the laptop at his throat, then smacks it hard with her forearm.

The guy drops.

She stamps on his wrist until he lets go of the knife.

Then with all her strength she brings the laptop down on his skull, aiming for the temple. She sees his head snap and spin and he slumps back against the wall.

He stops moving.

Ellen realizes she's breathing like crazy — too hard, too fast. She puts her hand to her hip. It comes away slick with blood.

She needs to stop the bleeding. And it's not helping that her heart is going like one-eighty beats a minute right now.

She takes a few seconds to examine the guy on the floor. His chest is rising and falling, but he's out cold. She doesn't know how long he'll stay like that. She lifts his mask for a second. Doesn't recognize him.

She drops the laptop and picks up the Ka-Bar knife. Then crosses to the computers and retrieves her pistol.

Gasps in pain as she tucks both weapons into her belt.

The reggaeton is still playing.

"Music off," she says.

Then there's just silence, and the sound of her own ragged breath.

And Reyes, dead, right in front of her.

26

Allentown, Pennsylvania

ELLEN CAN'T HELP but imagine Reyes's final moments as she looks at his body. She visualizes the guy standing behind him with the suppressor inches from the back of his head. And she sees Reyes, defiant, not giving him what he wanted, probably telling him to go fuck himself, right up until the moment of his execution.

She wonders if he was scared. If he considered giving up what he'd found, even giving up Ellen, to save his own life. Faced with the prospect of death, most people would have done that. But she knows Reyes didn't.

She imagines the pain this is going to cause his family when they find out. How they'll blame her for taking away their Ricardo — their son, brother, uncle, cousin. Maybe they're right. It was her fault. She vows to get justice for him, whatever that takes.

Ellen turns toward the man who killed him in cold blood, still unconscious on the floor. She considers dispensing that justice right here, right now. She could put a bullet in him while he can't defend himself, just like he did to Reyes.

Her hand moves to her belt. Her fingers coil around the pistol grip and she pulls it out as the fire inside her grows.

She takes aim at the guy's head.

An eye for an eye.

Then she stops.

Lowers the weapon.

This isn't her. She's not a murderer like him. Like the people who sent him. And like she's guessing the Keystone Boys are planning to become, if they're not already. Stopping them needs to be her focus. Saving all the lives they want to take. That's what Reyes would want her to do. That's the best way she can atone for his death.

She tucks the pistol away once more, wincing as her clothes brush against the knife wound. She goes to the kitchen, grabs a towel and binds it around her waist with Scotch tape she finds in a drawer. The bleeding slows a lot, but it hasn't stopped. There's still fresh blood, wet and glistening, slowly seeping through the material. She needs proper first aid, but this will have to do for now.

She should probably leave, given that a gunshot just took out the window. People will have heard that. Someone might even be on their way to the house right now to check what happened. She needs to get out of here.

But she recalls Reyes's text message.

He had something.

Her experience of working with Reyes told her that he was resourceful. Tech guys always find ways to solve problems, especially ex-military tech guys. When he realized someone was breaking in, what did he do? He managed to lock his screens, but might he have found a way to communicate what he'd discovered to her?

Ellen checks that the gun-for-hire is still asleep, then goes over to the computers. She feels sick to the stomach standing next to her friend, whose murder she caused, but she has no choice. She can't let his death be for nothing.

She pushes a button on the keyboard — one that doesn't have blood or brain on it. The screen prompts her to enter a password. For a moment, she considers trying to guess it. But Reyes knew cybersecurity. He's not going to have chosen "password123" or his birthday. She could be here all night trying to crack it, and the system would probably shut her out after multiple failed attempts anyway.

Her eyes dart around the desk. Reyes has scribbled a few sticky notes which he's put on the machines but, as far as she can see, they just contain technical stuff. None looks like a password, or any other clue as to how she might access his system.

There's a sound behind her. She whips around to see the guy shift a little, but he's still out. She knows she doesn't have long.

Ellen returns her attention to the desk. There has to be something here.

Then she sees it.

A ballpoint pen.

She hadn't noticed it earlier, when she first came in here.

Could Reyes have had the presence of mind to write something down for her in his final moments? She scans the desk again, but there's nothing. Checks the floor — again, nothing. She brings herself to slide a hand into his pockets, but they're empty, except for his cell phone. She decides to take the phone. Maybe the pen is a dead end, and he didn't write anything at all.

The guy behind her shifts a little more. He's regaining consciousness.

She needs to think.

She takes a step back, looks at Reyes.

Realizes that his shirt sleeves are down. Recalls that they were rolled up when she arrived.

Moving around his wheelchair to his left side, she carefully lifts one of his arms. She chooses the left one first, because she knows Reyes was right-handed. His arm is heavy and, as she peels back the shirt cuff, she can feel his skin is still warm.

Once more, grief rises up inside her, making her throat constrict and her eyes prickle with tears as the muscles in her face tighten. She wishes she could bring Reyes back, same as she wishes she could go back and undo what happened in Paris. But none of it can be undone, and she has to live with that.

"I'm sorry, Ricardo," she says quietly.

There's another movement from the guy on the ground. She has to work faster.

She rolls up the sleeve and sees the tattoos Reyes had once told her about. There's a large American eagle, carrying a stars-and-stripes in its claws. It's driving the pointed tip of the flagpole into the body of a snake whose jaws are open, its forked tongue flicking out. Reyes had said that it symbolized more than just the United States. It represented freedom.

The freedom for which he died, she thinks. Freedom that is now being threatened by an enemy within. By home-grown terrorists, born under that same flag.

Gently rotating his hand, she examines the inside of his forearm. At first, she almost misses it. But as she looks more closely, there's no mistaking the black ink of the ballpoint pen. Between a Puerto Rican flag and a pair of dog tags, inscribed with "Fallujah '04" and "never forget", scrawled in small capital letters, is a name:

LEANNE SPINOZA CLARION

Ellen stares at the words. Is this the identity of the person who posted about the Keystone Boys on the *Gigachan* board, under the alias *gotmilk2022*? A woman called Leanne Spinoza Clarion? What's her connection to the Keystone Boys? Ellen can't make sense of it right now. She needs to get online and do some research. But not here.

Memorizing the spelling of the name, she wets her fingertips and rubs the words off Reyes's arm, then rolls his sleeve back down. She feels horrible touching his lifeless body in this way, but she can't give whoever finds him here anything to go on. She needs to—

The police siren cuts into her awareness. Distant but getting closer.

She takes a final look at the room, and at her friend.

Then she gets out.

*

Route 737, Kempton, Pennsylvania

According to her GPS, Ellen is about twenty-five miles west of Allentown. She was lucky to get out when she did. By the time she reached the Camry, parked in the street behind Reyes's road, the police sirens were just a few blocks away. Another minute and they would have caught her.

Once out of the house, she'd had the presence of mind to pick up the food bag, and had moved as quickly as her injury would allow toward the car and bugged out, trying to put as much distance between her and the cops as possible. Between her and the man who'd tried to kill her. Between her and her dead friend.

She drove mostly one-handed, her other hand keeping the pressure on the open wound at her hip. It hurts like hell. The bleeding seems to have stopped, but she still needs to clean it and put a bandage over it, rather than a dishcloth. It might even need stitches. The prospect of that makes her even more nauseous than her anxiety.

Although no one but Luis knows the car she's driving, she's still kept to the back roads, weaving her way through a patchwork of farmland and forest. To stay off-grid, you have two options: merge into a mass of people in a city and hide in plain sight, or head to the absolute middle of nowhere and rely on the remoteness of your location for protection. She's taking the second option right now.

She's got to get access to the web to research Leanne Spinoza Clarion, but that can wait until she's fixed herself up. The mystery name makes her think of Reyes, and she remembers that she took his cell phone from the apartment. She takes it out of her pocket, removes the battery and SIM card, and tosses them all out of the car window into the pitch-black roadside.

How did they find her?

She tries to run through the possibilities. Did they discover that she took Mr Hamilton's station wagon, run the plates and catch her on some camera going north? Maybe, but that wouldn't have let them track her right to Reyes's apartment. Did they have her burner phone, somehow? Maybe her parents or Harry gave it to the cops out of concern for her safety. She considers ditching it, but right now it could be her lifeline, so she just switches it off and takes the battery out so it can't be tracked. Maybe they just spotted the car going north, checked her known contacts and guessed she was on her way to see Reyes. But, if it was a law enforcement operation to find her, they would have sent a SWAT team to capture her in Allentown, not an assassin in a mask.

Whatever means they used to find her, it's clear that the people behind this have resources. They probably have access to official systems, which means they've either hacked government servers or, maybe more likely, they have an insider. She recalls Detective Brennan back at the police station in Philly, and his unwillingness to believe her story. Is he working for the same masters as the Keystone Boys?

She can't make sense of it right now, except to acknowledge that she's up against something big.

Suddenly there's a break in the trees and Ellen sees the lights of a few buildings. She's approaching an intersection with a gas station on one side, and farm buildings on the other. The gas station looks closed, but there's a bunch of cars parked to one side of it in a field that opens right off the road. She pulls into the makeshift lot between two other vehicles, then kills the lights and the engine.

She waits, listening. There are no signs of life, although a hundred yards away she can see a couple of windows lit at the farmhouse.

Satisfied that no one knows she's here, she shifts into the passenger seat to give herself extra space and slides it all the way back. Then she snaps on the overhead light and fishes in her grab bag for the first aid kit.

Slowly, carefully, she removes the Scotch tape and towel from her waist. There's blood on her jeans and t-shirt, as well as streaks over her skin. The wound itself is about an inch and a half wide with a thick clot of blood across it. It's a clean cut, and not deep, but it's too big to leave untreated. She runs an antiseptic wipe over it, wincing at the sting. Then she prepares the needle and thread.

Psyches herself up.

DAY FIVE

27

ELLEN JERKS AWAKE, and a sharp pain flares at the wound at her hip. For a second, she feels nothing but confusion, as if she's still dreaming. Then the knocking at the window cuts through the fog in her brain.

Tap-tap-tap.

There's a guy standing next to the car. He's about her age. She sees the gun at his hip and her first thought is that they've found her. That she let her guard down by falling asleep and law enforcement have tracked her here.

Then she takes in his clothing: a plaid shirt over jeans and a gimme hat on his head, the words "I like big trucks and I cannot lie" printed on it, tufts of hair spilling out from beneath it. He has a couple days' stubble on his jaw.

He's not a cop.

"You all right, ma'am?" he asks, his gaze shifting from her to the interior of the car.

She looks down at her bloodstained clothing, then around her at the debris of her self-administered first aid and takeout food packaging. She remembers stitching herself up, then eating the food she'd brought. After that, she doesn't remember a whole lot. She figures exhaustion must've just overtaken her. At least she locked the car doors before losing consciousness.

"Do you need help?" the man says, when she doesn't reply.

Even though he's armed with what looks like a Smith & Wesson revolver, she decides he's not a threat. He's clearly a little surprised she's here, but he's not suspicious. And if he'd recognized her from the news reports, he wouldn't have approached and asked if she was okay. He'd have just called the police. She can trust him, for now, at least.

She cracks the window.

"Morning," she says, managing a smile.

"What're you doin' here, ma'am?" he asks, blinking.

"I, uh . . . I was driving, and I got sleepy, so I pulled in to get some rest. Must've drifted right off."

"Uh-huh," he replies. "Only thing is, you can't stay here. It's a private lot."

She wonders why all these cars are parked up at an intersection in a middle of a bunch of fields. Who do they belong to, and where did their drivers go? That didn't occur to her last night.

"Is it yours?" she asks. "The lot."

"No, this here belongs to Bad Farm. I just run the gas station."

"*Bad* Farm?"

"Yeah," he chuckles. "Ain't nothin' bad about it, it's just run by Beth and Dave. It's their initials, see? But they'll be pissed if they catch you. You know how it is, folks always tryin' to park for free."

"Yeah, right."

He sweeps a hand in the air. "These cars belong to their seasonal labor."

She looks past the vehicles and sees a few portable cabins behind the trees that she missed in the dark last night. More people around means more chance of being recognized. She needs to move.

"I should get going," she says.

He lays a hand on the doorframe. "You want some gas?"

She twists in the direction of the farm. She can't see anyone. "Sure."

"Bring her over, then." He hooks a thumb in the direction of the forecourt.

Ellen drives across and while the man is pumping the gas for her, she decides to get out and stretch her legs. There might be some useful stuff she can buy inside the little convenience store attached to the station.

"How much you want?" the guy asks.

"Full tank, please," she replies. She doesn't know when she'll get the chance to refuel again. She steps around the car.

"Whoa!" the guy exclaims.

She realizes he's looking at the blood on her clothes. She looks down too. It's a mess.

"You sure you okay?" he says.

"Yeah." She gives an awkward laugh. "It's, uh, my time of the month. I had a little accident in the car, couldn't get to a bathroom."

He looks shocked. Ellen wonders whether he's ever discussed menstruation with a customer before. Probably not.

"Okay. Well, ah, there's a restroom inside, if you need it."

"Thanks . . ." She tilts her head, inviting him to introduce himself.

"Nathaniel," he replies. "Nate."

"I'm Erica," she says.

"Pleasure to meet you, ma'am." He touches the brim of his hat and, in spite of everything, Ellen smiles at his old-fashioned manners. "Go right on in."

*

Having used the bathroom to clean herself up a little, Ellen places the granola bars, candy and potato chips she's selected on the counter, along with a large bottle of water and a t-shirt she's found. It was too much to expect a rural gas station to stock jeans, too, but at least if she can change tops, she might get fewer stares if she has to be seen by other members of the public. Though if they recognize her from the news, a bloodied t-shirt will be the least of her concerns. Nate seems blissfully unaware of who she is, and Ellen is grateful for his apparent lack of interest in the news.

The t-shirt she's buying is black with the Pennzoil logo on it — an old motor oil company long since moved to Houston. She remembers her Dad had a dusty can of the stuff in the garage when she was a kid. The gold letters of the brand name run over a red Liberty Bell, and Ellen thinks about how her week started, at Independence Hall. She gets a shiver at the thought of the guy drawing his weapon on her. Wonders if she could have avoided that incident and, in turn, everything that happened since. Perhaps there was no other way, and her life had changed the moment she overheard those guys in the hotel corridor. Or, more accurately, the moment she decided to do something about what she'd heard.

"Eighty-five fifty-four," Nate says. He's rung everything up on the register.

Ellen realizes her mind had wandered. She needs to concentrate. One mistake could cost her all the progress she's made so far. Which reminds her that she has no idea where she's going next. As she pays Nate with the bills from her grab bag, she notices he's got a computer behind the counter. It looks ancient. But, if it has internet, she doesn't care.

"Nate, can I ask you a favor?"

He counts her change and hands it to her. "Depends."

"My phone's out of battery, and I just need to check a couple things online. For where I'm going." She points to the machine. "Would you mind?"

He's caught off-guard, and she guesses no customer has ever asked that before.

"Uh, I'm not supposed to let anyone back here, you know . . ."

"It'd really help me out." She grins and winks, like it's a fun secret. "I won't tell your boss."

Nate frowns at her for a moment. "Well, okay, I suppose. If you're real quick."

"Thank you." She walks around the counter.

He opens a browser window on the computer, and it brings up what looks like a news site.

Ellen holds her breath. Then exhales in silent relief as she realizes it's ESPN.

"Don't be too long," he says, "sometimes my manager drops in to check up on me."

"Got it," she replies. "Oh, hey, any chance of a coffee?"

"I was about to put a pot on," he says pleasantly, and ambles over to a machine across the shop.

Ellen watches as he switches on a radio beside the machine. It's playing a country song, but it won't be long before there's a news bulletin. Suddenly, her anxiety kicks in and the slight sense of safety she felt here is gone.

She's got to work fast.

She goes to the Google Maps website to have something to pull up for cover if he comes back over, but then opens a private window and checks all the options so it doesn't log her sites and searches in the history. She knows a computer forensics expert would be still be able to find out every key she's pressed. But she guesses Nate doesn't have that skill set, so this is good enough for now.

She goes to the private browser and googles: *Leanne Spinoza Clarion.*

There's no one with that specific name.

But, after a few clicks, she finds a woman called Leanne Spinoza who lives in a town called Clarion. Ellen looks up the town.

It's a small place in western Pennsylvania, with a population of five-and-a-half thousand. There seems to be only one person there with that name. She has to be the woman Reyes found.

She clicks back and checks a couple of her original search hits on Leanne Spinoza. There isn't much. The image results show a bunch of different women, but the majority of the first two rows are of the same person.

Leanne Spinoza is pretty, with bleached-blonde hair and a wide-eyed expression that looks as if she's either high, or craving excitement, or maybe both. In one photo, she's singing in a bar. In another, she's at the front of a dance class, somewhere called the Millennium Studio in Clarion. A third image is a black-and-white head shot, professionally lit and edited. Ellen wonders if she was maybe a model, an actress, or pro dancer once, although there are no immediate search hits to back that up.

Is this really *gotmilk2022*, the person who posted about the Keystone Boys lighting up the sky on the Fourth of July? She doesn't look like a terrorist, although Ellen knows better than to judge a book by its cover. Still, she's starting to wonder if she's misunderstood Reyes's last message. Is she wasting valuable minutes on a dead end? Did Reyes make a mistake?

Then she catches herself. She realizes that she's talking about Ricardo Reyes, who was one of the best hackers-for-hire out there. If he chose to write something down for her in the final minutes of his life, then it was no mistake. She's got to——

"How d'you take it?" Nate calls over.

His voice causes another burst of adrenalin to pulse through her belly. She was so absorbed, she'd almost forgotten he was there.

"Ah, just cream, thanks."

"Comin' up." Nate is pouring the coffees, whistling along to the country tune.

She goes back to the hits and scrolls through a bunch of

people called Leanne Spinoza on social media until she finds the woman from Clarion. She clicks into the profile and, although she'd need to be logged in or "friends" to see it in full, Leanne hasn't locked her photos down in the privacy settings. Ellen knows it's a break — a potential chance to see who she hangs out with.

"Here you go," says Nate, approaching with a mug.

Ellen hastily switches to Google Maps. "Thank you so much," she says, taking it from him.

He stands beside her for a minute, looking at the screen. Slurps his own brew. "So, where are you headed?"

"That's what I'm trying to find out," she replies, willing him to go away. "I'll let you know if I need any local knowledge."

"Okay." He gets the hint and ambles away.

*

After a few more minutes, Ellen knows that Leanne grew up in Clarion, went to school here, and then moved to L.A. for a while before coming back to her hometown. It isn't clear if she has a job, but she likes singing and dancing. There are no obvious family members in her pictures, but she has spent a lot of her time in the past couple of years with her boyfriend, a man she's tagged as "Mitchy Mitch". To judge by the images, Leanne is really into him.

Mitch is clearly a big guy, and in good shape, a square-jawed jock right out of a teen movie. He reminds Ellen of Channing Tatum. But what interests her most about him is the tattoo on his arm. She can see it clearly in one photograph, where Leanne is sitting on Mitch's lap at a barbecue and he's wearing a tank top. And she recognizes the design. The eagle, globe and anchor that form the emblem of the US Marine Corps.

That gets her thinking.

Across the store, the radio news cuts in. The lead story is something about whether a gas pipeline in Pennsylvania should be extended despite environmental damage. It's state news. Ellen's heartbeat skyrockets. She should leave, now, but she just wants to do one more search.

She quickly googles 'Mitch' plus 'Clarion' and 'USMC' and drinks her coffee while she scans the first page of hits.

His name is Mitch Logan, a sergeant in the Marines. He's a hero. Tours in Afghanistan, Iraq and Syria, prestigious medals. A poster boy. But then he quits. There's a piece from last year in *The Derrick*, a newspaper published out of Oil City in western PA, that talks about him being discharged. But Ellen doesn't have time to read it, because right then she hears her own name on the radio.

Followed by the words *murder suspect*.

28

Clarion, Pennsylvania

PETER KNOWS HE should concentrate on what Mitch is saying, but he can't. It's not the fact that he's exhausted because he hardly slept last night, lying awake and staring at the ceiling, scared shitless. It's not the heavy metal that his brother is playing to mask their voices from the neighboring apartments, either. Or that, right opposite him on the couch, Leanne is wearing denim hot pants and a knotted t-shirt exposing her stomach. It's the scenes of death and destruction from Chernobyl that keep popping into his mind. Like the apocalypse at the end of the Bible, only worse.

Mitch is briefing them all on his plan to attack the Three Mile Island nuclear facility, in just two days from now. His brother is talking about it as if it's just another one of the hundreds of operations he did during his fifteen years in the Marines. Maybe it is. Peter guesses that blowing up a power plant is probably the exact kind of thing the military would do somewhere like Iraq, against a foreign enemy. But this ain't Iraq, it's Pennsylvania. It's their home.

His brother pulls up a satellite image on the screen of his

laptop and they all get closer. There's a bunch of fields and patches of forest with a wide river running down the middle. In the river is a long, thin island. The top half of the island is grey, and that's the power plant. There are four circles in it that Mitch says are the cooling towers, so big they're clear as day on the satellite photo. From the sky, it looks like a little piece of concrete in a sea of empty country.

Except it ain't empty.

Peter knows what's just a few miles north — Harrisburg. Fifty thousand people. And Philly's not too far away, either. One and a half million people live there. He checked the numbers online.

"Amphibious approach is an option," Mitch says, "but I discounted it, based on our cover."

Peter has no idea what he's talking about.

"And since we don't have a Black Hawk at our disposal," continues Mitch, to a few chuckles from the others, "that leaves entry by land."

Peter glances around at the others. Sherman and Randy are focused on the map. Leanne is gazing at Mitch.

"There are two ways onto the island in a vehicle." Mitch zooms in and indicates a thin strip which connects the mainland road beside the river with the island. "Our insertion is via the south bridge. It's the contractor entrance."

"Less security?" asks Randy.

"According to our intel, yes," replies Mitch. "The whole place should be operating on reduced staffing anyway, for Fourth of July weekend. We go in right after midnight on the fourth, just after the security shift changes."

Peter raises his hand.

"Pee-Wee," his brother says.

"Uh, yeah." Peter clears his throat. "I was just thinkin'—"

"Don't do that," Sherman cuts in.

"Let him finish," says Mitch. "Go ahead, Pee-Wee."

"Well, I was thinkin' . . . how're they gonna let us in the contractor entrance?"

"Because we'll be contractors." Mitch nods at Randy. "Dozer's hooking us up with some uniforms, hard hats, yellow vests, all that stuff. Leanne's making ID passes that look just like the real ones."

"Oh my God, they are *so* good," Leanne exclaims.

"We'll have our weapons in the toolboxes," adds Mitch. "And the EFPs in the back."

"But, uh, how do we know who to say we are, or what the ID passes even look like?" Peter asks. His head is hurting from trying to make sense of this against the backdrop of Black Crown Initiate's super-fast guitars and screaming vocals.

A smile forms slowly on his brother's face. "Because we've got a little help."

"From who?" asks Peter.

"Stop asking so many questions," Randy tells him.

"It's okay, Dozer. Pee-Wee's all in. We can trust him. Right, Pee-Wee?"

Peter looks at Randy, who's glaring at him. "Yeah, course you can trust me," he says, hearing the wobble in his own voice.

"We have a friend who supports our cause," Mitch explains, "who has access to restricted details about the plant. Someone way up."

"Hold on. A friend? Whose idea was it to attack this place?" Peter asks. "Ours?"

"It's the perfect target," his brother says.

"That's not what I—"

Mitch ignores him. "So, we hit the new guards with the fake paperwork and passes at the gate, right after midnight. We tell them it's a scheduled maintenance visit, and we go on in. I'll leave our friend The German here to tell us where the bombs go. Sherman."

"All right." Sherman sniffs, takes the laptop. "These buildings house the reactors, that's where—"

"Wait a second." Now it's Peter's turn to interrupt. "What if they don't let us in?"

"Then we open fire," Mitch says, matter of fact. "Shoot to kill."

He can't believe how cold his brother is. He's speaking about murder like it's a trip to the grocery store. "We what?"

"Why the hell you think we been puttin' rounds on targets with people drawn on them for the past four months, dumbass?" Randy says. "We're takin' down anyone who tries to stop us. It has to be done, and those folks are the enemy. Hell, even Leanne here understands that."

Peter's head is pounding, and he feels like he can't get enough air. "I need a minute," he says, walking out of the room.

"Leave him," he hears Mitch say.

*

Outside, it's a different world. Warm sunshine, people going about their business, students in and out of the college bookstore across the street. And no thrash metal.

"What am I doing?" he whispers to himself, wiping his hands over his face.

He joined the Keystone Boys all those months ago because, when Mitch asked him, it felt like the first time he'd ever been accepted into any group. His brother told him that they were going to strike back at the government that had betrayed them — betrayed so many Americans for so long — with its self-serving disregard for the Constitution. That the time for talking was done, and now it was time for action.

It had sounded good to Peter. Better than good. He was pissed at the system. More than that, though, he thought he'd finally have the chance to be respected. To be a hero, just like his big bro. He'd spent a lifetime trying to be like Mitch, and now, here was his opportunity.

Mitch brought them all together, united by their hatred for the oppression of federal government. Leanne was part of it, even Randy was being cool. Peter let himself get swept up and carried away. They were the freedom fighters, the revolutionaries taking the fight to the tyrants, just like their forefathers who founded the nation.

Now they're planning mass murder.

His cell rings in his pocket, and he pulls it out. It's his mom. "Hey, ma," he says.

She wants to know if he'll be home for lunch and whether she should make extra in case Mitch is coming too.

"Uh, I don't know," Peter begins, "we're doing some stuff now, and—"

The cell phone is yanked right out of his hand from behind.

He spins, sees Randy.

"Makin' a call, are we?" says The Dozer.

"Give it back," Peter protests. It's the school playground all over again, only now Mitch isn't here to stick up for him.

"Who is it?"

"My mom."

"And you just had to call her, right now?" Randy narrows his eyes.

"She called me." Peter reaches for the phone but Randy bats him away with a meaty hand.

Randy puts the cell phone to his ear. "Hello, Mrs Logan."

The big man's face suddenly breaks into a smile. "Oh, we're just fine, thank you for asking. How are you?" He glances at Peter and his grin disappears. "Yeah, we're at Mitch's apartment. Just hangin' out. No, I took the day off." There's a pause. "Sure, I'd love to come for lunch. What are you making?" His smile returns, broader this time. "Spaghetti and meatballs? My favourite. All right, see you soon."

He ends the call and tosses the phone back to Peter, who just about catches it.

"If Mitch says you're all in, then I have to believe you're all in," Randy says.

Peter swallows. He doesn't respond.

"Because if you're not," Randy goes on, "then I'll kill you myself and dump your body in the Clarion River. You got that?"

Peter blinks.

"And you know what?" adds the big man, stepping forward so that all 6'6" of him is towering over Peter. "Your brother just said that's fine by him. Because what we're doing here is more important."

Randy stomps back inside and Peter is left out on the sidewalk, holding his phone and wondering if Mitch really did just say that. Wondering whether his brother really does love him, like he told him the other day. Whether he'll always look out for him, like he promised he would.

Peter thinks about Leanne, about the bruising on her face. He thinks about Mitch planning the murder of innocent people, like it's just another day at the office for him.

And, for the first time in his life, he starts to think that maybe he's seeing his brother for who he really is.

*

Washington, D.C.

"I haven't got long," he says. "I'm due back in my office at quarter of one."

The kid checks his disgustingly expensive watch. "I have a video call at twelve thirty," he responds, as if it's a competition for who's busier and more important.

But he's done with competitions and games.

"Let's walk," he says, hooking his thumb toward the Washington Monument, rising up into a clear July sky a mile down the National Mall.

They keep to the trees for shade, and for a little more privacy. The kid tells him what happened in Allentown.

"So, where is she now?" he asks.

"We don't know," the young man answers. "But we'll find her. Obviously, you'll pass on anything that comes through from your side."

He bites his tongue. This isn't what he signed up for. In fact, he didn't sign up for anything. He was press ganged into it, every single step of the way.

"In the meantime," the kid continues, "we're looking at other options for locating her, since she's currently the biggest threat to the success of our plan."

"Other options?" He stops walking, turns to look at the young man. "What does that mean?"

The kid gives one of his fake smiles. "It's nothing for you to worry about."

"Well, what if it is?" He can feel himself getting mad, now, his temperature rising. He's balled one fist and part of him feels like smacking this little shit with it, teaching him a lesson. But he still has just about enough control to know that won't go down well. Not with all the tourists and bystanders. And not with their senior . . . what could he call them — associates? Colleagues? No, he should call them what they are.

Co-conspirators.

The kid doesn't answer him. Instead, he indicates the giant obelisk up ahead of them. "Pretty awesome, isn't it?"

"Huh?"

"Imagine having a monument to you, right in the middle of your nation's capital."

He imagines the kid would want exactly that for himself. Only bigger.

"Did you know," the kid continues, "that George Washington actually served in the British army, twenty years before he kicked them back across the pond? They taught him everything he knew about war, and he used it against them. That's justice, right?"

"Don't change the subject," he says.

"I'm not." The young man sniggers.

He grabs the kid's arm, his rage simmering. "What, you think this is funny?"

"Whoa, hoss."

"*Hoss?*"

"Okay, you need to chillax right now."

It's more than he can handle.

"Chillax?!" he yells. "Don't you fucking tell me to chillax, asshole! You have no fucking idea what this is like."

The kid's smirk disappears. In its place is the cold, hard, stare of someone who isn't used to being spoken to like that. He shakes his arm free.

"Have you forgotten who's in charge here?" the young man asks. "Because I can remind you, if necessary. And guess what? It's not you."

His desire to punch the kid is stronger than ever. To send him to his *twelve thirty* with a bloody nose. But he doesn't. He can't, because he knows the trust-fund baby is right. He has no power. They do. And there's a reason for that.

They know his secret.

29

Clearfield County, Pennsylvania

ELLEN HAS BEEN on the move for four hours, taking the smaller roads west toward Clarion. She's maybe an hour, hour and a half away from the town, now.

She's only stopped once, on an unmarked forest track, to change the dressing on her stab wound. It's not doing too bad. Her stitches are holding up, and it doesn't seem to have gotten infected, but it's still agony and she feels as though a sudden movement could tear it right open again. At least her ankle is a little better than yesterday.

Her cell phone is still off, so she's navigating with the hand-held GPS, which is taped to the dash. The long journey has given her plenty of time to think everything through, but she's still trying to get her head around it.

First, there's the fact that she's now a murder suspect. That means that the man who tried to kill her must have regained consciousness and escaped before the cops arrived. It also means they've connected her to Reyes — maybe with forensics from his apartment — and assumed she was responsible for his death. Which, in many ways, she was. But she can't dwell on that now.

If she thought being pursued for assault and breaking a commitment order was bad enough, it's going to be a whole lot worse being hunted for homicide. It means more cops, more media coverage, more images of her out there, and more people looking — not least the gun-for-hire sent to stop her.

She needs to consider changing her appearance in order to locate and conduct surveillance on the Keystone Boys in Clarion. It'll be tough to keep a low profile as a stranger in a small town, especially if you're Pennsylvania's most wanted.

Next, there are the Keystone Boys themselves. Ellen has no idea who they might be, beyond Leanne Spinoza, and possibly her boyfriend, Mitch Logan. She's not even sure what their deal is. Is Leanne involved, or was Logan just using her computer? Is he one of them?

Logan certainly fits a profile — the disaffected soldier who leaves the armed forces and becomes a terrorist. McVeigh, the Oklahoma City bomber, was like that. So was Rudolph, who bombed the '96 Atlanta Olympics. Weaver, from the Ruby Ridge siege, too. But none of those guys were elite soldiers. One way or another, they all washed out or quit the military after a couple years. Logan served for more than a decade. And he wasn't just a marine, he was one of the *best* marines. It's absolutely terrifying that someone with his skill set and experience could be planning an attack.

Even if she's right about him, she has no idea who else might be in the group, or how many of them there are. She could be facing a small army.

She knows she's going in blind, which is against every operational principle she's been taught. But she's on her own with this one, so there's no alternative.

As she drives, she wonders what Logan's motivation is. What his tipping point was. Whether he self-radicalized or was recruited to a cause.

Ellen thinks about the overseas deployments that she and Logan each made to counter foreign terrorism. She thinks about government agencies not listening and screwing over the very people who risked their lives to serve their country. She thinks about Leanne Spinoza and her choices.

And, like she often does, she thinks about Nadia.

*

Paris, five years earlier

"What are you going to do?" Nadia asks her.

They're walking by the river, a couple of miles north of Vitry-sur-Seine, on the Left Bank of the Thirteenth District. They've taken to meeting there — mainly at Nadia's insistence — to avoid being seen together by her husband, Jalil, or anyone who knows him, in their neighborhood.

"We're investigating as fully as possible," Ellen replies, feeling like a fraud before the words have even come out of her mouth.

Nadia stares at her for a long moment before looking away. "I don't want anyone to die," she says, gazing out over the Seine. The water is dark under low clouds that are threatening to burst open on them at any minute.

Ellen doesn't have an umbrella.

"I'll speak to my people," she says.

Only, she knows exactly what *her people* will say. They've said it already, a half-dozen times. When Ellen sent them the intel on Jalil speaking to known arms dealer Moustapha El-Amin about "catering" for a "party" they told her it was ambiguous. *Maybe he is having a party*, her boss, the section chief, had said. *Sometimes a cigar is just a cigar.*

Ellen argued back, pointing out that the online material was supported by human source reporting. *Unevaluated* human source reporting, her section chief countered. She had to agree, but said there wasn't time to fully evaluate Nadia as a source. That this investigation was the evaluation. *There are procedures*, her boss told her, firmly, *and procedures are there to be followed*.

The Agency had been burned by poor intel on WMDs in Iraq, and the world was watching Guantanamo Bay and demanding answers to allegations of special rendition and torture at "black sites". The Global War on Terror had to move slowly, Langley insisted. They weren't risking an international incident, and blowing her cover, as well as revealing the existence of a NOC programme in France, over one young woman's marital problems. Keep developing the asset, they said, and we'll see where it goes.

But Ellen can't tell Nadia any of that.

She can't even reveal that she believes Jalil is trying to buy weapons. That he may already have them.

Instead, she says, "You're doing an incredible job. You just have to keep going. See what else you can find out."

"But the more I push, the more he will suspect me," Nadia says.

"Well, remember the ways we discussed? Asking indirectly, letting him correct a deliberate mistake with new information, that type of thing?"

She nods.

"And, if you get the chance, you might be able to check his phone, in case he's—"

"I'm scared," she blurts. There are tears in her eyes. A few strands of hair have come loose from her hijab and are dancing in the breeze.

Ellen takes her hand. "I know. It's tough. But I promise you, you're doing the right thing."

"Will I be safe?" she asks quietly. She sniffs, wipes her eyes and nose on her sleeve. She needs to know this will be all right.

"Yes," Ellen says, automatically. She can't let Nadia believe there's any question of that, even though she knows it's not in her gift to give such assurance. Then, as if someone else is controlling her speech, she hears herself say, "I promise that you'll be okay, Nadia. I'll make sure you're safe."

"Samir, too?"

"Yes, both of you. You have my word."

It's a promise she can't guarantee to keep.

Nadia literally breathes a sigh of relief. "Thank you," she says.

Ellen nods, smiles, and draws this brave young woman into a hug.

But, inside, she feels sick.

*

Present day

Remembering what happened in France — especially to Nadia and Samir — makes Ellen think of the people she cares for most. Her family.

She imagines her parents, her husband, her *son* watching the news about her this morning. She knows that they won't believe it, because they *know* her, and they know she's not a killer — much less an executioner. But that won't stop it turning their worlds upside-down.

She sees Harry being chased by reporters and cameras as he makes his way to work. Harry, who advised her to stay in the psychiatric ward and follow the process. Not attack a member of staff with a home-made stun gun, steal her clothes and ID badge, and go on the run. He had expressed doubts, while she was committed, about her mental state. Not unreasonably, perhaps, after Paris. But surely he can't believe she'd cold-bloodedly murder a guy in a wheelchair, can he?

She pictures her parents, going out of their minds with worry. Pacing the living room, making calls to everyone they can think of to find out more. She just hopes the media don't discover their address in Doylestown, and descend on the street with their mobile news vans and lights and cameras. Josh would probably think that was pretty exciting, but he wouldn't understand the trouble she was in.

Josh.

She thinks of her son most of all. Left without his mom for almost five days, now. It feels like an eternity to her, with everything she's been through. She wonders if he feels that, too. She yearns to see him, to hold him tight, ruffle his hair and kiss him. Watch those cute dimples light up his little face. Fighting her mother's instinct to go to him takes every ounce of strength she has. She can barely resist it.

Ellen fishes in the grab bag for her burner phone.

Knows that any one of them — Harry, mom, dad, Josh — is just a call away.

And the urge to hear their voices is too much.

She switches it on, telling herself that it'll be harder to track her on the move, especially in a rural area. That she'll just tell them she's okay, that she didn't kill Reyes — if there was even a shred of doubt in their minds about that — and that she'll be back to them really soon. Once she's done what she needs to do, and what no one else seems interested in doing.

Once she's made amends for Paris.

The screen of the cell phone lights up, and two bars of signal appear as it connects to a base station. Out here, that could be miles away. She imagines a police alert being set off, but this is too important. They still won't know where she's going or what she's doing, and she can switch it off again right away, once she's called them.

She picks up the phone one-handed, the other still on the

wheel, and is about to call her parents when the notifications hit the screen:

> *18 missed calls*
> *5 new voice mails*
> *6 new messages*

Ellen taps into the call log and sees that ten of the missed calls are from her parents, along with three of the voice mails and two text messages. Seven calls are from Harry, as well as two voice mails and four texts. She doesn't read or listen to the messages now, because she's got to be quick. She needs to make the call and shut the phone off ASAP.

Then she sees another number in the log.

Unknown.

It's a cell which has sent her the last missed call — twenty minutes ago — with no voice mail, followed by a single text. At first, she thinks it might just be from the network. Something about a payment plan or a special offer. But she knows that's unlikely.

The dread starts to pool in her stomach, like ice water, sending a chill right through her. With a trembling hand, she forces herself to tap into the message.

Her breath catches in her throat for a second as she reads.

Then she screams.

The car veers to the left and she drops the phone, yanking the wheel back to the right with both hands as a truck comes at her, its horn blaring.

"No," she murmurs, "no, no, no, no, no . . ." Over and over, as if the word is an incantation that can undo what she's just read, make it not true. "No!" she yells, slapping a hand on the dash.

She's hyperventilating, she can feel it, and gripping the steering wheel so hard her knuckles are white.

She pulls the car off the road and grabs the cell out of the footwell.

Reads the message once more to make sure she's not hallucinating.

> *If you want to see your son again, call this number.*

And she screams again.

Louder, this time.

30

Clearfield County, Pennsylvania

ELLEN CAN'T BREATHE. She's sucking short gasps of air too quickly and she knows that makes it worse because it means she can't get enough oxygen. She remembers her shrink explaining that to her after Paris, when these kinds of panic attacks happened all the time. She forces herself to count while she inhales and exhales, even as the car interior begins to spin and blur.

At first, she doesn't even get to *one*. She sees her precious boy tied up and scared and not knowing what's going on and it's too much and she thinks she might pass out. The ceiling seems to be pressing down on her, the windows closing in.

Then a little voice in her head says, *I need you, mom*. And that makes the difference.

She counts *one* as she inhales, *one* as she exhales.

Soon enough, one becomes two. Then three.

Eventually, she's breathing in for four, out for four. Nice and steady.

She feels her heart rate slow and the air start to return to her lungs.

The inside of the car doesn't feel like it's suffocating her anymore.

She can breathe again.

She realizes she's broken a sweat, and her legs are shaking a little, too. Her system is still flooded with adrenalin, but she can't wait any longer.

She presses the phone icon to call the unknown number and shuts her eyes.

It's answered immediately.

"You switched off your cell," a male voice says. "I wondered how long it'd take you to check."

Ellen knows right away it's the guy from Reyes's apartment.

The one who murdered her friend.

"Where is my son?" she says, firm and clear.

"He's safe, for now," the man replies, "but that could change, if you don't—"

"Tell me what you've done with him, right now," she cuts in, "or I swear to God I will . . ." She tails off, unsure what she *would* actually do. Back in the apartment, she told herself she wasn't a killer. She switched her phone on partly to tell her family the same thing. But that was before this.

Maybe things have changed, now.

"As I was saying," the man continues, calmly, "unless you do exactly what I tell you, Josh is going to be a very unhappy little boy. I'm going to—"

"You sick bastard!" she blurts into the handset. "You fucking coward! Don't you dare threaten him, you—"

"Don't interrupt me!" he snaps. "Listen carefully, Ellen. If you want Josh to *stay* safe, then you need to come and get him. And by *you*, I mean just you. Alone. Do you understand that?"

"Where have you taken him?" she demands.

"I said, do you understand?"

She knows it's a trap. But this man has the trump card. She tries to swallow, but her mouth is bone dry.

"Yes, I understand. Where?"

"The Poconos," says the guy. "I'll text you the exact co-ordinates when you get closer. I assume you can navigate there, from wherever you are."

Ellen can feel her jaw tighten, her teeth grinding together.

"Be there by six tonight," he adds. "Or we will hurt him."

"You dare—"

"Think about calling the cops or any other agency, and we'll hurt him. Even the slightest hint you're not alone, and we'll hurt him. Have I made myself clear?"

"I swear to God," she growls, "that if you touch one hair on his head, I will fucking kill you."

The words come from somewhere deep inside her. She's not exactly sure where. All she knows is that she means it. She will kill this man if he hurts Josh. And she'll live with the consequences of that.

But the guy just laughs down the line.

"You're not really in a position to be issuing threats like that, Ellen."

"I'm not kidding. I will kill you." There's no doubt in her mind, now.

"You had the opportunity to do that," the man says, "and you didn't take it. You won't get the same chance again, believe me."

Ellen is already thinking about putting a bullet in him. Wishing that maybe she had done it back in Reyes's apartment, while the guy was out cold. Before he could kidnap Josh. She's kidding herself, though. She couldn't have done it, then. Besides, they'd have just sent somebody else.

Then it occurs to her where this guy would have found Josh.

"My parents," she begins, not even sure how to ask the question. If this guy has done anything to them . . .

"They grasped this situation a lot quicker than you," he answers. "They understand that if they reach out to law enforcement, or anyone else for that matter, their grandson will suffer. Unlike you, they did exactly what they were told right away. But they did have a handgun pointing at them." He chuckles.

Once more, Ellen feels the urge to make this guy pay.

She sees him turning up at her parents' place. Pictures them answering the door to him in good faith, maybe thinking that the person knocking was there to tell them something about her. Did he pretend to be a cop, or an old colleague, or someone from the hospital, offering an update on her? She imagines their shock and terror when he pulled out a weapon and began to threaten them. Did they try to stop him taking Josh? Did they think they were going to die?

Ellen's guts tighten, and the bile rises in her throat, leaving a sharp, burning taste at the back of her mouth.

Whichever way she cuts it, she's brought this on them.

She wonders if Harry knows, if her parents have dared calling him with this horrific news, yet.

Then another thought hits her.

The Poconos are a four-hour drive from here, right back the way she came, north of Allentown. If these people suspect she's headed for Clarion, could this be a decoy to pull her away from the Keystone Boys? At the moment, all she has is this guy's word that he's got Josh. Her training starts to kick in: always demand proof of life in a hostage situation. That's what they taught her at The Farm. She just never thought she'd be asking for proof of Josh's life. It makes her even more nauseous, but she forces herself to ask the question.

"How do I know you really have him?"

"You think I'm bluffing?" The man sounds amused.

"Prove you're not. Let me speak to my son."

"I can't do that," he replies.

"I need proof."

There's a brief silence before he responds.

"Okay, then . . ."

She hears footsteps, a door opening, movement. Then a scuffing, shuffling sound.

"Say hello to your mother, Josh."

"Mom!"

It's just one word, but she knows. It's him.

"Josh!" she cries, "I'm coming to get you, sweetie. Be brave, mommy is—"

"He can't hear you," the man says.

Ellen starts to cry, but she tries to keep quiet. She doesn't want to give this bastard the satisfaction.

"Let me say this one more time," he goes on. A door closes in the background. "If you try and screw around, any which way, your little boy is in trouble. You're smart enough not to go to the cops yourself, since you're wanted for murder. But if you call them, or try any of that shit you pulled in the cripple's house when you arrive, then I'm serious when I say your little boy is in trouble."

Ellen composes herself.

"And I'm serious when I say that if anything happens to him, I will kill you."

The guy laughs, and ends the call.

Then the tears come. Ellen allows herself to cry, now, to let it out. Big, heaving sobs, wails, cries of anguish. Kicks and punches to the car interior, hair pulling. It's several minutes before her anger and grief has subsided enough for her to think.

She's so close to Clarion, to the Keystone Boys. To finding out who they are and giving herself the chance to stop whatever they're planning, before it's too late. It's perhaps only two days before their attack. But it's no contest, now.

Whoever is behind this has won the battle. But there's still a war to be fought. And there's no way she's letting Josh or anyone else she loves become a casualty of that war. She swore she wouldn't let that happen.

She starts the engine, puts the car in gear. Pulls out and U-turns in the road.

Then she heads east, to the Pocono mountains.

To go find her son.

END OF PART TWO

PART THREE

PART THREE

31

Centre County, Pennsylvania

THE FIRST CALL Ellen makes is to her parents. She can hear that her mother's crying even before she's spoken.

"Mom!"

"Ellen . . ." her mother begins, but she can't say any more before her words turn into a primeval howl of pain. It's followed by a noise like coughing, but Ellen knows it's the sound of her mother's jagged breathing through tears.

"Mom, are you okay?" she says, loud enough to be heard over the noise of her mother's anguish. "Are you hurt?"

"Honey, I'm . . ." she hiccups, sniffs, swallows, and gasps, "I'm so, so sorry. We couldn't stop him, he had a gun. We let him in, and we shouldn't have, but we thought . . ."

"It's not your fault, mom. I'm the one who's sorry. I should never have put you at risk like that."

"Wh-what do you mean?" her mother asks.

"This is about Harry, isn't it?" her father's voice comes on the line, a little more distant. She must be on speakerphone. "I mean, they warned us when he was elected that this kind of thing could be a possibility—"

"No, Dad, this is on me," Ellen says. "They're doing this to get to me and to stop me. I can't explain everything right now, but it's connected to me getting attacked in Philly, to the commitment order, and to my friend's murder."

"The murder they're saying you're a suspect in?" he asks.

"That's right. My friend. He was in a wheelchair."

She gets a flashback to the apartment, to Reyes, his head dropped forward. The entry wound in the back of his head. The mess on the desk in front of him. A clip from Paris starts to play in her mind. It's the scene she found outside the movie theatre. Blood and bodies and shouting. Her panic rises again. She blinks, tries to focus on the road.

"Ellen?"

"Yeah, I'm here."

"We know you didn't do it, honey," her father says. "We know that."

"Okay, good. That's the truth. Hold on a second."

Ellen is approaching a junction. She checks her GPS, takes the left fork. Little clapboard houses built onto a hillside flash past. The town is so small that if she shut her eyes for thirty seconds, she'd miss it. Yet, she sees not one church, but two. They're the only new-looking buildings around. A message boards outside the larger one reads: *FEED YOUR FAITH & YOUR FEARS WILL STARVE*. Ellen isn't a believer, but it's the advice she needs right now.

She drives on.

"It's the same guy," she explains, "the one who killed my buddy — he's the man who's taken Josh."

"He said that if we reported it to the police," her mother says, "he'd kill Josh. We haven't said anything about it, yet. We only tried to call you, and Harry—"

"Did you speak to him?"

"No. He must've been in a meeting."

"Okay, I'm gonna call him right now. The main thing is that the two of you are okay, right? I mean, you're not hurt."

"We're fine, sweetie," her dad replies. "Just shaken up. And we blame ourselves." His voice cracks at those last words.

"Don't do that. Please. This isn't your fault. It's mine, and the bastards who did this."

"Is there anything we can do?" her mother asks. "Any way we can help?"

"No," she says. "I'm going to deal with this. You guys sit tight. Better yet, go someplace else, in case they come back, or send another guy, now they know where you are."

"All right."

"Do you have somewhere you can go?" she asks.

There's a brief exchange between her parents that she can't make out.

"Mom? Dad?"

"Yes, honey," her mother says. "Your father's cousin is just over the river, in Jersey. We can go there."

"Okay. Don't tell anyone where you are. I may not be able to call again for a little while."

"Are you sure about this?" says her father. "What are you going to do?"

"I'm going to get Josh back," she answers. "I have to do it. It's me they want. And if we go to the cops, they'll hurt Josh."

"Honey . . ."

"They've already killed my buddy, Ricardo. There's no way I'm giving them the chance to . . ." She can't even finish that thought. It's too awful.

"Okay, then," her father says, eventually.

"Be careful, sweetie," her mother adds.

They all know there's no other choice.

"I'll call you when I can," she says. "I gotta go, now. I need to call Harry."

"Ellen," her mother says.

"Yes?"

"We love you."

It's as though a hard lump is rising in Ellen's throat. And the tears are right back in her eyes again. Maybe they never really went away, she only managed to keep them at bay long enough to make the call. Her face is twisting, the muscles straining with the effort of not weeping once more.

"I love you both, too," she manages to say. "Okay, bye."

She hangs up.

*

She calls Harry as soon as she's composed herself again.

"Ellen, is that you?"

"Harry, oh my God! Harry."

"Ellen, what — where are you?"

"They've taken him," she says.

"Who? What are you—"

"Josh. They've taken him."

"*Josh?* Who has?"

"Whoever's trying to stop me. The same people I've been telling you about."

"Jesus Christ. Are you sure?"

"Yes. They snatched him from my folks at gunpoint. You didn't believe me, and—"

"I never said—"

"And now they've killed my friend and kidnapped Josh to get to me. It's real."

"Holy fuck. Is Josh okay? Is he hurt?" Harry asks, urgency in his voice. "What about your parents?"

"I think they're all fine. Traumatized, but unharmed. And these guys seem smart enough not to do anything to our son before I get there."

"Where?"

"The Poconos."

"The Poconos? What the f— Why there?"

"I don't know. That's just where they told me to go if we want to get Josh back. But it makes sense. Isolated location, few people. They can control the ground. Maybe they have a place there. A hideout or whatever, something off-grid."

"Please tell me this is not happening."

"It *is* happening."

There's a moment of silence as Harry processes this. Ellen can hear footsteps, voices echoing in a cavernous space. She guesses he's at work, maybe even in the lobby of The Capitol.

"Ellen, you can't do this alone. It's too dangerous. We have to go to the cops."

"We can't! They said they'd hurt him if we do."

"Oh my God. Are you serious? They actually said that? They threatened our son?"

"And now that I'm wanted for a murder they committed, I can't exactly go to the police anyway."

"I could do it."

"They'd still hurt Josh. They told my parents they'd kill him." It's like a punch to the gut, even saying that out loud.

"They wouldn't . . . They couldn't!"

"They could. Besides, we don't know exactly where he is. It's two and a half thousand square miles. I have to go to the area and get further instructions."

"There has to be some way . . . something we can . . . oh, fuck, this is crazy . . ." Harry tails off into a stream of muttered profanity. He's panicking. He's going through the moment she had right after the call to the kidnapper.

She needs to be the strong one, now.

"Try to stay calm," she tells him. "We'll find a way out of this."

"But . . . what are they going to do to you?" he asks, his breath heavy on the line. "When you get there, I mean."

"I don't know."

Except, she does know. She knows what they'll *try* to do, at least. But she can't bring herself to say that to Harry.

"Ellen, is there someone, you know, from your old work, that we could call? Anyone?"

"They've already killed the only person connected to the Agency I still trusted."

"The guy in Allentown?"

"Yeah."

Almost as a reflex, Ellen checks her rear-view. There's no one there.

"I have to do this alone, Harry."

"But . . . how?"

"I'll think of something."

"Let me come, too," he says. "I'll leave D.C., right now. I can take a cab, just tell me where to go."

"No, Harry," she replies. "It's too dangerous. They could be watching you, for all we know. And if there's a hint anyone else is coming with me . . . you know what they said."

"So, what can I do?"

"There is one thing, actually. In case I don't . . . in case I'm delayed," she corrects herself.

"Name it."

"The group I told you about, Keystone Boys."

"Yes." He doesn't sound sceptical anymore.

"That's why they're trying to stop me. Because I was onto them and whatever they're planning for the Fourth of July. My guess is it's either a mass shooting or a bomb attack, but I don't have any other details yet."

"Okay."

"I need you to do what you can about that, Harry. There's a

woman called Leanne Spinoza, in a town called Clarion, out west in PA. Got that?"

He repeats the details to her.

"Ricardo found out that the reference to Keystone Boys on the dark web came from her computer. She has a boyfriend called Mitch Logan, he's ex-Marine Corps. I think he could be a part of it."

"Okay. So, what do I do?"

"There must be a security person at work. Talk to them. Tell them it's a terrorism threat."

"But what do I say? There's no exact time or place or—"

"I don't know, Harry!" She snaps. "Just fucking tell them. I can't be in two places at once. And while I go rescue our son, I can't let Paris happen all over again somewhere else. Not when I could've stopped it."

"Ellen—"

"And maybe I could have stopped it a whole lot quicker if I hadn't been locked in a psychiatric ward for the past week!"

She takes a breath, realizes the tension is right below the surface.

"Just investigate, please," she says. "See what you can find."

"All right," he replies. "Love you."

"Love you, too. Speak soon," she says, and hangs up.

She needs to conserve the battery on her phone. But, before she puts it on power saving mode, there's one more thing she has to do.

She googles *hardware store*.

She needs some supplies.

32

Clarion, Pennsylvania

PETER FEELS AS though his home has been invaded. Except he has to recognize that this ain't really *his* home. Sure, it is in the sense that he grew up here, still lives here. But it belongs to his parents, as they often remind him. If he made enough money to get his own apartment, he could decide who came over. But he doesn't, so he can't.

Well, if their group gets caught, he'll be spending an awful long time – like, the rest of his life – in his own little place. One where they lock you in for twenty-three hours a day and you shit in a metal toilet next to your bed.

That's if he don't get the needle, of course. Pennsylvania hasn't executed anyone on Death Row in over twenty years, but that doesn't mean they won't. All it takes is a new governor. That scares the hell out of him.

Almost as much as those images of Chernobyl which keep popping into his head.

And there's nowhere he can escape from that.

What should've been a quiet lunch for Peter and his mom has turned into a big, long, awkward meal with unwanted guests.

After Randy accepted the offer of food, Sherman somehow got invited, too. It really sticks in his craw that The German is sat beside him, shovelling in spaghetti and meatballs and making nice with his mom. Randy has been staring at him the entire meal, and Peter knows that The Dozer is now questioning whether he can trust Peter's loyalty.

The one person who could've made this more bearable — Leanne — gave her excuses, saying she needed to go to a dance class. She and Mitch had rowed about that. She'd stormed off and Mitch had been real quiet since. Peter wonders if she'll have new bruises the next time he sees her. He wonders what makes his brother hit her. How long it's been going on. Whether Leanne wants out.

Without her, it's the four of them sat around the table with mom serving up seconds to Sherman and thirds to Randy, while insisting on baking a peach cobbler for dessert. Mom is fussing over them all, except Peter, as if this is the biggest event of the year. Pop isn't here, though. He came home, collected his food in a box, and went back to the auto repair shop. He had time to talk to Mitch, and even Randy, but he didn't say a whole lot to Peter.

Peter tells himself he's ridiculous for getting annoyed by this. He needs to get his priorities straight. He's pissed at sharing his mom's cooking with Sherman when they've just spent the morning going over an attack plan. One that involves murdering any security guards who try to stop them letting off bombs at a nuclear plant, which could kill or maim Lord-knows-how-many more folks.

At that moment, Peter wishes it wasn't happening. He closes his eyes and starts silently praying. If God is out there, up there or wherever, maybe he'll listen.

Maybe he'll do something.

"Pee-Wee, have you gone nuts?" It's Randy.

Peter opens his eyes.

"What in the heck are you doing?" the big man asks.

"Nuthin'."

"Looked like you were praying."

"Well, I wasn't."

"Goddamn freak," mutters Randy. But it's loud and clear enough for them all to hear.

Sherman sniggers.

Mitch is winding spaghetti onto his fork. He seems like he's on another planet.

Peter waits for his brother to step to his defence and say something to Randy.

But, for the first time in a while, he doesn't.

It reminds Peter of what Randy told him earlier.

I'll kill you myself and dump your body in the Clarion River . . . Your brother just said that's fine by him.

"Ma, may I be excused, please?" he asks, even though he's a grown man. It's habit. Same as Mitch sticking up for him. But maybe habits change.

"There's still peach cobbler, Peter," his mother replies.

"Yeah, but—"

"You know the rules," she adds, wagging a finger of warning at him. "If you get down, no dessert."

The others laugh, but she's serious. It's like they're kids all over again.

"Sorry, ma," he says, pushing his chair back and stumbling out of the kitchen.

*

Peter stares at the computer screen in his room as Chad Kroeger's voice rasps away in the background. He's put one of his old Nickelback CDs on the stereo. He could just as easily have played the same songs through YouTube on his PC, but there's something comforting about the old system.

He needs comfort right now.

He's been skipping around a few websites — news, sports stuff, a video game thing, even Pornhub — but not really focussing on any of it. He's been thinking that what they're doing ain't right, and maybe he should be the one to step up and stop it. He's just got no idea how to go about that.

He's not tough enough to confront any of them face-to-face, especially not after what Randy told him this morning. Leanne's the only one who might share some of his doubts about their plan to kill a bunch of people, but she ain't here. And even if she was, he don't suppose she'd say anything to Mitch or Randy or Sherman.

Peter knows he doesn't have the skills or the balls to do anything clever about it, either, like disarm their weapons or fix the bombs — these *EFPs* — so as they don't work.

Which leaves one option if he wants to act: a tip-off.

Or, as most folks call it: snitching.

He glances at the door, hears voices and laughter down the hallway.

Confident no one is near his room, he types *report terrorism* into the search engine, and a bunch of confusing stuff comes up. There's a report about terrorism, from the US State Department. Peter doesn't even know which state the State Department belongs to. Maybe it's Pennsylvania, maybe another one. It's not what he's looking for, though.

Next, there's a recent report in the *New York Times* about terrorism. He clicks into it and reads that last year, for the first time since the 1990s, experts said that *domestic terrorists, particularly far-right groups, pose a greater threat to the United States than foreign adversaries.* Peter looks up the word *adversaries*. It means enemies.

Is that what they are? Enemies of the United States of America?

Well, they're going to blow up an American nuclear plant, in America, and kill American people in the process, so he guesses they are.

Enemies of the state. Like that movie with Will Smith and that other guy, the old white dude who was in everything in the nineties. What was his name?

It doesn't matter, Peter tells himself. He needs to focus on this.

He goes back to the search hits. There are a bunch of tip lines, but he's not sure which one he's supposed to use. There's Pennsylvania State Police, whose website instructs Peter to *say something if he sees something*. Then there's Department of Homeland Security, which has its own tip line. Peter's not sure who they are, though. Then he sees the FBI page. Everyone knows the FBI. He's seen them investigating stuff on the news, as well as on TV shows like *Sleeper Cell*. That was a good show.

Peter throws another glance at his bedroom door.

He clicks on the FBI link.

Follows it to the online tip page. Checks one box to agree he won't hoax them, and a second to show he understands it's a crime to do that. Checks a third box to say he knows he should call 911 if it's an emergency.

Then he stares at the screen, his cursor hovering over the button that says *Next*. Once he's done this, he can't go back on it. He's snitching, including on his own brother. Will they really kill him if they find out?

His finger is trembling above the mouse button, and he feels hot.

Just then, the name pops into his head: *Gene Hackman*.

That's the guy who was in all those films.

Peter's door bursts open.

"Whatcha doin', Pee-Wee?" Randy is filling the doorway, his huge body tensed, like he's ready to attack.

"Nuthin'," Peter stammers, quickly closing a couple of tabs as he turns to face his uninvited visitor.

"What's goin' on?" says Mitch, appearing behind Randy, as the big man walks into Peter's bedroom.

Sherman comes in behind them.

"Let's see about that," Randy says, stomping over to Peter's little desk.

"Hey!" Peter yells, but not all that loud, and pretty soon Randy has the mouse and is looking at the screen. The others follow him in.

"Checking the Pirates schedule?" asks Randy. He sounds real suspicious.

"Uh, yeah. They've got the Brewers this weekend . . ."

"Why're you shaking?"

"I'm not," Peter answers.

"Yes, you are, man," Sherman chips in. "Like a leaf in a hurricane."

Randy tilts his head, stares at Peter. "Did you just close something?"

"No."

"Let's see what you closed, shall we?" Randy right-clicks the mouse and selects "Re-open closed tab".

"It's not what you think," Peter says. He shuts his eyes. Holds his breath.

Hears the laughter.

"So that's what you're hiding," Randy chuckles. "Little pervert."

Peter opens his eyes. Pornhub is on the browser.

The relief is so great, he could almost laugh, too.

"Got me," he says.

He knows that the FBI tip line link will still be in his History, but The Dozer seems satisfied with his discovery.

"All right," Randy says, releasing the mouse and standing up.

"Let's go, so Pee-Wee can finish jerking off. I'm gonna see if there's any more cobbler."

"Me too," Sherman adds.

"I want us all back at my place by fifteen thirty," Mitch announces. "We're going over everything one more time. Then we'll hit the range and put some more rounds down."

Normally, Peter hates shooting. But right now, firing that little Ruger sounds real good to him.

Maybe because he's the one who's just dodged a bullet.

33

White Haven, Pennsylvania

ELLEN GETS TO the location she's been given with ten minutes to spare.

Her GPS shows her that White Haven, the small town she's been brought to, sits at the edge of the Poconos region, a little way south of Wilkes-Barre and Scranton.

She scans her surroundings, trying to orientate herself.

She's in a parking lot on a dirt road beneath the two giant concrete strips of I-80. The highway is running east-west fifty feet above her on huge pillars and Ellen can hear the traffic thundering past overhead.

An information board in the lot tells her that this is the start of the Lehigh Gorge hiking trail. On the way, she'd passed signs for campsites, golf courses and state parks. There's even a ski resort someplace nearby, though she guesses it'll be closed for summer. It's an area of recreation, and the lot and trail are full of people. Couples and families on vacation are coming and going, in vehicles, on mountain bikes and on foot.

But there's no obvious sign of the reason she's here: her son.

There's no sign of the man who took him, either.

Despite what she saw in her Agency career, Ellen's not sure if there's such a thing as evil. It's too simple an explanation for why people do bad stuff. But a guy who murders somebody in a wheelchair and then abducts a kid at gunpoint must be getting pretty close to proving its existence. The thought of him preying on her friend and her son — both vulnerable people — makes her mad as hell. She wants to make him pay.

She tries to put a lid on the anger that's rising inside her and work out what's in the opposition's playbook.

She figures they won't be here, because it's too busy. This is probably just a waypoint in the scavenger hunt this bastard is sending her on to find her son. She guesses he's picked a secluded spot to take Josh, maybe a cabin out of town. Somewhere he can lure her on her own, with no witnesses. You wouldn't have to go far around here to find a place like that. Between the campsites and outdoor activity spots, it's just forest for miles and miles.

She knows the guy will try to kill her. Whoever is behind this has already tried twice, and twice she's gotten away. They're not going to let that happen a third time, which is why the guy is making her come to him.

She has no choice, not now he has Josh. She's got to do exactly what he tells her.

Her only chance is to catch him off-guard.

And she has an idea how to do that.

She calls the guy.

"You took your time," he says. "Your little boy was starting to think his mom had abandoned him."

Ellen doesn't believe that. "I made a few wrong turns," she lies, looking at the stuff she's spent part of the last hour buying. It's all sitting in plastic bags on the passenger seat and in the footwell beside her. Everyday items bought from a hardware store, a 7-Eleven and a gas station, paid for in cash with her ballcap pulled low and a hygiene mask from her grab bag over her nose and mouth.

"But I'm here now," she adds. "I've done what you asked. Where is my son?"

"We'll get to that. First, what color is the sign at the entrance to the parking lot?" he asks.

She cranes her neck to see. "White."

"And how many porta johns are in the lot?"

She looks around her. "Uh, two."

He's checking she is where he wants her to be. Making sure he's in control.

For a second, she wonders if he *is* here, and a shiver runs through her. She turns her head left and right, checks her mirrors. Can't see him.

"Okay," he says. "I'm going to send you co-ordinates. Go there, right now, and call me back."

"Where is my son?"

"He's here. And the sooner you get here, the sooner you can see him. Be here by six thirty. And don't make us wait. You know what'll happen if you do. Same goes if you bring backup. But you wouldn't be that stupid, would you?"

He clicks off.

Ellen stares at her cell phone for what feels like an hour, but is probably no more than a minute. Eventually a text arrives. It's longitude and latitude, same format as the first pair of numbers that led her here. She types them into the GPS. It's almost twenty miles east of where she is now. It'll take her a half hour to get there, depending on the roads.

She briefly thinks of the Keystone Boys, somewhere out west, making their preparations. All the while, she's getting farther away from them, and the window to stop them is getting smaller. She doesn't even know what they're planning to attack. But these assholes knew where to hit her hardest when they took Josh, and it's worked. She just hopes Harry will be able to do something with the information she's given him in the meantime.

Then another thought occurs to her.

The guy said, *us*. He said *don't make* us *wait*. Plural.

There's more than one of them.

*

On the way out of White Haven, Ellen passes a baseball field where some kids are playing. They look about Josh's age, and it reminds her of what her son should be doing on a warm summer evening — being outside with his friends, without a care in the world.

She recalls Josh and Harry tossing the ball between them in the backyard on a Sunday afternoon, two weeks ago, before all this started. She sees Josh catching with the mitt she and Harry gave him for his sixth birthday, his tongue poking out in concentration as he tracks the ball arcing through the air and into his glove. She hears her dad telling them the kid's got a hell of an arm on him for a six-year-old. Power and accuracy, a rare combination at that age. That he should think about pitching when he gets to Little League.

Those memories bring it right back to Ellen just how fucked up this all is. How much she misses her boy and her husband and her parents. How Josh is in danger, and she's the one who put him there and it's her fault this is happening to them. She starts thinking that maybe Harry was right. That maybe she should have let him go to the cops, despite the threats. That maybe what she's doing right now is madness.

That she'll get herself killed and they'll bury her in the woods out here, and that Josh . . .

Oh God, Josh. Her beautiful boy. Her baby.

Tears run down her cheeks. She wipes them away with her sleeve as she tries to get her shit together and concentrate on where the GPS is telling her to go. She digs deep, forces herself to focus.

A few minutes later, she's pulled through the moment of doubt. Her training is starting to kick in again, now.

She's got her game face on. There's a job to do.

She switches gears.

Gives it some gas.

*

State Game Lands Number 127, Monroe County, Pennsylvania

Ellen reaches the second waypoint bathed in sweat and with her heart beating at a hundred miles an hour, but slightly ahead of time. She's driven the Camry like it's a racing car in order to give herself a few minutes before her deadline to recce the location. And each of those minutes could make the difference between life or death.

Her life, Josh's life.

She cuts the engine and rolls to a stop on the single-lane road. The co-ordinates they gave her are a little way farther down, at what looks like the entrance to a track. She guesses there's a building at the end of it.

She needs to work quickly.

It takes her three minutes to rig up the firebomb, or improvised incendiary device — IID, as the military would call it. The core of her home-made munition is a can of gasoline. She's taped aerosol cans to it, to act as igniters. Then she cuts a length of twine and soaks it in the gasoline, to act as a fuse. Her problem is the timing. She can't set it off right away, because she needs to be somewhere she can see Josh when it blows.

So, she's used an old trick she learned at The Farm to create the delay — a bunch of cigarettes taped together into a cylinder.

They'll burn at around one inch every five minutes, so Ellen wraps the twine two inches below the tips and secures it all with tape.

Then she gets out of the car, closes the door quietly and sets off into the woods, carrying her makeshift device.

She moves as silently as possible in a semi-circle around the track until she can see the building.

It's an A-frame wooden cabin, built at the back of a clearing in the trees. There are steps leading up to a deck at the front, where a pair of glass doors give a full view onto the track. A Ford SUV is parked outside. She can't see anyone, but she guesses they're watching from inside.

She keeps moving.

At the rear, there's a small plot of ground between the cabin and the woods. Her plan is to put the device as close to the building as she can and set the fuse burning. When it goes up, it should create just enough of a diversion to let her attack.

Then she sees the propane tanks.

A pair of them, maybe ten gallons each, standing against the side wall, beneath a small window.

It makes sense, needing your own fuel supply all the way out here.

And it's just given her a better idea.

She creeps around until she's as close as possible to the tanks.

Takes a deep breath.

Then moves fast and low across the few yards of open ground until she's at the building. She's got her back to the wall and the window is above her.

She tries not to think about the fact that Josh is somewhere inside. She feels the urge to call out to him, to tell him that mommy's here and it's going to be okay. But she has to keep silent. Surprise is the only thing that's going to save him.

She empties most of the gasoline onto the tanks and the soil around them. Lays the can on its side between the tanks, the aerosols still taped to it.

The whole thing is a pressure cooker ready to go.

She unspools enough twine so as not to ignite the fuel immediately, and uses a lighter to set the cigarettes burning. Sets a timer for ten minutes on her watch.

Then she retreats into the trees and hustles right back the way she came.

She's breathless when she reaches the car.

It's exactly six thirty.

She makes the call.

34

State Game Lands Number 127, Monroe County, Pennsylvania

THE RING TONE seems to go on for a lifetime. Ellen wonders if she's made a mistake. If she was late, even by a minute, and whether Josh—

The guy picks up.

"Right on time," he says.

Ellen gives a silent sigh of relief. "Now what?" she asks, though she has a pretty good idea what comes next.

"You're at the entrance to the track?"

"Yes."

"Leave your car and advance up it on foot, slowly, with your hands raised. If you were dumb enough to bring a weapon, empty it and carry it over your head."

"Okay," she says. She anticipated they'd take the gun off her. But she's hoping the guy has forgotten about his Ka-Bar knife. The one he left behind in Reyes's apartment. The blade he stabbed her with, that gave her the hip wound she feels every time she moves.

"Start walking," he instructs her.

Then he ends the call.

She slides the Ka-Bar up the back of her sports bra, handle down, so it nestles between her shoulder blades. The thick elastic of the bra holds it tightly in place. If she tips her head back slightly, she can feel the point of the Ka-Bar at the nape of her neck.

She opens the car door and gets out.

Prays that her Plan A will work.

Because there is no Plan B.

*

Ellen isn't prepared for the sight that meets her at the end of the track.

She recognizes her boy from a hundred yards away.

Josh is standing on the decking. There's duct tape over his mouth and his arms are behind his back. She guesses his hands are bound. He's trembling and the dark patch around his crotch shows that he's peed his pants not long ago. It's absolutely horrific seeing her son like this. The only halfway good thing is that he doesn't look hurt.

Behind him, at least two feet taller than her son, is a man. Even at a distance, Ellen is certain he's the guy who murdered Reyes. There's no mask this time. As she gets a little closer, she can see the livid bruising on his face and neck, from where she hit him with a laptop. It's definitely the same guy.

Josh's eyes widen as he sees her.

She can't help but yell his name.

"Josh! Baby, it's me! It's Mommy!" she cries, picking up her pace to a jog. "I'm coming, sweetie."

The gunshot makes her freeze.

It echoes around the trees and sends a group of birds scattering into the sky.

For one awful second, she thinks he's shot Josh. Then she realizes he's pointing the pistol in the air. Just a warning shot, although it was close enough to Josh that all he'll be able to hear right now is a high-pitched tone.

"What did I tell you?" the guy calls to her. "Advance *slowly*. Or the next one goes in the back of his head." He turns the gun on Josh.

"All right, just . . . please, don't—" she calls back, the words catching in her dry throat. "You're the boss."

Josh makes a whimpering sound and screws his eyes shut.

This is more than Ellen can take, but she has to play along. For a little longer.

"Show me your weapon is empty," the guy barks. "Slow, remember."

With the barrel pointing upward and her forefinger outside the trigger guard, Ellen draws the slide all the way back and locks it. She rotates the pistol to show there's no magazine inside.

"Place it slowly on the ground," he says. "And toss the mag, too."

She does as instructed, dropping the magazine she was holding in her left hand.

"Show me your waist and ankles," he tells her.

He wants to make sure she doesn't have another gun concealed on her. She lifts her t-shirt a couple of inches above her belt and does a three-sixty, then raises the legs of her pants above her sneakers.

"All right," he says, apparently satisfied. "Keep moving."

She's maybe fifty yards away, now.

She wonders how her time-delay fuse is doing. If it's still even alight.

Up ahead, the guy calls something toward the open door of the cabin. A moment later, another man steps out.

The first thing Ellen sees is the submachine gun this second guy is holding. This far off, she can't tell exactly what type it is.

Maybe a Sig MPX or a Heckler & Koch MP5. It doesn't really matter. The most important detail is that it's now two guns versus none. And this new one is trained on her.

As she looks past the weapon and at the man, she realizes she's seen him before. He's the guy from Philly. The punk who tailed her and then drew his weapon on her at Independence Hall, right before she broke his finger and dropped him with a kick to the balls.

Michael John Smith. Or, at least, that's what his phoney ID said.

That makes two guys who probably want to kill her.

And two guys she wants to kill.

She glances at Josh.

Keeps walking.

*

Ellen makes a subtle check of her watch. It's been eight minutes since she set the fuse burning. She needs to buy another couple of minutes.

As she approaches the cabin, she tries to take in a few more details about it. Behind the SUV out front, she can see a grit bin on the corner of the building. There's a light on inside the cabin, and an internal door about halfway back. She guesses there are two rooms inside, most likely a living room at the front, kitchen and bathroom at the back. The beds are probably on a mezzanine level just below the pitched roof.

She's about twenty yards away from them, now. Taking one slow step at a time, her palms raised in submission.

"It's going to be okay, baby," she tells Josh.

He gives a muffled cry through the tape over his mouth. So, he can hear her a little, at least, after the gunshot.

"Shut up," the first guy says.

Ellen figures he's the one in charge.

"You can let him go, now," she responds. "Please, just let him go. It's me you want."

The first guy says something to the second.

She can't catch it, but the second guy nods in response and pats his jeans pocket. Ellen takes a few more steps and sees some strips poking out of the pocket. They look like cable ties, probably the same as they've put on Josh's wrists. If they get those on her, it's game over.

"Let him go," she pleads.

The first guy snorts a laugh. His head turns left, then right, taking in the wilderness enveloping them. "Where's he gonna go?"

Ellen knows he's right. There's no way Josh is getting out of here without her, or one of those guys, taking him — if their plan is to let him leave at all. The thought of that makes her pulse pound at her temple and her stomach knot.

"At least stop pointing your gun at him," she says. "Then I'll tell you what I know."

The guy doesn't move. "You can tell me what you know right now," he says.

She's ten yards out.

"He's just a kid," she protests, advancing toward the decking. She's easily in his firing range, now. But she needs to be even closer.

"Can you smell cigarettes?" the second guy says. He sniffs the air.

"Cigarettes?" the first guy queries. He lifts his nose, like a wolf scenting prey.

"It's stronger over here," the second guy adds, hooking a thumb toward the side of the cabin.

"You leave a smoke burning?"

"No. Obviously."

"You sure about that?"

"Yeah."

"Go check."

The second guy huffs, then lowers the submachine gun which he's been aiming at Ellen since he came out of the cabin. He walks around the side of the building and disappears from sight. He's going to find her device.

She returns her attention to the first guy while she waits for the inevitable. Closes the distance between them a little more.

"Hey!" the second guy calls.

"What?" yells the first.

But the second guy doesn't have time to reply.

The explosion rips through the stillness of the forest.

It's followed by a scream, and a hissing sound.

Ellen can see a jet of flames rising above the height of the eaves.

She looks back to the first guy. He's taken a step away from Josh and his whole body is turned toward the explosion.

She doesn't hesitate.

She reaches up into the back of her t-shirt, grasps the handle of the Ka-Bar. Draws it from the elastic strap of her bra.

Adjusts her grip slightly, takes aim at the first guy's back.

Imagines there's a bullseye right over his spine.

And lets the knife fly.

35

State Game Lands Number 127, Monroe County, Pennsylvania

Ellen watches as the Ka-Bar rotates in the air.

It seems to move in slow motion. One turn. Two turns.

Then it hits.

The blade sinks into the guy's back and his body bucks as if he's been shot. His arms shoot up and the pistol clatters to the decking as he staggers, trying to stay upright. He manages a few steps. Then he falls, face first.

Ellen takes her chance.

She lunges forward onto the decking and grabs the pistol. She pushes Josh towards the left side of the cabin, away from his abductor. Tucks the pistol into her belt.

Then she pulls the knife from the guy's back and, quickly but carefully, cuts the cable tie at her son's wrists. He half-peels, half-yanks the duct tape off his own mouth.

"Get in the grit box there, honey," she whispers to him. "I'll come find you."

He nods. There are tears in his eyes and he's shaking.

"Go, now," she says, physically guiding him away from her.

It's against both of their instincts to be separated. But Ellen needs to finish this.

She moves back across to the guy. He's still face down, bleeding. But he's writhing, trying to get up.

"You fucking bitch," he growls.

She kicks him back to the decking and steps on the wound. He yells out.

"This is for Ricardo Reyes," she says, kneeling beside the guy. He flaps a hand, clawing at the air. He manages to grab her leg. But he's too late.

She plants the Ka-Bar right in his kidney. Pulls it out.

He roars in pain.

"And this for my son." She stabs him again, hard and deep, through the ribcage. Leaves the knife embedded in his back.

There's a lot more blood now. It's seeping out of his torso and into the gaps between the wooden boards around him.

She stands and draws the pistol. Takes aim at the back of his head.

This is what he did to Reyes, she tells herself. *Do it.*

To her left, she hears Josh climbing into the bin and closing the lid.

Then she hears another noise. It's coming from the back of the cabin.

Movement.

She looks inside the glass doors. Can't see anything in the living room.

Creeping to the right-hand edge of the decking, she listens. Then whips around the side of the building, pistol raised.

There's no one there.

The propane tanks and gasoline can are still on fire, but the flames have died down now that the pressurized gas has burned off.

Ellen steps carefully onto the ground, aware of her shoes

crunching on the pebbles strewn in the dirt as she tries not to lose her footing on loose stones.

Keeping as close to the cabin as she can, she goes all the way to the back. Waits. Hears nothing.

She makes the same quick move around the corner, gun raised.

The guy isn't there.

But the back door is ajar.

She checks that the pistol she took off the first guy is still loaded. It is. She's about to move toward the door when all hell breaks loose.

Tat-at-at-at-at-at.

A flurry of bullets bursts out of the back wall of the cabin, splintering the wood. The noise is deafening.

Ellen throws herself to the ground and covers her head.

The barrage continues for several more seconds.

When it stops, she can barely hear herself think over the ringing in her ears, but she looks up. Sees that the first round to come through missed her by inches. The guy went too soon.

Ellen gets back up as quietly as she can. She guesses he's re-loading, then either he'll fire some more, or he'll come out to check.

She slips across the back wall to the far side of the door.

Moments later, the submachine gun muzzle pokes through the crack in the door. Followed by the hands holding it, and the rest of the guy. He's breathing loudly, almost gasping for air.

"Don't move," she says.

But he does move.

*

The submachine gun swings around toward her. There's no time to do anything but act instinctively.

Ellen kicks out at the door between them. It slams into the guy, knocking him off-balance.

Then she fires through the door, one round after another.

She thinks she's hit him, but she can't be sure.

Holding the pistol in her right hand and keeping it pointed in front of her, she reaches forward with her left hand and slowly draws the door back, stepping away as it swings toward her.

The guy is down.

He's looking vacantly up at her, his face red and blistered where she guesses the propane tank explosion caught him. He's still holding his gun but bleeding from at least three bullet wounds in his chest. He sucks in a breath.

Tightens his grip on the gun.

Ellen doesn't hesitate.

She shoots him again. And again, and again.

This time, she doesn't stop until she's certain he's dead, pumping round after round into his body.

Then there's silence.

She's panting, her heart a bass drum in her chest. She lets her arms fall slack at her side as she stares at him.

The man who tailed her through the streets of Philly is dead.

She killed him.

The reality hits her.

She's *killed* someone.

She's never done that before. She knew it was a possibility when she came here. She even told the other guy on the phone that she'd kill him. Her training at The Farm should have prepared her for it. But she wasn't sure she had it in her, not until now. She guesses you never know until the moment comes.

And that was the moment. It's one she's certain will stay with her for the rest of her life. Just like that scene outside the movie theatre in Paris.

Part of her knows she needs to go. To get Josh out of the grit box, get them back to her car, get back on the road. But she can't move. She's rooted to the spot, transfixed by this human body whose life is no more. Because of her.

He deserved it, she tells herself. He would have killed her and most likely he would've killed Josh, too.

Then a noise gets her attention, and she snaps out of her trance.

"Josh?" she calls. But even as she says his name, she realizes the approaching footsteps are too heavy.

The first guy drags himself around the back wall of the cabin. He's hurt bad, but on his feet, somehow. And he's holding her gun, the one he made her leave on the track. He starts to raise it.

Ellen whips the pistol in her hand up to firing position, sees the slide already locked back.

She's out of ammo.

She freezes as the guy takes aim.

"No!" she cries.

He closes one eye.

Then his head snaps around and he stumbles forward, fires into the trees, and drops.

The rock hits the ground beside him a half-second later.

"Mom!" yells Josh from the side of the cabin.

"Stay back!" Ellen shouts at him.

The guy her son just took out with a well-aimed rock is stunned, but conscious. Still moving.

She dives to the floor, right by the guy she's just shot dead. Snatches the submachine gun from his limp hands, then rolls left into a prone position and aims.

The other guy is lifting his pistol again.

Ellen fires. Hits him right between the eyes.

He slumps to the earth.

Stops moving.

"Josh!" she calls out.

"Mom!"

"Stay where you are, sweetie," she tells him. But she's too late.

Josh is already running to the back of the cabin, where two corpses are sprawled on the ground, one riddled with bullet holes and other with a dagger still stuck in his back. It's a sight no one should ever have to witness, much less a six-year-old. Her son stops and stares at the carnage, just like she was a moment ago.

"Get back, Josh, don't look!"

She races across to the second body, the guy with the Ka-Bar handle sticking out of his back, and takes her pistol off him. She's pretty sure he's dead, too, after she shot him in the head, but she checks the pulse at his artery, just to be certain.

She's right. He is dead.

She lays the submachine gun down and moves quickly around the corner of the cabin to where Josh is crouching.

"Come here, sweetie," she says. "It's over, now."

She pulls him into a big hug, wrapping her arms around him and holding on tight.

"It's okay, you're safe," she whispers, stroking his hair. She feels her tears start to flow at the relief. "I told you to stay in the grit box," she says. "Why didn't you stay in there?"

"He was gonna shoot you," Josh gasps. "I saw him go get your gun, and I had to stop him . . ."

"You saved my life, sweetie." Ellen smiles at him, her lips trembling. She squeezes his little bicep. "Your grandpa was right. You have got a hell of an arm."

She just wants to keep her little boy close to her like this. But they have to go. She doesn't know who might have heard the propane explosion and the gunshots. No one could mistake those noises for the sound of hunting.

And another thought has already occurred to her.

She needs to be dead.

Ellen releases Josh from what might be the biggest hug she's ever given him.

"Wait here a second," she says, guiding him up the side of the cabin. "Promise me you won't go back there."

"I promise."

She jogs over to the guy who was in charge, squats down and searches his pockets. Finds the cell phone. It's locked. She checks it, sees a fingerprint sensor. Forces herself to take the guy's hand. It's warm. She wipes the blood off his index finger as best she can and presses the tip to the sensor. Nothing happens.

She wipes it off again, tries once more.

The screen lights up.

She spends a few moments gathering what intel she can from the logs.

Then she sends a text message.

Finally, she leaves the phone with the guy's body and goes back to Josh.

"Let's get out of here," she says.

36

PETER IS BACK in his room, and this time he's sure he's alone. After the run-through at Mitch's place, and the session down at the gun range, the Keystone Boys have gone their separate ways for the evening.

Mitch went back to his apartment, with Leanne. They'd rowed about her teaching a kids' dance class when Mitch said she should be focussing on tomorrow night. Leanne had argued back that they needed to keep things looking normal, in case they were being watched. Mitch asked why anyone would be watching them. Whether she'd been shooting her mouth off online again. She swore at him and said that she needed the money for the class, anyway. He'd said they had money, thanks to the guy helping them and, besides, she wasn't even paying any rent to live in his apartment. So, she didn't need to teach class. They went back and forth like that, and Mitch called her selfish and dumb for putting herself out there and taking risks. Peter piped up to say he had a shift at the gas station tomorrow on his own, but Mitch just said that was different and told him to shut up. All the hollering had made Peter stay a little longer, figuring that him being there somehow protected Leanne. He didn't like to think about what might happen to her when he had to go home.

What might be happening to her right now.

Randy had gone over to the tavern to shoot pool, drink beer and — if Peter had to bet on it — try to catch Angie the barmaid's eye. The Dozer was under instructions from Mitch not to get wasted. But liquor seems to be the big man's way of dealing with stress right now.

Sherman had gone, too, off on his ownsome to do God-only-knows-what. Most likely reading that Nazi bullshit he loves so much and talking shit in chatrooms.

Peter's mom and pop are watching TV, separately. Probably both asleep. They won't bother him.

So, he finally has the place to himself.

And he's right back where he was this afternoon.

On the FBI's anonymous tips website.

One page further along than earlier. The page where you say what you want to report. There's a big empty white box on the screen and Peter is just staring at it. Thinking about what it means to fill it out.

What it means *not* to fill it out.

He's got Chad Kroeger on the stereo again. The track is *Hero*. It ain't a Nickelback song, it's a duet he did with Josey Scott, who's a dude, even though his name sounds like a girl's. They're singing about the world being saved by a hero.

It's the theme from an old Spider-Man movie — the 2002 reboot, directed by Sam Raimi, that was just called *Spider-Man*. Peter loved that movie. The Toby Maguire ones are his favourites in the franchise. They had Kirsten Dunst as Mary-Jane, the woman Peter Parker has had a crush on since he was a kid. Peter Parker, the ordinary, average guy who nobody, including Mary-Jane, really notices.

Peter can identify with that. It's kind of like him and Leanne.

But, in the comic books and the movies, Peter Parker gets bitten by a mutant spider and develops special powers.

He becomes a superhero.

Then Mary-Jane notices him.

Peter don't have no special powers. He ain't much good at anything, truth be told.

But he does have a chance to be a hero, now.

To save a whole lot of people.

To be noticed by Leanne.

This is his time.

He starts typing.

Sir

Then he thinks, what if it's a woman who reads it? He deletes, Sir, and writes:

Who may be concerned

He doesn't know if that's right. So he deletes it, too. *Get to the point*, he thinks. He types:

My brother and his buddies are

Then he realizes it's supposed to be anonymous. He tries again:

Theres a group called Keystone Boys and they gonna attack a newclear power plant on July forth at midnight. Its the one out on three mile iland in PA. They have bombs like the ones from Irak. Dont ask me how I no this cos I just do. Please stop them or a lotta people gonna die like in Chernobil on the TV. Theres Mitch and Randy and Sherman

He sits back and reads what he's written. The words are okay, but he can't believe he's actually doing this. Snitching on his brother. Then he wonders if he should put Leanne in there. She's in the group, but he don't want to get her in trouble. And should he put his own name down? He don't want to get in trouble either, but it'd look weird if he didn't write his own name and then the cops asked Mitch and Randy and Sherman who else is in the group.

He needs to think about this.

Chad is still growling in the background about that hero.

Peter wonders, for about the hundredth time today, what'll happen to him if he does this. Surely the others will know it was him. Will they kill him? Will The Dozer come for him with that big old Remington pump action and blow a hole the size of a baseball right through him?

And would Mitch just let it happen? Maybe. He recalls how cold his brother was when he came for breakfast yesterday. Peter has to face it – if he does this, their relationship is over. He'll lose the only real friend he's ever had in his life. The thought of that makes him feel lonely.

Then something else occurs to him.

What if they think it's Leanne who snitched, and she's the one they murder and throw in the Clarion River? Peter couldn't let that happen. No way. Not Leanne.

He realizes his leg is jiggling up and down like he's got ants in his pants.

He doesn't know what to do.

He's damned if he does, damned if he don't.

He deletes the message. Closes the web browser.

As Chad's song finishes, he stares at the wallpaper on his computer screen. It's a photo of him and Mitch. They're both grinning like a couple of idiots, beers in hand, drunk on Peter's twenty-fifth birthday. Mitch got leave and came home from Afghanistan, surprised him. It was one of the happiest days of Peter's life. Only, now he looks at the picture, he's not sure he recognizes his brother anymore. He thought his brother was a hero.

But Peter guesses he ain't no hero, either.

He's too scared.

*

Washington D.C.

He's still at work when the burner phone rings in the drawer of his bureau. Only two people have that number, and he can guess which one of them is calling him right now.

"Look, I've gotta go," he tells the person on his office line, a junior colleague trying to resolve some diary clash over his meeting schedule next week. "Let's do this on Monday, okay?"

He hangs up without waiting for a reply. *Monday.* So much will have changed by then. He yanks the desk drawer open, snatches the cell phone.

"Talk to me," he says.

"It's done," the kid tells him.

"Done?"

"Yup. The threat has been neutralized." The little prick sounds like he's speaking from some military command center after a drone strike. Playing God, which is exactly who he wants to be. Maybe who he thinks he already is.

"'Neutralized'? The fuck does that mean?"

"It means the threat isn't a threat anymore," the kid replies.

"Can you be a little more specific, for Christ's sake?"

"That's all I know." He can almost hear the shrug on the other end of the line. The self-satisfied withholding of information. Another bullshit power-play. "Their words," the kid adds, "not mine."

"Well, find out more."

The young man gives a light-hearted chuckle. "I mean, I can

ask, if you want. But that's not how these people work. They're professionals. They have their own ways of doing things."

"You're the one paying them, aren't you?" His voice is getting louder.

"Obviously."

"So, ask them what the hell 'neutralized' means, will you?" He slams a fist on the desk in frustration.

The kid sighs. "Fine. As a favor to you."

Favor? How about I do you a favor by not tearing you a new asshole? he thinks. But he knows better than to say that, pissed as he is.

Instead, he says, "Quick as you can." Hears the desperation in his own voice.

The kid ends the call.

He thinks he's going to throw up. This suddenly got a whole lot more real. Up until that call, he could have told himself it'd all be okay.

Now he knows it's very much not okay.

It's absolutely fucking terrible.

He'd stuck his head in the sand for months, convinced himself they'd be making a point, that was all. It wasn't a point with which he agreed, but his opinion didn't count. He'd told himself no-one would get hurt, that he was actually protecting the people he loved. Repeated that like a mantra, over and over, until part of him actually bought it. The truth is that the only person he was protecting was himself.

Did he really think that violence wouldn't be a part of it? Death? Murder? Well, now it very likely is. All of the above.

And he has to live with the consequences of his actions.

But he doesn't even know how to begin doing that.

It's like that sadistic experiment with the frog in a pan of cold water on the stove. It starts heating up, little by little, with no concept that eventually it'll boil to death. By the time the heat reaches the point that its pain is too much to bear, the frog can't move. It's trapped.

That's how he feels right now.

The water in his pan is about a hundred and ninety degrees and getting hotter by the minute. It hasn't killed him yet, but it will do soon.

The act that lit the flame underneath him was the deal he did with The Devil years back. He took dirty money from bad people to try to help good people who really needed it. At the time, he thought he was doing the right thing.

Evidently, he was wrong.

There's no going back from any of this. And he can't see a way out.

He only becomes aware he's crying when the salty tears reach his lips.

He gets up, crosses to the large window. Looks down at the street, four storeys below. The traffic, the people going about their business, oblivious.

He opens the window.

Climbs up onto the sill.

37

"IT SMELLS FUNNY in here," Josh says.

They're the first words her son has spoken since they left the cabin in The Poconos.

Ellen snaps out of the trance she's been in for the past half-hour. She's been driving steadily, trying to concentrate on not breaking the speed limit. The last thing she needs is to be pulled over.

She's still trembling a little from the adrenalin dump back in the woods as she fought for both her life and Josh's. Still seeing the images. The impact of the knife in the first guy's back. The glassy-eyed death mask of the second guy, after she shot him through the door. The moment where the first guy raised his pistol and she realized she was out of ammo. It was all so crazy that none of it feels real yet.

But it was real.

And she knows that Josh saw most of it, too. She has no idea how a six-year-old is supposed to process a scene like that. Right now, he's acting like he's just shut down. And she recognizes that response.

Her old therapist told her that, when some people are in a life-or-death situation, they do the human equivalent of animals playing dead. It's called *dissociation*. Your body is in one place, but your mind is somewhere else entirely. It's beyond fight-or-flight, a defence against trauma that's both overwhelming and inescapable.

She hopes she can help him out of it.

"Uh, well," Ellen says, clearing her throat, "that's just a little gasoline I spilled, sweetie. Open the window some more."

He lowers the window beside him, and the breeze makes his hair fly up off his forehead. He closes his eyes.

Ellen wonders what he's picturing.

She had asked him right away if he'd been hurt, and he said no. He'd just been scared, so much that he'd lost control of his bladder. Ellen took his pants off when they got to the car — it was warm enough without them and a whole lot more comfortable. She still thinks she should get him checked out by a doctor, but she doesn't know where she's going to find one when she's on the run.

Not to mention wanted for murder.

She wonders how long it'll be before someone notices their mercenaries are missing.

Before someone finds their bodies.

"Are you hungry?" she asks. Taking her eyes off the empty road for a second, she rummages in the grab bag, pulls out an energy bar. It's her last one. "You can have this if you want."

He opens his eyes, looks at her offering. Shakes his head.

"You not hungry? I think there's some potato chips in the back . . ."

"Uh-uh." He shakes his head some more.

"Okay. Well, we have snacks if you change your mind."

Josh doesn't reply.

"I know this is awful, sweetie. But we'll get through it. We'll be okay, I promise."

She's not in much of a position to promise anything.

There's still a-ways to go before they're safe.

*

Ellen checks her GPS. They're making good progress away from The Poconos, but she needs a plan.

When she and Josh first drove away from the cabin, Ellen's only concern had been putting distance between them and the two bodies she'd left behind. Now she has to work out what comes next.

She figures she's bought some time by sending a text to the contact of the dead men from the lead guy's cell phone. They were listed only as 'C'. She noted the number, then messaged to say that the *threat had been neutralized*. Hopefully, it's enough to let whoever 'C' is think that the mission to stop her has been accomplished.

Now, though, with the adrenalin and endorphins wearing off, she's starting to realize how totally exhausted she is. The craziest week of her life — maybe along with Paris — has taken its toll on her. She can't run on empty much longer.

If she's to stand a chance of finding and stopping the Keystone Boys, she needs to rest, eat a proper meal, rehydrate, and fix her hip wound, which has started bleeding again. And a hot shower would be nice.

Josh needs all of that, too, not to mention a proper medical examination. Probably a session with a psychologist.

But where the hell can she find a place to recharge in rural Pennsylvania, when her face is all over the TV and internet, her name in every news bulletin on the radio?

She's driven another five miles or so before the answer comes to her. She read a piece in a magazine, not long ago, about the concept of "digital detox". And one of the ideas it mentioned might just work.

She has to do a little searching on her phone and with the GPS, but then it's only thirty miles more until they reach the destination she has in mind.

Ellen stops the car at the entrance, reads the sign to make sure she's got the right place.

Verdant Hollow Bed & Breakfast

That sounds good. But it's the line underneath that seals it for her.

Amish Farm and Guesthouse

*

"Here you go," says the young woman, placing the plate in front of Ellen on the large wooden dining table.

Ellen is starving and the home-cooked meal of pork chops with apple sauce, mash and greens had her salivating before her host had even brought it out of the kitchen.

"Thank you," she says, and digs in immediately.

In their small, twin-bed room upstairs, Josh is fast asleep. He crashed out pretty much as soon as he lay down on the thick quilt.

"Do you need anything else?" her host asks. She's wearing a navy-blue dress, and a little white bonnet is perched on her head. It's an outfit that probably hasn't changed one bit in three hundred years.

"Just some water, please," Ellen replies, her mouth already full.

"Of course."

"What's your name?" asks Ellen.

"Sarah."

"Pleased to meet you, Sarah."

"You, too."

"And thank you so much for this. Really."

"You're welcome." Sarah blushes and heads back to the kitchen.

Ellen and Josh's unannounced, night-time arrival had under-standably caused quite a stir for the Hershberger family. The father, Jebediah, had stared at the pair of them with a hint of suspicion, stroking his long brown beard, as they first checked in. Ellen didn't blame him. Smeared with dirt and blood and stinking of gasoline, urine and gunshot residue, with just one rucksack between them, they probably looked more like wartime refugees than holidaymakers.

"We ran into a little trouble," Ellen had offered him by way of explanation.

He'd just nodded, stroked his beard some more.

His wife, Ruth, however, had recognized something. A need for help. Perhaps it was a mother's instinct, or just simple human empathy. She'd wasted no time getting a hot meal on for them and taking their clothes to wash, giving Ellen a full-length grey dress of her own, and Josh a small white shirt and dark pants to wear in the meantime.

Four children, two boys and two girls, had run downstairs and stared at Ellen and Josh with a mixture of surprise and fas-cination. Three of them had been sent back up to bed, while the eldest, Sarah, was sent to the kitchen to help with the food.

The language the family spoke to each other, Pennsylvania Dutch, sounded a lot like German, although Ellen heard a bunch of English words in there, too. But when they spoke to her and Josh, it was in fluent American English.

Despite living in Pennsylvania for more than half of her life, Ellen had never actually met any Amish before. She'd read about them, though, and heard a bunch of stories that she guessed were just myths and stereotypes. She knew they were a Christian group that originated in Europe and migrated to America — mostly Pennsylvania — in the early 1700s, way before the Revolutionary War and the Declaration of Independence. And more than a century ahead of Ellen's own Irish ancestors.

The quarter-million Amish in the US today live much as their forefathers had, working the land, going to church, and home schooling their kids until fourteen, when they were considered old enough to become farm hands. And, crucially for Ellen, their lifestyle keeps them pretty much off-grid.

They don't use phones, televisions, computers, radio, or internet. They don't drive cars, instead, they ride in buggies pulled by horses. They have no insurance, no social security numbers, no welfare. The Amish are a bunch of self-contained, self-sufficient communities, all but completely cut-off from the outside world.

Which is perfect for Ellen, because it means they have absolutely no idea who she is.

It also makes finding her here almost impossible.

By the time Sarah reappears with a water jug and a glass, Ellen has almost finished her food.

She practically inhaled it.

The young woman smiles at her. "There's more, if you like."

Ellen holds out her plate. Curbs her desire to shout *hell, yeah*, or *oh my God*. "Yes, please," she replies.

Sarah's mother, Ruth, has offered to heat some water in the tub so Ellen can take a bath after dinner. Then Ellen plans to tend her hip and try to get some sleep. With a belly full of food and a sense of safety in this quiet little home with its kind hosts, she starts to relax for the first time in days. She feels as though she could sleep for a week.

But a little voice in the back of her mind reminds her she doesn't have that long.

DAY SIX

38

Verdant Hollow Farm, Juniata County, Pennsylvania

ELLEN IS WOKEN from a deep sleep by a piercing scream. Her brain tells her right away that it's Josh.

She throws off the comforter and springs out of bed, rushes over to her son.

He's wide awake.

"Are you okay, baby?" she says, reaching out and squeezing his slim shoulder.

He screams once more, then sits up in bed and throws off the quilt. He's hyperventilating.

Ellen sits beside him and draws him into a hug. "Did you have a nightmare?"

"Uh-huh," he manages to respond, between jagged breaths.

"Oh, sweetie," she says, rubbing his back gently. "It was just a bad dream."

"There . . . was a . . . man," Josh gasps.

"It's all right," she whispers. "He's not here."

The images come all too quickly to her, now. Dead bodies. A knife handle protruding from a man's back. Another man staring at her, slumped in a doorway, riddled with bullet holes. Both killed by her. And both would have done the same to her if she hadn't acted. And one of them still might have shot her, maybe Josh, too, if her son hadn't hit him with a rock. Her heart rate starts to rise, and she tries to calm herself.

"They won't be hurting us anymore, honey," she adds, stroking his hair.

Josh leans into her, rests his head in the crook of her neck. His breathing starts to slow.

"Can we go home now?" he asks quietly.

It breaks her heart to think what he's been through.

What she's put him through.

"Soon, sweetie. There's something else I have to do, so your grandpa is gonna come here and pick you up today, okay?"

"I don't want you to go," he pleads.

Her heart breaks a little more.

"I don't want to either," she says.

They sit like that awhile, holding one another, until an incredible aroma begins to float up from the kitchen.

"Hey," she says, "can you smell what I smell?"

Josh wipes his eyes, nods.

"Want some breakfast?" she asks.

"Yeah, okay," he replies. Then, for the first time since she found him, he smiles. And seeing those beautiful dimples gives her hope that he might just make it through this.

*

"This is so good," exclaims Ellen. Next to her, Josh is shovelling in big mouthfuls, too. If they were at home, she'd tell him to slow down, take it easy, watch his table manners. Right now, though, she just wants her boy to eat.

"It's traditional Amish breakfast casserole," Ruth explains. "Eggs, bacon, hash brown, cheese, all mixed in together. Gives you the strength to keep going all day." She eyes Ellen knowingly. "I think you might need that."

Ellen meets Ruth's gaze, nods.

*

After seconds of casserole and two cups of coffee, Ellen heads back up to the bedroom. Josh is still downstairs, taking a bath in a big tub of hot water.

Ellen is sitting on her bed, gathering her things together and checking her kit when there's a knock at the door.

"Come in," she says, tucking her pistol inside the grab bag, out of sight.

Ruth enters, holding her clothes. Ellen's black Pennzoil t-shirt, jeans and underwear are clean and dry. It's like some kind of miracle, given how they looked when she arrived.

"I've left your son's clothes downstairs, so he can put them on when he's done in the tub."

"Thank you, Ruth."

"You're welcome."

Her host puts the clothes on the edge of the bed, then goes to leave, but hovers in the doorway and turns back to her.

"I know it's not my business," Ruth begins, "but you're running, aren't you? You and your little boy."

Ellen senses kindness rather than nosiness behind the question. And something tells her she can trust these people.

"Yeah, we are," she replies, although she stops short of telling Ruth exactly what they're running from.

"I've seen a few other folks pass through here in a similar predicament," Ruth says.

"You have?"

"Uh-huh. Women, with their children, who don't want to be found."

Ellen gets it. Ruth thinks she's a domestic abuse survivor,

who's trying to get herself and Josh away from a violent partner. It's impossible for her to imagine Harry doing anything like that to their family. But maybe it's better for Ruth to think that, than for her to know the real reason why she wants to be off the radar.

"What I mean is," Ruth adds, "if you want to stay a little longer, you can. I'll talk to Jebediah. We can come to an arrangement on the room rate. We want to help."

"I appreciate that," says Ellen, "but I have to go. My father is coming to pick up Josh. He'll be here in, like, an hour. Then I'm heading out."

"Okay. If you're sure."

"I'm sure, but thanks anyway."

Ruth hesitates, then says, "Do you know who Dirk Willems is?"

"Uh, no."

"He was a martyr of our religion, four hundred and fifty years ago, in Europe. The Dutch authorities put him in prison for his beliefs, but he escaped."

Ellen shifts on the bed, turns her body toward Ruth.

"When they realized he was gone," her host continues, "a guard came after him. Willems ran across a frozen lake to get away. The guard followed but fell through the ice. Willems heard his cry for help. And, being a good person, he stopped running. He went back and pulled the guard out of the lake."

"Wow. Really?"

"Yes. Willems saved his life. The guard wanted to let him go, but his boss overruled. Do you know what they did after that?"

"I can guess. You called him a martyr."

"That's right," Ruth says. "They tortured him. Tried to get him to recant his beliefs. But he wouldn't. So, they executed him. Burned him alive."

Ellen blinks. "That's some price to pay for your faith."

"When evil people hold power, the good have to do what they can to stay alive."

"Maybe."

"There's no maybe about it. So, whatever it is you need to do, do it while you have the chance." Ruth opens the door. "And don't look back."

*

Ellen and Josh watch from the bedroom window as the unfamiliar car approaches the farmhouse.

As the vehicle parks up, she recognizes her father's flannel shirt through the windshield. It's his favourite shirt, the green-and-black one she makes fun of him for wearing all the time. Right now, though, that familiarity is about the best thing she can think of, because it means he's here.

She's relieved to see he's done as she asked, borrowing his cousin's car. It was just a precaution, she'd told him, in case anyone happened to be looking for his.

By the time he gets out of the vehicle, Ellen is already crying. She can't help it. It's like a reflex, an automatic reaction to seeing him for the first time since her life changed ten days ago when she overheard those two men talking in the corridor of a D.C. hotel.

There have been several points in the past few days when she thought she might not see him again. Now, here he is, walking over to the house, as if nothing is different. His short grey hair is neatly combed in his usual side parting and, as always, he's shaved, despite the early start from Jersey. He happens to look up at the window and sees them. The moment their eyes connect is almost too much for her.

Ellen's hand flies up to her mouth and she stifles a sob.

"Come on," she tells Josh, and together they run down.

Ellen and Josh burst out of the front door before her father has even had a chance to knock.

"Dad!" she cries.

"Thank God you two are safe," he says, flinging his arms wide and wrapping them both in a strong hug. "Thank God," he repeats, his voice just a whisper this time.

"I'm so happy to see you." Ellen holds him tight in one arm, her other arm around Josh.

"I thought I . . ." Her father mumbles something as his voice cracks and Ellen pulls back a little from the hug. She sees that his eyes are wet and a little red. She realizes she's never seen her father cry before.

"What did you think?" she says gently.

"I said I . . ." He presses his lips together, inhales sharply through his nose. "I thought I'd lost you. Both of you."

"Oh, dad," is all she can say. She presses her head into his chest.

"How about you, little guy?" her father asks Josh. "How you holdin' up?"

Josh nods, but he doesn't say anything.

Ellen feels her son's grip around her waist tighten.

Her dad wipes his eyes with the back of his hand, composes himself. "All right," he says. "What's the plan?"

"Did you speak to Harry?" she says.

"I did." Her father grasps her shoulders. "He sounded bad when I got through to him. He's worried sick about you two. He wanted to come this morning."

"But you told him why he couldn't?"

"For his own safety, right?"

"Right," she says. "It's just that, people know who he is. It's hard for him to be low-profile. And, until we know exactly what we're up against . . ." She catches herself, knows it's too late to avoid her family being sucked into the cyclone. "Well, I wanted to keep you all as far away from it as possible."

Her father nods his understanding.

"Did Harry have any update for me?" she asks.

"What about?"

"About all this. I gave him a couple names."

Her father's expression is blank. "Not that he told me."

"Damn. Okay." Ellen wonders who Harry told about it, whether they took it seriously. "I'll find a way to call him later," she says. Her eyes flick from her dad to Josh and back. "You guys gonna be okay at your cousin's?" she asks.

He tilts his head. "Hang on, you mean you're not coming with?"

"I'm a fugitive, dad, remember? I want to be with you and mom and Josh, but——"

"We can call it in when you get home," her father protests. "Explain everything. Tell them about the kidnap, give them those names, cut a deal."

"It's a felony for you to be helping me. You shouldn't even be here."

He meets her gaze. "Nothing would have kept me away."

She gets that. "I know," she says, touching his arm. "But until we know more, I can't stop. I've got to keep going."

Her father sighs. "I was afraid you'd say that."

39

Route 36, Clearfield County, Pennsylvania

IT BROKE ELLEN'S heart all over again to see her father drive away, taking Josh with him.

She felt a powerful urge to stay with her boy, and almost as strong a desire to be close to her father, too. But she knew she had to let them go. Her dad would take Josh back to New Jersey, where they could stay with his cousin. She hopes it'll only be for a little while longer. Ellen's family is her world; being separated from them feels as if a piece of her has been ripped out, leaving a raw, gaping hole.

But there's no other way.

Even if law enforcement took Harry seriously and, based on her unverified intel and supposition, went to Clarion and arrested Leanne Spinoza and Mitch Logan, that may not be the end of it.

Ellen doesn't yet know how many people are in the Keystone Boys, or what they're planning to do on July Fourth. Even without Mitch and Leanne, the attack could still go ahead.

That's why, having settled up with her Amish hosts and got her stuff together, she's back on the road, heading for Clarion to find out more. Because her experiences so far have shown her that, with a handful of exceptions — Walter, Jada, Vang, Reyes — no one believes her story. Even Harry still doubts her.

In a way, she can't blame them. Nobody else seems to have heard of this group. There's barely any trace of them online, even on the dark web. There are no details about what they're going to do, or where they're going to do it. And then, she has to acknowledge, there's her personal psychiatric history.

It's no wonder Brennan, Schultz, Ratkova, and Nyborg didn't take her threat report seriously. And when she tried to tell them that she'd been in the CIA, to show them she knew what she was talking about, there were no records to back that up. Because Langley seems to have scrubbed her name from their books. She'd ended up looking like a crazed fantasist.

Would she have believed her, she wonders, if she walked in off the street with her story about the Keystone Boys?

She believed Nadia, she thinks, back in Paris, even though Langley didn't. She had faith.

It reminds her of Ruth's story about the Dutch martyr who escaped, and should have kept running, but went back to his enemy.

In Nadia's case, Ellen sent her back.

And she can never forgive herself for that.

*

Paris, five years earlier

Ellen had thought the bloodbath at the movie theatre was as bad as it could get.

She was wrong.

After Nadia's husband, Jalil, and his group had shot up the theatre, murdering a hundred and thirty-four people in cold blood — including a group of five American exchange students — they didn't blow themselves up or die in a shootout with the cops.

They reloaded, and moved on to another venue. This time, a bar.

Fifty-two more people lost their lives.

One hundred eighty-six murders, in total.

It all happened in under twenty minutes.

By the time the Paris police arrived, the attackers were gone.

Back at home, Ellen watched the rolling news footage during the night, cradling Josh in her arms. She was totally numb, barely able to comprehend the magnitude of the destruction those terrorists had caused. She wasn't sure how it'd happened so fast, with no warning from Nadia. But Ellen did know one thing for certain.

She was responsible for not stopping it.

And her boss at Langley was responsible for not listening to her.

The following day, Ellen met Nadia by the river.

Nadia was inconsolable.

Ellen hugged her as she wept.

"I didn't know what they would do," she wailed. "I didn't know."

"Do you know where your husband is now?" Ellen had asked.

But Nadia had simply bitten her lip and shaken her head.

Once Ellen had calmed her down, she managed to convince Nadia that the best thing they could do now was to find Jalil and the other attackers. To help bring them to justice. The police had identified them from security camera footage and a nationwide manhunt was underway. Any intel she could give Ellen would be crucial.

"You want me to find my husband, then turn him over to the authorities?" Nadia had responded. "The cops will kill Jalil, and put me in prison. Or his friends might kill me, then Samir will lose his mother as well as his father. I can't do it."

Ellen had held her firmly by the shoulders, looked her right in the eye, and told her a truth. "I'm sorry, Nadia, but you have to stop thinking of this man as your husband, and as Samir's dad. He's a terrorist and a mass murderer, and nothing will ever erase what he's done. That's not your fault, but helping find him is the right thing to do. And you know that, in your heart."

Nadia still hadn't been convinced.

"It's too dangerous. If I try to make contact, he will suspect me."

"We'll protect you," Ellen had promised, again. "You and Samir."

It took Nadia a week to locate Jalil. She got a friend to give a message to someone who knew someone, and eventually received an address. It was an apartment in a high-rise block across town, in a northern suburb of Paris. Nadia took Samir, pretending she was supportive of the attack. Once she'd visited, confirmed he was there, and left, she sent Ellen the address.

Meanwhile, Langley went into overdrive to manage the shitstorm. Ellen's asshole boss let everything slide right off him and onto her. He destroyed memos, erased voicemails, altered records. He blamed her for poor coverage of the Paris Islamist scene. He brought up her unauthorized spending on Samir's heart transplant. He denied that Nadia was an official Agency asset and refused Ellen's request to exfiltrate her and her son to the US.

He threw them all under the fricking bus.

At the same time, the CIA's report to Congress stated that the attack had been impossible to predict, given its small scale and independent initiation.

But Ellen knew otherwise.

She would have gone public, if it wouldn't have endangered Nadia and Samir even more. Instead, she committed another act of career suicide: rather than sending Nadia's intel on Jalil's hiding spot to her boss, she sent it to the French, anonymously.

Two days later, she saw the pictures on *France 24*. The GIGN,

France's elite counter-terrorist police, had stormed the apartment. Their entry had been met with armed resistance from the occupants. Jalil and a man believed to be one of his accomplices in the attacks were shot dead.

Nadia called Ellen the same day. She was terrified and pleaded for help to get her and Samir out of the country.

Ellen said she was doing everything she could. But it wasn't enough, and she knew it. Back in Langley, the CIA were already washing their hands of Ellen. And Nadia was just a post-script on a memo that had been shredded and sent to the incinerator.

It was three days after that call when Ellen tried messaging Nadia again.

There was no reply.

*

Present day
Clarion, Pennsylvania

The first thing Ellen sees when she finally arrives in Clarion is a cluster of fast-food restaurants whose giant plastic signs compete for her attention. They're part of a soulless expanse of concrete on the south side of town that comprises a Walmart, an AutoZone, and a couple of gas stations along with the food outlets. The parking lots are large enough for a bunch of semi-trucks, whose drivers Ellen guesses are taking a break from their east-west journeys on I-80, which she crossed a few minutes ago.

She figures that the area is sufficiently anonymous for her to stop, refill the Camry's near-empty tank, use the bathroom, and grab a sandwich. The Amish breakfast will keep her going a couple more hours, but she'll need something later, and here is as good as place as any to pick it up. There's also less chance of someone paying attention to her with all the vehicles coming and going. She chooses the Kwik Fill gas station, since it looks smaller and less official than the BP next door.

Ball cap pulled low and hygiene mask on, she fills the Camry. As she crosses the forecourt to pay at the Red Apple mini mart, she passes a middle-aged guy walking back to his car who stares at her like she's an alien, then shakes his head in apparent disbelief. She realizes it's the mask. It may be covering her mouth and nose, but it's actually making her stand out more. She takes it off.

Inside the mini mart, she reluctantly selects a shrink-wrapped cheese sandwich that's probably the least processed item in the refrigerator.

Ellen takes the sandwich and a bottle of water up to the counter. The guy behind it has his head down, absorbed in his cell phone. He's so small and skinny that, at first, she thinks he's just a kid. But when he looks up at her, the little lines around his eyes show he can't be far off her age.

The tag on his shirt says his name is Peter.

"Hi," she says.

"Oh. Sorry," he says, revealing a set of buck teeth. He lays his phone on the counter. On its screen is footage of an explosion that looks like an atom bomb detonating.

He rings up the sandwich and water on the register, then gazes out toward the pumps.

"You the Camry?" he asks. His voice is almost as high as her own.

"That's right."

"Don't see too many a them these days."

"Guess not." Ellen doesn't want to explain her vehicle choice — or lack of it — to this random guy.

There's a slightly awkward silence before he says, "That's seventy-seven twenty, please, ma'am."

She counts out eighty bucks from the grab bag. Realizes she has almost no cash left.

As Peter hands her the change, he takes a good long look at her, narrows his eyes.

"Do I know you?" he ventures.

"No, I don't think so," she replies quickly, taking her items. "Have a nice day."

"You too," he calls after her.

As she gets into the car, she throws a glance back at the mini mart, wondering if the guy has recognized her from the news, if he's calling the cops right now.

But he's back in the exact same position as when she walked in.

Head down, staring at his phone screen.

40

Clarion, Pennsylvania

PETER LOOKS UP as the nuclear bomb video on his cell phone ends. He watches the woman with the Camry drive out and take a right, headed north toward the town center, instead of back onto I-80. He'd swear there was something familiar about her face, but he can't put his finger on it. Then again, he can't put his finger on anything much, right now.

Hell, his concentration is so shot to pieces, he didn't even see her pull in, never mind pump her own gas. He normally prefers it when folks do that. After all, it's less work for him, especially since he's on his own today. But being alone hasn't meant any peace. It's meant a whole lot of time to think about what's going to happen tonight.

And he's done a whole lot of thinking.

Faced with the choice between saving a bunch of people at the power plant and protecting himself, he's still doing nothing. He's too scared to tip off the FBI, too scared to tell Mitch he wants out, and too scared to try rescuing Leanne from it all — before she wrecks her life, along with all the other lives they're going to destroy tonight.

He's pictured himself pulling up outside the dance studio this afternoon, telling Leanne to get in, that he's taking her away someplace safe, where it can be just the two of them. They don't even need to get together, like that, if she don't want to. He just wants to protect her.

But he knows it'll never happen.

Same as he'll never stand up to Mitch, and he'll never call the FBI. He knows he won't be able to pull the trigger tonight, neither, if the times comes.

When he didn't want to go for tackles on the football field as a kid, or when he shut his eyes on the plate as a fastball came at him from the mound, his old man used to call him *chicken shit*. Too much of a pussy to do anything. Twenty years later, nothing's changed.

Peter's just let himself be swept along by it all, desperate to be part of the crowd, to earn his brother's respect, to be noticed by Leanne. He didn't stop to think about what being in the Keystone Boys actually meant. Whether he really does want to be like Mitch. He didn't do anything, plain and simple.

And now it's almost too late to do anything.

But, instead of being a hero, he's just watching stupid videos on YouTube of nuclear bombs blowing up. That's not supposed to happen tonight — according to Mitch — but Peter don't trust Sherman the German to get it right.

He's read on a bunch of websites about an accident at the Three Mile Island nuclear plant, back in 1979. Apparently, it was just a little explosion. But they still evacuated one hundred forty thousand folks from a twenty-mile radius. President Carter got personally involved. It took fourteen years and more than a billion dollars to clean up all the radioactive shit in the area. There were "no nukes" protests all across America after that, even in other countries. A lot of talk about cancer.

And that was just a *little* explosion.

Tonight, they're planning to detonate a hundred pounds of military-grade C4 and blast copper slugs through the walls of all the main parts of the facility. Peter can't even remember their names, even though he's seen the diagrams and the maps dozens of times. The reactor-something, the turbine-gizmo, the cooling-whatchamacallit.

It ain't gonna be no little explosion.

Peter recalls the noise when they detonated two-and-a-half pounds of C4 a couple days ago. How he felt that blast go right through his body and shake his bones. How it cut clean through a block of concrete like it was butter.

The bombs they've made are six times the size of that, Sherman said.

And they got six of them.

He runs through the plan once more. His shift here finishes at four, they're meeting at Mitch's place at five, Randy is bringing the truck at six, and they're hitting the road by seven. Even allowing for a break and traffic, they'll be at Three Mile Island by eleven thirty, ready to hit the guards right after they change at midnight and it becomes the Fourth of July.

Independence Day.

Peter tries to imagine what'd happen if the cops or the feds are there at the bridge, waiting for them with a roadblock. He can't see Mitch backing down. He can't see The Dozer dropping his Remington pump-action and surrendering. And he can't see any of them getting out of that truck alive.

If he's going to stop this, he needs to do it before they get there.

He's got about six hours to decide. Maybe not even that long.

But all he does is tap on another nuclear bomb video.

Chicken shit.

*

Washington, D.C.

He almost did it.

In that dark moment, up on the ledge, looking down at the sidewalk below, it had seemed as though there was nothing worth living for. No, that wasn't strictly accurate. There were things to live for. It was that he didn't *deserve* to go on living. He'd thrown away everything he ever cared about — his family, his career, his integrity — because he was too stupid to take a stand earlier.

Too frightened, too selfish.

Even if, by some miracle, no one ever found out, the guilt would stay with him a lifetime. A colossal weight bearing down on him, every minute of every day. A demon sitting on his shoulder every time he hugged someone he loved.

It had felt as though the best thing he could do for the rest of humanity was to step off that ledge and let gravity pull him hard and fast into the concrete, into oblivion.

But something had stopped him.

The possibility that it's not all over, not just yet.

He could give G.I. Joe's name to any one of a half-dozen agencies right now. They'd be all over that little town in Western P.A. before you could say "domestic terrorism". But he'd be signing his own execution warrant. Those mercenaries would put a bullet in him by nightfall. He'd be *neutralized*, same as her. They might even make it look like a suicide, which would be ironic, after he chose not to kill himself last night.

Even if he grew a spine and sacrificed himself, it wouldn't matter. Because the Keystone Boys are just foot soldiers. If they're taken down, then the people above them, pulling the strings, will just find more pissed-off, poor rural white folks to do their dirty work.

"Those hillbillies haven't got a goddamn clue," The Texan had said, chuckling into his scotch. "They think they're starting a revolution. What they don't know is that they're actually stopping one."

It's the puppet masters that he needs to do something about. The Texan, The Ballbreaker, the old man with the grey moustache, and the kid. Maybe most of all the kid.

What can he do, though? He can't prove any of it.

Conversations in private rooms, calls on burner phones. No emails, no written instructions, nothing that can be traced back to them. He's the one who dealt with it all. He was the inside man. He obtained the technical documents, the specifications and plans for the power plant. He passed them on to G.I. Joe. And he made the money transfers.

Then it hits him.

Everything that's about to happen can be traced back to him.

He's the fall guy. He just didn't see it before.

He's even more of a fool than he realized.

And he's even more trapped than he thought.

41

Clarion, Pennsylvania

IN THE CENTER of Clarion, Ellen heads for the Millennium dance studio. It's the only definite data point she has in town for Leanne Spinoza. It's not exactly great targeting intel, but she figures she has to start somewhere. If the place is open, she can ask after Spinoza and go from there.

She stops a passer-by, a young woman with blue hair and a leather jacket, who is chewing gum and scrolling on her phone, and asks directions. She looks like the sort of person who might know where a dance studio is.

"It's right on Main Street," the young woman tells her. "You can't miss it."

Ellen finds it and parks up opposite. Ordinarily, she'd sit and wait. But she doesn't know how much time she's got, so she needs to make something happen. It's a risk showing herself inside, but one she has to take. She just hopes these people haven't seen the news item about the escaped mental patient who's also wanted on suspicion of murder.

That makes her think of the two bodies she left behind at the cabin in the Poconos. She wonders if anyone's found them yet, or whether anyone's looking for them at all. She guesses even killers and kidnappers must have family or friends who call to see how they're doing.

She goes through the front doors of the dance studio and immediately hears thumping music coming from a room off the reception. A few pre-teens, mostly girls, are milling around, chatting and practicing their moves. No one pays attention to her. They probably just think she's a mom here to pick up her kid.

She pushes away a thought of Josh, tells herself she'll see him again soon.

Then she approaches the desk.

"Oh, hey," she says.

"Hi," the woman behind the desk replies. She's got big hair and lip filler and fingernails like long pink claws. She stops typing. "Can I help you?"

"Uh, yeah, so, I'm looking for Leanne Spinoza," Ellen explains, affecting a voice that's all Californian upspeak and vocal fry. "Is she here?"

"And you are?" The woman raises her eyebrows. Inquisitive, but not suspicious. Not yet anyway.

"My name's Briana," says Ellen. "I knew Leanne in L.A. I'm passing through on my way to New York and, you know, Leanne said that if I was ever out here, I should come visit her."

"You don't have her number?"

"I think she stopped using the cell I had. She just said to come by this place. I mean, she still works here, right?" Ellen looks around and shrugs as if she's a little clueless. Then she gives the receptionist the broadest smile she can manage. Shows as many teeth as possible. Does her best to look easy-breezy, although her heart is pounding like the bass of the dance track playing next door.

The woman seems to be weighing something up. And then, she reaches a decision.

"Leanne's teaching a class at two this afternoon," she says. "You could come back then. I'll let her know you dropped by if I see her before. What did you say your name was?"

"Thank you," Ellen replies, ignoring her question, "but I'd prefer it if you didn't say anything. I want it to be a surprise for her. We haven't seen each other in years. It's gonna blow her mind that I'm here."

"Okay, you got it."

Ellen thanks the woman and leaves. She goes back to the car and gets in. There's nothing to do but wait and hope Spinoza shows up.

It's these periods of dead time which have been the hardest for Ellen this past week. Part of difficulty of just waiting is feeling the pressure to do something, the frustration of not being able to do anything. But part of it is also the way her mind wanders when there's nothing else to occupy it.

She sips her water and watches the entrance to the dance studio. But, in her head, she's right back in Paris.

*

Paris, five years earlier

At first, when Nadia didn't reply to her messages, Ellen wondered if she'd taken matters into her own hands and left Paris. Gone to ground, maybe with some relatives in another part of the city. Perhaps she'd headed down to Marseille, where she had other family. Or even hopped on a plane or boat to Algeria, where her grandparents lived.

After a day with no response, Ellen goes to Nadia's apartment to check on her. But she gets nowhere. The French cops are controlling access to her building. Ellen realizes they're probably treating Nadia and Jalil's home like a crime scene, stripping it and checking every single item for possible evidence.

She tries everywhere else she can think of: friend's apartments, the local cafés, Samir's school. Calls people she knows who know Nadia. Nothing.

She's in the apartment, feeding Josh on the sofa, when the story breaks.

The body of a twenty-five-year-old woman has been found in Vitry-sur-Seine. Lying in a dumpster, with her throat cut.

Ellen already knows who it is before the newsreader gives the name. A powerful feeling of nausea starts in her belly and spreads through her guts. Bile rises in her throat.

It's Nadia.

The woman has not yet been formally identified, but is believed to be Nadia Slimani, widow of the terror cell leader Jalil Slimani . . .

So far, there are no clear suspects, but the French police say they aren't ruling out a revenge motive for her murder, potentially by a far-right group, in retaliation for the atrocities last week.

There's no mention of Samir.

Ellen holds Josh a little tighter in her arms.

She gets up from the sofa, paces around the living room. She's fucked up, again, this time by not protecting her asset. She thinks of Nadia's last moments, of the fear she must have felt, of her anguish at being separated from Samir.

This is on her, too.

Ellen finds herself standing, facing the TV, with her back to the wall. Her knees start to give and she slides down to the ground, clutching Josh to her chest, as she begins to cry.

Harry comes in. He looks at her, looks at the news, and then comes over and, without a word, sits down beside her on the floor.

Puts his arm around her.

*

Present day

Ellen's sandwich tastes like it's been filled with plastic instead of cheese. Still, she forces herself to eat it, because she doesn't know when the next meal is coming. She's got maybe just a few hours left to collect the intel that could prove the threat from the Keystone Boys is genuine, and give law enforcement some actionable detail which they could use to stop the attack.

She refuses to let Paris happen again. Not here. And not on her watch.

Not this time.

She's resisted the temptation to switch on her burner phone and call Harry or her parents and Josh. She doesn't want to give the cops any more opportunities to track and arrest her before she can see this through.

Ellen is just wondering how much battery life she has left on the cell phone when a woman walks out of the dance studio. The same woman who walked in at quarter of two. Her blond hair is up in a high ponytail, and her face isn't totally clear at this distance, but Ellen is pretty sure it's Spinoza.

She starts the Camry's engine.

Spinoza waits on the street, glancing up and down. She takes out her cell phone, checks it, puts it back in her bag. She looks nervous.

Two minutes later, a pickup truck approaches and pulls over. It's a Chevy. Ellen can't see clearly who's driving, but it looks like a guy. Maybe it's Mitch Logan. Spinoza gets in and the Chevy moves off again, toward Ellen.

She turns her head away and waits until it goes by her, then she pulls out, U-turns and follows at a distance.

Five minutes later, the Chevy parks up beside a two-storey building on a smaller street. The first floor of the building is a real estate office, which is closed. There's a separate door to the side of the office, which Ellen guesses leads to an apartment on the second floor.

She pulls in across the road, about fifty yards back. Hopes she not too close.

The guy gets out and, even though he's wearing shades and a ballcap, she can see that it's Logan. He's openly carrying, a 9mm sidearm on his belt. He doesn't speak or smile or laugh, and there's no affection as he points Leanne toward the door beside the office, as if he's ordering her inside. She opens a single lock, then they both enter, and the door shuts behind them.

Ellen stays in her car. Watching, waiting.

Wondering how long she's got.

*

Twenty minutes pass before the front door to the apartment opens again. Spinoza and Logan both come out. Spinoza has changed out of the leggings and crop top she had on at the dance studio. Now, she's wearing a t-shirt and jeans. They get back in the Chevy. Logan backs it out, and drives away.

Ellen has a choice to make: does she follow them, or try to take a look inside?

They could be headed to meet their associates in the Keystone Boys. Or they could just be headed to the grocery store.

The apartment, on the other hand, might contain some intel on the group or their plans. But it could also be fitted with cameras or an alarm.

Ellen recalls the panic of trying to switch off the alarm after she broke into her own home. And she knew the code for that.

Attempting a covert entry of their apartment is a big risk.

She watches as the Chevy gets to the end of the street, slows, indicates left, then disappears from sight.

Time to decide.

She pulls two items out of her grab bag. Her pistol, which she tucks into her belt underneath her t-shirt. And her set of lock picks.

Then she gets out of the Camry and walks over to the front door.

42

Clarion, Pennsylvania

ELLEN LEARNED AT The Farm that there are two key stages to lockpicking. You have to lift the pins inside the lock, then you need to turn the barrel.

During the training course, they each got a set of picks and a lock made out of clear plastic, so they could see what was happening.

As with a bunch of stuff at The Farm, the recruits had stupid little contests among themselves. Who could do it fastest, who could do it blindfolded, who could do it tipsy, that type of thing. Ellen wasn't the best, but she wasn't bad, either.

She's just never needed to use her skills in the field, under pressure.

Until now.

Covering the lock with her body to shield what she's doing from anyone passing by, she inserts the turning tool and puts a little pressure on the lock barrel, twisting to the right. Next, she chooses a rake pick and slides it into the top of the key slot, wiggling it up and down to get each pin up and out of the way. She feels the first two rise, no problem. Then the third. The pick goes in a little further each time.

Her adrenalin is pumping and she can feel a tremor in her hand from the nerves, which isn't helping. Her palms are getting a little sweaty, too.

At the fourth pin, something sticks. It won't move.

Shit.

Maybe the pin is bent or something.

She glances around. An older couple is walking toward her, maybe thirty, forty yards away. They look like good citizen types, the sort who might ask a stranger what the hell she's doing trying to bust open a lock.

She makes a bigger movement with the pick and it slips from her hand. Hits the sidewalk.

Stay calm, she tells herself. *Breathe.*

She stoops and grabs the pick off the concrete.

The couple are twenty yards from her, now. Their footfall is getting louder.

Ellen re-inserts the turning tool, then the pick above it. Slowly, carefully, she works it in, up and down. This time, the fourth pin clicks, then the fifth. The lock pops. The door opens.

And she's inside.

*

Ellen braces herself for an alarm to sound, but nothing happens.

She glances around the entrance hall and can't see anything like a panel or a control box. No camera or motion sensor up by the ceiling. She concludes that Mitch Logan and Leanne Spinoza don't have any special security features in their apartment. In fact, they don't seem to have very much of anything.

As she moves through the narrow hallway, past a kitchen, into a living space, she gets a feeling of impermanence. What little furniture is here is bland, generic, flat-pack type stuff. There are few personal possessions, and no pictures on the walls. It seems like a place they haven't been in for long, and they probably don't plan on staying here too long, either. It's most likely rented, perhaps on a short-term lease, until they've carried out the attack.

Perhaps just until tomorrow.

Ellen takes a long, slow breath as the thought of that sends a bolt of adrenalin through her. The reminder of what will happen if she screws up, again.

She tells herself she needs to be quick, because Logan and Spinoza could be back any minute. She's got to make the most of this chance to gather intel. Except there doesn't seem to be much here of use, she thinks, as she moves into the living area. No maps or photographs of targets, no schedules, notes, or planning boards conveniently left out. The apartment isn't their base.

She wonders if she made the wrong call. If she should have followed them instead of breaking in here.

Then she sees the guns.

They're laid out on top of sheets of newspaper, on a coffee table between the sofa and TV. Beside them are a stack of cleaning materials — brushes, rags, and a can of oil.

Ellen approaches and studies the collection.

There's an AR-15, an AK-47, four Glock 9mm pistols, a little snub-nosed Ruger, and a Remington pump-action. She sees a dozen boxes of ammo, in all different sizes — 5.56mm, 7.62mm for the AK, 9mm and shotgun cartridges, both slug and buckshot. And, almost as an afterthought, there's a bunch of flashbang grenades on the floor.

Too much, surely, just for Logan and Spinoza. Ellen guesses the other guns are for their buddies. There are eight weapons, but she figures that whoever uses the Remington needs a sidearm, too, maybe same for the AR-15 and the AK. So, there's at least three of them, and maybe as many as six or seven.

And it sure looks like they're preparing for something.

Ellen immediately thinks of Jalil and his group in Paris, opening fire at the movie theatre and then at the bar. Unloading clip after clip from semi-automatic weapons into an unsuspecting crowd of civilians. The scene at the movie theatre comes into her mind and she feels her fight-or-flight system kick in.

As she moves off, she notices something under the coffee table. She has to get low before she can see what it is.

Body armor.

She counts five sets. So, that answers her question of how many of them there are. She imagines trying to take on five heavily armed attackers. One against five. Almost impossible odds, even if one of them wasn't a highly decorated ex-Marine.

She realizes her mouth is dry, and her tremor is worse than when she was trying to pick the lock.

She tells herself to focus. Keep moving, keep looking.

In the corner of the living room is a bookcase. It's almost empty, except for a handful of paperback thrillers, a couple of self-help books, and two photographs.

The photos are both small, six-by-four prints in little frames. One shows Logan and Spinoza together. The other shows Logan with a much smaller guy. They're at a baseball stadium. From the distinctive yellow bridge in the background, Ellen can recognize it as Pittsburgh. They've got their arms around each other's shoulders, but the pose looks a little awkward because of their height difference.

Ellen looks more closely at the second man in that picture.

She's seen him before. Earlier today.

It's the guy from the gas station.

Who is he? Logan's best buddy? It seems strange that Logan, who served for over a decade in a tight-knit military unit, doesn't have a picture from that time, or any other pictures, for that matter. Just his girlfriend, and this one guy.

Ellen isn't sure what to make of it, except that the lack of any-thing about the Marines might support her theory of his motivation — that he's disaffected, and that's why he left a stellar career behind to return to his hometown.

Maybe he even holds a grudge against the armed forces. Maybe he's chosen a military target for tomorrow.

She needs more information.

Heading back to the hallway and through the apartment, she finds a bathroom. A quick search of the cupboards yields noth-ing of interest.

She moves on to the bedroom.

One half of the bed is made, the side table and its contents neat and tidy, with nothing on the floor. The other side looks as if a hurricane has hit it, with underwear, hair straighteners, a wet bath towel, and Spinoza's outfit from the dance studio, all in a heap on the comforter, spilling onto the carpet.

Ellen checks the wardrobe and drawers, but nothing jumps out at her as useful.

She kneels down next to Logan's side table by the bed. Opens the little cabinet door at the front of it. Inside is a laptop. She carefully extracts it, places it on the bed, and lifts the lid. She switches it on but when it boots up a lock screen appears, asking for a password. She wishes Reyes was here with his tools. He'd be able to crack it. But she has no chance.

It's frustrating, because she's certain that if she could get into this machine, she'd find the details of what the Keystone Boys are planning for tomorrow.

She curses out loud.

Switches the laptop off again.

As she goes to replace it, she notices a thick, hardback book that was beneath it. She takes it out.

Clarion Area High School, the cover says. *Class of 2007 Yearbook*.

Something tells her this is worth a look.

*

Fifteen minutes later, Ellen is still reading. She's discovered that
Mitch Logan was one of two stars on the high school football
team, the other being Randall 'Randy' Kowalski Jr., also known
as The Bulldozer. If Logan was big, Kowalski was huge. Together,
the two seniors co-captained the team to a 12-2 record, and a
run all the way to the state championship semi-finals. They were
heroes, with both receiving all-area honors. Kowalski was third-
team all-state, the stuff of NCAA scholarships and pro dreams.

She's also learned that Leanne Spinoza was a sophomore at
the school that year. She was into all the theatrical and musical
stuff, and was already center stage aged fifteen, singing, dancing
and acting. No wonder she felt as though L.A. was calling to her.
And she had a serious crush on Logan, to judge from the message she's written on the flyleaf:

> Mitch, ur a stud! I wanna have your babies!!! Leanne xxx (Spi-
> noza, in case u forget)

Ellen has found a fourth person of interest, too. So unobtru-
sive, she almost missed him. A small kid, in the same class as
Spinoza, but whose presence barely registered on school life. He
wasn't a member of any club, society, music group or sports team.
He wasn't in any of the photographs on the montage pages.

It's the guy from the gas station.

His name's Peter Logan.

That explains the picture in the living room. If it wasn't for
that – and his handwritten message; Yo big brol – Ellen might
have just thought it was a coincidence that he and Mitch shared
the same last name. It certainly doesn't look as though they share
any DNA.

Ellen feels as though she knows these people a little better, now. The only problem is that it hasn't taken her much further toward identifying the Keystone Boys, or the target of their planned attack.

For that, she'll just need to stay on Logan and Spinoza, and hope that—

She hears an engine right outside. It roars, then cuts out.

Ellen freezes.

Car doors pop and slam. There are two voices.

Then a key in the lock.

It all happens so fast that Ellen doesn't have time to get out. She realizes she's trapped.

She closes the yearbook and shoves it back in the bedside cabinet, slams the little door shut. Looks around her, frantic. She goes to the bedroom window, peers out and down. One storey below, there's a small concrete yard with a few trash cans around the sides, plus a stack of FOR SALE signs. She can't see if it leads back to the street, but she's got no other option.

She hears footsteps on the stairs, getting louder.

She opens the latch on the window.

Now the voices are in the hallway.

They're heading for the bedroom.

43

Clarion, Pennsylvania

ELLEN STAYS ABSOLUTELY still, holds her breath. She knows that one movement, one sound, could give her away.

"The fuck, Leanne?" says Logan. "You left the window open." His voice is deep, with a rough, gravelly edge. Rage just beneath the surface, barely contained. He's standing right by the bed.

Ellen is underneath it.

"Huh?" calls Spinoza from outside the bedroom.

"I said, you left the goddamn window open, you dumb fuck."

"No, I didn't," Spinoza replies, coming in behind him. "I shut it."

"Well, it's open."

"I swear to God, Mitch, I closed it."

"And look at all your shit on the floor," he says. "I told you that if you want to be a part of this, you need to be disciplined. You need to follow my rules. That's rule number one."

"I am disciplined, I just—"

"And rule number two is test and check. Everything. That includes windows."

"I did check."

"Jesus Christ, how many times have I told you that?"

"I know, but I'm telling you, I shut the window."

"Clean this shit up. Right now."

"You clean it up," Spinoza shoots back.

From her hiding place under the bed, Ellen listens to their feet moving around her. Then there's a sharp movement, the hard slap of flesh on flesh, and a shriek.

"You want another one?" Mitch says.

Spinoza makes a whimpering sound.

"I said, do you want another one?"

"No."

"Okay, good. Pee-Wee and Sherman are getting here at five, remember? Dozer's bringing the truck at six. We go over everything one more time, then we're on our way. And you better be ready. You screw this up, I'll put a bullet in you myself. I don't give a fuck."

There's a silence.

Ellen carefully turns her head to the window side of the bed. Beside her, less than a yard away, Spinoza squats down and starts picking up items of clothing, wrapping the cord around her hair straighteners. Ellen can see her sneakers and her hands. She hears her sniff, her breath catching as she inhales.

"And quit crying," Logan adds, before walking out.

Ellen tries to process what she's just heard.

She guessed from the body armor in the living room that there were five members of the group. Now, she has five names: Logan, Spinoza, then three others — Pee-Wee, Sherman, and someone called *Dozer*. That last guy must be Randall Kowalski, aka The Bulldozer.

She also has some idea of their schedule. Whatever they're planning, the five of them are heading out together in a truck, around two to three hours from now.

She figures they're going to travel together to the location of their attack, or someplace nearby, maybe hole up overnight, and strike in the daytime. If their aim is a mass casualty attack, they might pick the moment the highest number of people are present. Rush hour on public transport, or lunch break in a city park, maybe.

Just like the terrorists in Paris chose evening time, when the movie theatre and bar were most crowded.

Bastards.

Ellen's learned one other thing, too. In addition to being a terrorist, Mitch Logan is a grade-A asshole in his personal life. A man who emotionally and physically abuses his smaller, weaker partner.

For that alone, Ellen has half a mind to roll out from under the bed and pull her pistol on him. But she knows that wouldn't end well. She can't hope to beat Logan in a firefight. She needs to outsmart him, or get some help.

Besides, even if she takes him out, the other Keystone Boys could still execute the plan.

"Piece of shit," Spinoza mutters, once his footsteps have faded.

A minute later, having shoved some items in drawers, Spinoza seems to get bored and kicks the rest of her clothing under the bed. A sock hits Ellen's arm.

Then Spinoza stands by the bed for what feels like forever.

Ellen prays that she doesn't change her mind and reach under the bed to retrieve the clothes.

"Mitch, I'm gonna take a shower!" Spinoza yells, eventually.

There's no response.

"Screw you, then," whispers Spinoza. She stomps over to a door which Ellen guesses is an en-suite bathroom. The door opens and closes, and a minute later Ellen hears a jet of water from the shower come on.

It's now or never.

She takes her chance.

Crawling out from under the bed, past Spinoza's discarded clothes, Ellen gets to her feet slowly, checks the doorway. There's no sign of Logan.

She listens, trying to pick out any sounds beyond the noise of the shower.

There's a faint metallic rolling of a gun slide being racked a couple times, followed by the dry click of a trigger being depressed with the barrel empty. She guesses Logan is *testing and checking everything*, once more.

Time to go.

Ellen stands, opens the window. Pushes it as far as it will go, which isn't all that far. Just about far enough for her to fit through.

Climbing up onto the sill and contorting to squeeze her legs into the gap one at a time, she lowers herself out as slowly as she can. Her arms are burning with the effort of holding her weight on the lintel as gravity pulls her south.

She glances down. It looks like a hell of a drop. Even though it's only one floor, it's high — maybe fifteen feet — and there's nothing beneath her except concrete. But there's no time for hesitation.

Ellen gradually turns herself around, until she's hanging off the sill by her hands, on the outside of the building. She grits her teeth, takes her weight on one hand and uses the other to push the window back to its original position.

Then she drops.

*

Since escaping through the window, Ellen has been sitting down the street from the apartment for more than two-and-a-half hours. She's restless, frustrated, hungry, thirsty, and tired. Her self-stitched hip wound is throbbing with pain, she rolled her ankle again when she landed on the concrete, and she needs to pee.

But, despite all that, she can't move, because something could happen at any minute.

So far, the others have more or less followed Logan's schedule. The first to arrive was a thin, strung-out-looking guy who, despite it being ninety degrees out, was wearing a trench coat. Her guess is that this is Sherman, because ten minutes after him, Peter Logan showed up, and she figures he's *Pee-Wee*. He probably got that nickname as a kid, and has been trying to shift it ever since. Obviously, that hasn't worked out for him.

Ellen wonders about Peter's involvement. Did Mitch recruit him to the Keystone Boys, or was it the other way round? Mitch is clearly the dominant one out of the two brothers — older, bigger, stronger. And he appears to be the leader of the group. But you never know. Peter didn't look like a terrorist, but Ellen's experience tells her that a whole bunch of other guys didn't, either. Until they attacked.

The French have an expression: *beware of the sleeping water.* It means that the quietest people can often be capable of more than anyone thinks.

Maybe that's what Peter "Pee-Wee" Logan is.

Sleeping water.

He and Sherman were followed just before six p.m. by a mountain of a man driving a white GMC cargo van. Although she was a way off, Ellen guessed he was at least 6-6, and probably north of 300 pounds. Though he'd grown a large beard since his high school days, there was little doubt in her mind that this was Randall Kowalski. And *bulldozer* may have been an understatement. He's built more like a combine harvester.

Since Kowalski went into the apartment, Ellen's been thinking about trying to break into the back of the cargo van to see what he's brought with him. But she can't risk it. Chances are there's nothing in it, anyway, and it's just their ride.

It occurs to her that she could call the cops right now. Use the last few per cent of battery life on her burner phone to dial 911 and report suspicious activity at the address. But what if the police arrive and find nothing more than the weapons? In Pennsylvania, you don't need a license for possession of a firearm inside your own home. There might be no other incriminating material in the apartment, and the truck could be empty.

Then what?

She realizes that having come this far and risked this much, she still needs more evidence. She can't give herself away just yet, either to the Keystone Boys, or the cops. She needs to wait a little longer.

Ellen's gaze travels from the white GMC van up to the apartment windows, where the blinds are down.

She wonders how long she can afford to wait.

How long before it will be too late.

44

Clarion, Pennsylvania

PETER FEELS LIKE he's drowning. He can't breathe, can't even see straight, and he's helpless. He's back in those summer days at the local pool when he was a kid, and the bullies held his head underwater because he couldn't stop them. And because they thought it was funny, until Mitch came along and did the same to them.

Now, it's as if Mitch is reaching down once more, lifting him up from that suffocating water to the surface, where he can get some air. Where the muffled sounds become clear again, and suddenly he can hear his brother's voice.

"All right, let's saddle up," Mitch says, closing the laptop he's just used to go through the plan one more time.

Peter barely heard a word of it.

His head is fuzzy, like a bad hungover. Except he ain't had any liquor, so it must just be his nerves playing up again. He can't think clearly, can't even hold on to a thought for more than—

"Let's go, Pee-Wee." Mitch's voice snaps him out of his latest trance. "Get your Kevlar on," his brother adds, pointing at the carpet, where there are two vests left.

Peter just stares at the body armor.

"I'll give you a clue," Randy says, "yours is the one marked *Small*."

The others chuckle a little, which relieves some of the tension in the room, but Peter doesn't reply.

Instead, he moves across to the vests with slow, jerky movements. *Just like a zombie*, he thinks. Like something out of *Night of the Living Dead*. Which is exactly how he feels. Alive and dead at the same time. Alive, because he's moving and breathing. Dead, because his life as he knows it is over.

Hell, he could take a bullet in just a few hours' time from a security guard or the cops or whoever else they might run into. It could be all over for him right after they go through those gates at the power station.

And if a bullet doesn't get him, maybe those goddamned atoms will, like in *Chernobyl*. Burning him from the inside, eating away at him, 'til there's nothing left but blood and guts.

And if he survives the bullets and the atoms, there's no way he can hope to outrun law enforcement, not once they work out who did it. The FBI will find him, for sure.

And if they don't kill him on sight, they'll throw his ass in jail.

And if the DA doesn't push for the death penalty . . .

Well, then he's going away for life, no doubt.

Peter struggles into his vest. It's thick and heavy and awkward and he can't coordinate his arm to get through the strap and now he's tangled up and he knows the others are watching.

"Your head goes through the middle hole, retard," Sherman cackles.

"Come here," says Leanne, stepping across to Peter and lifting the vest off of him. She replaces it correctly over his head, then pulls the edges of his t-shirt to smooth it out beneath the vest, before tightening the Velcro straps. "There you go."

"Thank you," mumbles Peter.

Part of his brain registers that this is the closest he's ever been to the woman he's had a crush on since ninth grade. He should be appreciating this moment, taking in every detail of it to remember later. But he can't. He doesn't even know what *later* will look like.

If there'll be a *later* at all.

And the moment is gone.

Next, Mitch has his arm around him and is guiding him to a corner of the room. Behind them, the others are prepping their weapons, loading the flashbangs into a holdall, putting the ammo in toolboxes.

"You okay, Pee-Wee?" Mitch asks him quietly.

"Uh, well . . ." This could be his last chance. He looks up at his brother, at that square jaw and those cold eyes that have seen so much death and destruction. And he can't say no. "I'll be all right," he says. "Just a little nervous, you know?"

He doesn't want to tell Mitch he's scared shitless, even though his brother probably knows that already.

"It's normal," Mitch responds. "I felt the same before my first operation."

"You did?"

Mitch nods. "Uh-huh."

"What did you do?"

"I took one of these bad boys." Mitch holds out a fist, then opens it to reveal a pill. It's small and white and has *D* and *5* stamped on it.

"What is it?"

"Dex."

"Huh?"

"Dexedrine. Five milligrams. It'll help you dial in, and that'll calm you down. Trust me, take it."

"Are you gonna give it to the others?" Peter asks.

"Maybe, if I think they need it," his brother replies. "But not 'til we're closer to the target."

"You think I need it now, though."

"Yeah."

Peter studies the pill. He knows he has no way out of the attack, now. But the next best thing is a way out of how he's feeling at this moment.

He picks up the pill, puts it in his mouth. Grabs one of the water bottles from the table. Takes a slug from it and swallows.

"Attaboy." Mitch claps him hard on the shoulder. "Now man the fuck up and let's do this."

"Showtime!" Leanne cries.

"Woo-hoo!" echoes Randy.

Sherman says nothing.

As they finish prepping and gather up their kit, Peter starts to feel a little more chilled and a lot more focused. Like everything is sharper, clearer. And that's when the thought hits him.

It's too late for him to tip off anybody, now. He's going to be in the same truck as these guys until the first shot they fire inside the power plant. So, if he wants to stop this, he's going to have to stop the others, including Dozer with his pump-action shotgun, and his own brother, the former elite soldier.

He wonders how he's going to have the balls to do that.

Grabbing his little Ruger pistol and a toolbox of ammo, he follows the group down the stairs and out of the apartment.

He still has the feeling that he's drowning.

Only now, the sensation is just a whole lot clearer.

*

Washington, D.C.

He knows he can't do anything to stop the attack.

Well, that's not strictly true. He knows the exact time and location, he knows the lead guy in the group. He could report all that information. He could even give the authorities G.I. Joe's cell number so they could track him in real time.

But he can't do that.

Not without risking more lives.

It's not so much about his own survival. Part of him thinks he deserves to be shot for what he's done for them — the kid, The Texan, The Ballbreaker, the older man with the moustache.

He's scared for his family's safety.

All he can hope is that the attack passes without loss of life, which *would* be possible, in theory. And that, as he instructed G.I. Joe, the bombs themselves don't actually damage the target. That they just send a message, scare some folks in charge.

He can *hope*.

But he needs to plan, too, for the fallout.

If they want to tie this thing around his neck and hang him with it, well, he'll be damned if he just lets that happen without a fight. It's time he faced up to the things he did a long time ago, accepted his punishment, and took away their hold over him.

It's time he got himself an insurance policy.

He positions his phone, starts the digital recording device beside it.

Then he calls the kid.

45

Clearfield County, Pennsylvania

ELLEN GLANCES OUT of the Camry's window at the green water of the Susquehanna river branch winding below her. She's on one of those gigantic concrete bridges that carries the I-80 freeway over any valley that dares to get in its way. There's deep forest as far as the eye can see in every direction. And she's trying to guess where the Keystone Boys are headed.

She's been following their white GMC cargo van for almost an hour, now. They hit the interstate just south of Clarion and have been driving east ever since. A steady seventy miles per hour, never going over the speed limit.

She recognizes that style of driving. *Just fast enough.* No need to go any faster, because you've planned your journey to have more than enough time. And no desire to risk drawing attention from law enforcement for speeding, because if you get caught, your mission is screwed.

Ellen has no doubt that this is the start of their mission.

She just wishes she knew what the end of it was.

If they were to follow I-80 all the way east, they'd get to New York City.

That's a possible attack location. Should she tell someone?

She takes out her burner phone. Switches it on.

There's six per cent battery life remaining.

About enough for one call, maybe two.

She considers calling Harry. See if he has any update from his contact with security at Congress.

Also, she misses him like hell and wants to talk to him. To say anything, or even nothing. Just knowing he's there, on the other end of the line, would give her a shot of hope, a sense of support.

She brings up his number on the screen.

Can almost hear his voice already.

Glances up at the Keystone Boys in their GMC, way up ahead, but still just about in view. Still cruising at seventy.

Then she turns off the phone.

She needs to keep those precious few per cent for a call when she knows what's happening. Just hearing her husband talk isn't a good enough reason right now.

She's got to wait until she has something more. Something concrete.

She drops the phone back in her grab bag.

Focusses on the white cargo van.

Tries not to think of her family.

Thinks of her family.

*

Reedsville, Mifflin County, Pennsylvania

They've turned off onto I-99, skirted around Penn State University, and now they're taking the 322, headed south.

Ellen was lucky, she almost missed it. She'd been a little too far back, keeping her distance to avoid them spotting her in their mirrors. Tailing them alone, on a big road travelling at seventy, she had no alternative. Her concentration had wandered when the turn came up, and she had to pull off a whole lot faster than she would've liked when she saw the van leaving I-80.

At that moment, it'd hadn't been her family she'd been thinking about.

It had been Nadia.

She had been right back in Paris, remembering the days following the attack by Jalil and his group. France was a nation in mourning for a hundred and eighty-six murder victims. Make that a hundred and eighty-seven, with Nadia dead.

And Ellen had felt responsible for every single death. She'd tortured herself, reading as much as she could find about each victim. The ones who had been officially identified, anyway.

During the aftermath, she'd at least been able to confirm that Samir was alive and staying with Nadia's cousins in Paris. That was some small consolation amid all the devastation.

The rest of it was a horror show, playing on repeat in her mind.

Now, she feels the panic rising in her chest at those memories. But she knows she can't let them get the better of her.

This time, she needs to use them as a reminder that she can't let anything like Paris happen again. Not here, and not now.

She checks her GPS, tries to reassess where the Keystone Boys are going.

She figures it's not New York.

South east from I-80 would take them towards Philly.

Suddenly, she's picturing a shooting spree downtown. Civilians screaming and running for their lives as that fully automatic AK-47 opens fire on a crowd outside Independence Hall and the Liberty Bell. Places that symbolize American freedom.

Perfect terrorist targets.

46

THEY'VE STOPPED.

This time, Ellen was ready to react. She followed the cargo van, maybe a little closer than she would have liked, as it swept around the outskirts of Harrisburg on the 22, before it pulled off the road and came to a stop at a retail park in the eastern suburbs of the city.

The place is a lot like the nondescript concrete-and-plastic commercial sprawl just south of Clarion, where she was served at the gas station by Peter Logan. Perhaps this one is even a little bigger, a little more soulless, if that's possible. Maybe that's just because it's late and there aren't so many people around. The fast-food drive-thru spots are still open, but the lot outside Home Depot, where they've parked up, is almost deserted.

She's taken a risk, following them in here. If they looked her way, they could see her. She's counting on them not paying attention to her banged-up Camry. And, desperate as she is to get out, move around, and use the bathroom, she needs to sit tight and watch.

One by one, the five members of the Keystone Boys climb

out of the GMC. Mitch Logan, Kowalski, and Leanne Spinoza are up front. Peter Logan and Sherman are in back. As the rear doors open, Ellen tries to get a look inside, but it's too far away, too dark, and then the doors are shut again.

From the way they did that, she guesses there's something important in the back.

The five of them stretch, shake out their limbs, pace around a little, drink some water. There's not a whole lot of talking. Sherman lights up a cigarette and Spinoza asks him for one. He hands her the pack. Kowalski takes one too. Mitch Logan refuses, but his brother Peter doesn't even get the offer, which Ellen thinks is interesting.

Maybe he has some kind of beef with Sherman.

Or maybe he's just refused a dozen times before.

Ellen notices that they're all wearing navy blue coveralls with dark work boots, and little ID passes on lanyards around their necks. They look like cleaners, or some kind of building maintenance crew, gearing up for a night shift.

She figures this is the cover they'll use to access the target. Possibly to get inside a location, if it's a controlled site, or a building. Perhaps it's simply to hang out in a public place without looking suspicious, until they're ready to strike.

Ellen feels the low rumble of anxiety in her belly. That feeling has been with her for a whole week now — make it ten days — but there's something about seeing them here, prepared, that takes it up a notch for her.

She wonders how long they're going to stay here. Are they planning to camp out until dawn, or is this just a quick pit-stop?

She wonders about the choice of location, too. Could this retail park be a staging post for the attack itself? Is central Harrisburg, just a few miles west, the target?

There's a logic to that. It's not as big or high-profile as Philly, but it's still symbolic — the state capital. Maybe the Keystone Boys want to make a point about Pennsylvania. It's in their name, after all. And there are certainly more than enough people in downtown Harrisburg for them to conduct a mass casualty attack, if that's their goal.

Ellen's mouth is dry, and she can taste bile at the back of her throat. It's the realization that this is no longer two men talking in a hotel corridor. It's no longer a name, whispered on the dark web. It's five real people, here and now, heavily armed, and preparing to attack.

But she has to remind herself that — other than possession of one fully-automatic weapon — she still doesn't have any direct evidence of them breaking the law.

As much as her fight-or-flight system is telling her to act, she's got to be patient. Because she's probably only got one shot at stopping them.

Keep sitting tight, she thinks.

Then the guy with the cigarette starts walking over.

*

Ellen freezes as he moves in her direction. He's staring at the ground, taking quick, hard drags on the smoke. He seems agitated.

She sits motionless in the car. Prays he won't see her.

Prays he hasn't already seen her.

Tells herself that, even if he has, he won't know who she is.

Maybe she should pretend to be asleep, or crying on her cell phone . . .

He's getting closer, now. Coming right at her.

What's he doing?

Ellen holds her breath.

Then he veers off toward a little outbuilding and tries to find a way in, but it's closed up. He goes around to the back of it, out of sight from the others. Has a few final drags, then tosses his cigarette. Unzips his pants, and takes a piss against the wall.

Ellen lets her breath out.

Sinks a little lower in the car seat, but keeps watching him.

He's turned side-on to her, hunched over, muttering to himself and shaking his head, like he doesn't agree with his own thoughts.

She studies the movements of his mouth in the half-light, but can't quite make out what he's saying.

This is the guy Mitch Logan called Sherman.

She doesn't yet know what his role is in the group. He's not a high school buddy of the Logans. She doesn't recall seeing him in the yearbook, like the other four. And he doesn't look as though he's ex-military, so he's probably not extra muscle.

What's his connection?

Then he says a few more words, more forcefully. Kind of spits them out, like he's angry.

And this time, she can lip-read one of them: *bombs*.

Did she get that right?

Bombs?

Maybe that's his role.

Maybe he's a bomb-maker.

In one terrible moment, her understanding crystallizes. She's been too focused on the firearms — and the memories of Paris they've triggered — to pay attention to the other possibility. One that had occurred to her when she saw the phrase *light up the sky*.

Suddenly, her brain starts to skip over a hundred leaps of logic.

Have they got a bomb in the back of the truck? Wait — or *bombs*, as in multiple devices? Is that why Peter Logan was looking at videos of explosions on YouTube this afternoon? Are they planning an Oklahoma City-type attack? Will it be against a civilian target? Are the weapons to make sure they gain access to it? And, if Mitch Logan has brought in a specialist, does that mean the device is more complex than something he could build personally?

If the answer to any of those questions spinning around her head is *yes*, then this is even worse than she thought.

If the answer to all of them is *yes*, then it could be worse than Paris.

Her pulse is racing as Sherman zips his fly, turns and walks back over to the van without so much as glancing in her direction. He lights another cigarette on the way.

When he reaches the GMC, he has an abrupt exchange with Peter Logan, who points in the direction of the little building.

Then he starts walking over toward her, too.

Stay calm, she tells herself.

She's pretty sure he's just going to pee in the same spot as Sherman.

Unlike Sherman, though, Peter Logan is walking with his head raised.

Alert.

47

Harrisburg, Pennsylvania

HOLDING AS STILL as she possibly can, Ellen watches as Peter Logan approaches. He's about seventy yards away from her.

She thought the building would give her a little cover, but now she's wishing she'd parked somewhere else. Anywhere else.

She waits as he gets closer. He's roughly sixty yards off, now.

Then it's fifty.

At forty yards, he sees her car.

He stops. Stares at the vehicle.

His eyes flick down to the license plate, then up to the windshield.

He looks right at her.

Ellen looks right back at him.

They stay like that, holding one another's gaze, for a few seconds.

Peter's features expand in surprise, before a moment of confusion passes across his face.

Then he blinks, snaps out of it.

Starts walking toward her again. Keeps looking at her.

He's maybe thirty yards from the Camry, now.

Ellen's right hand goes to her grab bag on the passenger seat.

She reaches inside for the pistol, slowly curls her fingers around the grip, then the trigger.

Wonders if this is the moment where all hell breaks loose.

Peter Logan puts his right hand into the hip pocket of his coveralls.

Ellen raises the pistol to just below the level of the windshield.

If he draws a weapon, she's confident she can fire first.

What happens after that is anyone's guess.

Peter starts to pull his hand out of the pocket.

Ellen takes up a little slack on the trigger.

She focusses on his hand as it appears.

He's holding a Kleenex.

He wipes his nose with it, stuffs it back in the pocket.

Then he breaks eye contact with her, peels off to the spot behind the outbuilding, and goes about his business.

Ellen tries to make sense of what just happened.

He saw her, and she's sure he recognized not only the car, but also her face.

Peter Logan may not have been trained at The Farm, but he's got enough common sense to know that seeing the same person twice in the same day, eleven hours and two hundred miles apart, on the day you're preparing a terrorist attack, isn't a coincidence.

Maybe he'll guess that she's FBI or something. Whatever he thinks, one thing is for sure. He knows that she's onto them. And yet he did nothing.

He saw her, and *he did nothing*.

There are two possible reasons for that.

One is the more likely of the two, and it's bad. He's going to go back, tell the others, and they're going to come at her, all five of them, maybe with the truck, right now in this parking lot. In which case, she's toast.

The other possibility is less likely, but it's a whole lot better. It's the slim chance that, whatever act of violence the Keystone Boys are planning to carry out, Peter Logan is not fully on board with it.

Maybe that was the reason for his snub with the cigarettes just now, the terse exchange with Sherman.

It's impossible to tell.

Peter finishes peeing, zips himself up and walks back to the cargo van without so much as a glance her way.

Ellen tries to steady her breathing. Checks her exits for possible escape routes.

She gets ready to start the engine.

Peter Logan reaches the group outside the GMC.

Nothing happens.

No one acknowledges his return.

They just kind of stand there. Talking, smoking, stretching out.

Peter is on the edge of the group.

Ellen wonders if it's been like that his whole life. If being part of this was the first time anyone let him into a group. If that was why he joined, perhaps desperate for approval, only to realize he was in too deep.

A few more minutes pass with Ellen on high alert.

Then Mitch Logan checks his watch, gives some kind of signal and they stub out their cigarettes, scoop up the butts, and get back in the van.

As they move off, Ellen breathes a long sigh of relief. She starts the Camry and slowly pulls out after them.

Peter Logan recognized her, and he didn't tell the others.

That means he wants her to follow them.

He wants her to see what their target is.

Maybe he even wants her to stop them.

*

Route 283, Middletown, Pennsylvania

The Keystone Boys have driven south out of Harrisburg and Ellen guesses that's not where the attack is going to happen.

Now, they're heading for the Pennsylvania Turnpike, which runs east to Philly.

A bunch of images flash through her mind. The carnage she pictured taking place at Independence Hall. Next, there's the Paris movie theatre, the blood and bodies. Then she sees the two men she killed in the Poconos yesterday. The open, empty eyes of the one she shot through the cabin door.

She blinks, breathes, flexes her hands. Tries to focus on the white GMC ahead of her.

As a junction approaches, the van suddenly changes lane and signals to turn off.

The sign overhead is for Harrisburg International Airport.

Oh my God, she thinks, as her heart rate goes into overdrive.

It's the airport.

They're going to shoot down a plane on take-off or landing. Or maybe try to blow up a jet on the stand.

Ellen takes out her burner cell.

Switches it on.

*

Royalton, Pennsylvania

They've passed the airport. So, it's not the target, either.

That's good, Ellen tells herself.

It also means she still doesn't know where they're headed. Which isn't so good.

They're continuing south, but this time it's on a small, single lane road that's flanked by neat, one-storey clapboard houses with white picket fences around perfect lawns.

Have they taken a wrong turn?

Have they spotted her, and are they trying to flush her out through a choke point?

Or is this their method of connecting up with a bigger road, like the 83, just across the river? Ellen knows that highway runs south to Baltimore, where they could hit I-95 down to D.C.

Maybe that's it — they're heading for the capital.

She thinks of Harry. She's not even sure if he's still in Washington, or if he's gone to New Jersey, to their relatives' house, to hide out with Josh and her parents.

She longs to call them.

As the cargo van starts to slow, Ellen hits her brakes, too.

She checks the GPS, zooms out a little.

Sees the island in the Susquehanna river.

And it hits her. She knows where they're going.

It's not a city or an airport or a monument.

It's a nuclear power plant.

Ellen curses herself for not anticipating it.

She thinks once more of the videos Peter Logan was watching on his phone at the gas station. They weren't just explosions.

They were *nuclear* explosions.

48

PETER IS SWEATING his balls off. The back of the cargo van is like a goddamn furnace. Dozer must've left it out full in the sun all day before he loaded up and drove over to Mitch's place. There are no windows to pop, no air coming through. And the combination of thick coveralls and body armor that he's wearing ain't helping, neither. Peter's t-shirt is soaked and plastered to his upper body. But he knows the temperature's not the only thing making him sweaty and nauseous.

Despite the pill Mitch gave him, Peter's still nervous as hell. So nervous that he feels as though he might actually shit his pants if he stops clenching.

It's because he knows they're only a few minutes out, now.

And because the woman from the gas station is tailing them.

Peter's gone over that a few dozen times in his head since he saw her in the Home Depot parking lot, but he still can't make no sense out of it.

He recognized her Camry from the pumps on the forecourt — a mid-nineties model, and you don't see so many of them anymore. He didn't recall the license plate, but he didn't need to.

The lady's face was clear enough behind the wheel. It was her, no doubt about it.

But who in the hell is she?

And what's she gonna do?

Peter wonders if she's some kind of special agent, one of them undercover folks from the FBI or whatnot. Except he never submitted the tip on the website, so how could the feds know? Far as Peter's aware, their group all stuck to Mitch's advice about security. Even Leanne, who lives half her life on social media, has kept schtum. And none of them has mentioned a thing about the Keystone Boys or their plan or any of it to no one.

It just don't make no sense.

Maybe Mitch's contact — the guy in D.C. who got them the details about the power plant — tipped them off.

Maybe it was Sherman. Peter's never trusted him.

He screws his eyes shut and tries to figure it out, but that doesn't help any.

"Wake up, Pee-Wee," barks Sherman, sitting on the wheel arch across from him. "We're almost there."

"I know," Peter replies, opening his eyes and staring at the floor of the van between them. Specifically, staring at the tarp that's covering six big IEDs. The bombs are lined up, side-by-side. Nearly a hundred pounds of military-grade high explosive packed into them.

"Everybody set?" Mitch calls out, turning from the front to check on the two of them in the back.

"Ready," Sherman responds, though Peter can see that his hands are shaking.

"What about you, Pee-Wee?" Mitch says.

Peter swallows. "Good to go," he lies.

"Weapons ready," Mitch commands. "But keep 'em covert 'til I say otherwise, okay?"

Up front, Leanne has gone real quiet.

Peter knows she's about to try pulling off the biggest acting job of her life. And, whether it works or not, Armageddon is coming. It's not a question of if, just when.

And that'll be the moment that Peter needs to make a decision.

Does he have it in him to be a hero?

*

South bridge, Three Mile Island, Pennsylvania

It's dark out and Peter can't see shit as they approach the plant. He sits up, tries to look through the gap between Mitch and Leanne's heads in the front. The GMC's headlights pick out a big white sign that reads: *CONTRACTOR ENTRANCE*. They bump over what Peter remembers from the satellite images is a railroad track, then they slow to a roll, and stop.

"Showtime," Leanne says.

"Go get 'em, baby," Mitch tells her.

Leanne drops the window. "Oh, hey there!" she calls out cheerily.

Peter hears footsteps approaching. He can't see the guy at the gate from where he's sat, but he can see Leanne turn her head and switch on that hundred-watt smile of hers.

The guy says something Peter can't really hear, but it sounds like a question.

"We're from Maxflow," replies Leanne. She pushes her chest out and lifts her little fake ID on the lanyard up for inspection. "It's a scheduled O and M visit. Part of the regular programme. It's listed right here." A piece of paper changes hands.

Peter can't remember what *O and M* means. Something and Maintenance.

His heart is beating like a jackhammer and his hands are so wet he has to wipe his palms on the coveralls.

The guy says he needs to check.

"What, nobody called you all about the time change?" Leanne asks. "Aww, shoot. We've driven all this way, on Fourth of July weekend, too." She gives a little laugh. "Sucks to be us, working the holidays, right?"

"That's a real shame, ma'am——"

"Call me Taylor," she says.

"Taylor," he repeats. He's starting to fall under her spell.

"And we gotta do the inspection," she continues, "or else our boss is gonna kick our asses. Plus, we only get paid for completed jobs."

The guy hesitates. "Ah . . ."

Peter knows that feeling. Being totally disarmed by Leanne. She does that to people. She's been doing it to him for sixteen years without even knowing it.

"Tell you what," Leanne continues, "why don't we go on through, like we always do, and your buddy at the guard hut can check us in while we call our out-of-hours guy to confirm? That way, we all save time. How 'bout that, huh?"

Peter can almost feel the heat of her smile.

The guy melts. He points her to the hut across the bridge, walks away, and opens the gate. It's a pretty flimsy thing, made out of aluminum poles and chicken wire, that they could ram their way through anyway, if needed. But Mitch said that the closer they can get to the targets without firing a shot, the better.

That works for Peter. But he wonders how much longer they can hold out.

And, as they drive over the bridge, he wonders something else.

Where's the woman in the Camry?

49

Three Mile Island, Pennsylvania

THEY COME TO a stop almost as soon as they've crossed the bridge. Peter tries to picture their location from the satellite images Mitch has shown him dozens of times. He knows they're on the island, now, and they've pulled up by a guard hut.

"Keep the engine running," Mitch tells Randy.

Peter hears a voice from outside, this time at the driver's window.

Leanne leans across Mitch and starts talking, but this time, it doesn't go so well.

"I need to check in the back," the security guard says.

"It's just our regular equipment," Leanne protests.

"But it's not a regular visit," the guy replies. "Maxflow's not due for another month."

"Our schedule changed," she tries. "The last shift shoulda told you guys . . ."

"I still need to check. That's our protocol," he states. He sounds like a hardass. Maybe an ex-cop or something.

Leanne's still talking, but the guard ain't paying attention.

"Mitch . . ." she whispers, urgently.

"Sit tight," says Mitch. "Randy, you know what to do."

"Uh-huh," Dozer responds.

"Ready in the back," Mitch adds quietly. He sounds calm as hell.

Peter listens as the security guy walks behind them. He catches some movement through the windshield, too. At least two more guards have appeared at the front. Peter snaps his neck to the rear doors as the handle pops.

One door opens and the guard peers into the darkness inside. He glances at the tarp, then at Sherman, then Peter. His eyebrows kind of press together.

"What is this?" the guard asks, his hand going to his pistol.

"Now," says Mitch.

Randy throws the gearstick in reverse and hits the gas. The guard screams as the truck slams into him and knocks him down. He disappears as Randy backs right over him with a thump. There's a muffled roar of pain from beneath them, an unholy sound.

At the same time, Peter hears shots from up front.

Two sets of two rounds. *Double-taps*, Mitch called them.

Peter instinctively covers his head, shrinks down. There's a high-pitched ringing in his ears from the bullets.

Over the noise, he hears his brother shout, "Drive!"

The tires screech as Dozer shifts gear and pulls away fast. There's a sickening crunch as they bump over the guard beneath the wheels a second time. But no more screams.

Peter looks back.

The back door is flapping open, and as they speed away toward the power plant, Peter sees three bodies lying on the blacktop. They're illuminated under the lights of the guard hut. White shirts over black pants. And they're all dead.

"Fuckin' A!" Randy bellows.

"Weapons ready!" Mitch calls. "Remember, we hit the reactor

first, then the turbine, then the cooling towers — the new ones, not the old ones, okay? Two EFPs per target."

Nobody says anything.

"Got it?" Mitch turns to the back.

"Got it," Peter says, automatically. A reflex reaction to a lifetime of agreeing with whatever his brother says.

"Expect armed resistance up ahead," Mitch adds. "And the guy from the first gate behind us. Pee-Wee, Sherman, get ready to fire at the rear."

Peter glances over at Sherman. The German has his head in his hands. Then his body heaves like he's been punched in the gut, and he spews up all over the tarp. It stinks. A little bit has splashed on Peter's legs.

"Jesus Christ," Mitch yells. "Sherman, get your shit together, soldier! This is your time!"

Sherman groans.

"We've probably got ten minutes, maybe twelve, before the cops arrive," Mitch tells them. "We wanna set off the EFPs and be gone by the time they get here. Understand?"

Randy says something affirmative.

Peter rubs his hands over his face, blinks.

The bodies are just little black-and-white specs, now. Then they disappear altogether as they round a corner. A mile up ahead, the lights of the power plant come into view.

*

The lights grow brighter as they hit the huge parking lot at the south end of the plant.

Peter recalls there's a concrete wall running across the island, probably to stop the exact thing they're trying to do right now. The only way past it is through a little barrier at a second guard hut.

"Spray 'em with the AK," Mitch tells Leanne. "Give 'em the full mag."

She lifts the weapon out of the footwell.

Peter can see it trembling in her hands.

"Then it's straight on through, Dozer. Ready?"

The big man grunts from behind the wheel, and floors the pedal.

Peter is thrown back as the van picks up speed. He grabs the wheel arch, steadies himself. Draws his Ruger pistol. Swallows hard.

"Now, Leanne!" yells Mitch.

Leanne raises the shaking barrel to the windshield and lets it rip. There's a deafening burst of fire and she screams.

Peter can hear Mitch firing as well. *Tap-tap, tap-tap.*

And he can hear shots from outside, coming at them. One pierces the side of the van, whistles right by his head and out the other side before he even knows what's happened.

Sherman is curled up like a baby on the cargo bed, beside the bombs.

They plough forward, Dozer hunched over the wheel, roaring at the top of his massive lungs like a crazy man. They hit the barrier and it snaps in two like a popsicle stick.

Leanne screams again, a different sound this time.

She's in pain.

"They fucking got me!" she wails. "Fuck, Mitch! My arm!"

Mitch says nothing.

Their momentum carries them up a few steps and then they're outside the power plant itself.

"Hit it right in the middle!" Mitch shouts, pointing at the perimeter fence.

The Dozer does what he did for years on the football field and just smashes his way through. The van rips the chain-link fence in two. Seconds later, they're by the buildings.

"Everybody out!" yells Mitch. "Go, go, go!"

Peter half-crawls, half-falls from the back of the van onto the concrete. His head is spinning. He looks back the way they've come. There are maybe four guys lying on the ground at the guard house, a couple of them still moving.

Then Mitch is beside him, yanking the tarp off and hauling out the first bomb. He hands it off to Randy, then picks up another one himself.

"Give us covering fire," he tells Peter.

"Leanne's hurt," Peter responds.

"Forget about her," Mitch says.

"But—"

"That's an order!" his brother barks. Then, turning back to the van, he reaches in and grabs Sherman. "Hey, German, let's fucking go. Now!"

As Mitch drags Sherman from the van, Peter makes his first decision.

He ignores his brother's instructions.

Instead, he jogs around to the passenger seat of the cargo van.

Inside, Leanne is holding her arm up by the shoulder. There's blood coming through the coveralls and onto her fingers.

"Peter," she gasps, her eyes wide. "Help me."

"I got you," he replies. He thinks of the first aid course he has to do every year at the gas station.

Stop the bleeding.

He pockets the Ruger and unzips his coveralls. Takes off his Kevlar vest, then his t-shirt. It's still dripping in sweat, but he ties it around Leanne's upper arm, right where the blood's coming out. Puts a twist in the knot, kind of like a tourniquet.

"Press on that," he tells her.

Ahead of him, in the headlights of the cargo van, Mitch and Randy are carrying the first two bombs over to the reactor building.

Then Peter hears the whine of an engine behind him. He spins around in the direction of the noise.

There's a car coming up the road, real fast.

He squints, focusses as it gets nearer.

It's the woman in her Camry.

50

Three Mile Island, Pennsylvania

"HARRY!" ELLEN FEELS the relief as he picks up, but she can't waste a second. "Harry, I'm—"

"Ellen! Where are you? What's going on?"

"I'm at Three Mile Island, Harry," she shouts into phone, set to speaker on the dash in front of her.

"Three Mile . . . you mean the nuclear plant? Why—"

"Yeah. Listen up," she says, cutting him off, "I have like two per cent battery left. My phone's gonna go any minute. I've been following the Keystone Boys, and they're attacking the power station right now."

"Holy shit. What, are you there, what are you—"

"Yes, I'm there. I'm driving right in after them. I knew they were planning it for the Fourth of July, but I didn't think it'd be literally after midnight—"

"Stop, Ellen, you hear me? Stop the car. Stop going after them. You gotta call nine-one-one."

"I just did. I want you to call FBI, Homeland Security, see if you can get onto that Fusion Center in Philly where they all sit. You know, the counter-terrorism unit?"

"Okay, I'll call them. Just stay back and let the cops—"

"There's no time, Harry. They're already inside the power plant. They're definitely armed, they've already fired shots, and I think they're preparing to let off a bomb. Maybe more than one."

"Then all the more reason to get out of there!" Harry yells. "Get as far away as you can!"

"No, Harry."

"What do you mean, no? Get the hell out, right now!"

"I can't let this happen," she says. "Not again."

"Again? Paris wasn't your fault, Ellen! Getting yourself killed won't change what happened, and—"

"Is Josh with you?"

"Josh . . . Yeah, but he's asleep. We're all here, at your dad's cousin's place. But you need to get out before—"

"Can I speak to them?"

"Christ, Ellen."

"Put them on."

Harry sighs. "Okay . . . gimme a second. None of us are sleeping . . . in case we heard anything . . ." He tails off and there's a shuffling sound, then a crackle on the line.

Ellen's car headlights pick out the three bodies outside the guard hut before she hits the other side of the bridge. There's one guard, alive, kneeling over a body, checking for vital signs. Maybe he was on the front gate. She swerves to the left-hand side of the hut to avoid them and accelerates toward the bend in the road up ahead.

"Ellen, honey, is that you?" Her mom's voice comes over the speaker. "Are you there?"

"Yes, mom, I'm here."

"Are you in danger, sweetheart?" her father demands. "Do you need help?"

"I just . . . I wanted to tell you," she says, ignoring the

question. There's nothing else her family can do for her, now. She just felt the urge to talk to them, in case—

A long, sustained burst of automatic fire breaks her thought. She hears more shots, up ahead. Small calibre weapons returning fire. She guesses who's winning. And it's not good news.

"I wanted to tell you all that I love you," she blurts. "A lot."

"Was that gunfire?" her mother asks. "Oh God, Ellen, honey, just make sure you're safe. Can't you—"

"I have to go!" Ellen shouts, as she hits the bend. The phone slides across the dash and she grabs it, holds it in front of her.

"Ellen!" It's Harry again, this time. "Turn back, and drive away, please. Please, just go, the cops will protect you, and—"

"I love you, Harry," she says in reply. "Make that call, now."

Then there's a commotion at her family's end, and they're all speaking at once before a single, small voice comes through, clearer than the others.

"I love you, Mommy."

It's Josh.

Ellen's heart leaps in her chest. Suddenly, she's fighting back tears.

"Josh, sweetie! I love you so much, and I'll be back home, just as soon as—"

The line goes dead.

Ellen snatches a glance at the phone screen. It's black. She stabs it with her thumb. Nothing happens. The battery's gone.

"Goddammit!" she shouts, tossing the handset into the footwell.

She pulls her pistol and accelerates toward the lights ahead of her, surrounding the towering structures of the nuclear reactor that the Keystone Boys are about to blow up.

She realizes that if they succeed, that may be the last time she ever speaks to her family.

But she'll be damned if she's going to let that happen.

51

Three Mile Island, Pennsylvania

IT ALREADY LOOKS like a war zone by the time Ellen reaches the power plant. Four bodies are lying on the ground. Two are completely still, two are still alive. The guard hut is riddled with bullet holes, and the barrier beside it is broken. She guesses the Keystone Boys rammed it with their vehicle.

Ellen pushes away the image of the Paris movie theatre that floods her mind and tries to focus on her surroundings. On the here and now.

She assesses the situation.

Past the concrete wall and up a set of steps, she sees a tear in the perimeter fence and, just beyond it, the white cargo van. The back is open, and she can make out a couple of the attackers moving away from it, toward a tower. They're each carrying something.

And she can guess what it is.

She has to act now.

Ellen slams on the brakes and throws the car door open. Pushes herself out, pistol in hand, and starts running.

She glances at the two guards who are alive by the hut. She

can see one of them is trying to press on a gunshot wound to the lower leg. The other is clutching his hip, writhing in pain. They both need first aid, for sure. But she has to make a decision.

She can't let the bombs detonate.

"Help is coming real soon!" she tells the guards, as she sprints past and up the steps.

Approaching the van, she gets her pistol stable in the cup-and-saucer grip, ready to fire. Then she sees a third figure in dark coveralls.

He's lying on the ground by the rear doors. At first, she can't tell who it is, because he's wrapped his arms around his head. Has he been wounded?

As she gets closer, aiming her gun at him, he turns to her.

It's Sherman. And he looks absolutely terrified.

"Please don't kill me," he whines. "Please."

"Do you have a weapon?" she demands.

He nods.

"Take it out slowly and toss it over here."

He removes a handgun from a pouch in the coveralls.

Ellen gets ready to shoot in case it's a trap or he tries anything dumb.

He throws it toward her, but it's a feeble effort that lands halfway between them.

Then she hears a groan from the front of the GMC. It sounds like a woman. It must be Leanne Spinoza. But where's Peter Logan?

Then she gets her answer.

"It's gonna be okay," says a high male voice from up front. "I got you."

"Stay there," she tells Sherman. "Hands on your head, face to the ground. Or I will shoot you."

He does as she says.

Rounding the side of the van, she gets a view of the two

figures, now positioning the objects they were carrying next to the tower. One's big, the other is a giant. It's Mitch Logan and Kowalski. They begin unspooling cord and backing up.

Ellen needs to stop them. But they're maybe fifty yards away, and she can't be sure she'll hit them at this range. She returns to the back of the van.

"Don't fucking move," she orders Sherman. He's still lying on his front, hands over his head.

She inspects the cargo bay. It smells like someone's thrown up in there. More importantly, though, there are four large, identical cylinders. They each have copper discs at one end, and blasting caps at the other. She recognizes them immediately.

Explosively formed projectiles. EFPs.

She quickly figures out that it's not a truck bomb they're going for. It's worse than that.

They want to punch a hole in the reactor wall, trigger a radiation leak.

Maybe set off a chain reaction.

Maybe even cause a meltdown.

She's got to stop them right now.

Ellen starts to run, but she's barely beyond the van when gunfire starts coming at her.

A whole lot of gunfire.

She dives to the concrete.

52

Three Mile Island, Pennsylvania

AFTER THE FIRST hail of bullets, Ellen looks up from where she's lying, prone, on the concrete.

A small team of armed security guards has arrived from the north side of the plant and taken Mitch and Kowalski by surprise.

The two terrorists have abandoned their det cord and devices and now they're taking cover by the buildings.

Mitch barks something to Kowalski, who grabs a long weapon that Ellen didn't even realize he had slung over his shoulder. Now she can see it's a pump-action shotgun.

She sees Kowalski rack the slide, then step out and fire five huge shots in quick succession.

He hits one of the guards outright, knocking him backward. Two others go to the deck and two throw themselves behind cover.

Mitch raises his rifle and calmly picks off the two on the ground.

Some part of Ellen's brain registers that she's literally just watched three men murdered right in front of her. Her fight-or-flight system should be sending her into panic mode. But, somehow, she finds herself thinking clearly.

Ellen knows she can't fight them with her little 9mm handgun. Her only advantage is that they haven't seen her yet. She gets up and makes a run back to the van, keeping low as the bullets fly.

As long as they're engaged in the firefight, they can't let off the bombs.

At the rear of the van, she jumps in, lays her pistol on the cargo bed, and turns her attention to the IEDs. She figures that at least she can sabotage the remaining four, right here. She'll worry about the other two once the gunfight outside is over.

She starts pulling the blasting cap out of the back of the closest IED. It's hard work, because it's embedded right in the explosive, which she guesses is C4. And there's a hell of a lot of it. She doesn't want to think about what'll happen if one of them goes off, let alone two. She gets the first cap loose, then moves on to the second bomb and does the same.

She can hear labored breathing from the other side of the seats, up front, just a few feet away.

She's wrenching the third blasting cap clear when she hears the click of a handgun cocking behind her, accompanied by a thin voice.

"Who are you?"

She turns slowly.

It's Peter Logan.

He's standing by the rear doors, topless, for some reason, his coveralls unzipped and peeled down to the waist. His upper body is pale and thin, almost boyish.

But he's holding a small pistol in trembling hands.

And the barrel is pointed right at her.

She raises her palms, gently extends them toward him.

"Peter," she begins. "My name is Ellen, and I wanna stop this—"

"Pee-Wee!"

It's Spinoza. Ellen guesses it's her in the cab.

"Hold still, Leanne," he calls out. "It's gonna be okay. Just stop the bleeding."

"Peter," Ellen says firmly, making sure she's got his attention, "I don't think you want to do this, and I want to help you—"

"How did you know about us?" he asks.

"That doesn't matter right now."

Behind him, Sherman gets up.

He's unsteady on his feet, but Ellen can tell something's changed. He's lost his fear.

She watches as he staggers over to his weapon, stoops to collect it, and comes back over to them.

"Shoot her, Pee-Wee," he says. "Or I'll shoot you."

53

Three Mile Island, Pennsylvania

PETER TURNS TO see Sherman holding a handgun. Aiming it at his face.

"I said, shoot her," Sherman repeats, "or I'll shoot you. It's pretty simple."

"I don't . . ." Peter stammers, "we don't even know who she is."

"It doesn't matter who she is," Sherman responds. His voice has gone kind of hard, now. "She's trying to stop us. So, we have to stop her. That's all that matters."

"But she—"

"Do it!" barks Sherman. "Now!"

Peter turns slowly back to the woman. She's crouching in the cargo bay of the van. From what Peter can tell, it looks as though she's taken apart two of their bombs. There's a pistol that he guesses belongs to her, but it's a little too far away for her to reach.

Gunshots ripple through the air over by the buildings. Mitch and Dozer are taking fire, and they're giving it back.

"Kill her!" Sherman cries. "Or are you too chicken shit to do it?"

Chicken shit. Exactly what his old man used to call him.

Without thinking, his finger tightens a little on the trigger. He shuts one eye, but the barrel is wobbling so much in his hands he can't hardly aim it right.

"Peter, listen to me," says the woman, calmly. "You don't have to do what he says. You can choose."

"I will shoot you, Pee-Wee, I swear," Sherman snarls.

"I know you're scared, Peter," the woman continues, "but I think Sherman is, too. And I think he's more scared than you are right now."

"Wait, how'd you know—" Sherman begins, but the woman talks over him.

"He wants you to do shoot me because he's too frightened to do it," she says. "But you're braver than he is, and—"

"Shut up!" Sherman yells. "I'm not scared!"

"You're in control, Peter," she tells him.

"Last chance, Pee-Wee," says Sherman. He cocks the pistol's hammer. "Do it."

Peter's guts are twisted in knots.

Will it be this woman's life, or his own?

Survival instinct tells him to pull the trigger. Fire and forget. Stay alive.

But he's already made one decision for himself tonight.

And he's about to make another.

"No," he replies, turning to Sherman and standing up a little straighter.

"*No?*" Sherman snorts. "What are you, some kind of traitor? A snitch?"

"I'm not a snitch, I—"

"Have you been working against us all along?" Sherman's face twists in disgust. "That's why she's here, isn't it, sabotaging our fuckin' EFPs? I should execute you for that. Or maybe Mitch is gonna want to do it himself."

"It's like I told you, Peter," says the woman, "Sherman hasn't got the balls to pull the trigger."

Peter turns back to her. She's closer than she was a second ago.

"Stay where you are," Peter tells her.

"He hasn't got the balls," she repeats.

"That's where you're wrong!" cries Sherman, switching his aim from Peter to the woman. "I'll kill the both of you!"

Sherman starts to squeeze the trigger.

Peter shuts his eyes.

The shot rings out.

54

Three Mile Island, Pennsylvania

IT TAKES PETER a second to realize that Sherman is lying on the ground.

There's a hole right between his eyes.

And he ain't moving no more.

It takes a few more seconds for Peter to figure out who shot Sherman.

She's kneeling on the concrete at the side of the van, holding the AK-47.

And she looks half dead herself.

"Leanne!" he exclaims.

"Peter, I . . ." she begins, but then she falls right over, drops the rifle, rolls onto her back.

He runs to her, cradles her head.

"Leanne, you okay?" He hears his own breath coming in short, sharp bursts. "You're gonna be okay, you hear me?"

But she just whimpers, shakes her head.

Her eyes roll back in their sockets, and the lids start to close.

"No," he says. "Stay awake. Stay with me!"

He gathers her up into his arms. It takes all his strength.

He feels something wet and warm against his ribs and glances down.

It's Leanne's blood.

There's a lot of it, soaking through his t-shirt, which has come loose, and into her coveralls. Their fabric has turned black around her shoulder.

"Don't you die, now," he says, his voice cracking.

She blinks her eyes open, looks up at him.

"He was . . ." she whispers, "gonna shoot you."

"You saved my life," Peter tells her. "And I promise I'm gonna save yours."

She gasps as he tightens the t-shirt tourniquet on her shoulder. But, as he looks more closely under the floodlights, he can see the problem. The angle on her arm means the material don't really cover the bullet hole. And the hole's worse than he thought, too. Bigger, closer to the blood vessels. And it's oozing red. He presses his own hand onto it and Leanne winces. It must hurt like all hell.

But she ain't got the strength left to holler.

"Leanne . . ."

He thinks she's about to pass out, but then she looks right up at him.

"You're not like the others, Peter," she tells him, her voice soft and low. "You're a good man."

He realizes that, for the first time in sixteen years, she's not calling him *Pee-Wee*. She's using his actual name.

His eyes are stinging with tears.

"Leanne, don't you go, now," he says, urgently. He pulls her a little closer to him.

Another burst of gunfire rings out across the way, then some shouting.

Then silence.

Peter glances up. He sees Mitch and Randy come out from the side of the building.

He figures they must've shot all the security guards dead.

Now they're walking back over to their bombs.

And Peter has another choice to make.

55

Three Mile Island, Pennsylvania

THERE WAS A moment where Ellen thought she was going to die.

She was pretty confident that Peter wouldn't pull the trigger, and she hoped Sherman was all talk, but she couldn't be certain of either assessment. Especially as their emotions rose. While they argued, she'd crept toward her pistol until it was within reach. She was about to dive for it when Leanne appeared and shot Sherman. She hadn't counted on that.

Nor had she counted on Peter's level of feeling for Leanne. It's clear the guy is in love with her, which is more than can be said for Mitch. Now, with Peter trying to save Leanne's life, and neither of them a threat to her, Ellen can get back to her task: disarming the EFPs.

She's working on removing the third blasting cap when the gunfire and shouting suddenly stop.

Ellen spins to look through the windshield of the van.

She sees Mitch Logan and Kowalski sling their weapons over their shoulders and head back toward the EFPs on the ground, over by the reactor building. She guesses they've either killed the remaining security guards, or the guards have abandoned their posts, and now they're going to finish setting up the bombs.

Grabbing her pistol, she leaps down from the cargo bay. She moves around the driver's side of the van, where the door is open, and scans the interior. The far passenger seat is smeared with blood that she guesses is Spinoza's. In the footwell, there's an open toolbox containing ammo, and beside it an unzipped black holdall.

Ellen reaches inside the holdall. It contains a bunch of stun grenades. She knows they're most effective indoors, in confined spaces, but what the hell. Beggars can't be choosers. She grabs one and stuffs it in her jeans pocket.

That's when she hears the first sirens.

They're a way off though, carried on the night air, and Ellen reckons she still has a couple of minutes before they get here.

More than enough time for Mitch and Kowalski to blow a hole in the reactor.

It's two of them against one of her, and they have superior weapons.

But she can't wait for backup.

She has to go for them now.

56

Three Mile Island, Pennsylvania

ELLEN SWITCHES THE pistol to her left hand, gets a little closer, then tosses the grenade at Mitch Logan.

As it loops through the air, she raises her pistol at the bulky figure of Kowalski, who's closer to her. There's a lot to aim for, but he's still forty yards away.

She shuts her eyes, dips her head.

The bang rips through the night and she sees the flash from behind closed eyelids, as if she's looking right at the sun.

When she opens her eyes, Mitch Logan is on the ground. Moving, but maybe concussed or disoriented.

Kowalski freezes. He's standing directly behind the EFP, and in front of the reactor.

Ellen doesn't hesitate. She fires, going for center mass.

The shot strikes him, knocks him down.

She exhales, blinks.

He gets right back up.

He's wearing Kevlar.

Shit.

He takes up his shotgun. Racks it.

Realizes he needs to reload.

He reaches into his pockets, starts fumbling with shells.

Ellen gets closer. She has to act fast.

Kowalski stuffs a cartridge into the shotgun breach.

Ellen knows if he gets off one round, she's a goner.

She also knows there's no point trying to hit Kowalski if he's wearing body armor. She needs to be smarter than that.

She might make a head shot, if she's lucky.

But then she has another idea.

She looks at the position of the EFP. Takes careful aim at the back of it, right at the blasting cap. It's just about within range, but still a long shot in every sense. There's no room for error.

She pauses her breath.

Beyond the device, out of focus, she's aware of Kowalski raising the shotgun.

She fires.

The blast is instantaneous. And so loud that it sends her staggering backward.

A cloud of smoke rises from where the EFP was, and floats over the concrete. When it clears, she can see Kowalski lying on the concrete. He's literally been sliced in two.

Ellen stares at his corpse in disbelief.

She forces herself to look away, behind him.

The reactor wall is intact. The bomb had been too far away, its aim a little off. And a part of its impact was deflected by The Bulldozer's huge, Kevlar-clad body.

She lifts her weapon again and, through the dissipating smoke, tries to zero in on Mitch Logan. She can't see him.

The bomb he was setting up is still there.

But he's gone.

Ellen checks left and right, but it's as if he's vanished. And she can barely hear anything over the buzzing in her ears from the EFP blast.

Trying to work out where he is, she turns right around to face the van.

Mitch Logan is standing next to it.

And his rifle is trained on her.

57

Three Mile Island, Pennsylvania

"WHO THE FUCK are you?"

Mitch Logan's first words to Ellen are almost the same as his brother's, just a few minutes ago, when Peter was aiming a gun barrel at her.

The difference is that, whereas Peter's voice betrayed his nerves and confusion, Mitch's tone is one of confidence and command. A man who's used to giving orders under pressure. Who's not used to his plans turning to shit.

And who would kill her without a second thought.

She figures he must've doubled back around the reactor to the rear of the van, from where he was able to ambush her.

"Drop your weapon," he adds. "Now."

She's got no choice. She stoops, throws her pistol down. It clatters on the concrete.

The whine in Ellen's ears has receded enough for her to hear the sirens again. They're louder, now, which means the cops are getting closer.

"Can you hear that, Mitch?" she asks him. "It's time to give up. Kowalski and Sherman are dead. Your girlfriend Leanne is dying, too, over there." She gestures to the other side of the van. "You've lost half your bombs, and the cops will be here in two minutes."

"That's enough time to finish what I set out to do," Mitch replies. "All I need to know before I shoot you is who you are, and why you're here."

Ellen tries to think. She needs to buy a little time if she can.

"You have five seconds to tell me," he says. "Then I'll put a bullet in your belly. Five . . . four . . ."

"My name is Ellen McGinley. Please don't shoot me," she says, trying to keep calm, even though she can feel her legs trembling. "I have a husband called Harry, and a six-year-old son named Josh. And I love them both very much."

Mitch narrows his eyes.

Ellen guesses trying to get empathy from a man like him isn't going to work.

"How did you know about this operation?" he demands. "Five . . . four . . . three . . ."

"I overheard some people talking."

"Which people? Where?"

"In a hotel," she gasps, "in D.C."

"Which people?" he repeats. "Five . . . four . . ."

"Two men. I don't know who they were."

Mitch looks like he's thinking. Trying to process something. Maybe re-evaluating who he trusted.

"Why are you doing this?" she asks him. "How could this be the answer to whatever you've been through?"

"Shut up," he replies.

"Who ordered you to carry out this attack?" she asks. "Who's behind all this? Who gave you the target?"

"I'm asking the questions," he tells her. "And I'm done. Which means you are too."

Mitch flicks a switch on his assault rifle and a red dot appears over Ellen's stomach.

She wonders if this is it. If this is the end.
She tries to think of something else to say.
But all she can think of is her family.
She stares down at that little red dot.
"Stop!"
Ellen's head jerks up at the cry.
It's Peter Logan.

58

Three Mile Island, Pennsylvania

PETER WALKS AROUND the front of the van. His revolver is out. He points it at his brother.

Mitch looks almost amused by the interruption.

"Pee-Wee, what the fuck? Put that down and grab another EFP out the van. Go."

"I can't let you do it, Mitch," he says.

"What?"

"I can't let you kill her, and I can't let you set off those bombs. You hear?"

Mitch grunts a laugh. "You'll do what I tell you, Pee-Wee. Like you always do."

"Not this time," says Peter.

Mitch lowers the weapon a fraction, stares at Peter.

"Seriously?" Mitch shakes his head. "What are you gonna do with that, li'l bro? There's no way in hell you can pull that trigger. Least of all on me."

Peter can feel his hands shaking. His whole body, matter of fact.

"I can, and I will," he says.

"Bullshit."

"Put the rifle down, Mitch," Peter urges. "We're gonna give ourselves up. And no one else has to die. Leanne needs a medic."

"Forget about Leanne," Mitch returns. "We've got a job to finish here."

Peter feels the anger rise up inside him, as hot as his brother is cold.

"I'll do it," Peter says, taking a step forward. He's maybe ten yards away from Mitch, now.

"No, you won't," his big brother replies. "You wanna know why?"

Peter doesn't respond. He just looks past the sight on the revolver, into his brother's eyes.

"Because you're *chicken shit*," Mitch says. "Just like pop always said. Ma said it, too. You ain't got it in you."

"I have, I . . ." Peter tries to respond, but his voice is as unsteady as his nerves are, now.

"Go on, then." Mitch lowers his rifle, spreads his arms, waits.

Peter presses his lips together. Shuts one eye.

But he can't do it.

"Like I thought," says Mitch. Then he turns back to the woman, raises his AR-15 rifle, and shoots her.

She falls to the deck like a sack of potatoes, gripping her stomach in both hands.

Then she screams.

Peter watches as Mitch walks over to her, kicks her pistol way out of reach, and looks down at her. Then he shoulders his rifle, and continues on toward the bomb he'd been setting up.

"Get me one more EFP, Pee-Wee," he calls, without looking around.

Peter curses his hesitation. His lack of courage. Now the woman is going to die, too. And Mitch is still going to set off the bombs.

He thinks of Chernobyl, of the death and destruction.

He thinks of Leanne, bleeding behind the van.

He thinks of the woman from the gas station, risking her life here to save others.

And he makes a decision.

He walks over to his brother.

Mitch has set up the bomb facing the reactor, a few yards off, and is now pulling the det cord back.

Peter lifts his pistol.

His brother grips the detonator switch.

Shouts, "Fire in the hole!"

Peter doesn't know why he shouts that. Maybe old habits.

But in the second he delays, Peter takes aim at his head.

Pulls the trigger.

His brother drops.

Peter just stands there for several seconds, staring. He can't believe what he's just done.

He's shot his big brother, his protector, his hero.

His own flesh and blood.

Shot him dead.

Guess I did have it in me, he thinks.

The sirens are getting real loud, now.

He looks up toward the road beyond the reactor.

A bunch of cop cars arrive, sirens wailing, blue and red lights swirling.

There's an ambulance, too.

Peter tosses his gun.

Raises his hands.

DAY SEVEN

59

Milton S. Hershey Medical Center, Hershey, Pennsylvania

WHEN ELLEN OPENS her eyes, she realizes she's in a hospital bed. For one awful moment she thinks they've brought her back to the psych ward at Norristown State Hospital. And the figure sitting beside her does nothing to immediately dispel that possibility. A bald, middle-aged man in a suit, whose tie is loose around his collar. The dark smudges under his eyes suggest he hasn't slept a whole lot more in the week since they first met at a Philadelphia P.D. station.

"I guess I owe you an apology," says Detective Brennan. "You were right."

"Where am I?" she asks.

"Hershey," he replies. "In a grade one trauma center. You were shot. Lucky for you, this place is only twenty minutes from Three Mile Island."

The images start to come back to Ellen, now. Snapshots, film clips. The EFP blast tearing Randall Kowalski in half. Then Mitch Logan ambushing her, raising his rifle. The red dot over her belly. Then the shot. Followed by another . . .

She shuts her eyes for a few seconds, takes a deep breath

to ground herself before she speaks again. "What happened after that?"

Brennan fills her in. Peter Logan shot his brother, Mitch, dead, right as he was about to set off the first bomb. Leanne Spinoza bled out before the medics could help her. Nine security guards were murdered, men and women with families who would now be grieving for a long time because of the Keystone Boys. But there was no damage to the nuclear facility. In that respect, at least, the terrorists had been stopped.

"And it was you that stopped them," he tells her. "Single-handed."

"It wasn't single-handed," she says.

The authorities may have ignored her, but Ellen knows she had a lot of help along the way. Walter, Jada, Vang and Reyes all played their part. Her father, the Amish family, and others besides — people who didn't even know how crucial they were. At one point, Josh saved her life by throwing a rock. Perhaps the most important role was played by Peter Logan, though. After all, despite Ellen's best efforts, Mitch could still have let off at least two EFPs at the nuclear reactor if Peter hadn't had the courage to stop him.

Brennan tells her an expert has already assessed that the potential bomb damage could have led to a level seven nuclear incident, which apparently is as serious as it gets. A massive radiation leak. Maybe even a meltdown. Without him, Three Mile Island might've been mentioned in the same breath as Chernobyl and Fukushima in years to come. And that's before you even begin to quantify the possible human loss.

"Peter Logan's a hero," she says.

"We're still trying to figure out exactly what he is," says Brennan. "We're holding him under the Patriot Act, but we don't know whether to lock the guy up for life or give him a medal." The detective explains that Peter is talking, helping them to understand the Keystone Boys and what drew its members into the group.

As for Ellen, Brennan tells her that she was shot in the abdomen. The high-velocity rifle round passed right through her liver and out the other side. It could have been fatal if she hadn't received immediate medical assistance. As it stands, though, she's doing okay. She just needs to rest while the doctors keep an eye on her.

"I should have taken you more seriously a week ago," he adds.

"Yeah, you really should have," she says. "So why didn't you?"

"Our Langley contact couldn't find any trace of you. Matter of fact, they still can't, and—"

"Maybe you didn't ask the right people."

"Impossible," he responds.

"So, maybe your security clearance isn't high enough."

Brennan frowns. "I work in a multi-agency counter-terrorism unit. My clearance is as high as it goes."

"There's always one level higher."

"I'll have to take your word for that." He shrugs. "Anyway, it wasn't just the no-trace. There was Doc Schulz's psych evaluation, too."

"That asshole's *psych evaluation* almost got me killed."

"Speaking of which, I've been told an inquiry is underway at Norristown State Hospital, looking at a number of patient safety incidents."

"Good."

Brennan takes a small notebook and pen from the inside pocket of his jacket.

"I appreciate you've been through a lot," he says, "but I still have one or two things to ask you, if that's all right?"

"Where are my family?"

"They're here."

"Where?" Ellen looks toward the door, searching for any sign of their presence. "I want to see them."

She sits up a little and feels a massive jolt of pain through the right side of her belly.

"Easy now," Brennan holds out a palm. "You were asleep, so they went to get coffee. They'll be right back. In the meantime, you mind if I ask you a few questions?"

Ellen sinks back into the pillows as the pain recedes a little. "Guess not."

"Peter Logan has already told us his brother had a contact, but Peter never met him. Do you have any further intel on other people involved in this plot?"

"Not really," she says. "Only that I overheard two guys talking about the Keystone Boys in a hotel in D.C., almost two weeks ago, now. An older man, who sounded southern, and a young guy." She gives him the rest of the details. "That's what started all this for me."

"And you didn't think to tell me this when I interviewed you?"

"I wasn't sure who I could trust, then. And it's not like you would have believed me, anyway."

Brennan inclines his head, as if to say *fair point*.

"So, who were they?" he asks.

"I have no idea. But from what I saw, the Keystone Boys knew exactly when to hit the power plant, and where to go once they were inside. The had fake ID passes and paperwork that was good enough to get them through the first gate. Someone gave them the intel to pull that off. I'm guessing that was Mitch Logan's contact."

"We'll investigate."

"Okay."

Brennan hesitates. "There's also the matter of a murder in Allentown. My colleagues up there think you did it."

"I know, I saw the news." She feels the grief welling up inside her once more. "Ricardo Reyes was my friend. I was at his apartment the night he died. And he was murdered because he was helping me. But the man who did it is in the Pocono Mountains. He's dead, too. Along with his buddy, the guy who was tailing me in Philly last week. Michael John Smith, or whatever he claimed his name was."

"Excuse me?"

"There's a cabin in the woods in Monroe County," she continues. "It's state forest land. I'll give you the co-ords. You'll find the bodies there, unless the people employing them have already cleaned it up."

"You killed them?"

"Those bastards kidnapped my son, Josh, from my parents' home — at gunpoint — and took him there, to get to me."

"What?" Brennan stares at her, wide-eyed.

"They threatened to kill him unless I went there, alone, without telling you guys. So, I did. And . . . well. Anyway, they're both dead."

"You killed them." This time it's a statement, not a question.

"Do you have children, detective?"

"Yes."

"So, you'll understand."

Brennan studies her, nods.

"Well, we'll need to take a full statement from you about that in due course. But if it was self-defence from serious harm, then you have the right to use lethal force."

"I know," Ellen responds. "This is Pennsylvania."

She wishes it hadn't had to be that way. That little Josh hadn't had to go through that ordeal. That she hadn't needed to shoot two people dead. She'll be reliving those moments for the rest of her life. She just hopes Josh won't be doing the same.

She starts thinking about re-contacting her therapist.

Then there's a knock at the door.

*

The door opens and Josh tumbles in, followed by Harry, then Ellen's parents. They all greet her at once. Josh rushes over, right past Brennan, ignoring Harry's warnings to slow down, and flings his arms around her.

Ellen winces, but she doesn't care. She'd give anything for this.

She almost gave everything for it.

"Are we interrupting, detective?" asks Harry.

"Not at all," replies Brennan, pocketing his notebook and pen. "We were just finishing up. Thanks for your help, Ellen. Hopefully I'll come see you again, tomorrow."

Ellen holds Josh close to her, smells his smell, strokes his hair. She glances at the machinery and monitors she's hooked up to. "I guess I'll be here."

Her family erupts into conversation again before Brennan has even closed the door on his way out.

"Are you in pain, honey?"

"What did the police say?"

"When are you coming home?"

"Have you eaten anything?"

And a bunch of other questions, none of which she answers.

She just reaches out, lets her family wrap itself around her and hold her.

Harry is on one side of her, clutching her shoulder, leaning in, touching his head to hers, kissing her.

Her mother is on the other side, gripping her hand, stroking her arm, bending to kiss the top of her head.

Her father is the only one not bear-hugging her, probably just because there's no space left by the bed. He simply places a hand on her mom's back, as if he can transmit his love through her. Ellen looks at him. He smiles, nods. She grins right back at him.

After a week of being tailed, arrested, committed, restrained, drugged, attacked, hunted, stabbed, and shot, the physical presence of her family here and now is almost too much.

It was the desire to save lives, to atone for Paris, that propelled Ellen to do what she did these past seven days. To risk her own life, time and again.

But it was the desire to protect her family, and to be reunited with them, that kept her going in the darkest hours. That gave her hope.

Now, her eyes are hot and wet with tears. She couldn't hold them back, even if she wanted to.

Her body feels as though it's been through a cage fight on top of a triathlon, with no food or sleep. The last time she felt this battered and exhausted was right after she'd given birth to Josh.

But she wouldn't change anything about this for the world.

Because it might just be the happiest moment of her life.

EPILOGUE

Two Months Later

East Norriton, Pennsylvania

ELLEN IS IN her kitchen, drinking coffee and reading the *Philadelphia Inquirer* on her tablet. Her recovery is going well, but the house feels awfully quiet now that she's on her own again.

Josh has just started back at school. He seems to be enjoying his first week in second grade, and isn't showing too many symptoms of the trauma he experienced back in July. He's been seeing a clinical psychologist who specializes in PTSD. They're keeping a close eye on him, but they think he's going to be okay. Children can be so resilient.

Harry is in D.C. for a few days, attending a major congressional hearing on the safety of America's nuclear power plants. No way was Ellen going to stop him going to that, although it's not as simple as she first thought.

What began as a review of security measures around nuclear sites of critical national infrastructure was quickly hijacked by some powerful lobbyists for the fossil fuel industry. Then an ancient senator — a man with a big grey moustache, who was probably alive when they first struck oil in the US — proposed a bill to shut down all nuclear plants and return federal funding for them to coal, oil and gas facilities.

The current administration, who had pledged significant investment in nuclear power, wasn't happy about it. But the momentum was with the "dirty" energy lobby, as Harry called them, who were riding high on a wave of public anti-nuclear outcry, following the foiled attack on Three Mile Island. It's been all over the national media.

So, in some ways, the terrorists might have got what they wanted. Only she's not sure she knows *what* they actually wanted.

Detective Brennan hasn't been able to tell her much more about that, either. According to Peter Logan, the Keystone Boys' plan had been simply about striking at government. He claims he didn't know why they chose a nuclear plant. Mitch Logan might have been able to say more, but he's dead.

Ellen thinks there's got to be more to it.

Brennan's Delaware Valley fusion center received additional resources from the FBI to investigate the origins of the plot. But they haven't been able to identify the older southern man or the younger guy from the D.C. hotel, whose throwaway remarks to one another in a corridor sparked Ellen's mission.

It seems as though the backers, whoever they were — including Mitch Logan's insider — covered their tracks pretty well. Brennan's team have tried to trace telecoms, money movements, transport, security camera footage and online activity. But all they've done is hit dead ends.

Ellen reflects on what Walter used to tell her about terrorism, and the three types of people who become involved in it. If the Keystone Boys were mostly type two, the foot soldiers, with Mitch Logan being type one, the ruthless killer, then who was type three, the leader, in this case? Who were the puppetmasters, pulling the strings?

She scrolls down the news page on her tablet, but there are no updates today.

Maybe she'll never know.

Maybe it doesn't matter.

Maybe it's Brennan's problem, now.

And, if she keeps telling herself all that, she reasons, maybe she'll even believe it.

Then she sees the headline:

Culture of abuse on state forensic psych ward, report concludes

Ellen clicks into the article. The investigation into safety at Norristown State Hospital has found that patient abuse was widespread within the secure forensic ward. It was perpetrated by numerous staff, including security guards and orderlies, over a period of several years. The report also found that many of the abuses were carried out at the direction of psychiatrist Dr Cornelius Nyborg and head nurse Ava Ratkova, under protocols that they referred to as *control measures*.

"Oh my God," she exclaims aloud, even though she's alone.

Reading on, she discovers that Nyborg and Ratkova have both been stripped of their licenses to practice. The state is considering criminal proceedings against them, and a class action lawsuit for damages has been filed by patients' families. The *Inquirer* says that Clinical Psychologist Dr Lee Vang — one of the whistle-blowers on the abuse — has been asked to head up a new team taking charge of the ward. A woman named Jada Robinson, who gave evidence to the investigation, has been released following a review of her case.

Ellen feels a glow at this news, at the sense of justice being done, and assholes who preyed on weaker people, getting what they deserved. The thought of Jada being reunited with her kids makes her smile.

She wonders if she should get in touch with Dr Vang or Jada, perhaps to contribute to the campaign and the rebuilding. If nothing else, she'd like to thank them both.

She goes through into Harry's study to dig out the documentation from her commitment order. She's not totally certain where it is, but chances are Harry's locked it in the drawers for their sensitive correspondence.

Ellen checks the first locked drawer, then the second, but it's not there. It's not in the third, either, although something does catch her eye. It's a digital voice recorder.

Harry sometimes uses them to dictate memos for his staff. He's a little bit old school like that. But this isn't the one he takes to work, now. It's an older model, the one he had back in Paris. It makes her think of the good times they had there, before the attack.

She picks it up, switches it on. Looks at the screen.

The last file was recorded two months ago. On July third.

Something tells her that's a little odd.

She presses *play*, listens.

No question, Three Mile Island's gonna be a game-changer . . .

Ellen hits pause. She knows that voice. It's that phrase, *game-changer*, that trips her memory. She rewinds, plays it again. Closes her eyes as she listens. Puts herself back in the place where she first heard the same voice utter that same phrase. Plays it a third time. Then she's certain it's him.

The young man from the hotel corridor in D.C.

Suddenly, her fight-or-flight system kicks into action.

Her mouth is dry, and she can taste metal at the back of her throat.

Her thoughts are going a hundred miles an hour.

Her hand is shaking as she hits *play* again and lets it roll.

A second voice comes over the speaker:

> *We're all in this together, it's important to remember that.*

The second voice is clearer than the first.

And she'd know it anywhere.

Because it's her husband.

Harry.

END OF PART THREE

TO BE CONTINUED . . .

ACKNOWLEDGEMENTS

Despite *Committed* marking a departure from my previous detective and psychological thrillers set in London, in some ways writing about themes of espionage and terrorism feels like completing a circle. My first, somewhat limited attempt at creative writing was a story along similar lines. That manuscript — from almost a decade ago — remains unpublished (probably best for all concerned) but my interest in those topics remained, and it wasn't until I had the idea for *Committed* a couple of a years ago that I was able to return to them. I'm glad I did, because I really enjoyed writing this book. But a novel is never a solo project, and there are several people I would like to thank for their contributions.

Firstly, I want to thank my editor Jack Butler at Wildfire for his vision for publishing *Committed* and ideas on how to improve it while always working collaboratively. Thanks also go to Rosie Margesson for overseeing publicity, and the rest of the team for their support. I'm very grateful to Russel McLean for his editorial input, both big picture and small details, which had a transformative effect on my original manuscript. A huge thank you goes to fellow author Matt Brolly for his advice, without which *Committed* may never have been published. I'm also indebted to Anthony Horowitz, who took time to read and comment on an early draft of the novel.

Committed is my first book set in the US and I'm grateful to my friends who live there for helping out with Americanisms, geography, food, music, and other details which hopefully make the story more authentic. In particular, I'd like to thank author Lisa Regan, and long-standing friends Per Besson, and Peter and Lynn von Koch-Liebert.

As always, I owe special thanks to all the readers who buy, borrow, review, and share my thrillers. I love hearing from you, so please drop me a line on social media or via my website if you'd like to get in touch, and I'll do my best to respond. I'd also like to shout out the community of bloggers, podcasters, booksellers, and festival organisers who help spread the word about my novels and let me take part in their events.

Finally, my biggest thanks go to my partner, Fiona, and to my parents, Jim and Rita, for their love, unfailing support, and encouragement in my writing career. I couldn't do it without you.